STILL MISSING

'An **astonishingly well-crafted** debut novel.
Still Missing will have you spellbound from the first page
until long after you close the book'
KARIN SLAUGHTER

'**Frank, fierce**, and sometimes even funny, this is a dark tale pin-
pricked with light and told by an **unforgettable heroine**'
GILLIAN FLYNN

'**Crackling with suspense** ... will have you glued to the page'
PEOPLE

'*Still Missing* runs deeper than the chills it delivers, the surprises
it holds and the resilience of its main character'
NEW YORK TIMES

NEVER KNOWING

'Chevy Stevens writes in a fresh, truly authentic human voice,
gripping you and **tearing your heart** from the very first page
to the last ... She is going to be huge'
PETER JAMES

'Stevens's **unnerving standalone thriller** about a woman's search for
her birth parents matches the intensity of her impressive debut, *Still
Missing* ... the skilful storytelling never flags'
PUBLISHERS WEEKLY

'Block off the weekend, grab a comfy seat, and prepare
for the **rocket ride of your life**'
LISA GARDNER

ALWAYS WATCHING

CHEVY STEVENS

sphere

SPHERE

Published in the United States in 2013 by St Martin's Press
First published in Great Britain in 2013 by Sphere
This paperback edition published in 2013 by Sphere

Copyright © Chevy Stevens Holdings Ltd 2013

A CIP catalogue record for this book
is available from the British Library.

ISBN 978-0-7515-4988-1

Printed and bound in Great Britain by
Clays Ltd, St Ives plc

Papers used by Sphere are from well-managed forests
and other responsible sources.

MIX
Paper from
responsible sources
FSC® C104740

Sphere
An imprint of
Little, Brown Book Group
100 Victoria Embankment
London EC4Y 0DY

An Hachette UK Company
www.hachette.co.uk

www.littlebrown.co.uk

For my brother, Steve

ALWAYS
WATCHING

Chapter One

The first time I saw Heather Simeon, she was curled into a ball in the seclusion room at the hospital, a thin blue blanket tight around her, the bandages sharp white lines circling her wrists. Her blond hair obscured most of her face. Even then, she still gave off a sense of refinement, something in the high cheekbones barely visible through the veil of her hair, the beautifully arched brows, the patrician nose, the delicate outline of pale lips. Only her hands were a mess: the cuticles raw and bleeding, the nails jagged. They didn't look bitten, they looked broken. Like her.

I'd already read her file and talked with the emergency psychiatrist who'd admitted her the night before, then gone over everything with the nurses, most of whom had worked in the Psychiatric Intensive Care Unit for years, and who were also my best sources of information. I might spend fifteen minutes to an hour with each patient during my morning rounds, but the rest of the time I was at my office in the Mental Health building, treating patients who are out in the community. That's why I like to bring a nurse with me when I first meet a patient, so we're on the same page with the care plan. Michelle, a cheerful woman with curly blond hair and a wide smile, was with me now.

Heather's husband had come home the night before to find her sprawled on the kitchen floor, the knife near her hand. When she was admitted to the hospital, she'd become agitated, crying and fighting the nurses. The emergency-room doctor ran a drug screen that came back clear, so she'd been given Ativan and placed in the seclusion room. She was under close observation on the monitor, and a nurse checked on her every fifteen minutes.

She'd been sleeping all night.

I knocked softly on the door frame. Heather stirred and opened her eyes, blinked a few times. I stepped closer to the bed. She gazed up at me, licked her lips, which were dry and chapped, then swallowed. Her mouth parted as if she were going to say something, but only her breath escaped in a long sigh. Her eyes were dark blue.

'Good morning, Heather,' I said in my gentlest voice. 'I'm Dr. Lavoie, the attending psychiatrist.' When I had my private practice up island, my patients called me Nadine. But since moving to Victoria to work at the hospital, I'd started using my title, had come to like the emotional distance – one of the reasons for my move in the first place. 'Would you like some water?'

She was staring somewhere over my shoulder, her expression blank, devoid of sorrow or anger. She might not have succeeded in checking out physically, but she had definitely disappeared emotionally.

'I'd like to talk with you for a little bit if that's okay.'

Her eyes skimmed past me, landing on Michelle. She pulled the blue blanket tight around her.

'Why . . . is she here?' Her voice was a whisper.

'Michelle? She's one of our nurses.'

On the psychiatry floor, the doctors are generally in business casual, the nurses dressed more for comfort. Michelle tended to favor fun clothes, today a funky striped shirt with dark denim dress jeans. Unless you noticed the ID badge around her neck, you might not realize she was a nurse.

Heather's body language was defensive, almost cringing under the blanket, her gaze flicking back and forth between us like a cornered animal's. Michelle stepped back, but Heather still looked overwhelmed. Some patients felt ganged up on when we brought a nurse in with us.

I said, 'Would you be more comfortable just talking to me?'

She gave a small nod as she worried a corner of her bandage with her teeth. Again, I was struck with the image of a wild animal trying to escape its bindings. I

3

glanced at Michelle, signaling that it was okay for her to leave.

Michelle smiled at Heather.

'I'll check on you later, honey. See if you need anything.'

I liked Michelle's warmth with the patients, had noticed it before. She'd often sit and talk with them, even on her breaks. When the door closed behind her, I turned back to my patient.

'Can you tell me how old you are, Heather?'

She slowly said, 'Thirty-five,' as she looked around, starting to become more aware of where she was. I saw the room through her eyes and felt bad for her: the small plastic window in the heavy metal door, the Plexiglas cover on the window with scratch marks down it like someone had tried to claw their way out – which someone had.

'And your name?' I said.

'Heather Duncan ...' She shook her head, catching herself, but the movement was sluggish, delayed. 'Simeon. My name now, it's Simeon.'

I smiled. 'Did you get married recently?'

'Yes.' Not *yeah* or *uh-huh*, but *yes*. She was educated, brought up to speak clearly. Her gaze focused on the heavy metal door. 'Daniel ... is he here?'

'He's here, but I'd like to talk with you first. How long have you and Daniel been married?'

'Six months.'

'What do you do for a living, Heather?'

4

'I don't do anything now, but I used to work in the store. We take care of the earth.'

I noticed her shift to present tense.

'Are you a landscaper?'

'It's our job to tend and keep the land.'

I felt an uncomfortable flutter in my stomach about the phrase. It sounded familiar, and she'd also said it like she was reciting an expression she'd heard many times. She was repeating it, not speaking for herself.

'I heard you had a bad night,' I said. 'Would you like to tell me what happened?'

'I don't want to be here.'

'You're in the hospital because you've been certified under the Mental Health Act. You tried to hurt yourself, and we don't want that to happen again, so we're going to help you get better.'

She pulled herself up into a sitting position, and I noticed how thin her arms were as she braced on the mattress, the veins popping. Her arms shook as if the effort of holding up her body was exhausting.

'I just wanted it all to stop.' Her eyes filled with tears that weaved down her face, dripped off her nose. One landed on her arm. She stared at it as though she had no idea how it got there.

'What did you want to stop?'

'The bad thoughts. My baby—' Her voice caught and she flinched, gritting her teeth as though something had stabbed her deep inside.

'You had a miscarriage, Heather?' According to her file, she'd lost the baby a week ago, but I wanted to see if she would tell me more about it herself.

Another tear slid down and dropped onto her arm.

'I was three months along. I started bleeding . . . ' She took a breath and let it out slowly through clenched teeth.

I paused, a beat of silence in honor of what she'd just told me, then said, very gently, 'I'm sorry, Heather. That must have been very painful for you. It's normal to have feelings of depression after losing a child, but we can help you manage your feelings so they aren't so over-whelming. Your file said your doctor prescribed Effexor last year. Are you still taking it?'

'No.'

'When did you stop?'

'When I met Daniel.' I caught the slightly defensive tone and knew she felt guilty that she'd stopped taking the pills, ashamed that she needed them. People with depression often stop their medication when they fall in love, the endorphins creating their own natural anti-depressant. Then real life kicks in.

'The first thing I'd like to do is put you back on the antidepressant.' My voice was casual: *This isn't a big deal. You're okay.* 'We'll start you off on a low dose and see how you do. Your file mentioned that you also went through a hard time a few years ago.' Her previous two suicide attempts had been with pills. She'd been found at

6

the last second in each case, but now that Heather had progressed to more violent means, she might not be so lucky next time.

'You were referred to a psychologist. Are you still seeing him?'

She shook her head. 'I didn't like him. Daniel, is he okay?'

'The nurses said he stayed here all night and only went home this morning to get some of your things. He's back in the waiting area now.'

Heather frowned, her face worried. 'He must be so tired.'

'I'm sure Daniel just wants you to get well. We're here to help with that.'

Fresh tears made her eyes seem even bluer, like sapphires set in diamonds. She was so pale you could see every vein in her neck, but she was still hauntingly pretty. People often assume that beautiful people have no reason to be unhappy. It's usually the complete opposite.

'I want Daniel,' she said. Her eyelids had begun to droop, the effort of talking draining what little energy she had left.

'I'm going to speak to him first, then we'll see if we can arrange a little visit.' I wanted to get a sense of what kind of emotional shape he was in, so he didn't make the situation worse.

'They can't find me in here.' She said the words to the

room as though she'd forgotten I was there and was just reassuring herself.

'Who are you afraid is going to find you?'

'I want them to leave us alone, but they just keep calling and calling.' She picked at her cuticles as she spoke, tearing at a small piece of flesh.

'Is someone bothering you?' Her file hadn't said anything about paranoia or hallucinations, but psychosis is sometimes possible with severe depression, which Heather was clearly suffering from. But if she was also having problems with some people in her life, we needed to know about it.

She started to worry the bandage with her teeth again.

I said, 'This is a safe environment – it's a place for you to get better. We can bar anyone you don't want to visit, and there's a security guard on the floor at all times. No one can get to you.' If there was a real threat, I wanted to make sure Heather felt secure enough to tell me what was going on. If it was just paranoia, she still needed to feel protected, so we could begin to treat her.

'I'm not going back.' The last part was said as though she was warning herself. 'They can't make me.'

'Who can't make you?'

She forced her eyes open, met mine with a flash of confused alarm. I could see her wondering what she'd just told me. Fear, and something else, something I couldn't name yet, rolled off her body in thick waves, pressing into me. I fought the sudden urge to step back.

'I need to see Daniel.' Her head lolled forward, and her chin dropped onto her chest. 'I'm so tired.'

'Why don't you get some rest while I talk to your husband.'

She curled up under the blue blanket in the fetal position, her face to the wall, shaking even though the room was warm.

Her voice now barely a whisper, she said, 'He sees *everything*.'

I paused at the door. 'Who sees everything, Heather?'

She just pulled the blanket over her face.

When I walked into the visiting area, a tall man with dark hair leaped to his feet. Even unshaven, with shadows under his eyes and a rumpled dress shirt hanging outside faded jeans, Daniel was an attractive man. He was probably in his mid-forties, judging by the laugh lines around his eyes and mouth, but I had a feeling he was one of those men who grow even more handsome with age. Their child would have been lovely. I felt a wave of sorrow for them.

He strode toward me, a brown leather bomber jacket hanging over his arm and a knapsack hooked over his shoulder.

'How is she? Is she asking for me?' His voice cracked on the last word.

'Let's go where we can talk privately, Mr. Simeon.' I led him down the hallway toward one of the interview rooms, skirting the janitor mopping the floor. I frowned when I noticed that the utility room behind him was unlocked and gaping, and made a mental note to mention it to the nurses.

'Call me Daniel, please. Can you tell me if she's all right?'

'I'd say yes, considering. She's having a hard time, but we're doing everything in our power to help her. This is the best place for her right now.'

'There was so much blood . . .'

I felt bad for him, knowing what he was probably thinking: *What if I'd come home ten minutes later? Why didn't I see the signs?* Families seem to fall into two categories: those that blame themselves and those that blame the patient. But they always need to blame someone.

'It must have been very upsetting to find her like that,' I said. 'Is there anyone you can talk to? I'd be happy to suggest someone.'

A quick shake of his head. 'I'm okay. I just want Heather to be safe.'

I thought about what Heather had just told me. *Was* someone harassing her? Or was his fear just related to what she had done?

'That's what we want too.' I unlocked the heavy metal door to the interview room and waved Daniel into a chair.

He sat across from me. People might think that the

ward would be decorated in soothing colors, a warm, nurturing environment, but the chairs, mismatched shades of pink, blue, and puce, have been there since the seventies. The desk was laminate, the edges cracked and peeling. A wood shelf stood against one wall with a few lonely books stacked haphazardly. Even the waiting area where he'd been sitting for so many hours was just a few chairs by the elevators. It's an old hospital. But the funding isn't there, and this isn't meant to be a holiday.

'Did she tell you why she . . . ' Daniel choked up, took a quick breath. 'Why she tried to kill herself?'

'I can't share anything Heather tells me without her permission. But I'd like to ask you some questions.'

'Sure, anything.'

'Did you know how depressed she's been?'

He rubbed his chin, his face bleak. 'Since we lost the baby, she won't eat or get out of bed. Most days she won't even shower. I thought it was postpartum, or whatever it's called, and she just needed some time . . . I keep thinking about how quiet she was when I left last night. I was late for work – I've been picking up odd jobs in the evening to make some extra cash – so I was in a rush.' He shook his head. 'If I'd stayed with her . . . '

He was the type who blame themselves. I leaned forward.

'This isn't your fault, Daniel. If you'd been there, she'd have waited until you weren't and tried again. People as troubled as Heather always find a way.'

11

He looked at me – long enough, I hoped, for my words to sink in – then his face clouded over.

'Her parents are going to take this really hard.'

'They don't know?'

'They're on an RV trip in Northern BC. I tried to call, but they must be out of range. She hasn't talked to them for a while.'

'What about her friends?'

'She never wanted to do anything with them, so they stopped phoning.'

I wasn't surprised that Heather had pushed people away, except for Daniel. A classic symptom of depression was detaching from friends and family.

'What do you do for a living, Daniel?'

'I'm a carpenter.' That explained his build, and his deep tan. He smiled as he looked down at his rough hands. 'Heather and I came from different worlds, but the minute we met, we had this instant connection, like on the deepest level. Neither of us had ever felt that way before.' He looked at me as if expecting skepticism.

I gave him an encouraging nod.

He continued. 'She'd just gone through a breakup – her ex was a real jerk. But we started hiking and doing yoga together. It seemed to cheer her up.'

It had been a good idea on his part. Exercise is one of the best natural aids for depression.

'So you noticed some signs of depression before you got married?'

'I guess ... She's the kind of person who's always trying to take care of everyone else, so it's hard to tell sometimes. She'd get really quiet or start crying, but she wouldn't want to worry me, so I wouldn't know what she was upset about. But when she got pregnant, she was really happy about the baby, picking out names, buying toys ...' His voice wavered. 'I don't know what to do about the baby's room or all the clothes she bought.'

My mind flashed to Paul painting Lisa's nursery strawberry red with apple green stripes because our child would be different, would skip to her own beat. Which she had, always – a trait I'd admired, until she danced away from me.

'Let's take it one day at a time,' I said, as much to myself as to him. 'You can work all that out later.'

'When can Heather come home?'

'She's been involuntarily admitted into the hospital so we can keep an eye on her. We can't release her until she's no longer a danger to herself.'

'What if she tries ... you know.' He swallowed hard. 'What if she tries to do it again?'

'We won't let her here. And we won't send her home until she's stable and has a good support system in place.'

'Can I see her? I brought some of her things.'

Normally, we're strict about visiting hours – they're only from four to nine in PIC, where everyone has to be buzzed in and out. We don't allow visitors before noon, so

patients can attend programs, and we can make our rounds. But he looked desperate, and I thought seeing him might help Heather settle in.

'She's resting right now, but you can say a quick hello.'

We didn't talk as we rode up the elevator to Psychiatric Intensive Care on the next floor. Daniel seemed lost in thought, and I was busy counting my heartbeats while focusing on my breathing. I've suffered from claustrophobia for years, a fact that would probably shock my patients. Various coping techniques help, from mental imagery to breathing exercises, but when I first heard the elevator seal shut, I had to restrain myself from hitting the panic button.

We were buzzed into the unit. In PIC, the nurses' station is behind glass, and a security guard is always at hand. One side of the unit is for high-risk patients like Heather, and the other is the step down unit, where they go when they don't need the same level of monitoring. If they continue to improve, they are moved down to the next floor, where they have more freedom.

The nurse searched the bag Daniel had brought for Heather to make sure there wasn't anything she could hurt herself with – the frame was removed from their wedding photograph, same with the tie from her robe. When the nurse was finished, I showed Daniel to an alcove in the lounge area, where they could have some privacy but still be in view, then went to get Heather.

As I entered the seclusion room, I gave her a quick visual. She was still curled in a ball, her pale arms wrapped around her torso with both small hands on her shoulders, as if she were trying to hold herself together.

'Heather, do you feel up to a visit with Daniel now?'

Heather twitched at the sound, then slowly rolled over. Her voice was pleading, and her eyes flooded with tears, as she said, 'I need to see him.'

'Okay, but you'll have to come out with me because we don't allow visitors in the seclusion rooms. Are you feeling strong enough to stand?'

She was already pulling herself up into a sitting position.

When we entered the lounge area, Daniel jumped to his feet – and froze as he took in the sight of his wife slowly shuffling beside me, the bandages on her wrists, the hospital blue pajamas, the blanket she'd wrapped around her shoulders like an old woman's shawl.

'Daniel!' she cried out.

'Oh, sweetie,' he said as he gathered her into her arms. 'You can't scare me like that again.'

Once a patient has been in for a few days we leave them alone with their visitors, but I wanted to see how Daniel and Heather interacted – in case Daniel was part of the problem. I sat in one of the chairs a little to the side.

Daniel gently helped Heather lower herself before

taking a seat. Heather rested her head against his shoulder, and he wrapped his arm around her back, supporting her.

'I'm sorry, Daniel.' Heather's voice was raw with emotion. 'I hate what I'm doing to you. You shouldn't have to take care of me all the time.'

A red flag. Suicidal patients try to convince themselves that people would be better off without them.

Daniel said, 'Don't talk like that. I love you. I'm not going anywhere. I'm going to take care of you forever.' As though to prove his point, he pulled the blanket up around her shoulders, tucking it around her neck where the hospital pajamas had drifted down, revealing the hollow of her thin collarbone.

She clearly wasn't frightened of Daniel, so I decided to leave and finish my rounds. Then Heather, speaking slightly under her breath, said something that caught my attention.

'I told the doctor about how they keep calling.'

'What did you say?' Daniel didn't sound upset, just a little worried.

'Not much, I don't think ... I'm confused, and my head feels funny. Are you mad at me?'

'I'm not mad, sweetie. But maybe you shouldn't think about any of that right now, just think about getting better. We can talk about everything else another day.' His face was earnest, making sure she understood.

'Do you think Emily knows ... what I did?'

16

'No, they probably wouldn't have told her at the center.'

Heather nodded, then glanced up at the camera in the corner. She'd also glanced at it when she first sat down, and I wondered if she'd been at a treatment center where patients were monitored.

'Is there someone you'd like me to contact for you?' I said.

Heather looked at Daniel. He shook his head, just a slight movement, but she nodded back, acquiescing to whatever he'd just silenced.

I said, 'It would help my treatment plan for Heather if you told me what program you were attending.'

Heather rested her hand on Daniel's leg, her eyes pleading with him. Daniel's were focused on her bandages, then he turned to me.

'We used to live at a spiritual center. It's out in Jordan River. We left when Heather got pregnant because she didn't want to have the baby there. Some of the members have been calling to make sure we're okay. They're nice people.'

I'd heard that there was a center out in Jordan River, a spiritual retreat of sorts that was well respected, but I didn't know much else about them.

Heather had started to cry again, her shoulders shaking.

'They made me feel like it was my fault I lost the baby.'

'They don't really believe it's your fault – no one thinks

17

that,' Daniel said. 'They're just trying to help, sweetie. You were doing so well.'

Heather was crying harder now, her face twisted.

'I didn't like how they're always telling us what to do. They—'

'Heather, stop – you don't know what you're saying.' Daniel's eyes shot to my face, his voice concerned and his expression helpless. 'They have rules, Dr. Lavoie, but they're so we can stay focused on the workshops.'

Heather and Daniel clearly weren't on the same page about the center, but she didn't want to contradict Daniel in front of me. She kept glancing at him. *Is it okay that I'm saying this? Do you still love me?*

She gazed at him now, her hands gripping her blanket tight around her.

'They wouldn't let me say good-bye to Emily.'

This was the second time Heather had mentioned Emily.

'Emily didn't want to leave with us, remember? She loves it at the center. I know you miss her, but you need to worry about yourself and the bab—'

Heather recoiled like he'd hit her.

Daniel said, 'Oh, sweetie, I'm sorry. It was just habit.'

Heather's eyes had gone dark and empty again, her hands dropped by her sides, palms up – defeated.

'It's my fault I lost the baby. You're mad at me.'

'It's *not* your fault, Heather – and I'm not mad at you.' In a voice so loving and sad it made my heart hurt, he

added, 'You're the most important thing in the world to me.'

'They said we should stay. They said it was better for our baby – and maybe they were right. I made you leave, and now the baby's dead.'

'Heather, stop.' Daniel was rubbing her back. 'Don't say things like that.' He put his face close to hers. 'Hey, look at me.' But Heather was just staring at the wall now, her expression blank.

I didn't want to push things too much, especially with Heather starting to dissociate from the conversation, but I was concerned about why she was blaming herself so much for the loss of her baby.

'Why did you want to leave the center, Heather?'

She began to rock, her arms wrapped around her body.

'They said that *all* adults are the child's parents. So everyone helps raise them, and they don't even stay with you.'

The horror in her face made it clear that this hadn't sat well with her.

'At the center, they believe it's better for the baby's spiritual growth to be loved by many hearts,' Daniel said. 'They have highly trained caregivers.'

This center sounded highly controlling. I turned to Heather.

'But you didn't want to share your child?'

She nodded and glanced at Daniel, who stared down at

Heather's bandages again. She looked like she wanted to explain herself more, but then she reached out and held Daniel's hand. He gave it a small squeeze.

'I think I was wrong, though,' she said. 'We should've stayed. Then I wouldn't have miscarried.'

I said, 'How can you know that you wouldn't have miscarried even if you *had* stayed? Did they actually tell you that you were responsible?'

'They didn't say it was our fault,' Daniel said. 'They were just worried that Heather had gotten herself too stressed out by moving.'

In other words, they had implied that it was her fault.

'What is this center called?' I said.

Daniel sat straighter, his shoulders proud.

'The River of Life Spiritual Center.'

Something tickled at the back of my mind, followed by an uncomfortable feeling of dread settling in my stomach.

'Who runs it?'

'Aaron Quinn. He's the director of all the programs at the center.'

Aaron Quinn. He said Aaron Quinn.

It couldn't be the same man.

Heather's voice was a whisper. 'Most of the members call it the commune.'

The commune. I hadn't heard that name in years. I hadn't wanted to hear it ever again. I stared at Heather, trying to think, my heart thudding in my ears.

'Dr. Lavoie?' Heather's blue eyes were full of sorrow and pain. 'Do you think it's my fault the baby died?'

It took a second for me to refocus my thoughts. *You have a patient, and she needs your help.*

'No, I don't think it's your fault. You made a decision you thought was best for your child – you were just being good parents.' I talked on for a minute or two, heard the comforting words coming out of my mouth. But all the while my head was filled with a dull roar, the sound of fate and life colliding. Because what I couldn't tell them was that I knew Aaron Quinn.

I knew exactly who he was.

Chapter Two

When I was twenty-five, I'd decided to go back to school and was attending the University of Victoria for a degree in science. I'd learned ways to deal with tight hallways and stairwells, mostly by avoiding them, but during final exams, all the outside lots were full and I'd been forced to park underground. I'd been over-whelmed by panic in the dark space and hadn't been able to step into the elevator. I had to walk the long way around, while hyperventilating in big gasps of air, my hair soaked with sweat, earning me stares from every student I passed. I'd missed the beginning of my exam and the door was closed, so I failed the course. It had been a humiliating experience, and I began therapy soon after.

While discussing my childhood with the therapist, I shared that my mother had run away with my brother and me to a commune when I was thirteen. The commune, led by a man named Aaron Quinn, had been built beside the Koksilah River on the outskirts of Shawnigan Lake, which is a small community about thirty minutes north of Victoria – on the southern tip of Vancouver Island. We lived there for eight months until my father came to get us.

My therapist had found this period in my life fascinating and wanted to explore it further. Especially because I'd been unable to pinpoint when my claustrophobia had developed, but I had more distinct memories of it interfering with my life after we'd moved back home. I slept with a night-light and my door open – I couldn't even clean the barn without hyperventilating, and Robbie, my brother, had to take over the chore for me.

Believing that my claustrophobia was linked to suppressed trauma, from something that had happened while at the commune, my therapist had suggested we try hypnosis as a way to unlock my memories. Recovered Memory Therapy was a popular treatment at the time, and he felt it was the best way to recover any lost memories. I'd been hesitant at first – I had enough painful memories already.

My family life hadn't been easy growing up. My father, a strict German, was hard to please but easy to anger. His temper often turned violent, and we spent much of our childhood hiding while he was on a drunken rampage, smashing his huge fists into the windows or knocking our mother around. If we intervened, she'd just scream that we were making it worse. He worked on a fishing boat, and my mother, who was unbalanced when he was around, became downright dangerous when he was away. She was either on top of the world, buying us gifts we couldn't afford and taking us on trips all over the island, or shut in her room for days, the curtains pulled down and the door locked. She'd often threaten to kill herself, the pills in her hands as we pleaded with her until she finally handed them over. Other times she'd take off in the truck, drunk or high on medication, not returning until the morning. Now I would diagnose her as manic-depressive, but back then all we knew was that my mother's moods were a slippery slope and we never knew where she would land.

The only person I could depend on was Robbie, my older brother by three years, whom I followed everywhere. He was my first best friend, my only friend growing up on a ranch where all our school friends lived miles away. Though we were very different, me with my love of books and school, he with mechanics and carpentry, we'd spend hours in the woods, building forts and playing army. Robbie wanted to join the army as soon as he turned eighteen, but I secretly hoped he'd change his mind. I didn't know how I would survive without him.

One February, just before I turned thirteen, my father was away on the boats, and we were at the local corner store with my mom. Robbie was waiting in the truck.

Mom was in one of her down phases, which meant she'd barely eaten for days – neither had we – and she was listlessly picking up items: Kraft Dinner, tomato soup, bread, peanut butter, wieners, hot dog buns, cereal. Her hair, normally a glossy, shiny black, was dull and limp. Mom's hair started going gray in her thirties, though she never lived long enough for it to turn completely silver. When I also started going gray young, I dyed my hair for years, wondering sometimes if it was more out of fear of becoming my mother than vanity.

That day there were a couple of young men in the store, wearing faded bell-bottoms and loose, caftan-styled shirts, ponchos for coats, strange knit toques, their hair almost as long as my mother's. Back then, in the late sixties, it was common to see hippies in town, but I still thought them fascinating. I flipped through some magazines at the counter while I watched my mom talking to the earnest young men. I was used to men paying attention to my mother, with her pale blue eyes and long dark hair, her body slim from working on the ranch; she always attracted attention, but something seemed different about the tone of this conversation. Though it was cold out, the men were wearing sandals, and I couldn't stop looking at their feet.

I don't know what they had said to my mom, but by the time we drove home, she had switched to her up phase. Laughing as she careened around corners, her eyes too bright, teasing us kids, who were terrified, for being 'scaredy-cats.' Robbie tried not to show his fear, but his knuckles were white as he gripped the truck door, his other arm around my shoulders, holding me in place. It wasn't the first time she'd taken us on one of her wild rides.

Years later, when I was twenty-six, my mother was killed in an accident. She'd slid on wet roads and lost control, hitting a tree doing a hundred. But I'd read the report, there were no skid marks: She never tried to slow down. She wasn't trying now either.

When we finally made it home, Robbie climbed out, and I slithered after him on wobbly legs. Mom had already leaped out, slamming the door behind her. We followed her into the house, a small rancher with cedar-shake siding, a sloping floor, and so many leaks we had buckets all over the house when it rained. Mom was in her bedroom, throwing clothes into a suitcase.

Robbie said, 'Mom, what are you doing?'

'We're getting out of here. Grab your things.'

Robbie said, 'Are we going on a trip?'

'Pack everything – we're not coming back.'

Robbie's face was scared. 'We can't just leave Dad—'

She stopped and turned to us. 'He leaves us alone for months – I can't live like this anymore. We're going to stay with some people out by the river.'

A kaleidoscope of confusing thoughts spun through my mind. Was she going to divorce our dad? What people? Did she mean the hippies we'd met?

She said, 'They're a revolution, and we're going to be a part of it. We're going to change the world, kids.'

Both Robbie and I knew that she wasn't going to change anything, except probably her mood in another day or so, but we also knew it was best just to go along with her. She would come down eventually, and then we'd go home.

Now she pulled some old suitcases out of the closet and handed them to us. 'Pack your clothes and anything else you want to bring.'

Robbie and I looked at each other, then he nodded: *Just do as she says, it will be okay.* I was scared, but I trusted Robbie.

All I brought were some clothes and my books. When we were finished, we found Mom outside by the truck, her suitcase and bags full of food already thrown in the back. Our dog, Jake, a black border collie mix with one blue eye, followed us out of the house, his tail wagging in concern, and an anxious whine leaking from his throat. Terrified she was going to leave him – we had two cats, Jake, and a couple of horses – I said, 'What about the animals?'

She paused in the middle of throwing some of Dad's tools in the truck, a confused expression on her face, like it was the first time she'd even thought about our pets. After a moment, she said, 'We'll take them. They should be free too.' She turned to us, her eyes lit up with frantic energy, her skin coated in a fine sheen of sweat. 'You kids

27

don't know how lucky you are. You're going to experience something *amazing*. Your lives are going to change forever.'

The commune was in a clearing alongside the river, hidden from the logging road, which leads up to Glen Eagle Mountain, by a thick wall of forest. The river wrapped around one side of the clearing and glimpses of jade green pools were visible through the trees. As we came into the center of the camp, the forest opened up beside the river to reveal a sandy beach, with the odd dead tree from winter runoffs littering the shore. One tree made a makeshift clothes hanger as a woman did her laundry in the water, soap bubbles frothing in the current. Across the river, the high bank was a sheer dirt wall, trees and ferns clinging to the earth as it eroded from underneath their roots.

There looked to be at least a couple of dozen people living at the site, the women dressed in loose dresses and skirts, their hair long. The men wore cut-off jeans, their chests bare, also with long hair and beards. Cats, dogs, chickens, and kids were roaming free, and there was a tangible air of excitement in the air. It was cold, and it had snowed the week before, but some of them were living in tents. Two old yellow school buses had been converted into sleeping areas, and there were signs that they were building more cabins. A couple of horses grazed in a meadow to the right of the main clearing. I also noticed a tractor, and pens with goats and pigs. A group came to greet us, pulling us in for hugs, touching and stroking our hair as they welcomed us to their camp. One blond woman, smelling of cedar and smoke, turned to my mother.

'Peace, sister. What's your name?'

'Kate. These are my children, Nadine and Robbie.'

The woman smiled. 'Welcome, Kate. I'm Joy.'

A tall kid with red hair and freckles, who looked about the same age as Robbie, came over and introduced himself as Levi. He clasped Robbie on the shoulder. 'Welcome to our camp, man. Want to meet some cool chicks?'

As they walked off, I said, 'Robbie, wait.' But he was already out of earshot, moving toward a couple of teenage girls, who looked happy to see Robbie. Since he'd turned sixteen, girls had been flocking to him – tall, with lean muscles from working on our ranch, shaggy black hair framing his face, and a perpetual tough-guy scowl, he looked like a moody rock star.

Mom was following Joy toward one of the cabins and gestured for me to come along.

I said, 'You said we had to unload the horses from the trailer.'

Over her shoulder, she said, 'We'll do it in a minute.' She turned back to Joy. 'Nadine's my little rule follower.'

It was true. I did crave the comfort of rules, of science and math. With a mother as mercurial as mine, I was constantly searching for absolutes. I stood near the truck, wishing Mom had left the keys. I didn't like the camp, the way it smelled, a bitter, metallic scent. The scent my mother gave off in her manic phase.

Then I saw an attractive young man, maybe early twenties, sitting on a log at the side of the clearing. The winter sun slanted down through fir trees and made his hair, a thick mane of chocolate brown, glow with rich tones and bathed his face in light. His dark brown eyes, with long eyelashes, had an almost sleepy look to them, and his cheekbones were high, creating shadows and hollows on his face. His mouth was full, the lips perfectly symmetrical and turned down at the corners. He also had a full beard, even darker than his hair, and he was wearing jeans, a tan corduroy jacket, and a string of leather tied around his neck. He was watching me as he held an old guitar, the embroidered strap across his chest. He smiled and motioned me over. I wanted to stay near the truck and shook my head. He shrugged, gave a wink, and started to strum the guitar, softly singing.

Jake, who'd been guarding my feet, sauntered over. The man paused his singing and ruffled the fur around Jake's neck. Jake didn't like anyone normally, but he rolled onto his back, wiggling on the ground. The man laughed and rubbed his belly with his foot. I was a cautious, distrustful kid by nature. But when the man lifted his head and said, 'What's his name?' I left the safety of the truck.

Chapter Three

I promised Heather and Daniel again that she was safe on the ward and reminded them that anything they shared would help me treat her. Then I finished my rounds and entered my notes on the patients' charts, all the while trying to ignore the dark feeling closing in around me, the question clamoring in my head.

Could it really be the same people?

Finally I had finished all my appointments at Mental Health, and my day was over. Each night when I got off work I'd take a detour down Pandora Street, where the homeless camp out, and search for the tall frame of my daughter, Lisa. She was turning twenty-five that March, and I wondered the same things I'd wondered every year since she had packed her bags at eighteen: Would I get to see her? Would she call? In the background there was always the more frightening thought: *Would she make it to her next birthday?* Each time the phone rang, I'd hold my breath, terrified the police were calling to say they'd found her body.

I parked my car and walked up and down the street, studying the clusters of street kids, wondering if their parents also lay awake at night worrying. It was cold, and I was tired and hungry, but I took another lap around the block, eyeing misshapen lumps sleeping under dirty blankets, straggly, unwashed hair, scarred arms, feeling a surge of hope when I'd see a young woman, followed by a crash of despair when I'd realize it wasn't Lisa. I had no idea how vast the streets of Victoria were until my child was lost on them. How many dark alleys and abandoned buildings there were, or how helpless it would all make me feel.

When I didn't find Lisa anywhere, I headed home. I'd moved from Nanaimo, a city about an hour and a half north of Victoria, on the first of December, in the hopes of connecting with her. Back in July, before I'd made the final decision to move, I continued with my practice for a couple of weeks, not wanting to leave my clients without a support system. Once I had referred any remaining clients to an excellent therapist in town, I took the rest of the summer off and traveled. That fall, I'd just put my house on the market, still considering opening a private practice in Victoria, when a job came available for an adult general psychiatrist at St. Adrian's Hospital. My house sold soon after.

Now it was February, almost two months later, and I

was still getting used to Fairfield, my new neighborhood in Victoria, a lovely community with tree-lined streets surrounded by Oak Bay, James Bay, Rockland, Beacon Hill Park, and to the south, the ocean shoreline of the Strait of Juan de Fuca. Normally I took my time, so I could admire all the heritage buildings, but today I was too distracted, and sighed in relief when I pulled in the driveway of my new home.

Set on a street of older Victorian homes, my house was an architect's funky blend of West Coast natural with Asian contemporary: all strong angles, golden-stained wood exterior on the lower part, steel blue HardiPlank siding on the top half, and broad sheets of glass windows, trimmed in thick white casings. An aluminum roof jutted down in a slash of silver, and there was even a penthouse deck for morning tea. Bamboo in big black ceramic planters lined the front steps and walkway, setting off the amber-stained wood fence and gates with their black hinges. The garage had been turned into a potting shed in the back, perfect for my new hobby – bonsai trees, an art form I've long admired and yet to master. I'd taken a class on a lark and ended up finding the discipline extremely relaxing. I spend so much time in my head that it was nice to do something creative for a change. The careful shaping and cultivating of a tree over a long period of time also reminded me to be patient with my clients.

Before I got out of my car, I did a quick check of all

my mirrors to make sure no one was lurking in my driveway. I'd been attacked outside my office that summer in Nanaimo — another reason for my move, though I had already been thinking about it. I hadn't broken any bones but I'd been knocked unconscious and never saw my assailant. A patient at the time had been involved in a situation with her birth father, whom we originally suspected of assaulting me. But as the investigation continued, it seemed less likely. Another of my patients had recently left her husband, who viewed her sessions as an abandonment of her wifely duties — something he communicated with his fist to her face. When her husband confronted me, I refused to tell him where she was staying. A week later, I was attacked. The police couldn't prove it was him, but I was sure of it.

I let myself into my house, stopping to notice a stray black cat, all skin and bones, saunter across the road and head toward Ross Bay Cemetery. I hoped she had somewhere warm to hide. My last cat, Silky, had passed away in June, and I hadn't been able to bring myself to adopt another, telling myself it was because I wanted to travel, knowing it was because I wasn't ready. Inside the safety of my home, I had a bath to wash away the smell of the hospital, put on my favorite dove gray yoga outfit, made a cup of tea, and then, and only then, did I let myself think about what I'd heard at the hospital — and what I was going to do about it.

*

My mother had told us that the commune moved down to Victoria not long after we left, and I'd assumed they'd eventually split up. Once, in my early twenties, I'd been driving on the mountain roads with a boyfriend, looking for a good swimming hole, and recognized the old entrance to the commune site. He'd wanted to stop and explore, having heard the rumors about a group of hippies that had camped there. I didn't divulge that we'd also lived there, but I'd been curious too. We'd walked around the site, now overgrown, and it had felt like visiting a ghost town. The barn and cabins empty, doors hanging open and windows broken, our voices hushed in the still forest. I'd become anxious the closer we got to the river, my heart beating fast and my chest tight, and had made him leave, assuming that it was just the silence and the dark woods that had frightened me.

Under my therapist's guidance a few years later, I had talked about the months I spent at the commune, sharing memories that I had of the place, the other members, my brother and mother, swimming at the river, the late-night campfires. But I never could recall any specific event that might've caused my claustrophobia, and hours of hypnosis never revealed anything further. There was just this murky sense that I hadn't liked some of the things that the adults were doing, and I'd been uncomfortable around Aaron, the young man I'd met that first day, and Joseph – his younger brother. Sometimes I felt like there might be things I was forgetting, gaps in my timeline, but nothing that I could put my finger on.

Now I couldn't believe that they were still in Victoria. I was curious about what the commune was like these days and whether the same people lived there.

That evening I spent some time online, reading about The River of Life Spiritual Center. It didn't take long to find their Web site, with its mission statement, 'Guiding you on your journey to enlightenment.' There were glorious photos of the commune, situated on more than 250 acres of land, where the river joined the ocean. I hadn't been to Jordan River for years, but I remembered that it was a small community about an hour west of Victoria. Originally a logging camp, there wasn't much in the way of a village, just a couple of cafés and a general store.

The commune land seemed to be mostly forest and hiking trails, but a big chunk was farmland, part of their stay-and-work program. It sounded like a fascinating place to visit, with its descriptive passages about the healing properties of the land, the intellectual and soul-fulfilling workshops on meditation, spiritual awakening, relationship building, living and dying consciously, blending East and West philosophies toward achieving your highest potential. There were sweat lodges and mineral pools, elaborate gardens, and descriptions of organic food grown on the property, all extolling the virtues of a simple, balanced way of living.

The Web site described the friends you'd make, the greater understanding you'd gain of yourself and life as you learned about the all-embracing world, your new-found self-confidence and personal satisfaction. There was a lot of emphasis on being a steward of the land, that humans must take responsibility for the earth. I thought of Heather's words the first time I met her. *We take care of the earth.*

They also gave back to the community and helped countries around the world. There were photos of people digging ditches, working in fields, building structures. There was a donation button, and I wondered how much money was actually used to help these struggling countries.

I was impressed – and surprised – at how professional they'd become since the sixties, and what they'd grown into. They were obviously a sizable organization now, with centers in three countries, and probably very wealthy. They had elaborate online catalogues, opening with a letter from their director, Aaron Quinn.

I stared at his photo. Gone was the long hair and straggly beard. His hair was now snow-white, neatly trimmed, and so was his beard, but he was still an attractive man. He was wearing a dark turtleneck and smiled kindly at the camera, a wise expression in his eyes. He looked exactly like what he presented himself as: a director of a center devoted to self-awareness and spiritualism. But as I studied his face, I felt myself drawing back in my chair, wanting to put some space between us.

I read his opening letter, about how he'd formed the center because he believed it was more important than ever, with the current global-warming crisis, to awaken people to the earth's plight. They commanded large fees for workshops and intensives, ranging from a weekend to a month – if you were accepted into the program. They would only take so many at a time. Members had to apply to stay on and live permanently at the commune. I wondered what that was evaluated on. I also wondered what had happened to Joseph. I tried to calculate his age, and if he was eighteen when I knew him, he'd be almost sixty now. Aaron, twenty-two, would be in his early sixties.

I looked again at Aaron's photo, his tranquil smile making me suddenly angry when I thought about Heather in the hospital, her wrists bandaged, blaming herself for the loss of her child. I turned my computer off.

Chapter Four

The next morning, I woke late and groggy. Though I had no appetite, I made myself eat a muffin on the way to the hospital, washing it down with a tea that I grabbed at the corner coffee shop. I was hoping to talk to one of my colleagues before my rounds. I'd decided it was probably better for Heather if she had a doctor who had no previous involvement with the commune, but I wanted to discuss it with someone first. As I headed down the hallway toward the unit, I ran into Michelle. She smiled and said, 'Good morning, Dr. Lavoie.'

I smiled back. 'Morning.'

She stopped and looked at my scarf. 'I love that. What a pretty color.'

I glanced down at the lavender scarf. I'd been distracted that morning and barely remembered putting it on. 'Thanks. I've had it forever.'

'You always dress so nice. Well, have a good day.'

'You too.'

She continued on her way, leaving me feeling lighter in spirit than when I'd first come through the doors. Michelle was a lovely person, always positive and complimentary. A few days earlier in the break room, I'd told her I was turning fifty-five this month. She'd paused with her mug halfway to her mouth, and said, 'You're kidding me. I thought we were around the same age.'

Michelle was probably only in her mid-forties. I laughed. 'I wish.'

She said, 'Well, you look amazing.'

'That's very kind.' I know that I look young for my age – I've taken care of my skin and eat healthy, though I struggle with an addiction to popcorn and peanut M&Ms. I balance it out with bike rides and yoga. Since I stopped dyeing my hair in my forties, deciding that it was just too much trouble, I'd come to like the silver, which was now in all different shades, ranging from nearly snow-white around my face to almost black on the underside. I used to wear it in a short, choppy cut, but I'd been letting it grow, and it now fell just past my shoulders.

To work with my coloring, I wear clothes in shades of gray and steel blues. I favor a bohemian style – long skirts with boots, loose flowing slacks and tunics, chunky silver jewelry, wraps and scarves, which fits with my love of art and traveling. Sometimes I wonder if I was a gypsy in a former life. But there's another part of me that just loves to be home. Paul used to say, as we bathed together and drank wine straight from the bottle, 'You're a complicated woman, Nadine. I'm looking forward to spending the rest of my life figuring you out.'

My heart panged, like it did every time my thoughts drifted to my husband, Paul, who'd passed away ten years ago from prostate cancer. I had the love of my life, but now my work and my patients were my relationship.

That morning, as I walked down the hallway, I was disappointed that I'd missed Maurice, another psychiatrist who worked in the unit. I'd wanted to talk about Heather with him, but he'd finished his rounds early. Still thinking about what to do, and considering other doctors, I almost bumped into Dr. Kevin Nasser as he stepped out of his office – as the staff psychologist, he had an office on the main ward.

Kevin reached out to steady me, his hand warm on my arm, then said, 'Good morning, Nadine. How are you?'

Many people just give the standard greetings without any real meaning behind the words, but from the first moment I'd met Kevin, I got the feeling that when we exchanged pleasantries, he was genuinely interested in my answer.

'I'm well, thanks. Is Erick in today?'

'He's off for the rest of the week.' My face must have revealed something because he said, 'Can I help?'

'I just wanted to get a second opinion on something.' I looked down the hallway, toward the ward. I was going to have to make a decision about this soon.

'Step into my office.' He opened the door.

I hesitated, wondering if I should work this out myself, then, still unsure of how to handle the situation with Heather, walked through. I hadn't been in his office before and it appeared that he'd tried to fix it up a little: a fern in the corner, a wall tapestry, which looked like it might be from the Middle East.

When Kevin caught the direction of my gaze, he said, 'Patients should have something to look at other than my ugly mug.'

He was far from ugly. True, he wasn't classically handsome, like Daniel Simeon, but he had an interesting face. His features were almost Lebanese-looking, his nose broad, his skin tanned, with deep-set dark eyes, the corners turning down with fine lines radiating out. I knew he was forty-five, but his hair was still inky black, not a trace of gray. He didn't dress very formal and tended to wear dark denim jeans with a nice shirt and tie, and then a casual blazer. He also wore clear-rimmed glasses with black metal earpieces that suited him. I'd only spoken to him a few times but thought him friendly and intelligent.

He said, 'So how are you finding working at the hospital?'

'I'm enjoying it. Everyone's been very welcoming.'

'Well, if I can ever help in any way, you let me know.'

I smiled. 'Thanks.'

He said, 'So what did you need a second opinion on?'

'A patient, Heather Simeon, was admitted a couple of

nights ago after an attempted suicide, and during our initial interview she revealed something that made me realize I might not be the best doctor for her. I'd like to refer her to someone else.' Though we need to keep the patients' information confidential outside of the ward, the doctors can discuss them because we work as a team.

'Can you tell me what she revealed?'

'We have a mutual acquaintance . . .' Why was I dancing around this? I was a professional, he was professional. There was no reason to be embarrassed.

'And you think this might make it difficult to be impartial?' His tone was kind and matter-of-fact. I could see why he was so popular with the patients.

'Yes, but it's more complicated than that.' I took a breath. 'She and her husband were recently living at a commune in Jordan River.'

He wrinkled his forehead. 'You mean The River of Life Center?'

'You know them?'

'I attended a yoga retreat there years ago.'

'What did you think?'

'They were a little intense and called a few times after, wanting me to attend other retreats, but besides that, they were okay. They seem to be heavily influenced by Eastern philosophy, mysticism, Hinduism, and Buddhism, and they're also dabbling in some Gestalt Therapy, but I didn't get the feeling they were married to any one belief.' He added, 'They've done some good

43

things for the community, recycling and conservation programs, planting a public garden.'

I thought over everything he said, which matched with what I'd learned from Heather and my own online research.

'So how does the center fit into your dilemma?' he asked.

'My patient and her husband lived there for a while as full-time members, and since they've left, it seems like some members have been harassing them.'

He looked concerned. 'What kind of harassment?'

'From what I can tell, it's mostly phone calls, similar to what you received, but they appear to be of a more pressuring nature. The center wants them to come back.'

'Do you know why they left?'

'She was pregnant.' I explained what Heather had shared about the center's beliefs and that she felt members were blaming her for the miscarriage.

'How's she doing now? Has she been showing any signs of paranoia?'

'She's understandably depressed. She also has some symptoms of complex post-traumatic stress syndrome, and she's very dependent on her husband.' My mind drifted back to the commune, the way my mother didn't want to go into town alone after we returned home, how she made my father go everywhere with her.

Kevin said, 'Is that what you wanted an opinion on?'

'No, it's about the center. I *knew* the leader. When I

was growing up ...' How much did I want to reveal? This wasn't something I talked about, even with my closest friends. 'My mother joined the commune with my brother and me when we were children. We lived with them for eight months.'

His eyes were sympathetic. 'I take it you don't have happy memories.'

The thing is, there were some good moments, swimming in the river, running around barefoot with the other kids, animals everywhere, but it was all clouded in darkness and a feeling of dread when I thought back to the commune.

'It was a difficult time in our lives and something I'd put behind me.'

Kevin said, 'And that's why you don't want to work with this patient?'

'I'm just concerned I'm not the right doctor for her.'

He gnawed on his lower lip. 'All the psychiatrists at the hospital are good, so any of them would be fine, and I understand why you might want to walk away, especially if you think there's any risk of counter-transference.'

I nodded. 'Of course, that's one of my main concerns.'

Kevin said, 'But as long as you think you can maintain objectiveness and appropriate self-disclosure ...' Another thing psychiatrists had to be careful of was not to share their own feelings. We can tell them we've had experiences with pain or abuse, to show we empathize, but we

45

can't share specifics. 'I don't see any ethical issues involved with you continuing to treat her, do you?'

I thought over what he said while studying the books on his shelf, noticing that he had a few on meditation. He specialized in Dialectical Behavior Therapy, which blended standard cognitive behavioral techniques with acceptance and mindfulness, mostly derived from Buddhist meditative practice. Judging by other titles, he was also interested in philosophy. But I was avoiding his question.

'No, I suppose not …' I'd been worried that my having memories of an upsetting time in my life might make it hard to be objective, but he was right – there was no ethical reason I couldn't keep working with Heather.

'Maybe I should stay with her and play it by ear.'

Kevin nodded in agreement. 'If you need to talk about it again, just let me know.'

'Thanks. I'll see how she does over the next couple of days.'

In the cafeteria, refilling my tea, I thought over the conversation. I'd left in an odd mood, uncomfortable somehow, but I wasn't sure of the source. Was it because I'd shared something personal with a coworker? Someone I barely knew? I reminded myself that I hadn't said much, and there was no reason to worry, but I still had the feeling that I'd just opened another door, one that it was too late to close.

Chapter Five

Looking back to those first months at the commune, before Aaron began to lead the group, I realize he wasn't that old, only twenty-two, but to my teenage mind he was much older. He was so sure of himself, so confident about his decisions and opinions. No matter what the problem was, a fire that almost got out of control, low food supplies, rats in the grain, a sick animal, he never seemed worried. He would just think for a bit and come up with a solution, and it always worked. I'd never met someone who smiled so much, who always seemed happy and excited. For a child with a mother whose moods blew all over with the wind, and a father who was perpetually angry, it was confusing to meet someone who woke up each day like the world was full of wonderful things waiting to be discovered.

It was shortly after my mom, Robbie, and I arrived that Aaron revealed a little about his background. We were sitting around the campfire one night, and he'd been playing his guitar, as he often did. It was amazing how he could pull a tune out of thin air, just from someone humming the first few bars of a song. Some of the little children were climbing all over him, as usual – they all loved him for the toys he carved out of wood and the piggyback rides he gave. One of them had fallen asleep leaning against Aaron, who stopped playing to pull the little boy into his lap. Another member asked Aaron if he ever wanted a family, and a distant look came to his eyes as he stroked the child's hair.

'You guys and Joseph are my family.' Aaron, who was from San Francisco, had joined the commune with his brother a couple of weeks before us. 'We don't have anyone else.' He glanced at Joseph, who was sitting quietly in a shadow by the fire, watching his brother. Aaron gave him a smile.

A female member said, 'You have no one?'

He shook his head. 'Nope, and good riddance. Our parents were just teenagers. After they had Joseph, my dad took off, leaving us with our mother. She was an alcoholic.'

Aaron handed the little boy back to his mother, then lifted up his jeans leg, showing us small round scars up and down his shins. 'These are from cigarettes.'

Some of us gasped, or made sympathetic noises, and Joy, whom we'd met the first day, reached out to touch his shoulder. 'That's terrible.'

'It wasn't as bad as this.' He lifted the back of his shirt, revealing long red scars, the flesh raised and jagged-looking. 'That's from when she dragged me naked over broken glass because I'd tried to feed Joseph, after she forgot.' His face was angry as he dropped his shirt back down. 'She only cared about herself.'

I had never heard someone talking so openly about their feelings and didn't know what to think. I had never told anyone about my own family's struggles. I noticed my brother also studying Aaron, admiration in his face.

Aaron said, 'She eventually split. We had to live with our grandfather, until he finally died.' He stared into the fire, poked at a piece of wood, his mouth a grimace. 'He was a real bastard.'

He fell silent, gazing into the fire. Joy, her voice soft, said, 'Where did you go after he died?'

He roused himself, blinking at her like he just remembered that he was still with people. 'We lived on the streets, then we met some people and were taken into an ashram. I studied under a guru for a few years.'

One of the male members leaned forward. 'You got to study with a guru? Is that how you learned to meditate?'

We'd all seen him meditating every day, and some were already joining him.

Aaron looked excited now. 'It was amazing, everything he taught me, how to live a spiritual life – you guys have no idea what you can do with your own power, it's untapped,' he said. 'I used to suffer from back pain every day. I couldn't even bend over, but my guru taught me

49

that I was creating my own pain by holding all my fear and anger inside. He showed me how to release it with meditation, and now ...' He stood up and stretched, touched his toes.

After that night it seemed the members grew more willing to follow Aaron's advice. None of us had much experience living off the land. Some of the other members were straight from the city, with vague romantic notions of roughing it and getting back to basics. It had been a tough winter, and many of them were losing heart. But Aaron wasn't just playing at the hippie lifestyle, he was *living* it. He must've seemed incredibly worldly to most of the kids who'd grown up in Canada and had never even been out of BC. He'd also gained a lot of skills – agriculture, carpentry, how to run a farm – and he was generous and patient about sharing that knowledge. Aaron showed the commune how to build a sweat lodge so we could cleanse our chakras, which when blocked or damaged could affect our physical and emotional health. He also held kirtana meditation ceremonies in the lodge, where we'd all chant as a group, sometimes using musical instruments and clapping our hands, but he mostly taught transcendental meditation.

The young men were always trying to impress Aaron with some feat of strength or bravery, working from dusk to dawn by his side, never complaining, even if they hurt themselves. The girls also followed him around, giggling if he glanced their way, and I'd hear them talking about how good-looking he was, how cool and fun. But it was more than that.

Aaron remembered details about each member, where they were from, what their family life had been like. He suggested that one shy young man take charge of the horses, and the man grew more confident every day, teaching others how to ride and look after the tack. Another member, a woman who always spoke in a whisper, was encouraged by Aaron to take over responsibility for all our meals when he realized how good a cook she was. She too blossomed, ordering the kitchen helpers about, loudly scolding us kids for stealing a snack.

He'd also trained in vibrational healing, the ability to move his own energy through others. When a member complained of back pain, a headache, or various other ailments, Aaron offered to take them for a private meditation in his tent. He'd use his hands to clear their meridians, and the pain disappeared. One man who struggled with arthritis was soon limber again, and a woman who'd had problems conceiving was quickly pregnant. Coyote and Heidi, who were Levi's parents, had also been told they couldn't have another child, but Aaron said he could help them, and she too became pregnant.

It was after Heidi got pregnant that Aaron told us the way to achieve enlightenment was through a strict discipline of daily rituals and that we needed a leader for it to work. Everyone voted for Aaron. He said, 'I'll only agree if you promise to think of me as the head of our family, not your boss.' He put us on the same schedule that he'd lived with at the ashram. First thing in the morning we'd practice meditation. Next we'd feed the animals and have breakfast – all meals were eaten in silence, so that we could savor our thoughts. The commune was also strictly vegetarian, but the table was always over-flowing with food: whole wheat bread, honey, brown rice, beans, blackstrap molasses, bran, fruit and nuts, goat cheese, vegetables fresh from our garden. We'd meditate again, usually in the meadow, where we were open to the earth's magnetic field. Then we'd do more chores.

After lunch, when we'd have a period for reflection, he'd send us out on long walks, so we could tune into nature's healing vibrations, or we'd chant in the lodge, and maybe take a swim in the summer. Then we'd work some more, building cabins, or out in the fields and gardens, followed by a silent supper, another session of meditation, and sometimes another swim or walk.

Not long after Aaron assumed leadership, those evening campfires changed. Instead of sitting around singing every night, we now sat in Satsang, a Sanskrit word meaning 'gathering together for the truth.' We'd talk about things we'd experienced that day in our practice, some members crying, or laughing, even angry. Aaron would explain how they could deepen their self-recognition and release any destructive emotions, awakening to their life's purpose. I was amazed to hear my mother admit that she'd finally let go of anger toward her father, who'd left her mother for another woman when she was a teenager.

We also spent a lot of time learning about the benefits of sustained living and making plans for the future, so that the commune could be completely self-sufficient. Aaron said, 'We're only stewards of the land, and we have a responsibility to treasure it.' He said that every environmental disaster was the earth groaning in pain – and he hated logging companies with a passion.

We were all willing to accept Aaron as our leader, but his brother Joseph was another story. He was quiet, but not in a peaceful way, more like he was about to explode over the smallest thing. He looked a lot like Aaron, but on him everything was slightly distorted. His lips more turned down, his skin paler, and his face, thin, angular. His hair was also thin, and he wore it braided and tied back with a leather strap.

The two brothers were close, though, and I never could tell if Aaron was even aware of how nervous his brother made everyone else. Aaron said his brother was an empath, who knew when someone was faltering. We'd be in quiet meditation when Joseph would suddenly stand up and scream at someone. Once he slapped Heidi in the shoulder, and we all sat there stunned. Coyote looked like he wanted to fight, his fists tense, but Aaron whispered something to him, then calmly took his brother off to his cabin to clear his chakras.

Aaron told us that Joseph could also feel who needed the most healing or who was struggling with a spiritual lesson. They were at risk for becoming sick, so Aaron would go off with them privately, while we continued with our chores or meditation practice. They were usually female members who needed his private counsel, which he explained was because we were more intuitive and therefore more susceptible.

Sometimes Joseph stayed in his tent for days, refusing food, and meditating for hours. Aaron would praise Joseph for his commitment, so then other members started doing the same thing. After some sweat-lodge ceremonies, Joseph would start ranting, 'There's evil spirits in the woods – I could hear them singing.' Sometimes he would also hear music.

Aaron said, 'Joseph is more sensitive to negative energy waves than most people, so he can hear things on another level.'

I now suspect that Joseph had schizoaffective disorder; untreated, the person may experience delusions and paranoia, and when he hid for days in his cabin he was probably suffering a period of depression.

After we'd been at the commune for a couple of months, Aaron had a vision in meditation about how he could reach a higher state of consciousness and asked that the sweat-lodge rocks be heated longer – they were always heated in the fire, placed in a pit in the lodge, then had water poured over them. He entered alone, saying that he didn't want anyone else to get hurt, in case something went wrong. He stayed there for hours, while we all waited outside, anxious, with water and fresh fruit for him. When he finally emerged, crawling on his hands and knees, flushed and disoriented, he ranted and slurred about finally reaching nirvana. Then he collapsed.

The members had rushed to him, soaking his body with cold water, trying to drop his body temperature. It took them a while to bring him back. When he was lucid again, he stood, refusing help from anyone, though he was swaying on his feet, and said, 'The most amazing thing happened. I died and crossed over to the other side. I did it, I really did it.' He broke out laughing, but in delight, like a man who couldn't believe his luck. The members were just looking at him in shocked silence, confusion in their eyes. His voice rose, still giddy. 'I felt myself lifting, then I was standing beside you all – I even saw Joy drop a cup.'

Joy gasped, her hand covering her mouth. 'It's true!'

'I saw each of you, could hear you talking, like I was inside your minds. Then I felt my body being pulled up to the sky, through a tunnel. At the end there was a bright white light, a glorious spiritual being. My body was filled with so much love and peace.' His face now reflected the pleasure he'd felt, his gaze rapturous and his voice almost awestruck with the memory.

Aaron said the Light asked him what knowledge he'd gained and how he had loved, showing him scenes from his life. Aaron said he could see some souls still stuck in the tunnel and that the spirit explained they hadn't learned enough and wouldn't be able to transition, so they'd be sent back to Earth, doomed to repeat their lives. The spirit also told Aaron that anyone who committed suicide wouldn't be able to cross over until they healed – they needed more time to understand the error of their choices, same with drug addicts. The Light then told Aaron that he had to share what he'd learned. Aaron said, 'I felt a pulling sensation, and I was flying backward through the air, then I was in my body again.'

When he was done speaking, there was silence. Everyone was amazed, awestruck that we had this person among us, someone as special as Aaron.

One of the male members said, 'Did the Light say what we needed to do so that we could go to the other side when it's our time?'

Aaron revealed that we needed to share all our belongings, to live as one and let go of society's quest for material possessions. We had to dedicate our lives to awakening our spirits, so we could become whole and help others. Then he asked members to donate some money for our cause, only those who truly believed, but everyone wanted to prove how committed they were and donated everything they owned. Some even contacted family members, asking for loans.

At the time, Aaron's vision of the other side had amazed and astonished me, but now, with an adult's wisdom, I see it for what it truly was. Many people who claimed to have 'crossed over' came back with a renewed belief and a deeper feeling that they were put on Earth for a certain purpose, something that was certainly true of Aaron. But in my opinion, most near-death experiences are just a series of physical reactions as the neurotransmitters in the brain shut down. In Aaron's case, his so-called near-death experience was likely nothing more than hallucinations caused by heat stroke. His vision of Joy dropping a cup could easily be explained by an auditory reaction. He was delirious and might've passed out, but his subconscious recognized the sound.

But back then, I believed. We all believed.

My mother, who used to take little white pills to help her moods, saying as she held the bottle in a shaky hand that she couldn't 'deal with us,' had stopped taking them when she began to have healing meditations with Aaron. Now she seemed to be perpetually high, going off with Aaron to his cabin for hours and coming out spacey, like she was in a trance, her eyes half-closed as she wandered around, stopping to pick a flower or a leaf, gazing at it dreamily. I didn't like how disconnected she'd become, living inside a bubble that I couldn't touch, but it was better than her dark moods, when I lived in fear that she would hurt herself. I didn't know if it was the marijuana, being away from our father, or the meditations, but she finally seemed happier. Robbie had also changed.

When we'd first arrived at the commune, he'd watched out for me, just as he had for years. With parents like ours, we'd frequently been left to fend for ourselves. When my father was away fishing, and my mother was sleeping all day, he'd make me dinner, and often my lunch for school as well. He'd also bring our mom food and do all the chores around the house, feeding the animals, chopping firewood, keeping things going until she finally crawled out of her room. I'd help as much as possible, but being older and stronger, a lot of it fell on his shoulders.

If our father was in a rage, Robbie would make me hide, or once even took the blame for something I'd done, saying, 'I knew he'd use the belt. I'm tougher than you. I can take it.'

At the commune, he made friends quickly, but he also made sure I was never sitting alone, and when he'd done his chores, he'd help me finish mine. In those first weeks and months, when the members would gather for Satsang or a campfire meeting, I'd look up and see him keeping an eye on me. He was my raft in an ocean of uncertainty, my only safe person in this new world, where all the rules had changed. But then he also started to drift away from me, spending all his time with Levi or the teen girls in the commune – a new one in his tent every night.

More and more, I was on my own.

We were starting to expand. Aaron wanted the young people to go into the village to sell produce we'd grown in greenhouses at the farm market and find other people who might be willing to join our group. It wasn't hard. The members were fresh-faced and wholesome-looking, our vegetables, herbs, homemade jams, baking, and eggs were always a hit. The members would explain that everything was organic and our chickens roamed free, while they handed out pamphlets on social consciousness. If someone stopped to listen, we'd tell them about the commune, how cool it was, how joyful and free we all were. We'd also pick up hitchhikers, and teenagers hanging around the corner store.

Aaron often went with us, and he could always sense right away who was a good target. Complete strangers would be telling him their heartbreaking stories in minutes. He'd hug them, reassure them, then bring them back to the commune, where we all greeted them with a plateful of food and a seat by the campfire.

While we ate, Aaron would talk about how we were all connected to every blade of grass and seed, and that it was our purpose to spread love and awareness. Everyone would be nodding and agreeing, passing a joint around, hugging each other. After the meal, he'd ask the new people to do a small task; they always agreed. They'd end up spending the night. The next morning, Aaron would ask them to help with something else, moving some equipment or planting, which would take all day, so they'd end up spending another night. Before they knew it, they were living at the commune.

No wonder people stayed. The commune was the perfect place to be if you were lost, afraid to take control of your life. It was the opposite for me. Something about Aaron made me shy and nervous, and I was frightened of Joseph. Looking back, I now understand it was because I was a child of abuse, too, and could sense volatility in others. Aaron was intense, and for a child who'd grown up with a manic mother and an alcoholic father, intensity equaled danger.

By the end of May, we'd swelled to sixty members, and the commune was a constant hum of activity. Aaron had handpicked two male members, Ocean and Xavier, to be Spirit Counselors to work with anyone Aaron felt needed more help, or whom Joseph had gotten a bad feeling about. Maybe that was when the tide started to turn, when things stopped being so simple. Ocean and Xavier would stand there, eyeing us and whispering to each other, as we waited, sick with tension, wondering who wasn't living up to their potential. Then Aaron slowly began to implement a system of punishment.

At first the infractions were usually something simple.

If a member had taken an extra share of food, they wouldn't be allowed to eat our next meal. If someone broke their meditation to go to the bathroom, they'd have to sit away from the group. Then things grew more serious. If a member argued with another member, they were tied together and had to work in the fields side by side. When a few members went to town for supplies, one later said he'd seen another use some of the commune money to buy a newspaper, something Aaron had strictly forbidden.

Hearing this, Joseph flew into a rage and started to whip the man's legs with a branch, screaming that he'd bring evil influences into the commune. We watched, horrified, until at last Aaron intervened, and it was decided that the man should be made to drag the plow through one of the fields for a day. We were all upset, but not at Joseph. We were angry at the man for disrupting our peace and harmony, and even after Aaron declared him rehabilitated, we ignored him for weeks.

When a young man smacked his girlfriend in the face because she'd been flirting with another member, he was told to pack his belongings. He was driven a mile away and left to find his own way back to town. No one ever checked to see if he'd made it.

Then Aaron created a small group called the Guardians, who were to patrol the commune at night, watching for wildlife or anyone trying to steal our supplies, especially once we started growing marijuana and magic mushrooms. Robbie was ecstatic to be chosen, along with Levi, for this task.

The women didn't have many roles – caring for the children, cooking, and working in the fields or greenhouses mostly. But they did a lot of hard labor, and our mother's arms became tanned and sinewy, her hands rough. I saw less and less of her that spring. Late in April, Aaron had decided that children over five years old should be kept in separate cabins, near another small building that was used for the school, and raised collectively. He said, 'Children belong to everyone. We're all their mothers and fathers.'

Some parents balked, but Aaron explained that this was necessary for our spiritual growth as we needed to connect to our true selves and not our earthly attachments. I remember being confused by this and ashamed. And so the parents agreed, terrified that if they didn't, their children wouldn't achieve the perfect state of spiritual insight and tranquillity that we were all trying to attain.

One morning, after we'd been there for several months, Aaron gathered us together after breakfast. The air still smelled like coffee and baked bread, fresh mint and sweet fruit, but I'd barely eaten. I was upset at my mother that day. I'd asked her if I could see some of my old friends from school, and she'd drifted away with a vague smile, saying, 'We have new friends now. Just be happy.'

Aaron warned us that it was easy to grow apart, even in a large group, and said we needed to practice a 'sharing' exercise, to bring us closer. He asked us to write letters, confessing any wrongdoings and negative thoughts, no matter how shameful or darkly hidden. He said it was to seek our own truths, an inner examination that no one will see, but when we were done, he'd gotten another vision. We needed to read them in front of the commune, to let go of all separation, even in our thoughts.

When people protested, he said, 'It's the only way to clear yourself from your past. If you aren't ready for this step, then you shouldn't be here.'

The crowd quieted. No one wanted to leave.

Aaron pointed to the young man who looked after our horses, and said, 'Billy, I know you're ready.'

Billy stepped forward, his face flushed, and read from his letter, admitting that he'd experimented sexually with a cousin when he was a teenager – a male cousin, and that he still had fantasies about men. We listened, embarrassed, as he stammered through it. We waited for Aaron's reaction, and when he reached out to embrace him, we all breathed with relief. Other people ventured forward to share their sins, and each time Aaron praised them. It was painful. People were sobbing, or silent, heads downcast. Others stared around with glazed eyes, looking shell-shocked.

Then it was my turn.

I confessed that I'd snuck food to the animals and had

angry thoughts about other members. My hands shook, and I was crying so hard I couldn't finish. Aaron grabbed the list and read my final confession. Then he handed the list back to me.

'You're not done.'

'I can't. Please, I don't want to.' I met his eyes, begging for leniency, but he was impassive, his only expression one of disappointment.

'Don't you want to be like the group? Everyone else shared theirs, and if you don't, you'll disrupt our harmony.'

I looked around at the angry faces, Heidi touching her belly, her face scared. I read my last confession, my voice quavering. 'I love my mom, but sometimes ... sometimes I hate her. I wish she was more like my friends' moms. I wish she was normal.' I searched the crowd, finding my mother, her blue eyes filling with tears. I held her gaze, my own tears dripping down my face. Trying to convey my thoughts: *I'm sorry. I didn't mean it. I was just angry.*

She turned away.

By the time we'd been at the commune for five months, I had retreated into myself, barely speaking. I spent all my time with the animals and began to have fantasies about running away. I might have tried if it hadn't been for Willow, a pretty, doe-eyed teenage girl, with caramel-colored hair that hung to her waist, who joined the commune that June. She told me about the places she'd hitchhiked to, the people she met on her way. She also told me I was going to be beautiful when I grew up. She gave me a beaded necklace, draping it around my neck, teasing me with her husky laugh for being shy. That day she'd been wearing faded bell-bottom jeans and a man's cinnamon-colored leather vest with tassels, which hung on her small frame, her feet bare, and one toe sparkling with a ring. I didn't know if I was going to be beautiful or not. I just knew I wanted to be like her. I wanted to be free.

Chapter Six

Before I started my rounds, I consulted with the nurses. Michelle told me that after Daniel left the day before, Heather had gone back to bed and slept through the night – she had to be coaxed out for a shower and breakfast. Then she'd gone back to the seclusion room and had been sleeping ever since. She was only responding briefly when spoken to and was still lethargic. I wasn't surprised that she'd retreated into herself after our initial meeting, as patients' moods often ebb and flow. When I entered the seclusion room, I found her in the same position as the day before – curled into a ball.

'Heather, can you come out for a little bit? I'd like to talk to you.' We can meet with patients in the seclusion rooms, as I had her first morning in the unit, but we try to encourage them to come out because it's better if they stay active.

She shook her head, mumbled something.

I kept my voice cheerful. 'I know you're tired, so I won't keep you for long. Then you can go back to bed and have a nice snooze.' When patients are first admitted, we focus on their basic needs, making sure they're drinking lots of water, eating, and showering, because they usually just want to sleep. Once they're more alert, we begin to work with them on a care plan. This conversation would just be a quick assessment to see how she was settling in.

Heather finally rolled over and slowly got to her feet. She didn't bother putting on the robe Daniel had brought, just shuffled behind me, her head down and her hair concealing her face.

In the interview room, I started off with some basic questions.

'How are you sleeping?'

'I'm tired.' She looked it, her head drooping, body slumped in the chair.

'You can go back to bed soon. Maybe this afternoon you'd like to come out and watch a little TV. What do you think?'

She didn't answer.

I asked a few more general questions: *How are you managing? Are you still having bad thoughts? Is there anything you need?* And got the bare minimum answers: *Fine; yes; I want Daniel.*

I said, 'I'm sure he'll be up this afternoon.'

'Can I go back to bed now?'

I ended our session at that point and led her back to the seclusion room. Based on her current state, she was still too depressed to do any real emotional work, so we wouldn't be able to discuss her care plan for another few days, which is when we'd also increase her antidepressant if she wasn't suffering any side effects.

Over the next couple of days, there was no change in Heather's condition. The nurses told me that she was still sleeping a lot, though she would come out for her meals, which she'd pick at. She'd show some signs of life when Daniel came to visit after work, and they would sit and watch TV together, her head on his shoulder. After she'd been in the unit for three days, she was more alert, so they moved her over to the step down unit, on the other side of the ward, but still part of PIC. On her fifth day, we increased her Effexor, and when she'd been in the hospital for almost a week, she was finally more communicative.

In the interview room, I said, 'How are you doing today?'

She was still rubbing at the bandages on her wrists, but I noticed that her eyes seemed brighter, and she was sitting up in her chair.

'Better I guess ... still kind of tired.'

'When you have more energy, we have some excellent groups you might like. Painting, life skills, relaxation exercises, crafts.'

She laughed, and though it was weak, it was the first time she'd showed much reaction to anything I'd said for a few days. 'Sounds like River of Life.'

'You had group programs at River of Life?' I made sure that my tone was casual, more curious than interrogatory. With Daniel not around, I hoped she might share more about the center.

'Aaron doesn't believe in medications. That's why I stopped taking my pills. He said I could heal myself, my meridians were just blocked.'

I wasn't shocked to hear that. He'd never liked medications, even in the early days of the commune, and wouldn't allow any of the members to consult doctors. It was amazing no one had ever died from medical complications.

'They had classes on how to be happy. They said you can use your mind to cure anything. It didn't help me, though.' She gave another hollow laugh.

'Depression is a disease, just like diabetes, or anything else. Even if you're feeling better, you can't just stop your medication. Let's talk about ways you can take care of yourself when you're feeling depressed. What were some things that helped in the past? Like exercise, or a favorite movie or book?'

She shrugged, scratched at her bandages. 'I used to do yoga.'

'So maybe that's something you can try again. We have group sessions a couple of times a week.'

She looked lost in thought. 'That's how it started. I met a woman at my yoga class, and she told me about this meditation retreat she was going to at the center. She said she had gone before, and it was the best experience of her life.' Her voice turned mournful. 'I just wanted to be happy, too, but look at me now.' She slumped in her chair, her earlier glimmer of energy snuffed out. 'What's the point of even talking about this? It won't change anything.'

My head filled with questions about the center. What happened during the retreats? How many members lived there? But I couldn't ask – this wasn't about me. I shoved everything to the side.

'We can show you how to stop your thoughts when they start spiraling down, like if you suddenly feel depressed, try to remember what you were just thinking. Once you identify the trigger, you can replace it with an alternative, more positive thought. Would you like to try some together?'

She stared at her knees. 'They said they could help me too. When I went to that first retreat, I *did* feel happier. Everyone was so nice – they complimented me and made me feel special. And they listened to everything I said, like my opinion actually mattered.'

What Heather was saying sounded like 'love-bombing,' which was something various groups and even salespeople did. They give you what they think you're missing, encouragement, compliments, validation, to make you feel good about yourself, which in turn makes you feel good about them. I thought back to the commune, remembering that Aaron would ask us to be extra nice to new members and show them how happy we were living at the commune.

Her eyes filled with tears. 'I hate myself for leaving. Why didn't I just stay there?'

I waited to see if she'd answer the question for herself, but she was just staring at her feet now.

'You didn't want anyone else to raise your child, which is perfectly understandable,' I said. 'Have you been having more troubling thoughts?'

She nodded and wiped her nose on her arm. 'I don't want to tell Daniel about them.' She took a shuddering breath. 'He's always worrying about me.'

'We won't tell Daniel anything you don't want us to. But you can talk to me. Is there anything you'd like to share?'

Her face grew sad. 'We did sharing exercises at the retreats. Daniel and I were partners the second weekend I was there – that's how we met. Aaron matched us. He said our energy was really strong together.'

'What kind of exercises?'

'We had to confess things.' She shifted her weight, tugged at the bandage on her wrist like it was suddenly too tight. 'I don't want to talk about it.'

My chest had also tightened at the word 'confess'. I wanted to ask Heather more about these exercises, to see if they were like the confession ceremony I had participated in or something even worse. Maybe there was a clue there as to my memory loss. I hesitated. It wouldn't be right to push Heather before she was ready – but she was the only person who could help fill in the blanks. I was still thinking about what to do when she continued on her own.

'They said they could help me, that all my problems were in my head.' Sounding wistful now, Heather said, 'So after a couple of weeks, I sold everything I owned, moved to River of Life, and started helping in the store.' I wondered what kind of store they had and whether it was at the commune.

'I wanted to be good at something.' Heather paused, thinking. 'Before Daniel came to the retreat, he'd been in Haiti, helping after the earthquake, and before that, he was overseas. He's done such amazing things with his life. I haven't done anything. I'm always quitting stuff – school, jobs. I have a trust fund, from my grandparents, and my parents bought me stuff and gave me money, so it just never seemed to matter. When I was at the center, though, I liked working at the store. I designed the displays – and I was good at it.' She began to pick at the bandage on her wrist. *Pick, pick, pick.* 'When we left, I couldn't find a job, because I was pregnant, so Daniel had to take two jobs. I was alone for hours.'

'How was that experience for you?'

'I hated it.' She stretched like she was trying to get

away from something, squirmed in her chair. 'Every minute seemed so long. I would watch the clock, TV, anything. But I was tired all the time, so I'd sleep. I tried to make him dinner when he came home but I'd make a mess and burn it.' Her eyes filled with tears, and she started shaking her head. 'He should have a wife who takes care of him. Look at me.' She held out her wrists. 'Who would want me?'

'Have you had more thoughts about hurting yourself?'

'I keep hearing a voice in my head.' She stopped. 'I don't mean like someone else's voice. It's mine, but it's saying that I should die and—' She broke off, her hand covering her mouth.

'It's okay, just take a moment. I know it's hard to talk about these feelings, but I can show you healthy ways to ease painful emotions rather than hurting yourself.'

She took a breath and started again. 'I call myself names.'

'Like?'

Her lips curled into a snarl, and her voice rose. 'You stupid bitch, I *hate* you. You can't do anything right. You're an ugly, worthless piece of shit.' Her voice changed back to normal. 'It makes me want to take a knife and gouge at my body, all over.' She pantomimed stabbing her legs, slashing at her body.

'Who is the voice?' I wondered if she might be experiencing some splitting, a form of dissociation.

'I don't know – me, I guess. I just want it to be over.'

'If everything is over, then you also don't get to experience anything good. There's no turning back.' I held her gaze. 'Death is a permanent decision. Your husband, your parents, they might never recover.'

'But then they could stop worrying about me – and my father can stop being disappointed.'

I wondered if that's why she'd been drawn to the center. A group that provided lots of encouragement and acceptance would have been very enticing. She was still searching for approval from an authority figure.

I said, 'Can you think of another time in your life when you felt depressed?'

Speaking in a flat tone, she said, 'When I tried to kill myself before.'

'If you had succeeded then, you wouldn't have met Daniel, right?'

'That's true . . .' She turned toward me, a flicker of awareness in her eyes. My words had connected.

'Well, that's something to keep in mind next time you're feeling depressed – wonderful things can happen. What's kept you going in the past?'

'Sometimes I'd want to kill myself, but I'd think about how angry my dad was the first time I tried, and that would stop me for a while.'

'Do you think maybe he was angry because he was scared to lose you?'

'He doesn't care about me. The second time I did it was *because* I wanted him to get mad – I just wanted him to see that I was hurting.' She shook her head. Though the sentiment was sad, I was pleased that she was showing some self-awareness. She added, 'You must think I'm so stupid.'

'It's not stupid to want your father to love you. But hurting yourself to get attention isn't the best way of going about it.'

'It didn't change anything anyway. They came back from their trip, and Dad made me see a psychologist, but then they just gave me money and left again. He's a lawyer, and everyone thinks he's this great guy.' Her mouth twisted. 'But he never spent any time with me. Neither of my parents did. When I was growing up, everyone thought my life was perfect because we're rich, but I was just lonely.'

'That must have been difficult. When you're depressed, being alone can make it even worse, so we can come up with some ways to combat that, okay?' I was willing to bet that loneliness was one of the main reasons she'd sought out the center in the first place – she'd wanted to belong somewhere.

'But it always comes back.'

'What comes back?'

'My depression – I'm so tired of feeling this way.' She faced me and the depth of pain, the hopelessness in her eyes made me catch my breath. 'Maybe I can't be cured. I've tried everything – antidepressants, yoga, therapy. I thought the center would help, but it just got worse. I don't think I can be helped.'

'You *can* get better. You started feeling depressed again

75

because you went off your medication, and you suffered a painful loss. That was a lot to take.'

'Aaron said that we create our own pain, and that you can't allow yourself to become dependent on medication. You can teach your body not to need it.'

I made myself take a breath before I spoke.

'Many people need medication for depression. There's nothing embarrassing or shameful about needing help. It's a difficult disease, but you can learn to manage it, just like you would any other health issue.'

'I'm not strong like that. Aaron said not eating or sleeping before we chanted would bring us closer to our true selves, and we'd learn to control our bodies, but I just felt confused.'

'How long did you have to go without food or sleep?'

'Sometimes days, I don't even know. It was just a blur. They'd talk to us for hours, about the center, their beliefs, how they could change our lives.'

It sounded like they were using alertness-stopping and programmed confusion, which was alarming – cults use it as a way of breaking down new members. While in university, I'd written several research papers about cultic groups and studied some of the more destructive ones. They didn't all have paranoid gun-toting leaders – some of the most dangerous ones paraded under the guise of human-potential groups. There was a great deal I didn't yet know about the center, but it did seem as though Aaron had progressed to new extremes.

'Was it like that when you went to the first retreat?'

She shook her head. 'They were just about how to slow down and come back to center. They were very relaxing. I'd walk around the grounds, and everyone would be smiling, or meditating on one of the hills. Everything was so quiet there, and the stuff that usually mattered, like cars or cell phones, movies, clothes, status stuff – no one cared about any of that. You ate all this healthy food, got fresh air, exercised, and just focused on stopping the noise in your head.'

'So when did you participate in the other chanting ceremonies?'

'Not until about the fifth retreat, after I'd asked to come live at the center. You had to prove you were committed.' Her arms tensed slightly, and she rubbed them, like she was cold.

'And that's when you fasted and went without sleep?' I was starting to get the feeling there were two sides to the center, one that was presented to the public, as a relaxing retreat, and the other a more intense version for full-time members.

She nodded, then started picking at her nails again, like she was nervous about having shared so much. 'Some other stuff too, but yeah.'

'Heather, anyone would start feeling depressed in that situation. Your blood sugar would plummet, and fatigue would make it even worse.' It would help Heather if she could see how she'd been manipulated, so that she'd be better able to stop the pattern of self-blame. I thought about how she said Daniel had to take two jobs after they left and wondered what had happened to her trust money.

I said, 'Did the center ever ask you to donate money to them?'

Now she looked even more nervous, her gaze flicking around the room, her chest rising as she started to take rapid breaths. She said, 'I shouldn't be talking about them. I told Daniel I wouldn't say anything.'

So they had, and judging by her reaction, she had complied. I wondered why Daniel had allowed them to leave. He'd obviously wanted to stay, and the behavior Heather had exhibited to this point, even her promise to her husband, showed someone more likely to submit to him. Either he'd given in to her feelings to keep her happy, or deep down, he might've also had his own doubts.

When she didn't elaborate, I said, 'I know you weren't comfortable with the center's beliefs about raising children, but was there anything else that you didn't agree with?'

She glanced at me nervously again, shrugged. 'Some stuff . . . it was just different how they did things – but it helped a lot of people.' She said the last part slightly defensively, and I wondered whom she was trying to convince.

I said, 'Like what?' I heard the words come out of my

mouth, and realized I'd asked because I'd *personally* wanted to know, not because I was worried about Heather. I felt a rush of anger at myself. This was not the kind of doctor I wanted to be, one focused on her own agenda. But it didn't seem like Heather had even heard my question.

She said, 'I keep thinking about when I was first there. How fun it was, and how happy everyone was. I felt really good, better than I had in years.' Her eyes filled with tears. It sounded like she was glorifying her first days there, in a sort of euphoric recall, like some people do about the beginnings of their relationship, after everything falls apart. 'Maybe I'm the problem. If I couldn't stay happy at the center, then maybe I'll never be like that. Maybe they were right, and I was just scared to let myself be happy. Why didn't I just stay?'

I repeated what I'd said on the first day I met her. 'You made a choice that felt right for you. You wanted to protect your child.'

'I don't know.' She looked confused. 'I was thinking that maybe I should go back. When I get out of here ...'

'I don't think you should make any decisions about that right now. This is a place for you to take a time-out from life, so you can focus on getting better.'

Her face was beginning to shut down as she pulled away from the conversation.

'Can you concentrate on taking care of yourself for now?'

She didn't answer, and I couldn't push harder without risking her shutting down completely, so I said, 'Would you like to talk about something else? You mentioned another girl, Emily. Do you want to tell me about her?'

Guilt washed across her face. 'When we'd been living at the commune for a few months, we were assigned people who came to a retreat – like a spiritual brother or sister. We had to go everywhere with them. Emily's only eighteen. She'd tried to commit suicide before too, that's why she came to the center . . .'

Where was this girl now? If she was suicidal, then the center might be the worst place for her. My concern was elevated even higher when Heather said, 'She was still depressed at the center – but I talked her into staying for another retreat, and now she lives there full-time. If you were able to get people who came to workshops to sign up for another one, Aaron would sit with you in a private meditation. I wanted him to like me.' Her eyes turned flat, despairing.

Trying to get visitors to sign up for more retreats also fit with the profile of many human-potential groups, including ones of a cultic nature, but it had been the mention of private meditations that alarmed me the most. I thought back to the commune and got a murky memory of Aaron leading female members off for healing sessions, his hand on their lower back, or resting on their shoulders, in almost a caress. Had he really just been trying to heal them, or something else?

I turned my thoughts to my patient, who still needed my help. I leaned forward and made eye contact. 'It's obvious that you're a very caring person, Heather. I'm sure you didn't want any harm to come to Emily.'

She looked down at her bandages. Then in a quiet voice she said, 'She shouldn't have listened to me. I'm useless. I couldn't even kill myself properly.'

Chapter Seven

On the way home from the hospital, I thought back to the commune and Willow, the first person to get me interested in medicine. She had a vast knowledge of herbs and plants, about which ones could be used for natural remedies, and quickly took over the greenhouse. If anyone had an injury or an ailment, they would consult Willow. She'd use lavender for just about everything – antiseptic, anxiety, insomnia, headaches, skin problems, upset stomachs. Stinging nettles helped with joint pain and as a laxative, comfrey tea for coughs. Yarrow could stop a toothache and was used as an astringent.

She always smelled like some herb or plant, rosemary one day, rhubarb or sage the next, but mostly lavender. She made soaps and lotions, shampoos and lip balms, pastes and oils. Food came alive with her herbs. I asked her once how she knew so much, and she told me that she'd grown up near a reserve and spent hours with a First Nations woman. When I inquired about her parents, her hand paused as it fussed with a leaf, and her mouth pulled down, so I changed the subject.

Joseph tried to bully her a few times, questioning her use of an herbal tea, claiming that she was trying to poison the members, but Aaron intervened and sent him to his cabin, while Willow watched, her face concerned. He then told Willow that she shouldn't use that tea anymore. She'd tried to explain it was harmless, but Aaron wouldn't budge. It wasn't the first time there'd been some tense moments between them. When people consulted Willow about an herb or some ailment, Aaron would make sure to give them a healing session right away. He'd thank Willow for her supportive treatment, but he'd stress that it was his clearing of their meridians or blocked chakras that had cured them.

That summer, Aaron had started to send members to sabotage logging equipment, where they were working in the mountain, then he'd had a vision that we should spike the trees, so the chain saws kicked back. Willow hadn't agreed with the idea, worried about hurting someone, and Joseph had been furious, shouting, 'The Light's going to punish us all if we don't obey his message.'

Aaron gripped Joseph's arm, holding him still as his body reared, like a young bull ready to charge the crowd. Aaron whispered something to him. Joseph studied the members, holding eye contact with each of us until we looked away. Willow was the only one who held his gaze, and I wanted to yell at her, to warn her that she was going to make it worse, but I was frozen in fear.

Finally, almost vibrating with anger, Joseph said, 'We have to destroy anyone who's hurting the earth. If we don't, something bad is going happen. I can feel it.' He grabbed his head in his hands. 'In here.'

His words sent gasps and murmurs through the group.

Aaron just said, 'Come on, Joseph. Let's hear what the others have to say.'

Joseph's mouth was open as he breathed heavily, his gaze going from person to person, but his voice was terrifyingly calm as he said, 'As you wish,' then walked off.

Aaron turned back to the group. 'Do you all agree with Willow?'

Tension rippled through the members. My body filled with dread as I waited for their answer. What was going to happen if they said yes? They'd never gone against Aaron before. Would he make her leave? I held my breath.

Then one member nodded, and another. The rest followed.

Aaron smiled and said, 'Then I'll meditate and find another way.' He then headed toward the lodge, his hands clasped in front of him, his head bowed.

The members stared after him, or looked at one another in concern. Though Aaron had appeared understanding, they were obviously worried that he was upset. I was also worried about his reaction, which had seemed too calm. Some members might've gone after him, but Willow turned to everyone with a smile.

'Let's go swimming before we melt in the heat!' The members, relieved to have someone tell them how to feel about the experience, started laughing and running down to the river. Robbie and Willow walked behind everyone, talking about something. I walked even slower, trying to hear what they were saying, but I couldn't make anything out. Robbie glanced back at me once, his face unreadable.

At the river, everyone stripped off their clothes and dove in. Most of the members were naked, as usual, but some men wore jeans shorts, and a few women wore bikinis. Coyote, who was Levi's father, was on the other side, climbing up the rock bluff at the end of the pool. Members called out, daring him to jump. Coyote, as wild as his name, would always take the highest dives into the river. He'd try to get Levi to join him, but Levi would only jump from the lower rocks, smiling when his father called him 'chicken,' but I'd see the hurt in his eyes. Robbie could leap from the higher rocks, but when Levi was there, he'd stay at the same level.

This day, I stayed on the commune side of the river with the other children, and, never a strong swimmer, I walked partway out, my knees numb in the cold water. Robbie was sunning himself on the shore on the far side, his shorts wet and his hair dripping. He shook his head like a dog, sending droplets onto Willow, who was nearby with the other women and my mother. She scooped up some water and threw it at him, the spray sparkling in the sun.

Coyote, almost at the top of the cliff, where an old log jutted out, stopped to howl. We all laughed, then fell silent when he crawled out onto the log. Levi, who'd been with the group of girls, made his way toward his father, his long legs flashing white as he jumped from rock to rock.

Coyote crawled farther out on the log, which was precariously balanced over the river. It wobbled for a moment, then righted itself. The group below let out a gasp. His wife, Heidi, called up, 'Coyote, come down!'

He grinned, checked that we were all still watching, and crawled out another couple of inches.

Robbie stood with his shoulders tense and his hand across his brow, blocking the sun. As Levi started to climb the cliff behind his father, his foot knocked a small rock off a ledge. It bounced, hitting against the cliff on its way down, splashing into the water. Coyote, distracted by the sound, turned in its direction, shifting his body weight. There was an audible crack as the log began to break away from the bank. Heidi let out a scream as Levi yelled, 'Dad!'

Coyote plunged into the water, the log crashing in on top of him. Levi scrambled back down the cliff. The other members, Robbie in the lead, were all swimming toward the spot where Coyote had disappeared. Robbie dove down. He came up, motioned for help, then Levi dove in beside him. They were down for so long that I began to sob, great gasping gulps of air. Finally Robbie came up, Coyote's limp body under his arm. Levi popped up next. They swam to the shore, pulling Coyote behind them. When they'd gotten him up on the rocks, Willow crouched down, motioning everyone back. Heidi was screaming. Robbie and Willow worked feverishly on Coyote: Willow giving mouth-to-mouth and Robbie doing chest compressions. Willow stopped, said something to Robbie.

Still standing in the water, my entire body shaking, I saw Coyote's head roll to the side, his hand limp and his mouth open, blood dripping from a gash in his forehead. Aaron was now running down the hill with Joseph, drawn to the screaming. When they got to the other side, Aaron tried to find Coyote's pulse, put his ear to his mouth. Then he looked at us and said, 'He's dead.'

Aaron and Robbie lifted Coyote and carried him back to the commune, laying him on the table. We gathered around, somber and quiet, some weeping. Heidi just moaned in broken grief. Water dripped off Coyote's wet jeans shorts, pooling around his body. He was the first dead person I'd ever seen.

Aaron motioned us to come closer as he stood at the head of the table. His face was grave and his eyes damp. 'We've lost a member of our family, and I know you're sad – I am too, I loved Coyote. But I promise you that he's in a better place.' He looked at Levi, who was staring at his father's body, rivulets of water from his wet hair mixing with tears and dripping down his face. Aaron clasped him on the shoulder. 'Coyote's not gone. His energy's all around us.' He looked at the group. 'But so are the negative energies that caused his accident.' The group made confused whispers, unsure of what Aaron meant. He said, 'One of the members denied my vision, and so we've been punished.'

Now everyone got it. Subtle tones of anger waved out toward Willow as they made the connection. Willow stepped back, looking fearful for the first time.

Aaron stared at her for a moment and turned away. 'We need to learn from this, or we won't be able to ascend to the next spiritual level and join our brother. Coyote has given us a great gift. We shouldn't grieve. We should be thankful.'

The commune murmured excitedly. We'd witnessed death, but Aaron's belief that Coyote's spirit was still alive gave us hope, and we grasped at it. No one wanted to face that we'd never see Coyote again.

He said, 'Now let's get back to work, and later in meditation, some of you may be able to connect with Coyote.' He focused in on Willow. 'We'll talk about your spiritual path after meditation.'

She nodded, her face concerned.

*

The police came and took statements, the coroner leaving with Coyote's body. A couple of hours later, Heidi miscarried. For the rest of the day, the commune was in turmoil, speaking in hushed voices, anxious for our next Satsang, and avoiding Willow. None of them wanted to end up like Coyote and Heidi.

Aaron had taken Willow into his cabin for a private meditation, and when they emerged, Aaron announced that Willow was now ready to 'accept his visions.' Willow agreed, but she still looked troubled.

The next afternoon, I noticed Willow frowning again during our Sunday spiritual class when Aaron reminded us that we had to share all our belongings or we weren't truly living as a family. Many of the members went to their tents and brought out belongings, swapping with other members, thanking them with smiles and hugs. After dinner, Aaron sent the group for our reflective walk but said that Willow was going to stay behind and meditate on her lesson from the day before. Joseph came with us, but Aaron was also going to stay and tend the animals.

As I followed the group up the trail, I glanced back and noticed Willow and Robbie talking at the edge of the forest. Then Robbie spun around and headed toward the logging road that led away from the commune. I caught a movement by the barn and realized that Aaron had been watching. Willow walked toward the river. Aaron followed. I wanted to sneak down to the commune and see what they were doing, but when I looked back up the hill, my mother was motioning for me.

The members splintered off into little groups, or found a quiet spot to meditate alone. Joseph drifted into the woods. One member was always appointed to stay back at camp and ring the chimes, signaling that our reflection walk was over. Aaron had said he'd do it. This time he left us to meditate for a long time, and when we got back it was getting dark. The group decided to have a late swim. I noticed that Willow and Robbie were missing, but Aaron joined us at the river. After the children were sent to their cabin, I stayed awake, worried about Robbie. I tried to make out voices at the campfire and could hear Aaron, and once in a while my mother and other members, but I still couldn't hear Robbie.

The next day at breakfast, I was excited to see that Robbie was back, but when I ran toward him, I realized something was wrong and stopped as though an invisible wall had slammed down between us. His skin was pale, his hair messy, damp tendrils sticking to his forehead. His eyes were also red-rimmed and bloodshot. And he was holding his hands funny, like they hurt, the knuckles skinned. I wondered where he'd been all night. Then my next thought was, *He should ask Willow for some salve.* When I glanced around, I couldn't see her.

Everyone gathered for our morning meditation, but before Aaron started leading us through the chants, he motioned us closer and told us that Willow had left early that morning. 'I tried to talk her out of going, but she wouldn't listen. She said she was tired of being in one place and wanted to travel again.'

When Aaron sent everyone off to meditate and clear the bad feelings that Willow's abrupt departure had created, I snuck to her tent, searching for a note, an explanation, something. All I found was a hand-sewn patchwork bag tucked under her pillow. Inside were a few items of clothing and homemade toiletries.

Aaron came in after me. 'What are you doing in here?'

I clutched her belongings to my chest as I stared up at him, my pulse loud in my head. 'I don't understand why Willow left.'

Then I realized he was wearing Willow's vest.

His face was calm, but his tone warning. 'She didn't like living as a group, so this wasn't the right place for her. Each member has to do what's good for everyone, not just ourselves, or we all suffer.'

A question flew out of my mouth before I could pull it back. 'Why do you have her vest?'

'She left it by the campfire this morning.' He looked down at it, fingered one of the tassels. 'The Light wanted me to have it.'

Some members were upset that Willow was gone, especially so soon after Coyote had died, but Aaron said that we shouldn't forget that her negative vibe led to Coyote's death and that she'd been causing problems in the commune. We'd get along better without her. The only people who ever seemed to have a problem with her were Joseph and Aaron, but now that she'd left, the group was quickly forgetting that detail. Aaron also reminded us that we couldn't let Coyote's death be in vain, and we had to try to learn from his and Willow's mistakes. Coyote's life had been sacrificed in the river so that we could save ours. That's when the commune started calling themselves The River of Life, and one of the men carved a sign for the tree at the entrance, two hands reaching up to the light.

I don't know how long we would've lived at the commune if a little boy hadn't died. His name was Finn, and he was eighteen months old when he wandered off during a late-night campfire ceremony. It was late September, and by the time his stoned parents, who also had a two-month-old baby, realized he was gone he'd been missing for hours. Everyone was woken up and we searched all over, but we couldn't find him. The commune had a meeting to decide whether to go to the police. It was a risk because they had marijuana plants drying in the barn, and we'd already garnered attention with Coyote's death.

Finally, Aaron meditated in the sweat lodge and said he'd had a vision that Finn was hiding somewhere warm and because he'd been taught to eat berries and find water, he'd be okay. In the morning, we still couldn't find him, so we meditated as a group, chanting to bring him home, but Aaron said our fear was blocking his connection with the other side now. Finn's parents took one of the trucks and went to the station. The police found Finn later that day, facedown in a puddle, his tiny hand still stained with berries. He had died of exposure.

Everyone was devastated. Aaron himself looked upset, holding the wooden horse he'd given Finn, but he stood tall and said, 'In my vision, he was okay. I thought it meant he was still with us, but I understand now that was a sign that he's safe on the other side.' In the days after, Aaron spent a lot of time working with us to reach Finn's spirit. His face intense as he led us in chants, his voice sure and strong. Sometimes in a meditation, Finn's mother would start to cry, saying that she'd seen him and how peaceful he'd looked, bathed in light. Others said the same, but no matter how hard I tried, I could never see him.

After Finn died, my mother started having long, private meditations with Aaron, but it didn't seem to help. She stayed in her cabin for hours, cried a lot, and I often saw her talking with the other women, her face sad. Since Willow had left, Robbie had been spending all his time fishing in the river. I tried to talk to him about Mom, and he told me not to worry about it. She was just upset about Finn. He'd speak to her. Not long after that, our father finally came to get us.

*

A truck pulled up at the commune when we were in the middle of dinner. I recognized it right away and got up from the table, saying, 'That's my dad!' Robbie also stood, but our mother was still sitting, her eyes anxious.

The truck stopped a few feet away. Dad got out, his dirty baseball hat scrunched down over his head, his face angry, and his hands tense by his sides.

Now Aaron stood and said, 'Can we help you?'

'I've come for my family.' Dad motioned for us. I took a step, but then I looked at Aaron, who held up a hand. I stopped. Robbie was also standing still, his expression full of relief as he gazed at our father. Our mother hadn't moved. I glanced over at her. Her eyes were wide and her mouth parted.

Aaron said, 'They have a new family now.'

My dad said, 'Kids, get your stuff.'

I felt a movement to my left. My mother was starting to rise, but slowly, cautiously, her face scared. She looked at my dad, then Aaron, hesitation in her eyes. I was shot full of fear. I wanted to leave, but I was afraid my dad was going to punish us for having run away. I couldn't tell what my mom was scared about – my dad or leaving. Robbie was moving away from the table now, toward his tent, but he was walking slowly, looking back at my mom, waiting for her. She finally started toward her cabin, but as she passed Aaron, he grabbed her arm.

'Kate, think about what you're doing. Your children are safe here.'

Standing by the truck door, my dad said, 'I wouldn't do that if I were you.'

Aaron glanced at him, then instantly let go of my mother. I looked at my father, and realized he was now holding a rifle down by his legs. He must've had it on the floorboards.

My dad said, 'My family's going to get their belongings and our animals. Then they're leaving with me. You got a problem with that?'

Aaron calmly said, 'Hey, man. We don't want any problems here. If they want to split, they can go anytime.'

The trailer was still parked behind the barn, and Mom and Robbie quickly loaded the horses. Terrified of what might happen once we got home and confused about why my father had shown up after all these months, I was standing transfixed, watching them. Robbie motioned for me to get moving. I grabbed Jake and the cats, putting them in the cab of the truck, with my bag of belongings. I kept glancing at the table, where the group was watching us, some of them looking confused, others upset. I wanted to say good-bye, but when I moved toward the table, Robbie grabbed my arm. 'We've gotta go.'

That was the last time I saw any of them.

Chapter Eight

The evening after my session with Heather, I went to grab my bike out of the shed, just like I had many nights since I moved there, but this time the small space made me break out in a sweat and my heart race. I gripped the handles on my bike and tried to back out quickly, but a garden tool fell over and jammed in one of the wheels. In a full panic now, I yanked on the tool, but my palms were slippery, and my hand slammed backward against the wall, scratching my knuckles.

After I finally got my bike out, I wheeled it down my driveway, sucking the small wound, angry at myself. Earlier that day, I'd also panicked when I was waiting for the elevator to the parking lot. The doors opened, and I hadn't been able to get in, even though there were no people standing inside. I had to take the stairs, fighting nausea in the cramped stairwell until I'd finally pushed the metal doors open and flung myself out into the light, breathing in big gulps of fresh air.

It was obvious my talks with Heather about the center were bringing back my claustrophobia, but I just wished I knew why, so I could face the fear head-on. I decided to bike down to the seawall to clear my mind. I'd paused at a red light, when a pickup truck idled up beside me. When I glanced over, I noticed an older man with a baseball hat, long nose, and dark, bushy eyebrows, like my father's. There was an empty rifle rack in the back window. The light turned green, and he roared off, but I was left frozen in a memory.

As we drive away from the commune, I glance back through the rear window. Aaron is staring after the truck, with hatred in his eyes like I'd never seen before in my life. My breath lets out in a gasp. Robbie turns to look, but by then Aaron's expression is blank again. He watches until we are out of sight.

A car pulled up beside me, the radio blasting, and I was snapped back into the present. I continued on my way down to the seawall, but I couldn't shake the pall my memory had cast over me. I'd forgotten that look on Aaron's face the day we left, how badly it had scared me. Now I remembered all the fear I'd felt as we drove off, that somehow Aaron would make us go back and that we'd be in trouble, but I was also happy to see my father, my mother sitting beside him again, all of us crammed into the front seat of the truck. We were going home.

We tried to settle back into our lives, and I'd tried to fit back into my school. One of the members had been a former teacher so we'd had some classes, but I had to work hard to catch up or risk being put behind a grade. I never really connected with my friends again. I'd changed. We'd all changed. Robbie had come back sullen and distant, getting in fights at school and drinking. Worse, he'd barely speak to me. Even our animals were different. The cats, half-feral now, moved out to the barn and wouldn't let anyone near them. Jake would run off, coming back days later stinking of carrion, his eyes wild and his fur matted.

Nothing was the same again.

The next couple of times I saw Heather she was more communicative, and Michelle told me she was starting to come out on the floor during the day, interacting with other patients, and had even joined a group session that Kevin was teaching on relaxation. Daniel was still visiting every day after work. Because Heather was on the step-down floor, and there didn't seem to be any risk of her running away, she was allowed to wear street clothes. She usually dressed in jeans and sweaters, the sleeves pulled down over her wrists, and they were expensive brands. I wondered how she'd fare if her parents ever cut her off financially.

Now that Heather was taking better care of herself – her hair always tidy and pulled back into a ponytail – she looked like a fresh-faced college student. Though she was often apologetic and insecure, she also had a really sweet side to her, asking how I was, expressing concern over another patient, and I could see why Daniel was drawn to her. I had come to like her myself, finding something about her sensitive, empathetic nature endearing.

I ran into Kevin one day in the hall outside his office.

He said, 'So how's it going with Heather?'

'She's coming along. I'm glad I stayed with her.' I was thrilled that she was doing better. Too often we see people who are chronically suicidal, hell-bent on destroying themselves no matter what. It was nice to treat someone like Heather, who was actually listening and willing to participate in her care plan.

'Good. I'm happy it worked out.'

I didn't tell him that it was having the opposite effect on me. My patient was getting better, but I was sinking. Now that Heather had opened the gates to my memories, I needed the light on at night again, or I'd toss and turn for hours, listening to every sound. At the hospital, I'd stopped being able to use the elevator and had to take the stairs. Even driving through a tunnel would leave me nauseous and shaking. After work, I couldn't stand the idea of going home to be alone with my thoughts, the walls pressing in on me, so I drove the streets, looking for Lisa.

When I'd first moved back to the city, I'd gone to the apartment building where one of Lisa's friends had told me she was living. But the landlord, a nasty piece of work, had evicted her. A young man told me she was staying with some people downtown, but that turned out to be a dead end. She had crashed on their couch for a while, then disappeared. When I asked if she was still doing drugs – meth used to be her poison of choice – they told me that she was trying to get clean and had mostly succeeded. But I knew that without following a program, her chances of success were slim, something we'd battled about many times before.

While her father was sick – Paul was diagnosed during my last year of residency – Lisa, fourteen at the time, had also started slipping away from me, barely speaking, dressing in baggy clothes, bleaching her hair, ringing her eyes in black, and hanging out with kids I didn't trust. Then, after Paul died, those dark days when part of me died with him, she grew even quieter, refusing to talk, staying out all night, sleeping all day, skipping class. Even her half brother, Garret, then twenty-one, couldn't pull her out of her shell. He'd only been five when I started dating Paul, and not too happy about it, though he'd come around eventually. When Paul was sick, Garret spent a lot of time with Lisa, taking her out for hamburgers, making sure she was occupied while I was at the hospital. When I'd get home she'd pick fights over everything. My heart ached for her, knowing how desperate she was for her father. But I was also angry at her for battling me when I was barely getting through the days, for doing drugs and destroying herself when I was doing everything I could to keep my family together.

I'd caught on quick: the mood swings, the bad skin, the agitation and paranoia. I hated the demon that was stealing away my sweet daughter, who used to foster animals and friends, who wanted to be a vet one day like her father. And I despaired when I saw her falling apart in front of me, her cheeks growing hollow, life disappearing from her eyes. When she was a toddler, she'd been a chubby little thing with round-apple cheeks. I used to pretend to nibble them, which would make her squeal with laughter, and her eyes were always her most expressive feature. Now I couldn't even get her to make eye contact.

I'd ransacked Lisa's room one day, finding the locked metal box in the back of her closet. I threw everything away, the little baggies, pipes, straws, ashtrays, and mirrors, and when she came home, threatened rehab. She'd begged for a second chance. I gave it, and within weeks, she was staying out all night again. Finally, out of sheer desperation, I sold our house and moved up to Nanaimo, hoping a smaller community might mean less trouble. Even there she found ways. In her last year of school she ran away three times. Still, she managed to graduate, albeit at the very bottom of her class. Now, I thought. Now she's turning her life around. But my relief was short-lived. The day school ended, she threw some things into a backpack and stormed out of the house. I later learned she'd moved back down to Victoria.

Since then, I've tried to keep tabs on her through parents of her friends. She came home one Christmas and spent most of it on her cell phone, while I tried to recreate the magic of her childhood. She'd promised to come home the next Christmas, even phoned a few days early to confirm, but then never showed up. She hadn't been home since. I've kept every present from every Christmas and every missed birthday. But I couldn't stop missing my daughter.

There wasn't a night that went by when I didn't wonder where she was, if she had enough to eat, if she was cold. I tried not to think about how she might be damaging her body, the things she might be doing to get more drugs. Mostly I struggled with guilt. *Was it because I was so consumed with my own grief? I should have talked to her more, should've found out what was going on earlier.*

And underneath that was the shame at my failure as a doctor. When she first started doing drugs, I thought I could help her. I was a psychiatrist, of course I could help my own daughter, but then, when every attempt failed, and she ran away, I thought, *What kind of doctor am I?* How can I hold myself out as a professional when my drug-addicted daughter is living on the streets?

Sometimes I wondered if the problems started even before Paul became sick. He was a veterinarian, and after we had Lisa I stayed home for a year, then worked part-time at the clinic. When she was five, I decided to become a psychiatrist, a long-held dream that Paul supported, so I went to medical school in Vancouver. Lisa lived with me and also started school. Paul would visit on the weekends. We moved back to the island when Lisa was ten, and I completed my residency at St. Adrian's. I did my best during those years to balance everything, to be a good wife and mother, but now I'd remember all the times I'd been short with Lisa when I was rushing to class, or told her to be quiet when I was studying – and her disappointed face.

The last time I saw Lisa was eight months ago. After I was attacked outside my office, one of my friends, Connie, had finally tracked her down through some of Lisa's friends. She'd visited me in the hospital. I'd been thrilled, had wanted to hold and hug her so hard that she could never run away again, but she was edgy, dark circles under her once-gorgeous blue eyes, her tall frame, so like her father's, painfully thin. Reminding me of Paul before he died. She could barely look at me and only stayed a few minutes, saying she had to meet a friend. I lost track of her after that, her friends changing as fast as her location.

After I moved down to Victoria and discovered that the trail stopped cold for Lisa, I visited the Victoria New Hope Society – they run three shelters for the homeless – with a photo of her, but they wouldn't give me any information. I wondered if I'd know my own daughter if I saw her. I didn't even know what color her hair was now. The first time she'd bleached it, I'd tried to understand that she was finding her own way, tried to applaud her individuality, but I'd missed the little girl who wanted to grow up to be just like her mother, who used to ask me to braid my hair like hers so we looked the same. We were never the same, though.

She was quiet, and I was communicative, always trying to get to the bottom of things, always wanting to know why people felt the way they did. I wondered if that was one of the many ways I'd gone wrong. Living in a family where nothing was discussed, I'd wanted openness with Lisa, encouraged her to talk about her feelings, to share her thoughts, but she'd always kept her own counsel. That had frustrated me when she was younger, as much as it scared me. It wasn't until after she moved out I realized that I'd wanted her to share her feelings so I could guide them and control her, so I could keep her safe.

Once in a while on my evening drives, I'd stop and show her photo to some street kids, wondering if Lisa would hear that I was looking for her, worrying that my attempts to find her might just push her away again.

I shouldn't have worried. It was always the same thing: just another group of kids, with their hoodies, baggy pants, and skateboards, not one of whom had ever laid eyes on my daughter.

*

That night, after my fruitless search for Lisa, I pulled in my driveway and as I walked around the corner of my house to my back door, I noticed the black cat stalking a bird. She spotted me, and with a clatter of garbage can lids, leaped on top of the fence. The cat glared down, her skinny tail flicking back and forth – not afraid, angry. I made kissing sounds, but she turned her back and began to lick her paws. I put some tuna on a plate and walked back out. She eyed me from her perch on the fence but wouldn't come closer, no matter how many enticing sounds I made. I put the dish up on the railing of my deck. In the morning, on my way to the hospital, I noticed happily that the plate of tuna I'd put out the night before had been licked clean. Tonight, when I returned home, I'd put out a blanket-lined box, so she'd have somewhere safe to sleep. My mind flowed back to Lisa, and I wondered where she was staying and if she was warm at night. I wondered if she ever thought of me.

The nurses told me that Heather wasn't sleeping as much and had joined another group session the day before, then spent the rest of the day watching TV with some patients – all good signs. During my interview, it was clear she was still struggling with self-esteem issues and guilt about leaving the commune, but I was able to get her to focus on staying in the present as we worked on her care plan.

'What can you do today that might help you?'

She said, 'I can join a group or take a walk around the ward.'

'Those are great ideas!' We talked about a few more things she could try, then I asked if she was still having thoughts of hurting herself.

'Sometimes, but not as much.' She looked around. 'It's different in here. I'm not as lonely. And the nurses, like Michelle, they're all really nice. I feel ...' She shrugged. 'Safer, I guess. Like I'm not weird or bad or something.'

'You're not. And I'm glad that you're starting to see that.'

'It's nice, having someone to listen to you.' She smiled. 'I used to listen to Emily when she was upset. We'd go to the barn – she loved horses.'

'Sounds like you were a great support for her.'

'I felt like her big sister.' She paused, thinking. 'I showed her how to ride bareback, and we'd go down to the river every day, just to talk.'

As Heather began to describe the trail they took down to the water, my mind filled with images and sounds, the forest cool in the summer, the creak of a saddle, the earthy scent of the woods and horses, and I was pulled back in time.

Willow and I are riding together, bareback through the woods. We pause to let the horses drink from a pool in the river. She's standing near me, her horse nuzzling her shoulder. She says, 'I watch Aaron with you some-times . . .'

My heart starts to thud in my ears, panic digging into my blood.

She's still talking. 'I saw you coming back from the river with him. You looked upset. If there's anything you ever want to talk about . . .'

Now my heart's hitting so hard against my chest, I can barely breathe. Shame, thick and hot, presses down on me.

My voice angry, I say, 'There's nothing to talk about.'

'If he hurt you—'

But I'm already turning, climbing up a log to jump on the back of the horse. 'Let's go.'

Heather's voice pulled me back into the present as she said, 'That's one of the reasons I thought about going back, so I could help her. I hope she's okay.'

I shook off my memory, though the emotions still lingered, fear and confusion sitting hard in my belly.

'She's probably okay, right?' Heather said.

'It sounds like you feel some responsibility for Emily, but she's an adult and can make her own decisions. Just like you made a choice to leave, now you can choose to follow your treatment plan and take care of yourself.'

She nodded. 'I know. I am getting better. I can feel it already.'

*

After I was finished with Heather, I met a new patient, a woman in her early seventies named Francine who was brought in after she'd been found wandering the neighborhood in her nightgown. She'd been diagnosed with dementia and didn't have any family. Dementia patients were always hard to treat as there wasn't much we could do for them, and they had to stay at the hospital until there was room in a nursing home. They were confused and upset by their memory losses and frequently tried to escape. Francine had spent the day walking around, testing the doors, begging us to let her go. She refused to be comforted, and we had to just leave her alone, until she calmed down on her own. When we met, I'd asked if she knew why she was in the hospital, and she'd laughed gaily and said she'd been on an adventure, then her face had turned grief-stricken and scared. She said, 'Why am I here? When can I go home?'

I gently said, 'Miss Hendrickson, you're in the hospital because you're having troubles remembering things, and we don't want you to get hurt.'

She was looking around the interview room, a confused expression on her face. 'I'm in the hospital?' Her eyes suddenly lucid and clear, she turned to me, and with a sad voice said, 'I'm never leaving here, am I?'

'You're just staying here a little bit longer while we run some tests.'

She grabbed my hand across the desk, her face lit up with a smile and her eyes sparkling. 'I had such a life! I was an artist and traveled the world to paint. I had friends in every country. I could tell you stories, so many stories.' Her eyes filled with tears, leaking into the deep grooves on her face, her white hair long and snarled around her face. Her voice quavered, filled with doubt and turned little girlish. 'I don't have anyone. No family, no one. I don't know where everyone went. What happened to all my paintings? Where's my pretty house? I just want to go home.' She started to cry harder. 'I can't remember anything.'

Chapter Nine

Back in my mid-twenties, when I was still living in Victoria and starting my second year of university, my therapist suggested that I talk to my mom and my brother about my experience at the commune, to see if they could open the window to my memories. But if anything, they slammed the door shut on them.

My mother never liked speaking about the commune after we left, especially if my father was around, but I caught her alone in the field one fall morning as she spread hay into piles for the horses. The sun was out, warming dew from the night before and making the ground steam. Mom was dressed in one of Dad's bulky work coats, her dark hair stuffed under an old cowboy hat. Even in that masculine garb, she was pretty.

I grabbed a flake and started to help her. After a moment, I said, 'Mom, I need to talk to you about the commune.'

She kept working. 'I don't like talking about the past.'

'I know, but this is important. I've been in therapy, for my claustrophobia, and my therapist thinks something happened to me at the commune.'

My mother stopped and looked at me. 'Like what?'

She was shorter than me, but she pulled herself up tall, her shoulders squared, work gloves on her hips. I felt a small thrill at her protective stance.

'Something traumatic that could have made me scared of the dark and small spaces. Like maybe I got stuck under something.'

'You've never liked the dark.' She took her hands away from her hips.

My thrill disappeared as I picked up the new tone in her voice. The one that said: *Is this what you came here to bother me about?*

'It's not just nervousness, it's more than that. I have panic attacks, and when I think back to the commune, I get uncomfortable sometimes.'

'About what?' She looked confused, her brows pulling together.

'I think I was scared of Aaron. I didn't like being around him.'

'Why on earth would you have been scared of him? He was so nice to you. When he took a few of us on that picnic up at the lake because we'd been working hard, you even got to sit in the front of the truck with him.'

I tried to think about a time we might have gone on a picnic, but nothing came to mind. I shook my head.

111

'I don't remember any of that.' But I did remember the fog my mom had been in back then. 'Are you sure it was me?'

'Of course it was you. You liked Aaron. After Coyote died, Aaron spent hours down at the river teaching you how to swim.'

I thought back. 'I can't remember that either.'

My mom looked like she couldn't understand why I was being so dense. 'We couldn't get you back in the river until he started helping you.'

'I didn't like him. He made me nervous.'

She sounded surprised now. 'He's the reason you know how to swim.'

I was embarrassed that I had no recollection of any swimming lessons, and that I'd voiced my uncomfortable feelings about Aaron – feelings she obviously didn't share.

'Do you remember a girl named Willow?'

She paused for a minute, thinking, and then nodded. 'What about her?'

'She was just really nice to me. The commune, some of the people there, for a kid it was scary. But I liked her.'

She said, 'Aaron could get carried away with all that New Age spiritual stuff, but they were all just harmless hippies.'

It was the first time my mom had ever given an opinion on the commune's beliefs, and her tone made me wonder if she hadn't been on board with them as much as I'd thought. I said, 'Maybe, but I just wanted to go home.'

She looked upset for a moment and almost defensive, as she said, 'You had it a lot better there than at home.'

Feeling defensive myself, I said, 'Then why did we leave?'

Her whole body flinched, like I'd hit her, and it took her a moment to speak. 'That little boy . . .' Her eyes were sad. 'He was so sweet, just a baby still.' I was surprised by her emotional reaction after all this time, the sorrow in her face, and thought she might cry. But then she took off her glove and rubbed her hand across her nose, tossed her head with an angry jerk. 'Social services were involved, the cops. It wasn't good for you kids to be there anymore. Your dad said he was going to be home more, and I wanted to give our marriage another try.'

Though Dad forgave her for running away, and he quit working on the boats, their marriage had never improved. If anything, it was worse. I couldn't count how many times we had to buy plates because they'd thrown them at each other. Eventually, Dad had started spending all his time hunting, or at the pub, until Robbie came to collect him. Mom spent all her time with the horses.

Mom put her glove back on and took another flake out of the wheelbarrow, dumped it on the ground. 'The commune left after that – moved down to Victoria.' She held my gaze. 'Don't go looking for trouble, Nadine. You'll only cause yourself pain.' She touched my cheek gently, the glove rough on my skin. 'I might make a lot of mistakes, but that one I know for sure.' She grabbed the handles on the wheelbarrow and headed back to the barn.

It was only a few weeks later that she died in the car accident.

I didn't have any more luck with Robbie. Back then, he was living in a rental house with two guys in the village. They worked for the same logging company, building roads. I caught him alone a while later, changing the oil on his truck.

He stopped, lit a cigarette, took a long drag. 'What's going on?'

'I was just out at the ranch talking to Mom.'

'Yeah? What about?' He took off his baseball cap, ran his hands through his sweaty hair and jammed it back down, black tufts winging out by his ears. He was twenty-nine at the time and still handsome, in a tough don't-mess-with-me way, though he was uncomfortable in his body, pacing restlessly, especially in social situations, like he couldn't wait to escape. And he never seemed to date, or have a girlfriend, that I knew of anyway.

Since I'd moved to Victoria after high school, we didn't spend much time together anymore, only seeing each other at family dinners and holidays, where I'd sit, depressed, staring at my father's and brother's beer cans on the table, their stony faces as they dug into their mashed potatoes and gravy. Mom, mixing wine with whatever pills she was taking, just picked at her food. If Mom and Dad hadn't erupted into a fight by that point, she'd disappear to the barn after dinner, and Robbie would head outside for a smoke. I'd follow him, making small talk that hurt my heart as I babbled about my life, trying to find something that would interest him. Once in a while I'd make him laugh, then, mistakenly thinking that meant we were on the same team again, I'd say something about being concerned about Mom and Dad, who was having trouble keeping a job since he'd left the boats. Robbie would angrily butt out his smoke, and say, 'They're fine. Worry about your own life.'

Now I said, 'I was asking her about the commune.'

He took another drag before he said, 'She doesn't like to talk about it.'

I didn't know he'd tried to talk to Mom about the commune and wondered what they'd discussed, if anything.

'I know, but I've been seeing a therapist, and I underwent hypnosis, so I can—'

'You're letting some guy hypnotize you?' He raised an eyebrow, a smirk playing at the corner of his lips.

'It's called Recovered Memory Therapy. It's a real thing. He thinks something happened to me when we lived there, and that's why I have claustrophobia and have to sleep with the light on.'

'You were always freaked out about the dark. When you were little, I had to give you my flashlight to sleep with.' Now I remembered Robbie sneaking into my room when I was crying one night. He'd whispered, *What's wrong?* I'd told him there were bad things in the dark.

'But it seems like it got worse when we came back.'

He shrugged. 'I don't know anything about that.'

I said, 'Do you ever think about the commune?'

'Not really.' But he took another long drag and looked away.

I said, 'Remember Willow?'

His face was blank, but his eyes narrowed, like he was wondering where I was going with my question. 'What about her?'

'It was weird how she left. Did she say good-bye to you?'

He shook his head. 'As far as I know, she didn't say anything to anyone.'

'Don't you think that was strange?'

'No. She probably knew everyone would give her a hard time.'

'Why do you think she left?'

Another shrug. 'She was probably sick of the commune, being told what she could and couldn't do. She was a free-spirited kind of chick.'

'She left her stuff, though ...'

'She left *one* bag.' He sounded annoyed. 'She probably forgot it.'

'I guess ... There's some other stuff that's freaking me

out. Mom told me about some picnic we all went on and how Aaron taught me to swim, but I don't remember any of it.'

'Shit, there's tons of stuff I don't remember from when I was a kid.' He took another long drag. 'You gotta stop letting this doctor mess with your head. He's *giving* you problems.' He blew his cigarette smoke out in a laugh. 'If you weren't fucked up before, you will be now.'

I went home that day more confused than ever, wondering if Robbie was right – my therapist was trying to make something out of nothing. A theory I started to believe more when he never could unlock my trauma. Instead he taught me some coping techniques for my claustrophobia, and I was eventually able to sleep with the lights off. We ended our sessions, and I moved on with my life.

In my last couple of years of earning my Bachelor of Science, I worked part-time at a vet clinic and fell in love with Paul. We married as soon as I graduated and had Lisa a year after. There were new challenges, raising a family, finishing medical school, commuting, but we were happy for the most part.

In the nineties, Recovered Memory Therapy was discredited, and I grew even more convinced that there hadn't been any mysterious trauma in my past. But once in a while, when my claustrophobia was triggered, by a small room, someone standing too close, or even a busy shopping mall at Christmas, I'd think back to those sessions with my therapist. Was he right after all? *Did* something traumatic happen at the commune? I always managed to push the doubts away.

Now I remembered something else my therapist had said, that my psyche was protecting me, and when I was ready, the memories would come back. They might be triggered by a scent, photo, or even a voice or phrase.

If they were coming back now, I wasn't sure I was ready.

Chapter Ten

The day Francine was admitted, I came home exhausted, and still confused by the memory that had surfaced that day. I needed to talk it out with someone, so I called Connie, my best friend in Nanaimo, also a psychiatrist. We met at university and have been close ever since. Even when we were both married, we tried to vacation together once a year. Sometimes we only managed to meet up at a conference, but we had fun together, spending as much of the time as possible in our hotel room, eating ourselves silly on junk food and watching bad movies.

Connie had been traveling in New Zealand for a couple of months with her husband and had just arrived back, so we caught up. We'd emailed while she was away, but I shared more about my move and new job. Then I explained about Heather, leaving out her personal information, but divulging that it had stirred up some memories of my time at the commune. I'd never shared that part of my life before with Connie, or that it could be the cause of my claustrophobia, so it led to another long conversation. I finished by telling her about my recent flashback of Willow. At the end, I said, 'Many of my memories center around her.'

'She obviously meant a lot to you.'

'I was painfully shy then, and she was kind to me. We spent a lot of time in her greenhouse.' Another memory fluttered forward. I was in the greenhouse with Willow and she was explaining how the First Nations cured leather. I asked about her vest, if she had made it herself, and she told me it was a gift from her brother, who died in Vietnam, the only thing she had left of him.

I told Connie about the glimpse. 'Strange that I just remember that now.'

'She'd confided in you about something important to her. You must've felt special – and probably very abandoned after she left.'

'It was confusing, I do recall that. So was that memory of being at the river with her and the horses. I don't know why I reacted so badly.'

Her voice softened. 'Do you think that Aaron may have done something to you? And that's why you were so ashamed to talk about it?'

'I've been considering that possibility all afternoon, and it's deeply upsetting to think that he might've molested or hurt me in some way. But I just don't see how he could've. There were always so many people around.'

'Did he ever take you anywhere?'

'I don't know. My memory is still murky about so much.' I thought back, remembered the conversation with my mother. 'He apparently taught me to swim, so I suppose I would've been alone with him then, but I don't recall anything about that, certainly nothing bad or him being inappropriate with me or any of the other younger girls. I was just uncomfortable around him. I do remember that.'

We were both silent for a moment. I'd stepped away from viewing this as something that might've happened to *me* and was just looking at the situation analytically. I didn't want to react to anything until I had more information.

I said, 'His center has become very successful. If he was a pedophile, I find it hard to believe there have been no other reports over the years.'

'His success could be part of the problem. Victims might be scared to speak up.'

'I don't know, maybe … Or maybe something happened to me during one of the lessons. Perhaps I got trapped underwater.' I told her about Coyote.

She said, 'It certainly would've been traumatic if you'd nearly drowned after already witnessing a death and definitely could cause claustrophobia.'

'Exactly. I've never been comfortable near rivers since.' More memories came back now, how I always wanted to swim in a lake or the ocean, the time I'd made my boyfriend leave the old commune site. 'It's the more likely scenario. Willow might've witnessed my coming back from a lesson when I was upset.'

'That's also very possible.'

We talked until Connie's husband came home. By that time, I'd had a headache and had to take some Tylenol. Later, resting on the couch with my eyes closed and the fireplace warming the room, my mind drifted back to the memory of Willow's leather vest. She'd loved that vest; why would she just leave it by the campfire? And why didn't she say good-bye to anyone? She knew we would be upset. Then I thought back to the last time I saw her, talking with Robbie at the forest's edge, when the rest of us were leaving for our walk. I narrowed my focus, tried to think of her face. How did she look? I got an image of Willow seeming annoyed, her forehead pulled in a frown and her hand gesturing, an angry motion. That's when Robbie had left. Then I flashed to the memory of Aaron watching her as she walked down to the river, the malevolent energy in the air, the sick tugging in the pit of my stomach, my body full of dread.

I opened my eyes, stared up at the ceiling, a thought stopping my breath. *Did Willow really leave the commune? What if Aaron did something to her?*

I wanted to turn away from the question, at the impossibility of it, but then I began to consider the facts. He was the last person to see her, and her departure had been odd. She'd had many friends at the commune, and no reason to walk out without saying good-bye or explaining her decision. The only person she had a problem with was Aaron. There'd been lots of tension between them, especially the day before she left. He said they were okay after their talk, but what really happened that day? And why did he follow her down to the river?

I sat up abruptly, my mind filled with terrifying images: Aaron and Willow in an argument, him striking her, or hitting her with a rock, maybe even strangling her. I tried to stop my runaway thoughts. *Quit it, this is ridiculous.* What would he have done with the body? She would have been found by now. Then again, would she have? That mountain was remote, the river wild, there were many spots that had probably still never been seen by human eyes. Unless a hiker or someone with a dog had come across her, she could've remained out there for years. I wondered if her body was in the woods somewhere, rotting alone in the leaves and dirt, animals carrying her bones off into the mountain.

I thought about it until exhaustion finally took over and I fell asleep. Hours later, I woke, rain pounding on my roof, my heart racing, the scent of lavender in the air, and Willow's husky voice in my head: *Don't let him follow me.*

Chapter Eleven

Over the following week, Heather continued to improve, and we moved her to the floor below, where she would have more freedom. Noticing she had no visitors other than Daniel, I asked about her parents, and she said they still hadn't gotten hold of them. I got the feeling they weren't trying too hard and that she probably didn't want them to know what had happened. I'd walked by her room one day when Daniel was visiting and heard them laughing. It made me hopeful that we would be able to stabilize her enough that she could go home and continue to improve on an outpatient basis. Daniel also seemed optimistic, and I told him if she continued to do well, she might be home in a couple of weeks.

On the weekend, I forced myself to take a break from everything and made plans with a friend. I hadn't had more memories surface that week while working with Heather, but I was still struggling with the suspicion that something could've happened to Willow. I needed a distraction. I met up with a friend, a retired psychiatrist, to celebrate my birthday, though I wasn't much in the mood. We decided to catch a romantic comedy at the movie theatre. Elizabeth's also widowed, and we joked that it was the closest either of us had come to romance in years. But as I watched the characters fall in love, I had a little ache of loneliness, a remembrance of what it felt like. Then I flashed to Kevin and wondered if he was seeing anyone. That surprised me – was I interested in Kevin? I thought he was intelligent and always enjoyed our conversations. I'd also noticed that I'd started to scan the parking lot for his vehicle in the morning. So maybe I did find him attractive, but I quickly reminded myself, there was too much of an age difference.

My thoughts drifted to Paul, how secure I'd always felt with him. Our relationship hadn't had the intensity of the ones in my youth – men molded after my father, distant or dominating, usually drinkers – but the sweet comfort of being so connected to another human being you could coexist in harmony, supporting each other while still being your own person. Then I realized that as much as I missed Paul, I also missed being married and wondered if I ever would be again. I shook off the idea. That time was over, and though it was difficult to find pleasure in any aspect of my life when my daughter was on the streets, I tried to remind myself that it was okay to enjoy the good things in my life. I loved my house, my job, and I was blessed with wonderful friends who I could travel with, and – I glanced over at Elizabeth – laugh with at the movies. But it was still hard.

That was another reason I'd decided to work at the hospital – I'd wanted to be part of a team. Private practice can be lonely at times. There's also a bigger risk of connecting with your patients because you might relate to their issues. There's less chance of that in a hospital, where you work with people who are more acutely ill. At least that was the plan until I met Heather. But watching her get better reminded me of why I'd gone into psychiatry in the first place. I was profoundly pleased that I was able to have some impact on Heather's life and believed she had a strong chance of making it.

Then we got news that her parents had been killed.

It was Michelle who phoned me at home that Sunday evening. Daniel had called the unit, saying he had some bad news to tell Heather, and he needed help. I called him back right away.

'They were asleep in their RV when it happened,' he said. 'Apparently, fumes from their propane stove had leaked in. A hunter found them – they'd been dead for several days, and he noticed the smell.'

It was a terrible image, their bodies rotting alone in the woods, but without the smell it might have taken days longer.

'The police want me to tell Heather.' Daniel sounded frantic. 'Do we have to?'

'She's in the best place to find out. Would you like me to tell her?'

'I think I should do it – she'd want to hear it from me.' A long pause. 'But what if she tries to hurt herself again?'

It was a very real concern and something that had worried me the instant he told me the news. 'We'll put her under close observation and move her back up to PIC, where we can keep an eye on her until she's over the worst of it. But we shouldn't tell her tonight. Let's wait until tomorrow. Try to get some rest.'

'Okay, thanks.' He sighed into the phone. 'I just wish I could take away the pain for her.'

'I know.' I felt the same way. I wished I could take away Heather's pain, and Daniel's.

In the morning, we met in the visiting area. He was pale and obviously nervous, constantly rubbing his unshaven jaw or running his hands through his hair, his whole body keyed up. He met my eyes and said, 'This is going to be the hardest thing I've ever done.'

'Would you like me to be with you when you tell her?'

'Thanks, but I think I should do it alone.'

'I'll be close by in case you need help.' I held his gaze. 'I know you're scared, but she'll get through this, okay?'

He took a deep breath and squared his shoulders. 'Okay.'

The nurses had already placed Heather in one of the interview rooms, and she thought she was waiting for our morning session. When we walked in, she was reading a book, sitting cross-legged on the chair, her feet tucked under her jeans-clad legs. The book was a course guide for the university. She was making plans for her future – a future we were about to turn upside down.

She looked up with a smile. 'Daniel! I didn't know you were coming in.'

Daniel sat in the chair beside her and held her hands. He tried to smile back at her, but his lips were tight, his eyes sad. She searched my face, then Daniel's. She said, 'What's wrong?'

I said, 'Daniel would like to speak with you. I'll leave you two alone.'

Just as I sat nearby at the nurses' station, where I could observe on one of the monitors, Daniel leaned close to Heather. I couldn't hear anything, but his face was gentle, and I could tell that he was explaining what had happened.

Heather's body rocked backward, her hands across her mouth, which was opened in a silent scream.

Daniel was still talking, his hand on her shoulder. He was obviously trying to comfort her, but right now Heather wasn't able to absorb anything. She was just shaking her head back and forth, trying to block him out. Daniel pulled her in for a hug. She pushed him away, then pressed her hands against her ears.

Daniel looked up at the camera in the corner, his face helpless.

I knocked on the door and walked in. Heather turned to me, her expression beseeching. 'They're *dead?*'

'I'm very sorry, Heather.'

'Maybe it wasn't them. Maybe it's a mistake.'

'The police are positive, or they wouldn't have notified Daniel,' I said.

She stared at me for a moment as my words sank in, then she started to sob, in loud, choking gasps. She doubled over, clutching her stomach. Daniel rubbed her back while I handed her the Kleenex.

When her sobs had finally eased, and she was sitting back up, I said, 'I know you're hurting right now, and this must be very overwhelming, but we're going to support you through this. You're not alone.' I explained that her parents would want her to focus on her treatment and reassured her again that she would have help through this difficult time. Then I left them alone for a while and got the nurse to give Heather some Ativan. When I came back, Heather was still sitting beside Daniel and holding his hand, the occasional shiver vibrating her body. She looked like a storm had swept through her: tear tracks down her face, hair half pulled out of its ponytail, the expression in her eyes dark and empty.

I said, 'How can I help you, Heather?'

She looked up at me. 'It's too late. They were right. If you leave the commune, everything falls apart.' Her voice was so sure and calm, almost prophetic. The hair on the back of my neck stood up. This wasn't good. She sounded like she was giving up. Something I didn't want to see happen.

Echoing my thoughts, Daniel said, 'It's not too late. You're going to keep getting better, and we're going to have a wonderful life together.' He bit out the last words, not angry, but desperate to convince her, to cement her in this world.

I said, 'I understand that it feels like things are stacked against you right now, but you can get through this. It will just take some time—'

'It doesn't matter anymore.' Her voice was flat, resigned. 'The baby, my parents. They all died after I left.' She rubbed at her arms.

Did she think she was being punished? I said, 'You haven't done anything wrong, Heather. What happened to your parents isn't your fault.'

She just kept shaking her head and repeating, 'They were right.'

I waited for a moment. Beside her, Daniel was also silent, his body rigid and his face concerned, but she didn't say anything else. I was still worried, but it was obvious she wasn't going to share anything further, so I moved on. 'Your parents' death was a terrible tragedy, but you will get through this. We're going to put you in another room, okay? It's closer to the nurses' station.' I'd wanted to put her back up in PIC, but all the beds were taken. Each floor had a seclusion room, though, so she'd still be on camera and closely monitored. 'If you have any thoughts about hurting yourself, I want you to tell somebody.'

She nodded, but her expression was bleak, her chest heaving with the occasional sob. Daniel sat with her until the Ativan started to work, and I finished my rounds. By the time Daniel left, and the nurses moved her into the seclusion room, she was calmer, though still shell-shocked, her face pale and her eyes vacant. While I made my notes on the charts, the nurses kept a close eye on her, and I peeked in again before I left for Mental Health. She was curled into a tight ball, sleeping. The next day, the nurses told me she'd slept fitfully for most of the day, waking up crying and wanting to talk, which meant she was at least processing her emotions. But she'd become upset and agitated when Daniel arrived later, sobbing that he was going to die next, so the nurses had given her another dose of Ativan.

When I met Heather in the interview room the next morning, I said, 'You had a bad blow yesterday. How can I help you? Is there anything you need?'

Her voice hollow, she said, 'I still can't believe they're dead. I hadn't talked to them for months. The last time . . .' She caught her breath, started to cry. 'The last time I spoke to my dad, he was mad at me for getting married when they were away. I hung up on him. I didn't even say good-bye.'

131

She began to sob again, big, painful gasps that shook her whole body. It was hard to watch without crying myself, especially when I remembered Lisa and Paul. Toward the end of his life, Paul had shrunk to a shadow of himself. It had been awful seeing him like that, and Lisa and I usually left the hospital in tears. The day Paul died, Lisa hadn't wanted to come up to the hospital. I'd let her go to a friend's, thinking it would be good for her to have a break. Paul took a turn for the worse and died in my arms. When I told Lisa, she screamed, 'I never got to say good-bye!'

I forced my mind back to the present.

'It's natural to think of things you could've done differently, but this isn't your fault, Heather. Your parents would want you to be happy. The best thing you can do for them now is to continue with your care plan and live a good life.'

'I always thought that my dad would be proud of me one day, once I got myself together, you know? That's why I was starting to feel better last week. I was thinking that I could go back to school, maybe for design, get a good job, and show my dad that I was married to this amazing husband. Now there's no point.'

'Those are still great goals, Heather. Continue doing them for yourself.'

She shook her head. 'There's *no* point. I'm never going to be happy.'

'I know it feels like that right now, but trust me, you

will feel happiness again in your life, and things *will* get better. You just have to give it some time.'

She stared at her feet, her eyes filling with tears. 'I don't care if it gets better. I just don't ever want to feel like this again.'

The rest of the session I worked on reassuring her that the pain would pass, but she was still despondent and wanted to go back to bed. Sleep was probably the best thing for her right now, so I didn't push her to engage too much. The next day she was sad, but not as lethargic and depressed as she was when she'd first entered the hospital. She'd been in the ward for more than three weeks at that point and was on the full dose of Effexor, which seemed to be helping her cope. When I asked if she'd been having any thoughts of hurting herself, she said no, even repeating it while she looked me in the eye. That was a good sign.

Over the next couple of days, they kept a close eye on her at the hospital. I was off for the weekend, but I called in and asked about her a couple of times, relieved to hear that she was managing. Though she was obviously grieving about her parents, she was willing to come out on the floor and watch TV with the other patients, and three days after we'd given her the bad news, she participated in one of Kevin's meditation groups. I ran into him out in the hall at lunch on Monday.

He said, 'I was happy to see Heather made it to my

group today.' Along with MMPI testing, which is figuring out personality types, as well as IQ testing, Kevin also worked with anxiety groups and did some 'one-to-one' counseling.

'Yes, the poor thing's been through a lot.'

'I'd say, but she's processing her feelings well.'

I was glad for the validation, and my shoulders unknotted. I didn't realize until that moment just how worried I had been about her. 'You think so?'

'We talked after group, and she thanked me, said it helped.'

'That's wonderful!'

When I saw Heather the following morning, she was still lethargic and speaking slowly, but she told me that Daniel was going to bring some vacation brochures that afternoon because they'd never had a honeymoon.

I said, 'That's exciting. Maybe you can put up some photos of where you'd like to go on your trip and things you'd like to do, like a vision board.'

'Maybe.' She met my eyes. 'You're a good doctor.'

Surprised by the comment, I said, 'Thanks.'

I waited for her to explain, but she didn't say anything else. I asked a few more questions: How was she managing? Was there anything she needed? Anything she wanted to talk about? Had she any thoughts about hurting herself?

She stared at her feet and just kept answering 'No' to everything, so we finished the session there. She was grieving, but in proportion to her recent loss, and I was hopeful that in time the supportive environment of the hospital would bring her back to where she was before. Then we could continue her treatment so she could go home and finally take that honeymoon with her husband. When I said good-bye, I added, 'I'm going to want a postcard from your trip.'

She smiled wistfully and gave me a little wave.

Chapter Twelve

I went home after work that night, pulled on my overalls, threw my hair into a careless topknot, and worked in my potting shed for a while. Normally I loved the *snip, snip* of my pruning shears, keeping beat with Leonard Cohen's 'Hallelujah' playing in the background – it was my therapy. But today tears dripped down my cheeks as I thought about Heather, my daughter, and Willow – all the lost girls of the world. I rubbed at my face, leaving streaks of dirt behind, and stared at the bonsai tree I'd been trying to shape. I gave up and went inside for a shower, but first I checked the cardboard box I'd left under the back steps for the cat, noticing that there was a fine coating of black hair on the blanket.

After watching some TV for a while, I talked on the phone with Connie about how I was starting to over-identify with Heather's emotions, which was making it harder to remain a compassionate observer. Being there when she was given the news about her parents had also reminded me of the agony of telling Lisa her father had passed. I felt more at ease by the time I went to bed. I'd grown fond of Heather over the last couple of weeks and was glad she was doing better, but it would be good for both of us when she was released.

I read for a while, then I switched off the light. My heart started pounding, but I continued with the calming self-talk – *You're okay, just keep breathing, this won't kill you* – until the panic eased.

Though it was still early, I drifted into a sound sleep.

Two things happened at once: There was a loud clatter like the garbage can had been knocked over, and the phone rang. I bolted up in bed, my heart crashing into my rib cage as I tried to figure out what was happening. I heard a couple of cats screeching and realized they were fighting. The phone shrilled again. I turned on the lamp and grabbed the handset on my night table, noticing it was nine forty-five.

It was Michelle. She was trying to tell me something, but she broke off crying. Still half-asleep, I was confused for a second, thinking my worst fear was coming true, and she'd phoned to tell me Lisa was dead.

Then Michelle gathered herself together long enough to say, 'Heather Simeon committed suicide tonight.' My blood roared in my ears as Michelle tried to describe the brutal scene, but she kept dissolving into tears, and I'd only catch snippets of phrases. 'There was blood everywhere –

we didn't know she was in the utility room. I called code. But it was too late. She was already dead.'

'What happened? How did she get in there?' My own voice sounded high and strained as I tried to make sense of what I was hearing.

Michelle, calming down a little now that she was being asked direct questions, explained that a fight had broken out among some patients on the ward when they were having their evening snack. All the nurses were needed to break it up, and the janitor, in the middle of gathering supplies, had left the utility room unlocked while he went to clean up the dining room, where some trays and drinks had been thrown. In that brief fifteen-minute span, Heather had entered the utility room and, finding a coffee-can lid on the janitor's cart, which he'd been about to take downstairs with some other items, had slashed her wrists. Perhaps remembering that she was interrupted before completing her last attempt, she then drank cleaner. When that still didn't work fast enough, and she'd vomited liquid, comprised of bile and tissue from her burning esophagus, all over herself, she shoved rags down her throat. She had finally suffocated to death, her body's last struggle for air drowned out by the sounds of the fight on the floor.

Michelle said, 'Everything happened so fast – after I found her. I just saw the blood. It was awful.' Her voice changed from a frantic, shocked tone to a hushed and eerie resolve. 'I'm never going in that room again.'

*

As soon as I got off the phone with Michelle, I pulled on some clothes and rushed to the hospital, where the nurses were trying to calm the patients down. Michelle was sitting in the nurses' station, pale and shaking, as another nurse handed her a mug of tea. Until the coroner had finished his initial investigation, Heather's body was still in the utility room. Noticing that the door had been left ajar, and not wanting anyone to peer inside, I went to close it. Before I got it shut all the way, my eyes were assaulted with the brutal image of Heather's body on the floor, her back still leaning against the wall, and her thin, pale legs and arms all akimbo, like a broken doll. Her face was to the side, so all I could see was her hair. Thick, red blood pooled around her wrists, a bucket was kicked over by her feet, and there were smears of blood over her nightgown.

Then my eyes were drawn to the wall above her head. Written unevenly in blood were the words: *He's watching*.

I quickly closed the door.

The coroner was already interviewing everyone, including me. I sat through his questions, numb, my mind spinning. How had this happened? There'd be an inquest and a quality care assurance, as there always is when there's a death on the floor. I would have to call MCAP, my insurance provider, and they'd advise me on what to say and how to say it. There'd also be group grief-counseling sessions in the coming days, but I didn't care about any of that right now.

All I could think was: *How am I going to tell Daniel?* I would rather have done it in person, but I couldn't risk Daniel arriving in the morning before anyone had a chance to tell him. There was still too much chaos on the ward, so I walked over to my office at Mental Health, delaying for a few more moments. Then I sat at my desk, staring at a photo of Lisa, thinking that at least Heather's parents were spared this call, feeling sad that so much tragedy had befallen one family. I couldn't stop going over my last conversations with Heather. What had I missed? Was I clouded by my own feelings about the commune? Should I have referred her to someone else? I remembered seeing the utility door unlocked weeks before, remembered thinking I should mention it to one of the nurses. But I'd been so upset after hearing Aaron's name that I forgot.

If I'd said something, she might still be alive.

Finally, I looked up Daniel's number, took a deep breath, and made the call. As I dialed, I realized my hand was shaking.

His voice was husky from sleep but also tinged with fear. He must've seen the hospital name on his call display.

'Hello, Daniel, this is Dr. Lavoie . . . I . . .' I was at a loss for words, my head aching and close to tears myself. How was I ever going to tell him that his wife had died? I had assured him she was safe – *assured* him.

'Dr. Lavoie?' Daniel sounded more alarmed. 'Is everything okay?'

'I'm calling to talk about your wife.' I had to say this as gently and as swiftly as possible. 'There was an incident on the ward tonight, and Heather was found unresponsive. We tried to revive her, but it was too late. We don't know the exact cause of death, but it appears to be self-inflicted. I want you to know that we tried everything we could to save her.'

There was a sharp intake of breath on the other end, like he was strangling for air.

'I don't understand. What happened?' His mind was grasping, spin wheeling. The weight of my words hadn't hit home yet.

'We'll know more when the coroner finishes his investigation.' I took a breath and steadied myself. I didn't like that I couldn't give him details, but the potential for a lawsuit was too high. The hospital would appoint someone to handle all future communications.

'How did she die?' His voice was horrified, shocked.

My mind filled with visceral images of Heather, writhing in agony on the floor, clawing at her throat. Her esophagus burning.

'I'm sorry. I don't have that information right now.'

'I just don't understand. I saw her this morning. She was better than she'd been in days – she kept telling me how much she loved me.'

His tone was heartbroken confusion. The mind tries to reason, to find a justification: One plus one equals two. I did the same after Paul's diagnosis. He just had to eat right, get chemo, and think positive. He would beat cancer. But life doesn't work like that. Good men die before their time, and patients, despite getting our best care, still find a way to destroy themselves.

'Yes, she did seem to be doing better.' I didn't have the heart to tell him that it's when suicidal patients start feeling better that they sometimes complete the process — they now had the energy to follow through. Even though she'd told me that she wasn't thinking of hurting herself, she'd likely had a plan for a while and was just waiting for an opportunity. She'd been so convincing, and seemed so genuine, but I regretted believing her. I thought about how desperate she must have been to choose such a painful way to die.

I flashed to an image of her face the last time I saw her, the wistful smile. *You're a good doctor.* Was she trying to make sure I didn't blame myself for what she was about to do? I also thought about Kevin, how she had thanked him that day. Even her loving words to Daniel could now be interpreted as a good-bye.

Daniel's voice turned hard and accusing. 'You said she was safe — you *promised* that nothing would happen to her.'

Anger and blame were the next steps. I had expected it, but I still felt the blow, ached with my own guilt and regrets.

'I realize this has been an incredible shock, and you're upset—'

'Upset? My wife just *died* – when you were supposed to be watching her.'

I chose my words carefully, struggling with my need to comfort him and my need to protect the hospital. 'I'm truly sorry for your loss. Someone will be in touch with you soon. They'll help you with the next part of the process.'

I was glad I didn't have to go through it step by step with him, didn't want to brush past her death and move on to the particulars: picking up her personal belongings, her remains. My eyes stung when I thought of everything he was going to have to face in the coming days. 'You shouldn't be alone right now. Is there someone you'd like me to call for you?'

This time there was no anger in his voice. He just sounded hollow and defeated as he said, 'Heather was all I had.' Then he hung up.

Chapter Thirteen

The next few days were a blur, but I needed to be on the ward, with the support of the team, all of us still reeling from the tragedy. We had a couple of group counseling sessions, most of the nurses breaking down at one point. A few times I came close as well. The young woman whose room was next to Heather's was having a particularly bad time. Jodi suffered from anorexia and was extremely underweight, below ninety pounds. She had to have meal support, where a nurse sat and ate lunch with her. Heather had befriended Jodi and also sat with her at meals. Now Jodi was refusing to eat again.

The staff who saw the scene in the utility room were also struggling. One nurse mentioned having nightmares about all the blood from when Heather had cut her wrists, and I flashed to an image of Heather's writing on the wall: *He's watching*. The moment I first saw the words was still burned in my own mind – the streaks of red, the violent shock to the eyes. I'd been so upset by Heather's death I hadn't had a chance to think about the meaning of them. Now a quick snapshot of a memory came rolling out of the dark: Aaron at one of the late-night teaching sessions, the smell of a campfire, his voice raised in a fervent warning: *The Light sees everything we do. He's always watching over us.* What had he been talking about? I calmed my mind, tuned out the voices around me, concentrated on that moment. Then, with a stab of fear, a sharper memory came into focus.

I'm hiding under a cabin watching a ceremony that's just for adults, a cat clutched in my arms. Joseph's face is angry in the glow of the fire as he kicks a man on the ground, his voice punctuating each blow. 'Aaron warned you. The Light's always watching – he knows what you did.' The man moans and curls into a fetal position as Aaron pulls Joseph away. Members mill about, some faces concerned, others excited – sharks smelling blood in the water.

I yanked myself out of the memory, shaking off the cold fear that had crawled up the back of my neck. *That was then, this is now. You're not a child anymore, you're safe.* I turned my mind back on the current problem. Why had Heather written *those* words? I couldn't remember her saying anything like that in our sessions. So why had she taken the time to leave them as a final message? Was it related to the commune? Maybe guilt over having violated some of their rules or teachings? Or had Heather been trying to tell us something else? For a brief moment I considered if anyone from the commune could've gotten into the ward. No, the security was too tight. It was most likely my original thought: She couldn't fight her guilt about the miscarriage any longer, and she probably viewed her parents' death as her fault somehow. If Aaron still taught his members that the Light was watching, her grief-stricken mind might have felt she was being judged.

I tuned back in to the meeting. They were talking about procedures, what we could've done better. I thought about the unlocked door, and regret spread through me again. I wasn't the only one replaying events.

Michelle said, 'I keep seeing her face – her body just lying there. I can't sleep. Every time I close my eyes I see ... that.' She made a motion with her hand over her face, our minds filling in the blanks: the chemical burns around Heather's mouth from when she vomited, lips pulled back in a grimace, her skin mottled, and the ends of rags still visible in her throat. We were all quiet for a minute, and I had to close my eyes, blinking hard. When I opened them, Kevin was watching me, his face full of sympathy.

I went home for lunch, and when I came back, I was just getting out of my car in the staff parking lot when Daniel suddenly materialized by the hood. Heather's bag was over his arm, a box in his arms, and their wedding photo, which she'd kept by her bed, clutched in his hand. Had he been waiting for me?

'Daniel. Are you okay?'

His eyes were red-rimmed, his hair a mess, and his face unshaven. It was clear he hadn't slept in days. When he met my eyes, I almost stumbled backward from the grief burning in his gaze.

'No, I'm not okay, Dr. Lavoie. But you don't really care about that, do you? Your job is done, so what do you care about my life now.'

There was something in his voice that scared me, a ready-to-snap, dangerous edge. Adrenaline rushed through my body, making my stomach pull up hard under my ribs. I gripped the key fob in my hand, finger over the panic button.

'Of course I care, Daniel. I know this must be a very painful—'

He took a step closer. 'You don't *know* anything. Not about me, or my wife. She was just another patient to you, but she was everything to me.' His voice cracked, and he stopped, then shook his head and pulled his chest up high. 'You people let her die. I'm going to sue every damn person in this hospital.'

I was pinned between my car and the one beside me, blocked from behind by a cement wall. I hoped a security guard would notice, or someone parking their car, but when I looked around, the lot was empty.

I kept my voice low and soothing. 'Would you like to go inside and talk about this?'

'What's left to talk about?' His face was angry, his

breathing rapid. 'She's dead, and nothing's going to bring her back.'

I wanted to help him, wanted to explain about depression and chronically suicidal people, about the damaging effect a center like River of Life could have on someone already struggling with a mood disorder, but I was thrown by the situation and the despair in his face, by my own feelings of remorse and sorrow. According to the hospital lawyer, I shouldn't even be having this conversation.

Daniel was smart enough to realize that and said, 'It'll be lies anyway. You're not going to tell me what really happened – no one at this hospital will.'

'Daniel, I truly am sorry, but—'

'I don't want to hear any more apologies. I trusted you.' The words hit hard, and fear followed when he took another step forward. 'I thought she was getting better.' His voice had started to rise. I was scared, but I was also hoping he'd attract attention. 'What happened? I don't understand what happened.' His hands on the box were shaking now, tears leaking from the corners of his eyes.

A strong male voice rang out, 'Hey, you all right?'

Then Kevin was walking briskly toward us. I sagged with relief against the side of my car. Daniel backed up, slowly, wiping at his eyes. When Kevin reached Daniel's side, he said, 'Can I help you?'

'I'm done with all of you.'

'Then I think you'd better go home now.'

Daniel turned and took a step toward me. I held my breath, and Kevin's body also tensed. But Daniel just held out a photo.

'I want you to have this.' He thrust it toward me again. I took the photo. He nodded once, then turned and walked toward the main parking lot.

Kevin and I were quiet for a moment, watching him, then Kevin looked at me. 'You okay?'

I nodded. 'I'm fine.'

He met my eyes and raised his eyebrow. He knew perfectly well I was upset. I gave a sheepish smile.

He said, 'Do you have time for a coffee?'

I hesitated. I'd wanted to get started on some paperwork. But I was shook up. It might be nice to talk to someone who understood what I was going through.

'Sure, that would be great.'

We sat in the cafeteria for a while, and I shared my guilt over Heather's death, how I was struggling with it, wishing I'd done more. The wedding photo of Heather that Daniel had given me rested on the table between us as we talked. My gaze dropped down to it often, my mind still trying to make sense of her death, as though her face, captured forever in a smile from a happier time, might hold all the answers. Kevin shared that he'd also lost a patient before.

He said, 'I started wondering if I had what it takes.'

I nodded. 'I have to admit that's how I'm feeling right now. I'm second-guessing myself with every patient.'

'Completely natural. It took me a while to get my confidence back. I traveled for a while, trying to reconnect with myself. Then I starting thinking about all the people I *had* helped, and all the ones I could still help. It's impossible, I think, to save everyone, but if we help even one person in our lifetime, then we succeeded.'

'That's a good way to look at it. But I still feel like I missed something. I should've placed her on a one to one, but we'd just had the meeting about funding ...'

One to one is when a nurse is assigned to monitor a patient constantly. We usually reserve that for high-risk cases because of budget restraints. And in Heather's case, she hadn't indicated she was having suicidal thoughts again.

'If you'd requested it, it would've been shot down.' He was right, but I still wished I'd tried. 'You did the right thing by putting her back in the seclusion room. Even if she'd been up in PIC, it still might've happened. You know as well as I do that if someone wants to complete, they'll find a way.'

'True. But even one day can make such a difference.'

'And then something could've tipped her back the other way.' He held my gaze. 'You did your best.'

I stared down at my coffee, fiddled with the cup, avoiding the photo, and Heather's blue eyes, which now seemed accusing and angry, her mouth saying all the things I was thinking. *You should've saved me. You missed the signs.*

Kevin leaned over the table. 'Hey, you didn't do *anything* wrong, okay?'

I searched his expression for any insincerity, found none.

He repeated, 'You're not responsible for her death.'

I gave him a smile. 'Thanks. I really appreciate the support. This has hit me even harder than I realized at first.'

'We should—' He stopped as his pager went off and glanced down, made a disappointed face. 'Duty calls.' He looked directly at me. 'If you want to talk again, let me know.'

'I will.'

After he'd left, I sat there for a minute, looking at my reflection in the window, wondering what Kevin had been about to say. I tucked Heather's wedding photo into my pocket, then picked up our cups, Kevin's still warm from his hand.

Chapter Fourteen

Heather's obituary was in the paper the next day, along with an announcement for her funeral, to be followed by a burial at the memorial gardens. The same place Paul was buried. A heavy pressure settled on my chest as I remembered the sound of each shovelful of dirt falling on his casket while I stood numb by his grave. Then I thought about Daniel and how hard it was going to be for him. I wanted to go to Heather's funeral to pay my respects but wasn't sure it was a good idea even though it's appropriate for a doctor to attend a patient's service. I didn't want to add to Daniel's distress. In the end, I decided to visit Paul's grave the same day – I hadn't been for a while – and if I could, watch Heather's burial from a distance.

The afternoon of the funeral was sunny but cold enough to make the skin on my cheeks tighten and my hands ache. I wore my black trench coat, a gray-and-cream scarf

Paul loved, and big sunglasses. I set some tiger lilies on Paul's headstone and saw that someone had planted a small flowering shrub at the base of the stone. I knelt and spotted a tiny plastic dog nestled in the roots – white, like our beloved husky, Chinook, who'd passed away a year before Paul. My eyes welled up. Lisa must have left it for her father.

Then, in the distance, I saw a small procession moving toward Heather's grave, which wasn't far from Paul's. There weren't a lot of people, but I wasn't surprised. Heather had mentioned that her parents didn't have much family, and Daniel had told me she'd pushed her friends away.

When the ceremony was over, people said a few words to Daniel before drifting off. Daniel stood by the grave for a while, his head bowed, then turned and walked down the path toward the parking lot. I made my way down to Heather's plot with my bouquet. I placed the white roses on her grave, remembering her sweet smile and sad blue eyes when she'd look sideways at me through the veil of her hair.

I'm sorry I wasn't able to help you.

Behind me, a man's voice said, 'What are you doing here?'

I spun around. It was Daniel.

'I just wanted to pay my respects. Sorry if I've intruded.' I brushed away tears and turned to go.

'Wait,' Daniel said.

I turned back, my body tense.

His eyes met mine, and this time there was no anger in them, just a tired sadness.

'I owe you an apology.'

My shoulders relaxed, and I loosened the grip on my shoulder bag. 'You don't owe me—'

'No, I do. The things I said to you in the parking lot.' He shook his head. 'That wasn't fair. It's just seeing all her stuff in that box, our wedding photo . . .' He stared down at the flowers on the grave, swallowed a few times. 'She tried to kill herself when she was living with me – and even before that. I'm not going to sue the hospital. It's my fault anyway. I should've brought her back to the center sooner.'

'I don't know if that would have helped, Daniel. They seemed to upset her.'

'She was doing great there – it's when we left that she fell apart.'

'That may be so, but it seemed like Heather felt they were harassing her to come back. And they didn't appear to respect her boundaries or wishes.'

'They weren't *harassing* us – they just wanted to make sure we were okay.'

'Do you think it was just that? Or were they hoping you'd come back for another reason? Heather mentioned donating money.'

'But we *wanted* to donate. Is that why you came here today?' His voice sounded tight, defensive.

'No, it's not. I apologize if I've upset you. I just wanted to pay my respects. Heather was a special woman. I'm sorry I couldn't help her.'

Daniel took a breath and let it out in a sigh.

'You tried. You were the only doctor at the hospital who helped her at all. She liked you a lot.'

The only one . . .

An image of dark water, the smell of sand and earth, something familiar about the words. I focused in, grabbed at it. I was at the river with Aaron, cold rocks digging into my knees. *You're the only one,* he whispered.

I was looking at Daniel, but my mind was elsewhere.

'You have to help me, or I won't be able to heal her.' Aaron's naked, and I'm kneeling before him. He takes my hand and puts it on his penis, then grabs the back of my head, pushing my face toward him. I say, 'I don't know how . . .'

'Dr. Lavoie? Are you okay?'

Daniel was staring at me. He looked worried.

I tried to think of something to say, but my head was spinning. It all made horrific sense now. Were there other victims? What about the women he took for private meditations, those long walks with other girls in the commune? He'd said something about being able to 'heal her.' Who was he talking about?

Daniel. Focus on Daniel.

'Sorry, I was just thinking how much I liked Heather too.'

We held gazes for a moment. Our grief binding us.

Then he bowed his head again, covering his face with his hands while his body shook with the effort of holding in his sorrow.

I stood beside him, my hand on his shoulder.

I don't know how I made it home. I only remember getting undressed and climbing in the shower. The water beat on my head as I stared down at my body, wondering at the secrets it still held. *What else did Aaron do to me?* I stayed in the shower, scrubbing my skin over and over, until the water turned cold.

Sitting on my couch later, I tried to calm down and consider the facts. If Aaron had abused me, then it would explain why I'd been so uncomfortable around him, and it also probably explained my claustrophobia. But why did the memory finally surface *now*? Was it real? It had felt real, but now, without any other supporting evidence, a time line, a sense of when it started or ended, and the memory already fading, I wasn't so sure. It was possible that being immersed in memories of the commune for the last three weeks, then dealing with the strong emotions that Heather's death had triggered, distorted my true memories. Like a dream that had no meaning and was simply a representation of other emotions. Could it be that my suspicion of Aaron and what he was doing at the center had manifested in this way? I viewed his actions as a betrayal of trust, even as a child, and so my psyche was portraying it as an even more intimate violation?

Some therapists, while using Recovered Memory Therapy, accidentally planted memories in their patients' minds. One of the reasons it was eventually discredited. Is that what I had actually recovered? A long-buried manipulation?

I tried to hypnotize myself, counted backward several times, focusing on the flame of a candle, but I couldn't get to that memory, the images that had seemed so sharp were now blurred. I didn't know what was real anymore.

Chapter Fifteen

That night, I spoke to Connie about my experience at Heather's funeral. We also discussed my concerns about the commune, the damaging effect they could have on the mental health of their members, and that if my memory was indeed real, there could be more victims of sexual abuse. I considered making a report to the police. In the end, I decided that I wasn't ready to share my story – it was deeply upsetting, but I still wasn't confident enough in my facts and wanted to think about it longer, see if anything else surfaced. I did, however, want to make them aware that they should look into the center's operations. Hopefully, when they saw that things weren't on the up-and-up, they'd investigate and shut it down.

After work the following day, I stopped at the police station. In other places in BC, the RCMP service the area, but Victoria and the township of Esquimalt, which borders Victoria, are handled by municipal police. I spoke to a pleasant officer, who listened patiently, then said, 'Do you know of anyone being harmed at the commune?'

'No, but if they are convincing people to stop taking their medications, they're at risk. And there are other concerns.' I shared how they'd harassed Heather after she left, and that she'd been donating large sums of money. Also that I feared Aaron was using mind-control techniques.

He said, 'Did your patient say that she was held against her will?'

'Well, no, but—'

'Did they force her to give them money, by means of a threat or any other intimidation tactic?'

'Not that I'm aware of. It's more about pressure and manipulation.'

The officer said, 'If no one at the center has made a complaint, then our hands are tied. The River of Life is a respected business in this community. We can't just go in there and ask a bunch of questions without a good reason.'

I thought about my memory of Aaron at the river. They obviously weren't going to look into the commune's activities without more evidence of a crime. I hadn't wanted to open this can of worms when I was still uncertain myself, but if it was real, and other girls *were* being hurt . . .

'What if the leader was abusing underage girls?'

'Is he?'

I couldn't waver now or signal any uncertainty. I had to go forward.

'He has ... in the past.' I took a breath and briefly explained about my recovered memory and my previous experience with the group as a child.

When I was finished, the officer didn't give me a sense of whether he believed my story, but his face was sympathetic. He said he could take a statement from me, but it would get sent to the RCMP in Shawnigan, where the crime occurred. His careful explanation that they wouldn't be the ones following up told me that he personally believed I should make the statement directly to the police who would handle the investigation. When I suggested as much, he said, 'It's up to you. I'm sure it's been hard for you to come in here today, and you might want to just get it over with. But they'll probably still want to interview you, so you'll have to go through it twice. If you don't mind driving up there, it might be better—'

'I'll go to Shawnigan.'

I left feeling exhausted – it had been difficult and embarrassing to tell a stranger that I'd been abused, especially when I still didn't have many memories of the experience. It was like feeling around in the dark, stumbling into sharp edges. The officer told me that someone would be in touch soon, but I still wasn't sure how far I wanted to go with it personally. I just wanted them to check into the center.

I wondered if I should tell Robbie – in case the police needed to speak with him. He wouldn't be happy about it. Robbie isn't the type who likes to discuss his emotions at the best of times, even less so with me, and he'd probably rather drive off a cliff than talk to the police about anything. Still, I didn't feel right about not sharing this with him. In the end, I decided I'd tell him after I'd met with the police.

The next morning, I got a call from Corporal Cruikshank, a female officer who sounded very professional and matter-of-fact. We arranged to meet the following Friday afternoon at the station. That day, I finished work early and drove up the Malahat Highway to Shawnigan, which is about forty minutes from downtown Victoria. The Malahat could be treacherous in winter, with its winding turns through Goldstream Park, rugged steep slopes, and the occasional waterfall cascading down a sheer rock wall, but that day it was clear and the traffic light. I would have enjoyed the drive if my head hadn't been consumed with thoughts of the commune, my brother's reaction, what Aaron might do after he found out I'd made a statement. My body tense with dread, I reminded myself that there was no sense worrying until I had more information, but a small voice still niggled at the back of my mind. *Are you sure you're ready for this?*

I took the turnoff to Shawnigan, just before the summit of the Malahat, and followed Shawnigan Lake Road down through the mountain into the valley, noticing that they had logged some of the area. Once I reached the junction at the south end of the lake, I stayed right and headed into the village on the east shore, which is where the police station was located, passing numerous summer cabins on the way. Shawnigan has a population of only about eight thousand people, and most of the vacation homes are owned by residents of Victoria, taking advantage of the quick commute and the lake's beaches and waterskiing.

The village itself was still small, with two general corner stores, a gas station, barbershop, video store, coffee shop, and a couple of restaurants. If you keep going past the west arm of the lake, it was mostly farmlands and forest, also, from what I remembered, a popular area for hunters and four-wheelers.

The police station was built out of red-toned bricks. It wasn't very large and reminded me of an old schoolhouse. I could see most of it from the waiting room as I sat on the wooden bench, watching officers come and go in their uniforms, the odd laugh breaking out as they joked about something. After a few moments, a young woman in a dark blue suit came through the door with a pleasant smile. Her blond hair was pulled back in a bun, and she had a heart-shaped face, with big brown eyes. She walked with a certain swagger that made me think she must be an athlete. She also didn't look much older than my daughter, which didn't inspire much confidence in her abilities.

I felt a flash of shame at my unkind thought. If she'd achieved this level in her career, then I was sure she was more than capable.

She said, 'Good afternoon, I'm Corporal Cruikshank.'

I shook her hand. 'Hello, I'm Dr. Nadine Lavoie.' *I'm not making this up. I'm a doctor.*

We sat down at a metal table in a small gray room, a camera in the corner. She leaned in. 'So I understand you'd like to make a report?'

'Yes.' My throat was dry, cracking slightly as I spoke. She offered me some water, and when I said, *please,* she brought back a bottle.

'We're going to record you so we can make sure we have everything, but I'll also be taking notes, just in case there's anything I need to ask you more about.'

'That's fine.'

The policewoman, proving she was more in tune than I'd given her credit for, said, 'I know how uncomfortable this must be for you, and that the crime was a long time ago, but it's important you try to give me as much detail as possible. I'd like you to close your eyes and walk me through it. Try to use all your senses, scent, anything you heard, all of this can help.'

I nodded, not trusting myself to speak – the idea of closing my eyes in the small room suddenly terrifying.

She studied my face. 'Just take your time.'

I took a deep breath, waiting until the pulse in my throat had settled down, willing myself to relax, then closed my eyes and began to speak. First I explained how we came to the commune and what it was like living there, opening my eyes to make a point every once in a while. She nodded encouragingly but never asked any questions, just made the occasional note. 'My mother said that he used to give me swimming lessons, but I'm not sure if that's when it started . . .' The room was so quiet I could hear the officer breathing – the walls pressed in, the sudden urge to run. I opened my eyes. 'Can we leave the door open?'

She looked startled.

I said, 'Or is there a bigger room? I have claustro-phobia.'

'We can open the door, but officers will be walking past. Unfortunately, this is our only interview room. Would you like to take a break?'

'Just give me a minute, please.' I centered myself, taking three deep breaths. When I was ready, I began again. 'We were down at the river . . .' My eyes closed, I noticed a rhythmic sound, a pattering against the roof, and realized it must've started to rain. My body relaxed, and I drifted back into a memory.

Now I remembered how it had all started.

We haven't been at the commune for long, maybe a couple of months, when Aaron starts paying special attention to me, making eye contact at the campfire, giving me an extra piece of fruit, his hand lingering on the back of my leg when he shows me how to sit for meditation. I'm shy with him, barely speaking when he asks me a question, and my mother scolds me, telling me to be nicer to him.

I'm alone in my cabin, having snuck away from the other kids. One of the dogs, a spaniel, has puppies under my bed. I've just slid their box out, and I'm holding one, rubbing my nose against its soft fur, when Aaron comes in the cabin.

He says, 'Are you okay? I noticed you weren't with the other children.'

I stumble over my words, confused and flustered by his attention. 'Yes, I just ... I just wanted to make sure the puppies were all right.'

I can feel him watching me as I kneel down and slide the box back under the bed. When I stand up, he studies my face, his gaze lingering on my mouth.

I'm uncomfortable at the way he's staring and want to move away, but I don't want to offend, remembering my mom's warning to be polite.

He says, 'Come to the river with me. I want to show you something.'

I follow him down to the trail as we push our way through shrubs and bushes, wet from the rain that has now stopped. As we pick our way over the slippery moss-covered rocks on the shore, our footsteps are drowned out by the roar of the river. Finally, he finds a spot around the bend, blocked on both sides by dead trees. I shiver in my sweater and jeans, *my breath cloud puffs in the air. He comes close and puts his arms around me, burying my face in his coat. I stand still, my heart hammering loud in my chest, wondering why he's touching me.*

I pull away, peeking at him nervously as I look around. 'Why are we down here?'

He spreads his arms wide and smiles. 'Life, it's in every leaf and every drop of water.' He tilts his face to the sky, inhales deeply. 'Can't you smell it?'

Confused again, and wanting to give the right answer, I tilt my own face up, take a breath, and say, 'It smells good.'

He eases himself down on a flat rock, crossing his legs, and motions for me to sit in front of him. I hesitate.

He tugs at my hand. 'Let's meditate together. It will be fun.'

I sit, cross-legged, our knees brushing. I bow my head and close my eyes, waiting for him to lead the chanting.

He leans toward my ear, his breath, smelling of sweet marijuana, hot against my neck as I stare at the ground, frozen. He whispers, 'Look at me.'

I raise my face toward his, confused and nervous. I've never meditated alone with Aaron, and I'm worried about making a mistake.

He says, 'I had a dream last night about you.'

'Me?'

He nods. 'You're very pretty.'

I blush, embarrassed and uncomfortable that he's telling me this.

His face clouds over. 'You don't like me very much, do you?'

'No, I like you.' I was even more embarrassed that he'd sensed my discomfort around him, wanted to assure him. 'I'm just shy.'

He smiles, looks relieved. 'You don't have to be shy with me. We're friends, right?'

I smile back, feeling more relaxed now. 'Sure, we're friends.'

'Okay, close your eyes and we'll meditate. It'll be cool, trust me.'

I close my eyes again, waiting for him to start chanting. He cups his hand around the back of my head, holding me in place. Then his mouth presses against my lips, his beard scratching. I struggle, panicked by the unfamiliar sensation of someone's lips against my own. His tongue slides into my mouth, the taste of him making me gag. Scared now, I push him hard in the chest. He pulls his face away, his eyes surprised and angry, his lips tight.

'I thought you said you liked me?'

'I do. I just . . . I thought we were meditating.'

His face softens. 'We are. This is a special meditation. It's just for us, so you can't tell anyone. It'll be our secret.'

I feel another surge of fear. This isn't right. I start to get up.

He grabs my hand, his face now furious. 'Where do you think you're going?'

'I don't want to do this.'

'You don't have a choice. Not if you want your mother to keep getting better. You remember how she used to be, don't you?'

I catch my breath. I remembered too well, the dark moods, the threats of suicide. Aaron must've seen the terror in my eyes, the moment he had me, because he says, 'I can help her, Nadine. And you can help me.'

Then he unzips his pants.

Now, years later, my eyes closed, I described in detail everything he'd done – and everything he'd made me do. 'He wanted me to perform oral sex. But I didn't know how, so he made me open my mouth, then he put it in. And he also touched me, mostly just my breasts. He kept asking if I liked it – I remember that.' I also remembered how terrified I'd been, shaking and crying, not understanding what was happening. 'After he was done, he said that if I told anyone, my mom would get sick again. He said . . .' I opened my eyes. 'He said that she'd kill herself.'

I began to cry, reliving all the fear I'd felt in that moment, believing that my mother's life was in my hands, that if I made one mistake, she'd die. She'd finally crumble under the weight of all her sadness and dark thoughts. The same feeling I'd had most of our childhood, be good, take care of our mother. But who had been taking care of me? Robbie, yes, but he'd only been a boy himself.

And I'd been just a little girl, on her knees in front of this man, scared and helpless, knowing that the things he was doing were wrong, a horrible sick feeling of shame in my stomach, that I was dirty now, that something was wrong with me.

The officer got up, came back with some Kleenexes. I didn't try to stop the tears. I gave in to them, allowing my grief. For the little girl who didn't have anyone to protect her. I'd been taken advantage of in the worst way. Manipulated by fear and guilt, trapped and unable to say, *No, this isn't right, stop now.* And there was no one who could save me, to even see what was happening. To care.

Finally I took a breath, blotted my tears, and blew my nose, feeling wrung out, the emotions still thick in my throat as I struggled to accept what he'd done to me. I now understood why I'd blocked out the events. It was common in sexual abuse cases where the victim had been threatened, but I was still having a hard time grasping that it had happened to me. I was also scared what else might have happened – I still couldn't recall how the abuse stopped, or if it did.

The officer said, 'Were there any other occasions? Did he ever take you anywhere else?'

I remembered my mother's confusion. *Don't you remember the picnic?* It came back now. He'd taken us to a lake that had an old fishing cabin. Everyone had fun, but I hated the place. I'd already been there, with Aaron and another girl, whose name I couldn't recall, but she'd been about my age. He'd encouraged us to take off our clothes and go skinny-dipping in the cool lake water. I hadn't wanted to, but the other girl had, so I followed. Later, he'd wanted us to play hide-and-seek, naked, while he watched. We'd balked, we were too old, but he said it would be fun. The person counting had to sit on his lap. I could still hear his voice in my mind, *One, two, three . . .* and feel his hand under my towel.

I shared the memory with the officer. 'I think it was usually at the river, though, and maybe just a handful of times over the first few months . . .' I paused, thought back. My mother was right, after Coyote had died that summer, I became deathly afraid of swimming. Aaron offered to teach me, but it had been a ruse so he could spend more time with me down at the river, with lessons every week. I had vague recollections of him starting off kind and friendly, showing me how to swim, encouraging me, but I'd be filled with dread, knowing how it would end.

I told her about the lessons. 'Sometimes . . .' I took a breath, swallowed hard. 'He, uh, he would make me touch myself. He liked watching. Then he'd always make me give him oral sex.' My mind filled with the image, his noises and grunts. My crying and my eyes closed, pretending I was somewhere else.

I wiped away some tears now. 'That's all I remember at the moment. There could be more, though. I don't know if my claustrophobia was because of what he did to me or something else.'

The officer said, 'It may still come back, now that you've opened up. You did a great job. I know that was very difficult.'

I let my breath out in a sigh, emotionally drained. I said, 'Is anything going to happen to him? I'm sure now that there are more victims.' I explained some of my other fears regarding the commune's tactics and belief systems.

'We'll bring him in for an interview and take it from there.'

'Without any other evidence, what are the chances of you arresting him?'

'Our job is to gather information. Then we present the facts to the Crown, and they'll decide if there's enough evidence to lay charges.'

'But if he denies it, and I don't have any witnesses . . .'

She looked down at her pen and paper, assessing the notes she'd made, like she was trying to decide something.

I added, 'I understand how these things work.'

She met my eyes, her gaze kind. 'Unfortunately, without any physical evidence, or additional statements by other victims or witnesses, the burden of proof won't be met, and the likelihood of conviction is slim.'

'You mean nonexistent.'

'When we bring him in for an interview, he may reveal new information.'

'Will you tell him my name?'

'He has the right to know who his accuser is, and we can't properly question him unless he knows what he's supposed to have done. You're not a minor, and unless he has directly threatened you . . .'

'No, not that I recall, but I've witnessed his brother being violent. I believe he might have a mental illness. I don't know where he is now . . .'

The policewoman made a note, said, 'Can you tell me what happened?'

I explained about Joseph's attacks on members who broke the rules. 'Aaron had a temper as well, but he was better at hiding it. I don't think many people picked up on it. There was also a teenage girl named Willow who left the commune.' I hesitated. Should I voice my fear that she might have met an untimely end? I didn't want to sound like a lunatic. 'Is it possible to find out if she was reported missing? I think she was from Alberta.' I hadn't even remembered that until it came out of my mouth. I told her everything else I knew about Willow, adding that I thought it was odd how abruptly she'd left.

When I was finished, she said, 'Back then, a lot of teenagers were transient. They'd stay with a group for a while, then move on to the next.'

'I understand. I'd just feel a lot better if we knew where she'd ended up.' I flashed again to the image of Aaron watching her when she fought with Robbie. Then a new memory clawed its way out of the dark. When Aaron had joined all of us at the river after our walk, he'd been sweaty and dirty. Was it from working in the barn, or a far worse possibility? What had he been doing?

She said, 'We'll look into it. But it might take a while to find the records because of the length of time that's passed. Hopefully she's alive and well and living in California.'

I hoped so too.

Chapter Sixteen

When I was done at the station, I drove out to our old home, around the west arm of the lake. We had a couple of acres that backed onto the old railway tracks. After our mother died, Dad lived there on his own for years. Robbie had checked on him every week until he'd found him dead one day, still sitting in his chair. Dad had some stocks and bonds, which went to me, and to my schooling, while Robbie took the place. I'd only been there a couple of times over the last few years, when Robbie and I would have awkward visits, trying to find things to talk about.

I hadn't seen Robbie for at least a year now, only speaking to him briefly at Christmas, which he spent with friends – he'd been doing so for years. I always sent him a care package of meats and cheeses. When Lisa still lived at home, Robbie joined my family at Christmas and Thanksgiving. He'd wolf back his food, then eye up the door – but he loved Lisa. When she was little, she could only say 'Unka Wobbie' as she followed him everywhere.

He'd take her for rides on his mini excavator, their faces serious, neither of them saying a word.

Robbie had worked for a logging company most of his twenties, building roads, then he bought his own equipment. He now owned a backhoe and excavator business, and was doing fairly well, or as well as he wanted. He'd never been motivated by money. After Paul died, one fall day I'd found myself driving up to Shawnigan, just wanting to get away from my thoughts for a while. Robbie had been building a rock wall at the ranch – he's torn down the old barn, and it's now a two-bay shop. I stood in the cold, misty rain watching him, thinking how confident he looked running that machine, the bucket grabbing at boulders, then gently setting them down, his hands on the levers, sure and fast.

He'd said, 'Hop on,' then showed me how to operate the foot pedals and levers. When I'd gotten the hang of it, he jumped off and watched me: awkward, jerking the levers, banging the bucket into the ground. He just laughed and made a motion with his hand, so I'd know how to correct myself. Then he'd shouted over the noise of the machine that he had to take care of something in the shop. He left me alone there for a while, digging a pile of dirt, lifting and pulling, feeling more in control of that machine in that moment than I did of anything in my life, while tears dripped down my face. I'd glanced over my shoulder and caught him watching from a distance. When I'd finally finished, my hands cold and cramping, and had destroyed the bank, he'd shown me how to warm my hands over the exhaust pipe. We hadn't talked about Paul or anything that was happening in our lives, but I drove home that day feeling more at peace than I had in months.

This time I found Robbie working in his shop. When I didn't see him at the house, noticing that he'd fixed it up – new cedar-shake siding and aluminum roof, a large deck circling one side – I walked behind to his shop. A big German shepherd woofed deeply and trotted over to me. I held out a hand, let him sniff it. 'Hi, buddy.' He bumped his cold nose into my palm.

Robbie came out from a door at the side of the shop, wearing red-strapped jeans, a two-tone green plaid Mack Jacket, which all loggers on the island wore, and a black baseball cap. 'Hey, what are you doing out here?' He didn't sound annoyed at my interruption, just confused.

'I had to take care of some business. Who's this?' I pointed to the dog.

'Brew.' He took his hat off, rubbed sweaty hair from his brow. He was mostly silver now, like me, but his hair had never thinned like a lot of men his age. He was also lean and broad-shouldered, his forearms thick with muscles, and though his face was lined, he was still an attractive man. I used to hope that he'd meet a nice woman and settle down one day, but somehow my brother had become a confirmed bachelor.

'When did you get him?'

'Last year. Someone dumped him at one of the job sites.'

I felt a wave of sadness that I was so out of touch with my brother that I didn't even know he had a dog now.

'I was hoping to talk to you about something. Got a minute?'

'Yeah. Come into the shop. It's warmer.'

While I eyed a calendar with some half-naked pinup girls, Robbie grabbed a beer out of an old fridge, then held it up with a questioning look.

I said, 'No, thanks.'

He spun the cap off, took a swallow, and poured a little bit into a bowl beside the workbench, which Brew lapped up instantly.

I laughed. 'I see he comes by his name honestly.'

Robbie said, 'He gets cranky if you don't share.' He took a pack of gum out of his pocket and popped a piece into his mouth. Then I caught sight of the distinctive green label on the package and realized it was Nicorette.

'Did you quit *smoking*?'

I was shocked. After our father passed, I was so scared to lose my last family member, and any chance of us ever repairing our relationship, I used to nag him about it constantly, reciting various medical facts, which usually resulted in his face going cold and flat. This time he just looked defensive when he said, 'It was bothering Brew's eyes.'

I shoved a smile of amusement down into the back of my throat as Brew glanced up at me as though to say, *That's right, lady. I'm running the show now.*

Robbie said, 'So what did you want to talk about?'

I was not looking forward to this. 'Well, remember years ago when I told you I was undergoing hypnosis so I could recall what happened at the commune?'

'What about it?' His voice was guarded, and his neck muscles taut as he took a long pull off his beer.

'I had a patient come into the ward recently. She'd been staying at a commune in Jordan River, near Sooke – it's led by Aaron Quinn. It's now called The River of Life Spiritual Center. It's a much bigger organization than when they were here.'

'Mom said they moved down there.' He didn't look surprised by my information, and I wondered if he'd kept track of them over the years.

'Right, she told me that too, but she wouldn't say anything else.'

'She didn't like it when you pushed her to talk about that crap.'

They had discussed me? It still stung all these years later, the feeling that he knew our mother better than I did, that they'd shared a closeness that we hadn't.

'When did she say that?'

He shrugged. 'Whenever you came up, you were always asking her stuff, or telling her things she should do with Dad, or the property.'

I tried to explain my thoughts. 'I was just asking about my childhood, so I could better understand some things, and I gave her advice, but only to help.' I remembered how hard it had been to get my mom to talk about anything serious. How she would tell me it was better to leave the past in the past – her favorite line. But I don't think my mother had found it so easy herself.

He gave a quick, impatient shake of his head. 'It's not the questions. It's *how* you ask them – you pressured her. It got her all upset.'

Guilt spread through me when I thought about the conversation I'd had with her about the commune – two weeks before she smashed her car into the tree. Had I upset her that much? Had she told Robbie? Was that what he meant?

'I didn't *pressure* her.' I caught the defensive tone in my voice, was surprised at how familiar this felt: my trying to prove myself to my brother.

He took another pull off his beer. 'You do, even when you think you don't. We're not dumb-asses. We know what you're getting at.' He leaned against the bench behind him.

Now I was frustrated – and hurt. I lived in a world where sharing your feelings was encouraged, but I came from a world where it was considered a weakness, an annoyance. My family was all about shutting things out.

But I hadn't come here to argue with my brother. In fact, I hadn't realized until that moment that I'd come for solace, then wondered why I still thought he'd be able to provide it when we hadn't been close for decades. I mentally stepped back and refocused on my goal.

'You're right, I'm sorry. I know I come on a little strong sometimes. I just wanted to tell you something about Aaron . . .' I braced for the next part, everything in my body recoiling in embarrassment about sharing this with my brother. It felt wrong, but it *all* felt wrong – what Aaron did, and having to talk about it. I used that anger to push the words out. 'He sexually abused me.'

Robbie was just staring at me, his face stunned, the beer halfway to his lips. My own mouth was so dry I was tempted to rip it out of his hand. Then a red wave started to crawl up Robbie's neck as he came off the bench he'd been leaning on, his body squared, like he was getting ready for a fight.

'That fucker. When did he do that?'

I'd expected him to deny that Aaron would've touched me, and had been mentally preparing an angry response. But he'd surprised me. I felt a surge of relief; now I realized that part of me had also wondered if he'd known. If that's why he'd stopped looking me in the eye.

'Down at the river – when he said he was teaching me to swim, and there were some other times. I only remembered recently. That's why I'm here. I made a police report.'

He said, 'You sure that was a good idea? It's been a long time, and things could get ugly. Might screw up your life.' His face was worried.

'I had to do it.' I said it firmly, daring him to tell me

that I'd been wrong. 'I'm also trying to find out if there might be more victims. Do you remember him being inappropriate with any other girls?' I thought of the girl in the cabin with me, where she was now, and if Aaron had done anything else to her.

'No.' He leaned back against the workbench, but he didn't look relaxed, his limbs tense. 'He was always screwing someone, but no kids that I know of.' His words were tight, clipped.

'Did you ever see him, you know, acting strange with me?'

Robbie looked down at the beer in his hand, rolled it around. 'You spent a lot of time with him, but I thought you liked him . . .'

My face flushed hot, knowing if anyone who lived at the commune back then testified that was probably what they would think too – that I'd liked him.

'I did when we first met him, but then *he* did things that he shouldn't have. Do you know if anyone from the commune still lives in Shawnigan?'

He shook his head, took a gulp of beer. 'Don't think so. Most of them are from the city – they run away up here for the weekend.'

That reminded me of another runaway. 'I also told the police about Willow. They're going to check if she was ever reported missing.'

'Why would they think she was missing?' He looked surprised.

'I don't know that they do. I just think it's odd how she left so suddenly, so they said they'd see if they could find her.' I didn't know how much of my suspicions I should share, still wondering if I was jumping to conclusions, and crazy ones at that, so I just said, 'I'd like to talk to her, see what she remembers.'

Now there was an edge of concern to his voice. 'I don't think you should go talking to a bunch of people about Aaron. They were into some weird shit, and they're probably *still* into weird shit. If I was you, I'd just stay out of it.' Brew whined. Robbie ruffled his head, trying to soothe. But his face was stressed.

Sounding calmer than I felt, I said, 'The reason predators like him get away with things like this is because most people are too scared to say anything, they're afraid of the public humiliation and being doubted. I feel the same way, but I also believe he's destructive – and there are probably more victims.'

'If they're this big organization now like you say, people aren't going to like you going around making accusations.'

I was starting to get angry. He was my brother. I wanted his support, not warnings. 'I appreciate your concern, but I understand the possible repercussions, and I've made my choice. I just wanted to know if you remembered anything.'

'No, and I'm not talking to the cops about anything – and don't tell them fuck-all about me.'

That threw me. I'd never even suggested it as a possibility.

'I'm late,' he said. 'I've gotta get to a job site.' At the words, Brew's ears twitched, and he loped to my brother's black Silverado, JAEGER EXCAVATING painted on the side in red. Brew circled at the passenger door, barking.

Robbie walked toward his truck. At the door, he turned and looked at me, his face serious. 'Those guys are screwed up – you should just stay away from them. It's shitty what he did, but you gotta move on with your life.'

Move on? I sucked in my breath, his words hitting hard and deep.

'I could say the same of you. What's keeping you here? Mom and Dad have been gone for years.' I don't know where my question came from. No, that's not true. It came from hurt, but it hurt more when I saw the angry flush cross my brother's face, and the look in his eyes. He opened the passenger door, and Brew leaped in. Then Robbie got in the driver's side and, without looking at me, gunned the engine, spun his tires, kicking up gravel, and roared out the driveway. Brew hung his head out the side window, glaring balefully back at me, barking into the wind.

Chapter Seventeen

Frustrated about our visit and regretting some things I'd said, I'd planned to head straight back down to Victoria, but I drove around the east side of the lake, back through the village, so I could fill up on gas. While I waited in the car for the attendant, I caught sight of the corner store, a cream-colored wood building, with blue trim, where my mother had first met those commune members. Dread ran over my body as I remembered how anxious I'd been that day, watching her talk to them and sensing danger in the air. The store had changed over the years. Now a small outdoor café was attached to the side, where some teenagers sat on the tables, braving the cold for a cigarette, laughing, and texting on their phones.

I flashed to waiting in our old pickup truck, while Robbie and Levi approached a pair of teenage girls as they rested on the front steps of the store with their backpacks, drinking Dr Peppers in the sun. Their lives had probably changed forever when they decided to climb into the back of our truck and come out to the commune for a swim. I tried to think of their names, but they just blended with the other young women at the commune, all tanned with long hair, blissed out on pot and freedom. The only one who ever stood out was Willow. I wondered how she came to be at the commune, tried to think back, but nothing came to mind. Then I remembered that the community museum was just around the corner. After I paid for my gas, I parked my car in front of the small yellow building, thinking that I'd just pop in and see if they had any photos from the sixties.

The door jangled as I pushed it open. A woman, maybe early thirties, with blond hair pulled back in a ponytail, was sitting behind a glass counter covered with calendars and postcards. Below in the display case, logging tools, a railway spike, and books rested on red velvet. Behind her on the wall there was a framed artist-drawn map of Shawnigan Lake. There were also some photos of the Kinsol trestle, one with the old train crossing, steam billowing out from behind.

The woman set down the book she'd been reading and smiled. 'Welcome to the Shawnigan Lake Museum.'

I smiled back. 'Hello.' As I browsed around, I focused on some black-and-white photos hanging on the wall, rich people summering at the lake. Lost in thought, I heard her say something but didn't catch the words.

I turned. 'Pardon me?'

She said, 'Are you visiting Shawnigan for the first time?'

'No, I grew up here.'

'Oh, yeah?' She studied my face. 'Where did you live?'

'Out toward the trestle – but it was a long time ago. I live in Victoria now.'

'It's being rebuilt.' I'd already noticed all the photos of the Kinsol trestle, happy to see they were fixing it up. It had been one of my favorite places when I was growing up, somewhere I went for comfort. It was the largest wooden trestle in the Commonwealth and one of the highest in the world. Years ago it had been burned in the middle by some students, and it came with its own tragic past. A young man had committed suicide by hanging himself from a beam.

I said, 'Actually, maybe you can help me. There used to be some hippies living out by the river . . .'

'You mean the commune?' She cocked her head, waiting for the rest of my question.

Fear crawled down my legs, the sense of opening doors that should be left closed. 'Do you know anyone in town who might remember them?' Other than me, who wasn't sure she wanted to remember.

'Hmm. Don't know . . .' She wrinkled her nose.

I glanced down at the book in her hand – it was a book on the history of the Malahat and Shawnigan Lake.

Noticing the direction of my gaze, she said, 'I'm obsessed with history.' She smiled guiltily and shrugged.

'Well, there are certainly plenty of stories and legends about Shawnigan.'

She leaned over the counter, her eyes wide. 'You mean like all the drownings?'

Growing up, I'd heard that the First Nations refused to come anywhere near the lake, saying it was cursed. Legend had it that there'd been a war between two tribes that took place in the center of the lake. The boats had capsized, drowning everyone, but their bodies had never been recovered. When we were young, and our parents took us to Mason's Beach to swim, I'd been terrified, thinking the weeds touching my legs were ghostly arms reaching up from below. I assumed that was what she was referring to now, but I said, 'The First Nations drownings?'

She nodded. 'Those, and two others as well. One couple was killed in a speedboat accident. And there was a logger who drowned waterskiing. They couldn't find the bodies, so they had to dynamite the lake ... then they floated up.'

We looked at each other. I imagined bloated white bodies drifting up from the deep, felt the skin tingle at the back of my neck.

She added, 'There've been lots of suicides too.'

I thought of my mother, wondered if the locals considered her death one of the tragedies or one of the suicides. The museum walls pressed in on me, my chest tightened, and I felt hot all over. I had to get out of there.

Take a moment, relax your throat. You are not your panic.

After a couple of beats, when I pretended to be studying a photo on the wall while I waited for my heart rate to settle, I said, 'Yes, Shawnigan does have a fascinating history. I was hoping to find out a little more myself. That's why I asked about the commune. I'd love to talk to some locals who lived here back in the sixties, and who might remember them. I'm looking for some old friends.'

'You know who you should talk to? Larry Van Horne. He still lives out on Silver Mine Road.' She pointed to one of the walls. 'He donated some of the photos.' I looked in the direction she had pointed and noticed a photo of a logging truck. 'That was his. He called it Big Red.' She laughed. 'If you want some stories, he'll have them. But he can be kind of grumpy.'

'That's great. Thanks for the lead.'

I purchased one of the framed maps of Shawnigan, wondering if I should ask for her silence, but I had a feeling that it might just draw more attention to the matter, so I decided to leave it alone. As I walked out of the museum, I noticed a tall, ginger-haired man using the pay phone on the front porch of the corner store. He caught my gaze, then turned around. I had an odd feeling of connection, like I knew him somehow, but he laughed into the phone, and the moment was gone.

The woman at the museum had said Larry was in the big log house at the end of the road, and she wasn't kidding – it was huge. I parked out front and walked up to the front steps, where I was greeted by an old white cat who hobbled out on stiff legs.

The door opened, and a short man, barrel-chested and wearing a gray wool Long John top with denim jeans, suspenders, and a faded blue baseball cap squished down on sparse gray hair, said, 'Yes?'

I came up the steps. 'Hi, Larry, my name is Nadine Lavoie. I was just—'

'Do I know you?' He squinted at me, and I wondered if he might've seen me in Shawnigan when I was a child, but surely he wouldn't still remember me.

'I don't think so. I was just at the museum and the woman there—'

'Beth.' His voice was gruff, his body language tense as he sized me up.

'Well, Beth said that you'd be a good person to talk to.' I was starting to wonder about that theory. But I wasn't sure if his grumpy demeanor was genuine or just a defense mechanism, so I pressed on. 'I'm trying to find some people who remember a commune that was here in the late sixties.'

Bushy gray brows pulled down over watery eyes. 'Why you asking?'

'We knew some people there, when I was a child, and I'm hoping to track down some old friends.'

He continued to assess me, looking at my car, then back at me. Finally, he said, 'Come in.' He shuffled into

189

the house, reminding me of a sailor as he rolled from side to side. I followed him to his kitchen, noticing as I passed that the living room was dark, the curtains pulled. On the kitchen counter a small TV was blaring a hockey game, which he switched off, and there was a little table pushed against one wall, with a cheerful sprig of flowers in a glass Mason jar. He caught my gaze, said stiffly, 'Just 'cause I'm a bachelor doesn't mean I don't like pretty things.'

I smiled politely, but thought it better not to say anything.

He looked around his kitchen, like he was trying to remember what you do when you have a guest. Then he said, 'Coffee? Just made a pot.'

'Sure, I'd love some.'

He poured two cups, motioning for me to sit when I made to help. He shuffled over to the table, his gnarled hands shaking as he carefully set a mug in front of me.

'So what do you want to know?'

I took a sip of coffee, wondering how to form my question. I decided it was better to start off casual.

'Well, it was a long time ago, but I just wondered if anyone was still in town.'

'Not that I know of. They all moved down to Victoria. They were there, and then next time I drove by the site with my truck, they were gone.'

'That's right, Beth mentioned the truck. I heard some of them sabotaged logging equipment . . .' I'd heard it myself at the commune, but I left that part out.

He sat back in his chair, his big hand plucking and pulling at his suspender, like it had suddenly grown too tight. He studied my face again. 'You still live around here?'

'No, Victoria, but I have family in the area.' I didn't want to give him too much information, so I just said, 'We lived near the commune and used to ride our bikes out there to swim sometimes. My brother and I, we got to know a few of the kids. They were nice to us, but I remember rumors.'

'They were a strange bunch. Okay for the most part.' Again he gave me a look, like he was evaluating me, trying to figure out what I was really about.

'You met them?'

'Yeah, I stopped my rig and hung out by their campfire a couple of times. I was trying to tell them that they shouldn't hobble the horses.'

I'd forgotten how scared I'd been for the horses when I was a child, knowing they could break a leg easily on all the trees on the ground. But I couldn't remember ever seeing Larry at the site. I was surprised Aaron allowed it.

He was still talking. 'They liked to lecture me on logging, so I'd let them. Heck, why not, pretty women with hardly any clothes.' He smiled, his face slightly turned away, looking at me from the corner of his eyes, gauging my reaction. 'I used to give them rides when they were hitchhiking into town. They'd accept a lift in a logging truck, and then all the way to the village they'd give me holy hell for killing trees.' He laughed, but he started coughing so hard he couldn't catch his breath. He reached for some cough drops on the table, I pushed them toward him, about to get him some water, but he motioned that he was okay. His cat climbed up on the table, and he pulled it into his lap. It made me think of the stray near my house. I'd been checking her box every day since the catfight but there'd been no sign of her.

When the coughing spell had stopped, he shook his head, and wheezed, 'Getting old isn't any fun.'

'No, it isn't.'

The polite exchange over, he met my gaze. 'That all you wanted to know?'

It was clear he wanted me gone, so I had nothing to lose. 'Do you remember a girl named Willow?'

He stared off like he was thinking. 'Don't think so . . .'

'She had long, caramel-colored hair, big brown eyes, she was only about seventeen. Maybe you gave her a ride into town, say late July?'

'That was over forty years ago. I'm lucky if I remember what I did yesterday.'

'I'm sorry. I know it's a stretch.'

'I'd say. But I wished I did remember her, she sounds like a looker.' He gave a bawdy laugh and instead of it being amusing, it struck me as wrong, this old man mentally leering at a seventeen-year-old. He said, 'Why you asking?'

'She was just someone I remembered. I wondered if

she was still in Shawnigan. I think she ran away from the commune or something.'

'Far as I recall, most people were running *to* the commune, not away from it.'

We held gazes. Again I wondered if he recognized me. Or had he known my mother? I looked down at my mug, took the last swallow of bitter coffee, and said, 'Well, I've used up enough of your time. I should get going.'

I stood up, and he followed, shuffling behind. I paused at the door when I noticed a painting of a small boy picking berries. It reminded me of Finn, and I wondered if Larry knew anything about the case.

'I heard a little boy also died out there . . .'

His eyes widened, but then closed back down. He nodded. 'That was a bad bit of business. Parents smoking too much wacky tobacky, and the kid dies in a puddle.'

'That's so sad. Do you know if anyone was ever charged?'

'The cop who worked the case, Steve Phillips, he's retired now, but he's still in Shawnigan. You'd have to ask him about that.'

I nodded. 'Thanks for the information. It was interesting.'

He just grunted.

At the bottom of the stairs, I turned around. 'I'd love to talk to that officer. Do you know where he lives?'

We held gazes again, his revealing nothing, then he

said, 'He lives by the provincial park. Big white house at the end of Minnow Lane – he's got a camper in the front.'

I knew the area well. In the summer evenings, after we'd been hauling hay all day, our dad would stop at the park and we'd race through the dark trails in the forest, over the open field into the water, washing away the hay and sweat.

'Thanks, that's very helpful.' The words were barely out before he'd shut the door. But a corner of his blind lifted up as I backed down the driveway.

I felt him watching me until I'd turned around and driven off.

Chapter Eighteen

It didn't take me long to find the white house, but when I knocked on the door I was greeted by silence. As I walked back to my car a man, trimming branches off a tree in the next yard, shouted, 'Can I help you?'

'I was hoping to speak with Mr. Phillips. Do you know when he'll be home?'

'He's off fishing. Won't be back until next Friday.'

Thank God for small towns, where most people still trusted a friendly face.

'Thanks, appreciate that.'

I had planned on heading straight back to Victoria, but instead I sat for a minute at the end of the driveway, the car idling. *Maybe I should go out to the commune site and see if any memories pop up.* My heart rate accelerated immediately at the idea. Then, angry at my fear, I turned my car in the direction of the commune. When I passed my brother's driveway and made a left at the north end of the lake onto Renfrew Road, I wondered if he ever went out there. When we were in our teens, he used to go four-wheeling up in the mountains for hours at a time, but I had no idea if he ever visited the site or even thought about it.

Five minutes later, I hit the junction at the end of Renfrew Road, where it turned to gravel, and stayed right – the other side is mostly used by logging trucks. It was also where my mother had her accident. A light mist blanketed the forest, making the houses and ranches look spooky, the chill March air causing me to turn my heat up. I drove slowly, so I didn't bottom my car out on the rough road, but I was also dreading the emotions and memories I might find ahead. Finally, I passed the old gravel pit and came to another junction in the road at Burnt Bridge – so named for the forest fire that destroyed the first one. I made a left, and a few more miles down the road, there it was.

I wasn't sure how overgrown the forest might be since I'd been there with my ex-boyfriend, or if I'd even recognize the entrance, but the wooden sign with hands reaching toward a light, *River of Life* written in blackened letters across the bottom, was still hammered into one of the big Douglas firs at the top of the driveway. Though the carving was now aged and weather-beaten, it sent a tingle of anxiety down my back. I was surprised that no one had taken it down, wondered if it was respect or fear that made them leave it alone. Three big boulders had been placed at the entrance, blocking any vehicles. I wondered if it was still Crown land – the commune members had been squatters.

I pulled over on the side of the road. Even with my windows closed, the river was loud, full from winter runoff. I took a deep breath and climbed out of my car, glad I'd decided to wear flat shoes and jeans. It had been sunny all week, but it was still cold, and even more so at the side of the woods, where the dampness crept into my bones. I wrapped my scarf around my neck and grabbed my gloves out of the car before making my way along the smaller dirt road, which went down a hill, then toward the river and the commune.

Other than some motorbike tracks, it was clear the road hadn't been used in years, grass and saplings growing down the middle. The old-growth forest had an eerie feeling; a standing snag leaned sideways like a great fallen beast, draped in moss, everything dark and shadowed and silent, which was intensified by the realization that I was alone out there. That thought was interrupted by a vehicle roaring by on the road above. I turned, listened for it to stop, but it kept going. I continued deeper into the forest.

The trees – Douglas firs, hemlock, red cedar – were dense and thick, the woods still. I made myself take some deep breaths as I felt my throat close up, concentrating on the beauty not the fear: the moss-covered trees, the ground blanketed with ferns and deep thickets of salal.

The shrub, with its thick, shiny green leaves, was common in the Pacific Northwest, but we'd used the dark blue berries as a sweetener. Fiddlehead ferns would be popping up soon, which we used to fry with butter, along with wild mushrooms. We'd also cook stinging nettles like spinach, and pick sweet, tangy huckleberries for pies and jams.

When I entered the main clearing, I was surprised to see that a lot of the old buildings were still there. There were signs of campfires, blackened logs, the odd beer can and cigarette butt, like someone had been having parties. The cabins were falling down, with their roofs sagging, windows smashed, and some were completely collapsed. The old bus was gone. One rusted rim, though, stood against the side of a tree, riddled with bullet holes.

The fences had also come down, and the pens were overgrown with weeds and brush. I followed the path through the center of the commune, remembering how it all used to look, thinking that this was my history, good or bad. This place made me who I am today: I rarely eat meat, prefer organic food, soaps, and sundries from the health-food store, and I love jewelry and art inspired by nature. If Aaron and Joseph hadn't been here, it would have been a heavenly place to grow up.

I stopped in the center of the commune, where we'd eaten all of our meals at a long table. The cabins were built in a circle, radiating out like a fan from the fire pit, and the old sweat lodge, now gone. I slowly spun around, taking it all in. Then I closed my eyes, awakening my senses. I caught the scent of charcoal from old campfires and skunk cabbage on the breeze, remembered sitting around the fire with Robbie and the others, listening to Aaron sing and play the guitar.

I thought of Willow, how great she was at encouraging everyone to join in, even Robbie, who hated to sing but had a strong, deep voice. He'd laugh and refuse, but he'd always give in eventually. Now that I thought about it, he spent a lot of time with Willow. He'd been friends with a few girls in the commune, and more than friends with a lot of them. But something about their relationship felt different. Robbie had been casual when I asked about her, like she was just one of the members, but now I wondered if they might've been closer than I realized. I made a note to ask Robbie if he knew anything about her background.

I was about to leave when my gaze landed on the trail down to the river, now overgrown. I paused, thinking I should follow it and see if more blocked memories came back. Then, in the distance, I spotted the barn, and a jagged shard of a memory sliced into my psyche: Aaron, behind the barn in the woods on the left, digging into the ground. He turned to look at me, his face angry. Then the image stopped. What had he been burying? An animal? I tried to focus on the moment, using all my senses, but I just remembered feeling scared and anxious, like I wasn't supposed to be there. Where had Robbie and my mom been, the other members? I got the feeling it had been hot out, and it was late at night – I was supposed to have been in bed. But I still couldn't focus my mind's eye on the ground, couldn't see what he had there.

My skin turned cold, my stomach full of dread, but I forced myself to walk over to the spot in the woods. I searched the ground, looking for any strange depressions or rises, but didn't see anything more than a normal forest floor.

I turned my attention back to the barn. It was in bad shape, one of the walls had collapsed, the roof nearly tumbling to the ground, ferns and trees growing up through the old stalls, every railing coated with damp green moss. The closer I got, the more my throat tightened. And by the time I reached it, my stomach was rolling with nausea.

It's just a barn, it can't hurt you. You're safe.

It almost worked, but when I took that first step into the relic, keeping an eye on the ceiling to make sure it didn't fall down, my heart felt like it had slammed up into my throat, and someone was gripping my chest tight, my breath coming in quick, short pants. For a moment I thought I might actually pass out as darkness closed in on me. I was hot all over and cold at the same time.

In here, something happened in here.

I turned and ran, getting halfway through the commune before I stopped myself, feeling like a fool. I looked back at the barn, my heart pounding and my breath still wheezing out of me. *Stay calm, Nadine. It's just a barn.* But it wasn't just a barn. Every cell in my body was telling me it was dangerous, that something could hurt me in there – something *had* hurt me.

Not something. Someone.

I closed my eyes, focusing on the rise and fall of my chest, channeling my energy, concentrating on the feel of the ground beneath my feet, the cold breeze against my face, trying to remember: *What had happened?*

Then the hair on the back of my neck lifted, as though from an unseen hand, at the same time as a bird flew cackling up to the sky to my left.

My eyes shot open, and I stared at the dark woods, my body rigid, blood roaring in my ears, wondering what had startled the bird. I began to slowly back up, keeping my eye on the spot, searching the thick underbrush for an animal. Behind a large stump, just out of the light, there was a shadow, tall, like a man. Was someone there? I called out, 'Hello?' No one answered. I stared at the shadow, sure that I felt someone's gaze on me. I spun around and made my way swiftly back to the car, barely stopping to take a breath until I was inside and had locked the doors. I sat, waiting for my system to settle down, telling myself I was foolish – no one had been watching me. But when I looked back down the trail, I felt an overwhelming urge to get out of there as fast as possible.

I started up the car and reversed so quickly my tires slipped on the loose gravel, almost shooting me over the side of the bank. I put the car in drive and sped away. Not slowing down until I reached the turnoff down to Victoria. I'd finally found the source of my claustrophobia – but not the reason. I told myself it was just childhood memories blown out of proportion. I'd probably fallen down the haystack, or maybe got trapped in one of the stalls with a horse. That's all. But still, I heard a voice in my head. *Something bad happened in that barn.*

Chapter Nineteen

The next day, Saturday, I was still trying to shake off the events of the afternoon before. I spent the morning going through some moving cartons that I hadn't dealt with yet, unpacking, rearranging, storing the boxes in the basement, wishing it was that simple with memories. I stirred up some more when I opened a box from Paul's office. I picked through his favorite pen set, medical books, the model plane that he'd wanted to fly one day. I remembered that I still had his old tool set. They hadn't interested Garret at the time, but I'd kept them, thinking he might want them when he was older. He'd be thirty-two now. The last time we spoke, when I first moved to Victoria, he mentioned that he was house-hunting as well. It reminded me that we'd also talked about going for lunch in the New Year.

We'd kept in touch at the holidays after Paul died, but when Lisa moved out, the calls dwindled. I'd sent Christmas cards for a while, but then they started coming back with *Return to Sender* scrawled across the front. His mother had been a nightmare – moody, histrionic, passive-aggressive, and controlling. We'd tried to take Garret as often as possible, and Paul always made sure he was still part of his life. I'd also tried to bond with him, remembering my own longing for a family. But Garret was a temperamental child, and he hadn't made the transition easy. He'd resented Lisa terribly, and with seven years between them, they hadn't had much in common. But when Garret was around eighteen they'd finally developed a friendship and become quite close. That's why it was so sad when she also stopped communicating with him after their father died. Garret had tried a couple of times to find her when she moved back to Victoria, but she'd cut both of us out of her life. I'd also missed Garret. Then, finally, when he hit his late twenties, he started calling me once in a while to chat, and we'd go for lunch or coffee when I was in Victoria, and we'd talk about his dad and Lisa.

When I'd done all I could in the house, I headed outside to get my bike, holding my breath when I spotted the black cat perched on the roof of the shed. She was still, her body tense, watching me. She looked thinner than last time, one ear missing a chunk. A battle scar from the fight? I went back to the house and got some food from the kitchen. Then I cautiously walked to near where she was sitting, eyeing me. I reached up and set the little blue bowl on the lowest edge of the roof. We stared at each other. I blinked first, then backed up, but stopped halfway to the house, still partly in the driveway.

If you want it, kitty, you're going to have to eat it when I'm here.

The cat nimbly made her way down the roof, then strolled over to the bowl, head high, saying, *I'm not scared of you.* She gobbled up the food but still stopped every once in a while to stare at me, tail flicking. After a few moments, when I continued to talk soothing nonsense, telling her how pretty she was, what a good kitty, the tail flicking slowed to a calmer rhythm, and toward the end, a low purr at the back of her throat. When she was done, she sat, licking a dainty paw. *I may be a street cat, but I'm still a lady.* Then her head snapped up, she stared over my shoulder, streaked across the roof, leaped over the fence – and was gone.

I spun around, wondering what had startled her. I didn't see anything at the end of my driveway, or at the front of the house. I frowned, all my nerves standing at attention as an edgy feeling of being watched spread over me. Was someone there? Ever since I'd made my police report, I'd been jumping at every sound. Then a man called his dog from the end of the street. So that was what scared her – a dog running by. I let out my breath.

I grabbed my bike off the back deck, where I now stored it instead of the shed, tossed my purse in the front basket, and pedaled down to the waterfront walkway along Dallas Road. I paused to watch the winter waves against the breakwater. In the summer, enormous cruise ships docked at Ogden Point, and the Inner Harbor teemed with camera-happy tourists and the clip-clopping of horse-drawn carriage rides. Victoria came alive with music and arts festivals, concerts in the parks, fireworks celebrations, float planes zooming in and out of the harbor, boats from all over the world dotting the water. I was looking forward to the summer season, but I also enjoyed these last few days of winter, when Victoria still mostly belonged to the locals.

I took a moment to breathe in the fresh air, glad I'd decided to get out of the house. After a moment, I continued on to Fisherman's Wharf. Paul and I had often taken the kids there to feed the harbor seals – you could buy a bucket of fish for a dollar. Lisa had been obsessed and talked about becoming a marine biologist for years. She'd loved animals ever since she was little, begging to come to the clinic with her father, sitting up with a sick animal. Many nights we had to drag her home. We'd been sure she'd become a vet of some kind, but that was another dream that had fallen by the wayside. I still liked to go down and see the seals myself, though it was lonelier now.

I grabbed a London Fog tea at the Moka House, then wheeled my bike down the ramp to the wharf. The fish-and-chip place was boarded up for the winter, but I was happy they were still in business – we used to take Garret and Lisa there, but Lisa would feed half her chips to the seagulls and the other half to the seals, so we had to keep an eye on her. Still lost in my thoughts, I noticed a young woman sitting on a picnic table, wearing a faded green cargo coat, a thick black knit scarf wrapped around her neck, tight jeans with ripped knees, old black Doc Martens with the top laces removed, and wool socks pulled up over the bottom of her jeans. Her face was turned, looking down at a seal bobbing in the water in front of her, so I couldn't see her features. Then the woman glanced at me.

I was staring into my daughter's face.

There was also instant recognition in hers. I fought the urge to rush forward and gather her in my arms, knowing she would just push me away. We were silent for a moment, assessing each other, collecting ourselves. I was happy to see that her skin was clear, with no sores – and no makeup, but she'd never needed it. I'd hated it when she circled her eyes and lips with black, never understood why she was hiding her beauty. Her eyes, the same blue as mine, were ringed in black eyelashes, but her facial structure was more angular, like her father's. She'd grown her dark hair out and it was thick and wild around her face, ending far past her shoulders in light auburn tips; whether from sun or bottle, it suited her.

I smiled. 'Lisa, I'm so glad to see you.' I felt a stab of grief that I should be talking to my daughter like a stranger, followed by bitter irony that I'd been searching the streets for her but never thought to look at one of her favorite places.

'Hey.' She turned back to the seal, reached into the bucket beside her, tossed a fish.

I stood awkward. She hadn't told me to go away, but she hadn't provided an invitation either. Now that I finally had her within my reach, contact I'd craved for months, I was unsure of myself. I inched forward, standing near her but still maintaining some distance, nervous about saying anything that would make her bolt. A pulse fluttered in her neck, and though her face was calm, I wondered if the pulse belied her own inner turmoil. My head was filled with anxious questions. *Where are you living? Do you need food? Are you still doing drugs?*

She twisted slightly, glanced at me.

I pretended to watch the seal, smiling at her antics.

She said, 'They can live up to thirty-five years, you know.'

I did know, but I said, 'Really? I wonder if she's the same one we used to feed.'

She shrugged. 'Not like she'd remember us.'

I waited for a beat, hoping she'd elaborate, but she was focused on the seal. I said, 'I didn't know you still come here.'

She looked at me, one brow raised. The message was clear: *You don't know anything about my life anymore.*

'I'll have to visit her more often. I live in Victoria now . . . ' Throwing out a hook.

She glanced at me again, pulling her coat tight around her body as the wind came off the ocean, her hair picking up at the ends, her cheeks pink. I ached at how beautiful she was, seeing Paul's and my love in every cell of her body. Her long hands: his. Her coloring: mine. Her legs that went on for miles: his. Her love of the earth and animals: ours. Her pain: mine.

I said, 'You look well.'

It was meant as a compliment, but she caught the tone of relief.

'You mean I don't look like an addict.'

'That's *not* what I meant.' But it was.

She snorted, turned back to the seal. 'Why did you move down here?'

'I got a job at the hospital. And I wanted to be closer to you.' She didn't say anything. But her cheeks flushed. Pleasure or anger? I added, 'It's your birthday coming up. Would you like to go for dinner? Anywhere you like. Or you can come see my new house.' I gestured toward Fairfield. 'I have a potting shed in the back. I've been trying to grow bonsai trees, but I suck at it.' Did I really just say *suck*? What was I trying to prove? That I was cool? That she should love me? But I still couldn't help adding, 'There's an extra room if you ever need a place to crash.' I was disgusted with my desperate attempts to relate.

209

'I'm doing okay. You don't have to worry about me.'

I laughed, trying to ease the tension. 'It's hard for a mother not to worry about her child, even if the child is grown-up and making her own decisions.' She didn't smile. I changed my tone. 'But I'm happy to hear you're doing well.'

She tilted her chin back, looking at me with those soulful blue eyes that had lied to me so many times, and said, 'I've been clean for a couple of weeks.'

I was a psychiatrist, trained to say the right things at the right time, but now my mind spun with the worry of saying the *worst* thing: sound too encouraging and risk sounding patronizing; ask the wrong question and risk angering her; don't say enough and risk sounding uncaring.

I settled on, 'That's great. Are you in a program?' The last part had slipped out before I remembered what a hot topic it was for her, how much she'd hated the rehab I sent her to as a teen. She'd called, crying, but I'd refused to pick her up, telling her she'd made a commitment. She broke out. Garret and I had found her hitching, just about to climb into a truck with three guys. I sat frozen in the car, terrified about what could've happened to her, wanting to lock her up for life, knowing that anything I said would just make it worse. Garret got out and talked to her until she finally got in the car. She hadn't spoken to me for weeks, only telling me she'd stopped doing drugs, only to start again a month later.

'I don't need a *program*. I'm doing it on my own.'

'I'm proud of you – that takes a lot of discipline.' And rarely works. 'If you did ever want to get treatment—' Her jaw tightened, and I quickly added, 'On an out-patient basis, of course, you could stay with me. I'd be happy to pay for it.'

She stood up. 'You just can't stop yourself, can you? You think you're so helpful – you don't help *anything*.' And with that, she grabbed her packsack and stormed off. I stood there for a while afterward, my face hot with embarrassment, my eyes stinging with tears, and my heart full of regret.

I looked down at the seal. She turned and dove under the water, only the ripples on the water showing that she'd ever been there.

Chapter Twenty

The rest of the afternoon I stayed close to home, puttering around in my garden, licking my wounds. My daughter's words, and also my brother's, had hit home. I knew there was some truth to what they were saying. I'd always had an urge to fix everything and everyone I came across – the same urge that had driven me into psychiatry. I'd turned that trait into a skill and learned that you could only give people tools. They had to do the work themselves. But it was a lot harder to remain a compassionate observer when it came to my own family.

That also made me remember Garret, how frustrated he'd been as a child, angry at his parents' separation, how hard I tried to connect with him. When Paul and I first started living together, Garret often raged against me, even hitting at one point – saying that he hated me. One of the many reasons it had meant so much when he finally accepted me into his life. I thought again about my plan to give him some tools. When he answered the phone, I'd forgotten how much he sounded like Paul, and grief, sharp and poignant, stopped my voice in my throat.

'Hello?' Garret repeated.

I pulled myself together. 'Garret, hi, it's Nadine.'

'How crazy is this. I'd just been thinking this week that we needed to get together soon.' He chuckled and the warm sound, lighter than Paul's deep laugh, relaxed me and helped separate them. It had been even harder after Paul first passed away – they looked so much alike, both blond and fair. Though, Garret had his mother's delicate artist's hands. Paul's had been large, yet gentle when he held a scalpel, or a small kitten. Garret had wanted so much to be a vet like his father, but he'd been nervous around animals, having been badly bitten once. Instead he'd picked up a camera and had become very good with it.

I told him that I had his father's tools and asked if he would like them.

'That would be great. I just bought a house, and I'm building a studio.'

'So you did buy a house. Good for you. And your photography business is doing well?'

'Yeah, it's going great. Phone's been ringing off the hook.'

'Oh, that's wonderful. I'm thrilled for you – you have such an eye.'

'Thanks! You should come by and check out my studio.'

'I'd love to.'

'How's Lisa? Have you heard anything?'

I paused, wondering how best to answer that. It was the same feeling I got whenever anyone asked about my daughter. Sorrow, but also shame at my own failings.

Realizing that Garret was still waiting for me to answer, I said, 'She's still living on the streets, somewhere downtown Victoria.'

'Do you think she's also still doing drugs?'

Part of me wanted to rush to defend my daughter, against the concern in his voice, but also the hint of judgment – and if I was honest, what felt like judgment against me as a mother. *How could you let this happen? You're a doctor, and you couldn't help your own daughter?*

I said, 'I don't think she's using at the moment, but I'm not sure.'

Garret said, 'That's too bad – I know it's really tough on you. I think about her a lot too. But you can't blame yourself. She's made her own choices.'

I'd never stop blaming myself, but it was still nice to hear that from him. Then I realized that Garret was almost the only family I had left now, certainly the last link to Paul. We talked for a while longer, making a plan for him to come by one evening that week. I hung up the phone, glad I'd called.

For the rest of the week, I focused on my work, though I hadn't stopped searching for Lisa every night. I'd caught a glimpse of a tall woman entering an alley, with dark hair and a similar way of moving, and had parked in a hurry. I'd then run down the alley, only to find a prostitute in the middle of shooting up. She'd yelled obscenities at me as I quickly apologized and fled the scene. One night, I got a call from a private number, and when I picked up there was just a dial tone. Was it Lisa? I could only hope.

I bumped into Kevin at the hospital a couple of times, and he was always friendly, asking how I was doing. We had coffee together again one afternoon when we both had a break. I shared my passion for gardening, and he said, 'I grow more weeds than vegetables.' I promised to show him some of my bonsai trees, and he promised to teach me to play guitar. I was amused to learn that he was in a band with some of the other doctors, who called themselves 'On a Good Note.' I teased him about groupies.

'Hey, we're hot stuff.' He laughed. 'We even put on a show at Christmas and in the summer. The patients love us – and not just when they're medicated.' I laughed along with him, and it felt good to be taken out of my thoughts for a little while, to remember the good things in life.

*

We had a staff meeting one day, and my director pulled me aside afterward. Elaine was almost in her mid-sixties but didn't show any sign of wanting to retire soon – she often came in on her days off. She was respected for her fairness to the staff and her low tolerance for any drama, but she also didn't miss much.

'You doing all right? You seemed distracted today.'

'Sorry. I didn't sleep well last night.'

Her expression concerned, Elaine said, 'You've looked tired a few times this week. Losing a patient is traumatic, if you need some time off—'

'Thank you, but I'm fine.'

'Okay. Door's open if you ever need to talk.'

Despite my answer, I had a feeling she was going to watch me closely, and she was right to be concerned. I *had* been distracted and tired at work recently.

A couple of nights that week, I'd woken up, sure that I heard the rumble of a car slowing down outside. One time, I got up and opened the front blinds, spotting a green truck, which sped off when I flicked on my outdoor light. And a few times when I'd come home from work, I was sure I felt someone watching me as I got out of my car, but whenever I looked around, I couldn't spot anyone.

It wasn't just my personal life that was weighing on my mind. Francine, my dementia patient, wasn't doing well on the unit, refusing to eat and trying to run away daily. She was also becoming violent, biting and kicking, and had to be sedated. Sometimes I'd come in, and she'd be staring out the window, her face empty, a trapped bird.

We'd also had a young man admitted who'd tried to hang himself after losing his job and his girlfriend in the same week. Young men have a particularly difficult time with depression as they don't have the emotional skills to work through it. Brandon was struggling, with no idea what he wanted to do with his life when he was released.

'You have lots of options, Brandon,' I told him during our sessions. 'This is just a bump in the road.' And we'd talk about employment resources and where he could get help on his resume. I often thought about Heather when talking with Brandon, her ghost still lingering in the hospital halls, smiling at me through his blue eyes. I spent longer than normal with him, hoping to avoid another tragedy.

Thursday, Garret came over. Seeing his grin when I handed him his father's tools solidified my belief that he should have them. He stayed for coffee while we reminisced. It was sweet when he said, 'I'm sorry I was such a brat as a kid.' And I laughed when he said, 'You should pose for me sometime,' enjoying the man he'd grown up to be. He showed me his new business cards, and it was clear he was trying hard with his venture. We also talked about Lisa again. It was nice to share my dashed hopes and dreams with someone who also cared for her. I told him about my run-in with her down at the wharf.

His concern was obvious in his face, but he just said, 'It might be better to leave her alone. She'll probably come around on her own one day. I did, right?'

He smiled, reminding me so much of his father I had to smile back.

Friday, I heard from the Shawnigan Lake RCMP – they'd talked to Aaron. I stood with my hand still on the pile of clothes I'd been in the middle of putting away, waiting for the news while my heart thudded in my ears, already knowing instinctively that it wasn't going to be good. My premonition was confirmed a moment later when Corporal Cruikshank told me that Aaron denied everything, and he had also refused a lie detector test, which they couldn't force him to take. She explained that without further information, the case would be archived.

I'd hung up the phone with a mixture of defeat and anger, trying to find some peace in knowing I'd done the right thing. Still, a part of me couldn't shut out the fear that there were other victims out there. I also couldn't ignore the feeling that one day, maybe even soon, someone was going to get seriously hurt at the center, either by some of his techniques like fasting and sleep deprivation, or by their not letting someone seek medical treatment for some ailment in time.

On Saturday, I'd finished my shopping and house-cleaning when my mind drifted back up to Shawnigan. The retired officer, Steve Phillips, would be home from his holidays now, and I wondered if it was worth talking to him. He'd worked on Finn's case before the commune moved. But if he even remembered one small thing . . . They couldn't get Aaron on the sexual-abuse charges, but perhaps there was something else relating to Finn's death that would make them take a closer look at the center.

I also couldn't stop thinking about that image I'd had of Aaron burying something behind the barn. When I had mentioned it to Corporal Cruikshank on the phone, she'd promised they'd check into it, but I was sure that was said just to pacify me. They weren't going to search the woods because I thought I remembered Aaron burying something forty years ago. But this officer, Steve, he'd seen and talked to Aaron, and he might have a different impression of him. I also wondered if he'd ever run into any of the members in town, namely Willow.

That was another thing Corporal Cruikshank, or Amy, as she'd asked me to call her, had said. They had no record of any missing women by the name of Willow. In case that wasn't her real name, they had checked missing women fitting her description and still hadn't come up with anything. I hadn't had a chance to ask Robbie whether he had more information about Willow that might help us find out if she was alive. And I knew he'd want to know why this all mattered so much. Why now, after all these years?

Obviously, I wanted to make sure that there weren't other victims, but there was also still a feeling that I'd let Willow down. I didn't know if the feeling came from my argument with her at the river or from walking away that last day, but I feared what else my memory had blocked. Maybe by solving some of these other mysteries, I'd find out what happened to me all those years ago.

Just to be sure, I slept on it overnight, but first thing the next morning I woke up clearheaded – and resolute. I was going back to Shawnigan. I made myself eat a healthy breakfast, taking it easy on the caffeine so I wouldn't add to my already jangled nerves. Then I made the drive up to Shawnigan, feeling calm and centered. I was just going to talk to the retired officer and visit my brother – if he was home. I'd called his cell but only got voice mail. There was no harm in asking a few questions. But I reminded myself that if this trip still didn't shed any light on the situation, I was going to have to accept it and move on with my life.

This time, when I pulled into Steve Phillips's driveway, there was a blue Ford truck parked near the camper and a man was unloading some fishing gear into his garage. When he heard tires on his gravel driveway, he turned around. I climbed out of my car and walked over. He was tall, a little stooped in the shoulders and gray-haired, but he still sported the short hair of the RCMP and a thick mustache. He was also wearing a windbreaker with the RCMP logo on it. He might be retired, but he hadn't stopped being an officer.

As I got closer, he said, 'Can I help you?'

'I'm hoping so. My name is Nadine Lavoie, and I grew up in Shawnigan.'

'Okay . . . ?'

'I was wondering if you could help me. I have some questions about a little boy who died in the mountains in the late sixties. His name was Finn.'

He eased himself down onto his bumper, like all the energy had just left his body. 'Yeah, I remember the case. It's not one I'll probably ever forget. Why you asking?'

'I was living at the commune when he died.'

His eyes narrowed as he gave me an appraising look. 'You don't look familiar. Did you stay in Shawnigan?'

'I was only thirteen at the time. My mother and my brother, Robbie Jaeger, were there as well – Robbie still lives in town. But I moved away.'

I wondered if he might know Robbie, but he gave no indication, just said, 'So what can I help you with?'

As I talked, he finished unpacking his truck. He stopped when I described how Aaron took me down to the river and what he made me do, giving only the basic facts, which was hard enough without adding details. He motioned for me to keep talking while he rinsed out his coolers and hung up fishing rods. His face was

221

contemplative as he listened. Finally, I was finished, and so was he.

He said, 'Let's go into the house. It's getting cold out here.'

His home was neat and clean, but it was clear a bachelor lived there, with the rugged masculine energy of brown leather chairs and a stainless-steel kitchen. In the living room, he threw another log on the fire and motioned for me to sit. The burst of warmth was nice after the cold. While he stoked the embers, I stared out at the lake through a big picture window as a thick layer of fog rolled across the dark surface.

Finished with the fire, he settled in the chair across from me and leaned forward, his elbows on his legs. His voice was gruff, almost angry, when he spoke.

'I was the one who found the boy's body. His parents kept saying that he was in a better place now.' He paused, his lips tightening. 'There was something wrong with them – Aaron especially. I thought he might've had more to do with the boy going missing than he was letting on, but we couldn't pinpoint anything. And some of the members vouched for his whereabouts.'

'Do you remember which ones?'

He sat back, stared up at the ceiling. 'No names coming to mind. We had one witness who'd seen a woman dancing with the little boy in her arms, then walking off with the child. Later, the witness said he'd been high and had just been confused about the timing.'

'Do you think someone told him to take it back?'

'That's a pretty good bet.'

'What was his name?'

'Levi.'

I had been praying he wouldn't say Robbie's name, but I was just as jarred by his answer.

He caught my expression. 'Something I should know?'

'No ... it's just.' I strained my memory, thought back. 'I can't really recall much from around the time Finn died, but Levi and my brother were good friends. I'm surprised I don't remember that.'

'He recanted fast.'

'You think they were covering up something about Finn's death? Do you ...' I cleared my throat, suddenly tight with emotion. 'Was he murdered?'

'No, there were no signs of trauma. He died of exposure. His parents had another child – social workers took the baby away ... always wondered what happened to him.' We were both silent. Then he said, 'We were sure they were growing marijuana, but we couldn't find anything to bust them on.'

'They *were* growing drugs. That's why they didn't go to the police right away. They were afraid you'd search the barn.'

He shook his head. 'We figured they'd gotten rid of it, but there was no sign of burning, nothing. We could never figure out what they did with it all.'

I paused, trying to think. 'That's strange. I don't know what they did with it, either. They made all the kids go to bed. I was scared for Finn, thinking of him out there alone. Aaron kept saying our positive energy would bring him home.'

'The parents were stupid, but their main crime was listening to anything Aaron had to say.'

'He was very convincing, and manipulative. That's why I'm concerned now about what's happening at the center and that there could be more victims.'

'Pursuing sexual abuse cases isn't easy, especially when someone is well known, like him. That center is a big deal now. Brings in a lot of money, and he has lots of supporters.'

'I realize that.'

He held my gaze, like he was testing my resolve. I didn't look away, but he was right. Again, I asked myself how far I wanted go with this.

He continued. 'I've kept tabs on the group since they left. Two young girls, sisters, back in the nineties, claimed Aaron had made them do some things, sexual things. One of my buddies worked the case.'

So there had been more. My breath caught in my throat as I thought of another young girl with Aaron, knowing all too well things he'd probably made them do with him, all in the name of spiritual awareness. 'What happened?'

'They had a good case, looked like they might even be

able to arrest Aaron. Then the girls got scared and recanted. File's closed now, but it's always bugged the hell out of Mark – he had a bad feeling about Aaron. I could get their names.'

'Do you think they'd talk to me?'

'Hard to say, but I can ask. They're older now. Sometimes knowing there are other victims can change their minds. There's safety in numbers.'

I nodded and said, 'It's worth a try.' I didn't want to get too hopeful, but if the sisters realized there were more victims, they might be inspired to reopen their case. Then the police might finally be able to nail Aaron.

I wasn't sure how much to tell him about Willow, and I didn't want to lose the ground I'd gained by having him dismiss me as paranoid, but I casually said, 'There was a girl, Willow, who left the commune rather quickly. The police haven't been able to find anything about her whereabouts.' I told him the rest. I didn't give an opinion on what might've happened to her, just let him come to his own conclusions, and that he did.

He tugged on his mustache. 'So you're thinking she might never have left at all? That something happened to her?'

'I'm not sure, but I'm concerned.'

'Can't do much without any evidence of a missing girl. The RCMP won't perform a search without more information.'

'I understand, but I wanted to get your take on it.'

225

He said, 'Let's see if we can get those names for you. Meanwhile, maybe I'll take a walk around out there and see what I stir up.'

'That would be great.'

He draped both his arms on either side of his chair, and said, 'Sorry about your mother. Kate was an interesting woman.'

His words caught me off guard, and so did the shot of pain that her name, spoken out loud for the first time in years, still sent into my heart. I took a moment to gather myself. 'You knew her?'

'My buddy bought one of your horses.' I remembered now. When we came back from the commune, Mom sold both of our horses. She'd eventually gotten more, but it was like she couldn't stand to look at anything that reminded her of the commune, including me. Only Robbie seemed able to crack her shell.

Steve's face was grave as he smoothed his mustache. 'I was one of the first officers at the scene of her accident.'

My head filled with imagined horrors. Police lights shining. Steve, younger, peering into the mangled metal. Mom slumped over the steering wheel, one bloody hand hanging down. I still remember the police coming to the door, my father's big shoulders shaking as he dropped to his knees, Robbie and I running toward him, sensing something terrible had just happened, that life would never be the same. I swallowed hard, tried to say something to Steve: couldn't.

Steve changed the subject. 'Levi's still in Shawnigan.'

Glad for the distraction, I grabbed at it. 'I thought he'd left with the commune.'

'He came back. Runs a water-ski school on the lake now, rents boats, Jet Skis, paddleboats, things like that. He might be willing to talk to you. He's always been friendly.'

Levi had always been good-natured and fun-loving, but my memories of him were entangled with Robbie, the two of them talking and laughing with girls, or working together in the field. I'd blamed Robbie's moodiness when we'd come back home on missing his friend, but now I remembered that in the days before we'd left, just after Finn had died, they'd barely been speaking. I tried to focus in on that time, searching for an explanation, a fight or disagreement, but nothing came to mind. I wondered if Robbie knew that Levi was back in town. He must, but why hadn't he mentioned him when I asked about former members?

Steve added, 'There's someone else you could talk to, but she might be a tougher nut to crack.'

'Who's that?'

'Mary. She was also one of the commune members, but she stayed behind after they moved down to Victoria. She has a homestead out toward the river, on the left side at the junction. Hang on. I'll draw a map.'

He got up and grabbed some paper from a kitchen drawer, then roughed out a diagram. While he was busy, I tried to think of which member was named Mary but couldn't conjure a face. I was surprised we'd never run into her as kids, and that Mom and Robbie had never mentioned her.

Steve passed me the map.

'Thanks. Maybe I'll head out there now.'

For some reason I didn't feel ready to see Levi yet, my mind instantly balking at the idea. Instead my psyche latched on to this new information: There was another woman who'd left the commune. Other than my own family, Willow, and Heather and Daniel, I didn't know any former members.

'Good luck – she's a cagey one. I had to talk to her a few years back about some robberies out that way, and she kept one eye on the nearest exit. I'm sure she's got some stories, but she might not be willing to share them.'

His assessment didn't surprise me. If she'd decided to stay behind, she might have a very good reason. I was definitely interested in talking to her.

Steve and I exchanged numbers, and he walked me out to my car. I climbed in and started it up. He tapped on the top to remind me to put my seat belt on. When I rolled down the window to thank him again, he leaned over and said, 'Drive safe. And hang in there. Let me make some calls and see what I find out.'

'Thanks. I *really* appreciate your help tracking down the sisters.'

'I'll do my best.'

*

I was glad that Steve had validated some of my concerns, but I was upset to learn of the other young girls who might have been abused. How many more could there be? I remembered a recent case of sexual abuse that had gained a lot of media attention because the abuser had been a powerful official at a university. Once one victim had finally come forward, another dozen had followed suit. I thought about all the girls who'd been at the commune the same time as I had been. I tried to think of their names but couldn't recall many. Some were older, around sixteen or seventeen, most of them runaways. There were also younger ones there with their families, some maybe around eleven or twelve, and some even younger still.

Then another snapshot image came back. A thin girl, with long legs and limbs. Her parents had called her Dandelion because of her fair hair and skinny body. We'd called her Danny for short, and she was only eleven, but bold and talkative. I vaguely remembered arguing with her one day and struggled to focus on the memory. It seemed like it might've been later in the summer – and I got the feeling I was sad, so it might've been after Willow left. I concentrated harder on the memory. It was something about Aaron; he'd asked Danny to help him pick berries, and I hadn't wanted her to go. Was I scared for her? I had another brief image, a flash of her calling me jealous or stupid, or something like that, then running off to join him. More hazy images followed: Danny sitting by Aaron at the table, her face smug. I remembered being confused and upset about something, but there was also a feeling of relief.

Now, looking back, I felt sick, wondering what she had endured to earn that privilege. Was that why the memories of the abuse stopped? Aaron had left me alone because he found a new target? It was possible, but I still had a feeling that I was missing a piece of the puzzle, something that would explain my claustrophobia. Something else that had happened that summer.

Chapter Twenty-one

Five minutes later, I found Mary's place. The railings around her property were old and peeling, bleached by the sun to a faded gray. A rusted metal saw blade was bolted to the top of her front gate, the bottom lined by tire rims. The gate was open, and I pulled in her driveway slowly as two dogs, one a black Lab, the other a sheep-dog, came running from behind the house, barking. The underside of the sheepdog's fur was wet and sandy. As I parked my car, I noticed the dense forest surrounding the house, and in the distance the familiar hum of the river. I imagined the dog following the trail of a deer, or river otter, barking at crayfish.

As I climbed out of my car, a woman with snow-white hair, long and braided to hang over the front of her shoulder, came out and stood on the porch of the home. Smoke billowing from the chimney scented the air. She was wearing a man's denim jacket, a few sizes too large, with a fur collar pulled tight around her throat. Her skin was pale but looked weathered and tough, her face lined. Her hands were in her pockets as she watched me walk toward her. The dogs circled and growled, causing me to pause a few times, but she never called them off. I pushed my way through them, and they fell back, the sheepdog leaving a streak of sand and fur on my legs. As I came closer, I studied the woman's face, trying to place her. She had to be in her early sixties. I couldn't recall her, but she'd been pretty, and was still very attractive. Her features strong, her cheekbones high, and her eyes a bright and sparkling green.

Finally, she spoke. 'Do I know you?'

It wasn't a casual question. It was a demand. Did she recognize me?

'I'm not sure. That's what I'm here to find out.' I smiled pleasantly. She didn't return the gesture. 'I lived out at the commune for a while . . .'

Her body stiffened. The hand that had been reaching for one of the dogs was stuffed back into her pocket, leaving me wondering if it was a nervous reaction. When she caught my gaze, she turned away and abruptly said, 'I have to collect the eggs,' then walked toward a little coop at the back of the house.

She hadn't told me to go away, so I started to follow, then on the left I noticed a barn with a corral, where two horses munched on hay, their heavy bodies shifting back and forth, the plumes of their breath in the air. I caught the smell of horse and was drawn toward it, wanted to run my hands through their thick manes, breathe in the musky warmth at their necks. But then I picked up another odor from the barn, something familiar, old manure and musty feed, damp earth. I felt ill with it but didn't understand why. Still wondering at my body's reaction, I hurried after Mary. 'You used to live at the commune too?'

She glanced at me again, without breaking stride, then gazed up at the sky and said, 'He's always watching.' I was thrown by her words, by the eerie tone, then the way she was holding her head as she looked upward struck me as familiar. I stopped dead in my tracks. My brain superimposed my memories over her face – and I recognized her.

'Cedar, your name was Cedar.' She'd been a devoted member, always singing at the campfire and meditating with Aaron. Something else clung to the corners of my memories, twisting in my guts, my heart thudding a warning.

Bad, something bad.

She stopped and pivoted, took a step toward me. I took a step back, my heel catching on a rock, causing me to stumble.

Her eyes were filled with anger. 'I *used* to be Cedar. My name's Mary.'

She spun around again and continued on to the chicken coop, where she picked up a bucket outside the door. I hesitated, and then followed, gagging at the thick

233

odor of chicken manure and dander as she pulled eggs out from underneath squawking hens, her back to me.

Over the shrill squawking, she said, 'I was young and stupid. We really thought we were changing the world.' She laughed. 'We weren't changing anything. Just getting high and screwing our asses off.' She laughed again, but in a raucous, fun way, and I began to relax slightly. Something about the woman's rawness appealed to me. Felt real and authentic. What she might say could hurt, but she'd tell it like it was. I was proved right a moment later, when she turned and said, 'Your mother was beautiful – you've got her looks.'

I kept my face composed. 'You remember my mother?'

'Kate. Sweet woman, but a little . . .' She made a motion by her head. I was caught between wanting to defend my mother and knowing it was true. I decided not to say anything, but Mary must have seen something in my eyes because she said, 'Don't get me wrong, I liked the woman. But it had to be hard growing up with your mother's head in the clouds all the time.' She assessed me again, looking hard in my eyes like she was trying to see into my life, what I'd become. She said, 'Commune wasn't a good place for kids.'

I took the opening. 'That's what I was hoping to speak with you about. Do you know much about Aaron, or Joseph, since they left?' I said the last part cautiously, in case she was still in touch with anyone.

She shook her head vehemently. 'No. I've put those days behind me.'

'So you don't know about the center in Victoria?'

Another quick shake.

I told her everything I knew about the commune while she continued collecting eggs, then I said, 'I'm not sure where Joseph is these days, or if he's even alive, but I think Aaron's been sexually abusing young girls.'

She turned, frowned. 'Why do you think that?'

'There have been a couple of cases that were dropped, but I have good reason to believe they're true.' She didn't ask anything further, just went back to her task, so I added, 'Do you remember Aaron being inappropriate with any girls?'

She looked at me again, her hand still under a hen, who was pecking at the skin on top. I cringed, thinking of the pain, but Mary didn't even flinch.

'Don't recall anything like that,' she said. 'But I was only twenty at the time. Running away from my rich parents because I thought I had it so hard.' Another laugh, which stopped abruptly as a bitter expression passed over her face, like she'd just opened a painful memory. Her tone changed, dropped low. 'If you're going around talking to people about them, you better be careful.'

'What are you afraid might happen?'

'People like that, they don't like it when you don't see things their way.'

So she also knew there was another side to Aaron. I wondered what had happened to her at the commune.

'Do you think they'd come after someone who spoke about them?'

Mary didn't say anything for a second, then just nodded.

I didn't know if she was afraid of a lawsuit, or that they might choose some sort of violent means of silencing potential witnesses, but I certainly didn't want her to be scared to speak with me.

'I can understand that you might be concerned, but I don't believe he would risk drawing more attention to himself – not now.' I explained about my own abuse and that I'd made a report.

She said, 'Sorry to hear that he messed around with you, but it doesn't surprise me. Lots of sex and drugs at the commune. People telling themselves that what they're doing is okay as long as it's all in the name of love and peace.'

'Yes, and I don't think he's ever stopped, just moved on from victim to victim. We may never know how many lives he's ruined over the years.' I added, 'There was a girl, Willow. I'm trying to find out what happened to her.'

'Willow? I thought she left?' Mary's expression was puzzled.

I decided to hold back on my suspicions for now, until I knew more about Mary. 'Yes, but I'd like to know where she ended up. I'd love to reconnect with her.' I held her gaze so I could read any change in her expression.

Her eyes narrowed, like she was trying to understand what I might be getting at. She pulled her hand out from under the hen and rubbed her forehead.

I glanced at her hand. And that's when I noticed one of her fingers was missing. Seeing the direction of my gaze, she snatched her hand back down by her side and closed her fingers in a fist, holding it protectively against her stomach.

It was too late. The memory came rolling back in.

It's night, not long after Willow left. I'm awake in my cabin, thinking about running away to find her. I hear strange sounds from the campfire. I sneak out the door, then creep along the dark edge until I can hear raised voices. Joseph is kneeling behind a blond-haired woman, also down on her knees, with her hand strapped to a chopping block and a gag in her mouth. He's holding a machete. The woman is crying in muffled sobs and trying to pull away, but Joseph holds her in place.

Aaron is standing near, his face alarmed. I can't make out the words, but he's talking to Joseph, his hands reaching out, and I have a feeling that he's trying to get Joseph to give him the machete. Joseph hesitates, but then he looks up at the sky. He says something to the air. There's a flash as Joseph raises the machete, then a quick thwack as it comes down hard. I quickly slap my hand over my mouth, to hold in the scream, but a moan leaks out. Aaron, now pulling the machete out of his brother's hand, as the woman sobs at their feet, has noticed. He starts toward me as I cower in the shadows, but the woman is crying louder, nearly choking on the gag, and he turns back around, whispering to Joseph, 'Shut her up.'

I crouch low and scurry to the cabin.

In the morning, I skirt around the campfire, noticing the scuffle marks in the dirt, the dark splotches of blood. During our breakfast meditation, Cedar sits alone, not speaking to anyone, a large bandage wrapped around her hand.

My mother whispers, 'Aaron said she caught her hand in a blade, after he warned her to be careful. Now she's chosen to sit in silence and reflect on her decision, so she can learn from her mistake.'

I glance at the woman again. Her eyes meet mine. And in the back of them, I see something. She's not sorry. She's angry.

Now, years later, I saw that same look in Mary's eyes. I said, 'Joseph did that to you. I remember now. But I don't know why.'

Mary didn't say anything, just turned away and moved to the next chicken.

'You must've been terrified.'

She paused for a minute, studying the eggs in her bucket, her good hand holding the handle. I wondered what she was thinking. Finally, her voice raw and angry, she said, 'I'd wanted to leave the commune at the end of the summer. One of my cousins was living in California, and I thought it would be fun. I'd told Aaron that night, after everyone had gone to bed, but Joseph heard us talking . . .'

'Joseph cut your finger off because you wanted to leave?'

She nodded abruptly, her neck muscles corded. 'He said he had a vision of my finger being a snake full of venom. That it was poisoning my thoughts.'

'Why didn't you leave after they hurt you?'

'Aaron . . . he said he needed me, that we were a family now, and families don't leave each other.' Her face took on a reflective expression. 'I think about that sometimes, how beautiful he was when he smiled. He could make you believe anything. It was like I was high all the time, on everything he was teaching – meditating, the pot, the singing and chanting, the walks, all the sex and love, it was like walking around in a dream.'

'Why did you finally leave?'

'After Finn died, there was lots of police attention. Aaron didn't like it. I told him I'd stay here to keep an eye on the situation. He forgot about me. I was just one of many of his women.' There was no tone of bitterness, just factual, with a hint of relief.

'You haven't heard from him since?'

'No, and I want to keep it that way.' This time her tone was a clear warning. 'That's a time in my life I'd rather forget.'

'I can understand that. I feel the same way, but I had a patient recently . . .' Without giving away too many details about Heather, I explained what had drawn me back into the past. 'There are more young women at the commune, and I'm afraid that he'll keep destroying lives unless we find a way to shut him down.'

She didn't say anything, but her face, from what I could see of it as she worked her way down the line, collecting the last of the eggs, was thoughtful. I wondered what her life was like since she had left the commune.

I said, 'Do you have any children?'

She thrust her hand under a chicken, making it squawk in protest. 'I have a son.' She said it protectively – no doubt concerned about what I was going to do with the information, but there was also pride. She loved her son.

'Do you get to see him much?'

'He travels, but we keep in touch. He doesn't like me living out here by myself. I've done it for over forty years – told him I was leaving over my dead body, and he's going to have to bury me in the manure pile.' A cheeky grin.

'That's nice, that he worries about you. I have a daughter, but we're not close.' I heard the catch in my throat. Mary did as well.

She studied my face, questioning.

I said, 'She lives on the streets in Victoria. I worry about her.' It was an understatement, but the best I could do with the sudden tightness in my throat.

'Only time we have control over our babies is when

they're in our womb.' She looked at me with under-standing. Two mothers who missed their children.

'That's one of the reasons I'm so concerned about the center. Aaron takes girls like her and preys on their emotions. I keep thinking about their mothers, how no one has any idea what he's really like or what he might be doing. Like I said, I very much understand your concerns, but if you did tell the police about your finger, they might get more serious about the investigation.'

She paused, her hands on an egg, holding the delicate shell in her rough hands as she rolled it around. 'I'll think about it.' I had a gut feeling that she didn't plan on speaking to the police for one second, but I didn't want to push her. Truth is, it would be hard pursuing any sort of assault case after all this time, and I couldn't blame her for not wanting to go through the process.

Before I left, she kindly gave me a carton of eggs. I drove slowly down her driveway and over the potholes until I was back on pavement. I was still thinking about Mary when I realized I was at the corner where my mother had had her accident. I pulled over and looked at the tree that had taken her life. It had grown, but the scar was still there.

I stopped at Robbie's on my way back to Victoria, so I could ask him about Willow, and whether he knew Mary lived nearby, but his truck was gone, and the house dark.

Chapter Twenty-two

On my way to the hospital Monday morning, I stopped at the organic coffee shop on the corner for my usual green tea infusion. As I turned to leave, paper cup in hand, I suddenly noticed Daniel sitting alone in the corner, his back to the wall as he read a paper. When he felt my gaze, he glanced up and with a small smile waved me over.

I said, 'Good morning.' I was pleased to see him. I'd been thinking about him, wondering how he was faring. 'I didn't know you lived in this part of town.'

'I don't.' He nodded in the direction of the hospital. 'I had to sign some release forms.'

He might have released the hospital from responsibility for Heather's death, but I still wished we'd been able to help her. Daniel looked like he needed some help himself. He'd lost weight since the funeral, his skin was pale, with dark shadows under his eyes, and it was clear he hadn't shaved for days.

I said, 'How are you doing, Daniel? You holding up okay?'

He shrugged, a sad, defeated motion.

I gestured to the chair across from him. 'Would you like to talk for a moment?' He wasn't my patient, and it wouldn't be appropriate for me to treat him, but I didn't feel right about walking away without offering some solace.

'Please.' There was a look of confusion in his eyes that I've often seen in the grief-stricken in the weeks that follow a death. When someone first passes, there's the business of notifying people and planning a funeral, a focused activity.

Then there are no more distractions, only silence and loss.

After I sat, he said, 'I'm back at work, and I make myself go for runs, but I just miss Heather so much . . . I haven't been able to pack up any of her things.'

I thought about Paul, how it took me months to give away his clothes, how I slept in his pajamas for years.

Daniel shook his head. 'I shouldn't be bothering you with any of that stuff. You probably have to go and do your rounds or whatever.'

'It's okay. But I would suggest you speak to someone if you're having a hard time. What about a grief-support group? There's one that meets at the hospital. I can email you a contact name.'

'No, I'm just finishing up this last job, then I'm going back to the center.'

It made sense that Daniel was being drawn to the comfort of the familiar, but I was still alarmed to hear his plan.

'You remember being happy at the center,' I said, 'so you think going back there will help you escape the pain. Unfortunately, there are no shortcuts with this kind of loss. I wouldn't want to see you carry this with you for the rest of your life. It's hard to find true happiness when you have unresolved grief.'

Daniel said, 'Everything just made sense in there, but out here . . .' He shook his head. 'In there, I had a purpose. I was helping people.'

'Daniel, I understand that right now you're searching for answers, and you're in pain. But sometimes people who are experiencing grief try to replace the loss, without processing their feelings—'

'I'm not trying to replace her. I just have nothing out here. But I have friends in the center, people who care about me, and they want me to come back.'

'What they want from you and what you might need may be two different things. I know you did a lot of work for them, and—'

'That's not why they want me back.' He frowned. 'Why do you hate the center so much?'

I paused, thinking how best to answer. 'I don't hate the center, Daniel. I'm just concerned that Aaron's beliefs are dressed up to be spiritual but are really self-serving and might just cause more pain for you and others.'

'What do you mean?' He set down his cup.

It wasn't the ideal time to open up a subject that would anger him, and upset me, but I also felt he needed to know the truth. I took a sip of tea, composed myself. 'The center, Aaron, he's not what you think. In the past . . . ' I hesitated, thinking of how to put it. 'He sexually abused a young girl. There may be other victims.'

'That's impossible.' His face was angry, shocked. 'Aaron would never do something like that.'

'It's true. I wish it wasn't, but it is.'

'If there's a victim, why haven't we heard anything? He's never been arrested. It sounds like someone is lying.' He shook his head. 'It can't be true.'

'There's been a report made with the police.' I wondered why he was still so loyal to Aaron, whether in his grief he just couldn't deal with another loss.

Now his face was confused, his brows pulling down as he tried to take in the information. 'Have they arrested him?'

'Not yet, there's not enough evidence, but I've been talking to some people in Shawnigan.' I gave him the basics, about the girls who'd recanted, and Mary, leaving out Willow. 'I'm confident that more information will come out.'

'Are any of them pressing charges?'

'Not at the moment, no.'

His face was earnest. 'So it *could* be lies.'

245

As I looked across the table at him, I realized again how this would be many people's reactions, *Not Aaron, he wouldn't. He couldn't.* But I know he did. I considered sharing my story but didn't feel right about it, not given our history and his connection with the commune.

'I doubt it, Daniel. I know for a fact that he has molested at least one young girl.' I held his gaze.

He sat back in his chair, pushing his cup forward as though to block my words. 'No way. I still don't believe it.'

He didn't *want* to believe it. I sat back in my own chair, suddenly very tired. Since I'd seen the green truck outside my home the week before, I'd woken up several times throughout the night, listening to every vehicle as it drove past, holding my breath until it was gone. The previous evening, I'd gotten two more calls from a private number, and each time they hung up when I answered. In case it was related to my attack in Nanaimo, I talked to the police up there, but they had no new leads. They told me that I could start marking the calls by pressing *57, and then my phone provider would release the information to them. But they could only do something if the person started to verbally harass me when I answered. They couldn't do anything about hang-ups.

'There was a reason you left,' I said, gently. 'I think if you'd really wanted to stay, you would have found a way to convince Heather. Is it possible that you've had your own doubts about some of their methods and beliefs?'

Daniel flinched, his face pulling as he wrestled with his emotions.

I said, 'I know you're hurting, Daniel, and you want to be part of something that brings meaning to your life, to all of this, but the center isn't it.'

He was already shaking his head before I was finished speaking, refusing to hear me or the doubt-filled thoughts that were creeping into his mind.

'You don't understand. The whole point is to trust the process, to have faith you're on the path to enlightenment, or it doesn't work. Questions are just fear, trying to distract you from your path.' He got up, and before he walked away, he paused by my chair, not looking down, as he said, 'I'm going back.'

The next evening after work, I looked for Lisa again. I was encouraged when a homeless woman told me about an abandoned house downtown where she might be staying, but when I got there, the place was empty. I thought about trying to find the commune store, but I needed a break from thinking about that place. I stopped by a store window, seeing an angora scarf in a blue that would look wonderful with Lisa's eyes. I went in, fingered the soft material, wishing I could buy it for her birthday, which was the following weekend, but realized it would probably get stolen on the street if she didn't sell it first. I opened a bottle of perfume, inhaled the woodsy aroma, and remembered how excited she was the first year I'd given her a perfume set. Did she still like the sweeter scents, or would something stronger appeal to her now?

While I browsed the store, I reminisced about how I'd tried to make every one of her birthdays a celebration when she was growing up, baking special cakes and decorating the house top to bottom, singing to her at the top of my lungs. Then I remembered that we hadn't celebrated birthdays at the commune – Aaron said that we were ageless. I felt a sudden surge of anger at my parents, at the choices they made, how they'd let us down. Then I wondered if Lisa also felt that way. What did she blame me for? Her drug addiction? Her father's death?

On my way out, I spotted a stuffed husky who looked just like Chinook. Lisa was long past toy animals. I bought it anyway.

In the morning, Steve Phillips called me at the hospital. When I dialed him back, my hand kept pressing the wrong buttons. I had to slow down and start again a couple of times. I was nervous, in hope and in fear of what I might learn.

He said, 'I got those names for you.'

'That was fast. I really appreciate this.'

'My friend's been hoping for a break in this case for a long time. The girls are Tammy and Nicole Gelsinki. He talked to Tammy. She's living in Victoria, and she's willing to speak to you, but she's pretty edgy. Got a pen?'

I wrote down Tammy's number, and he filled me in on what Mark had told her about me, and that Tammy wouldn't reveal where Nicole was living. I wondered if she might feel more comfortable telling me than the police.

When he finished, I said, 'Did you take a walk out by the commune?'

'Sure did, and had a look around the barn.' My stomach contracted at the memory of my own recent visit there. 'And at that spot you mentioned, but I couldn't see much visually. We'd need a cadaver dog to take a sniff around.'

The words 'cadaver dog' hit hard. It was one thing to go from speculating about what happened to Willow to honestly considering that her body might be on the commune grounds. I took a second to gather my thoughts again. Then I said, 'Well, there's no way the RCMP are going to get involved with that.'

'If you get me more information, I might be able to call in a few favors. Let me know what you find out.' He clipped out the last words, still a sergeant.

I said, 'I'll try my best.'

'Be careful.'

My nerves came alive, remembering the sound of that truck slowing down, then speeding away. 'Of anything in particular?'

'Just make sure anyone you're talking to about the commune tells you more than you tell them. If they're still connected to anyone, you don't want it getting back to Aaron.'

'He's already aware I made a report.'

'Right now he knows you can't go anywhere with it, but if he finds out that you're talking to previous members, and you get too close, he might take off. He owns communes all over the world, which means he's a flight risk.'

'Okay. I'll keep that in mind.'

'Don't say anything about Willow either – I'd like to keep that one under wraps for now. Let's see what other information they produce on their own.'

His reasoning seemed sound, so I said, 'Got it.' But as I hung up the phone, I heard Willow's voice in my head. *If there's anything you ever want to talk about* ... I tried to think back to that moment, wondered why those words haunted me, and realized it was because when she'd asked, I had wanted to tell her what Aaron had been doing, but I'd been too scared. Now I wondered how different things might have turned out, for her and for me, if I'd spoken up.

After I finished my rounds, I called the number that Steve gave me and was greeted by a cheerful female voice, 'Hello?'

'Hi, my name's Nadine Lavoie, and I was hoping—' I broke off as I heard a loud crash in the background, then the wailing of a child.

'Oh, jeez, hang on.' The clatter of the phone being put down, then shushing sounds. She came back. 'Sorry about that. My little guy had a fall.'

'Hope he's okay.'

'He's fine.' Talking quick, wanting me to get to the point, a busy mother.

'I was hoping I could speak with you about a personal matter.'

Her voice turned cautious. 'Who's this?'

'I believe the RCMP told you I might be calling. I'm a psychiatrist in Victoria, and I'm looking into something that happened when I was a child . . . '

'Oh, right.' Now she sounded more curious.

Steve's friend had already told her that I'd lived at the commune and was trying to find former members, but until we were face-to-face, I didn't want to give more details. I just said, 'I was really hoping we could speak in person.'

She was silent again, her baby starting to fuss in the background. 'I'm not sure. My husband's away right now . . . ' There was nervousness in the words. Insecurity, but also something else. She had given her number, so she obviously wanted to talk. Maybe she was uncomfortable meeting in public.

'I can come to your house.'

'Is there a way I can, like, verify who you are?' Embarrassment now.

'Of course.' I gave her my number, then told her to call

me back at the hospital. But she didn't. After ten minutes I started to wonder if I'd lost her. I was almost ready to give up and head to my appointment when the phone rang.

'Sorry about that. My son needed his bottle. Can you come over later? My husband has hockey practice on Wednesday nights.'

It was interesting that she mentioned her husband not being home that night, and I wondered if he knew about her former life. 'Absolutely.'

I took down her address, then hung up the phone. I cautioned myself to remember that she'd recanted before and that this was a sensitive subject, laden with shameful emotions she still might not be ready to face, but I was hopeful that she might share her story with me.

I was still struggling with the memories of my own abuse. It had made me look at my life differently, made me question everything. Like the fact that I'd never been comfortable alone with a strange man and how long it took me to trust someone. Paul and I had worked together for a year before we started dating – our friendship had turned to love one night when we both snuck in to check on a dog who'd just had surgery. We'd ended up staying at the clinic for hours, talking in the quiet, our hands accidentally touching as we patted the soft fur of the sleeping animal. Even then, it took a while before I was willing to be intimate with Paul.

Was I just a person who liked to take her time? Or was

it a symptom of the abuse? Everything that I had taken for granted, my reactions, my dislikes, things that I had just accepted as quirks of my personality were all a question mark now.

At lunch, I grabbed some soup in the cafeteria and was just setting it on a table when I noticed Kevin in line with his tray. He was looking around for a seat in the busy room. I caught his eye and motioned to the chair in front of me.

He sat down with a smile. 'So this is where you've been hiding.'

'From the big bad wolf?'

'I think I might be treating him.' We both laughed, and he said, 'So how've you been? I haven't seen you around much.'

'I've been busy, looking into some things happening at River of Life.'

'Yeah? Like what?'

I hadn't planned on telling him – or anyone at the hospital – what was happening in my personal life, but he seemed genuinely interested, and he'd been very helpful before. I shared what I'd been going through since I'd first met Heather, still leaving out big portions, like about my brother and Lisa. I also said that I'd been having flashbacks of being abused by Aaron and was concerned that there might be more victims, using my clinical voice, trying to detach from the emotions of the words.

While I spoke, he mostly just listened, only occasionally paraphrasing something I'd said, asking if he'd understood correctly. At the end, he sat back and took a swig of coffee, his eyes warm and compassionate.

His face was serious as he said, 'Do you think you should be digging into this by yourself? It might be better if you leave it to the police from now on.'

I thought about what he'd said. 'It's certainly the easier approach, but I'm concerned that the case will be dropped. And then Aaron will keep on abusing girls. The police don't really have the time to do this kind of legwork. If I find enough evidence that something's not right, then I can push them harder.'

'Do you think this could be dangerous, though?'

'Not at the moment . . .' I told him what I'd also told Mary, that Aaron wouldn't want to draw negative attention. But while I spoke, I thought again about the green truck, the feeling of being watched, and wondered if Aaron *did* have someone keeping an eye on me. I decided to keep that possibility to myself.

When I was finished speaking, Kevin nodded in agreement. 'Yes, that makes sense.' He paused, thinking as he chewed a bite of his sandwich, his eyes narrowed. 'The members I met from the center seemed decent – I'm sure they have no idea about Aaron's sexual abuse or his brother's history of violence.'

'That's my thought too, that there's the center – and then there's Aaron.'

He nodded again. 'Still, it might be a good idea to be careful who you talk to and what you say.'

He was right. I needed to be more careful, especially if Aaron was watching me, but I couldn't stop now, not when I was finally getting somewhere.

'I will. Thanks.'

We talked for a while about a program he was starting for young men who have lost their jobs, something he connected with because of his own experience as a youth, and how he found relating to them to be the first step in gaining their trust. We also spoke about my patient, Brandon. I found his project interesting and a good diversion from thinking about the commune. We'd been talking for so long that I was startled when I glanced at my watch and realized my lunch hour was over, a thought that was followed with disappointment.

'Shoot. I should get back to work.' I stood up, grabbed my empty tray with one hand. 'Thanks for keeping me company.'

Kevin also looked disappointed, which made me happy for some inexplicable reason. He said, 'Sure. If you ever need an ear – you know where to find me.'

'Thanks. I'll keep that in mind.'

I had walked all the way to the elevator and was starting up to the first floor before I remembered my next appointment was on the ground level.

Chapter Twenty-three

After work, I went home to grab a quick bite to eat, forcing myself through the motions, my stomach muscles tight with the idea of talking to another woman who shared my experience. Tammy lived in Fernwood, an older neighborhood near downtown, and not very far from my place. When I knocked on the back door of her lemon-colored Victorian house, I noticed that most of the paint was peeling, and they were in the process of fixing up the back deck. An older car sat in the driveway with two flat tires. Tammy opened the door, a smiling blond baby boy on her hip. She was a sweet-looking woman: round-faced, no makeup, brown hair pulled back into a scattered ponytail, and a fine dusting of freckles that gave her a youthful look. But she was probably in her mid-thirties, judging by the lines at the corners of her eyes.

She said, 'Come in. House is a mess, though.'

'That's perfectly fine.'

I walked into the kitchen, carefully taking my shoes off, and said, 'Your home's gorgeous.'

She turned around from the coffeepot, her face pinking with pleasure. 'Thanks. It's going to take a long time to get it where we want it, but you know.' She shrugged. 'Babies take priority.'

'It looks like you've done a lot of work already. I love the treatment on the cupboards.'

'Thanks.' She smiled as she glanced at them. 'I did that myself.'

She'd done a nice job. I imagined her carefully painting each cabinet, screwing on the glass doorknobs, making a home for her family. I felt a twinge, remembering that when I was pregnant with Lisa and close to my due date my nesting instinct had been so strong, I'd made Paul repaint most of the house, something he did with a smile, even while cursing my hormones.

Tammy put her baby in a playpen in the corner, poured us each a coffee, and sat across from me. She studied my face, hers intent, with her body leaning forward – a good sign. She was open to talking.

She said, 'So you lived at the commune too?'

I nodded. 'Yes, back in the late sixties, when they were in Shawnigan Lake. I was hoping you could tell me about your experience. You have a sister?'

She gnawed at her lips and glanced at the door. I followed her gaze. 'Does your sister live with you?' Maybe she was expecting her home.

'No. She went back to the commune.'

I stared at her in surprise. I hadn't anticipated that.

She said, 'I didn't tell the cop because I didn't want him to try to contact her in there and get her upset at me. She doesn't call anymore because she knows I want her to leave.'

'Why *do* you want her to leave?'

Now she sat back in her chair a little, putting some distance between us. Hands tight around the mug as she eyed me, suspicious.

I said, 'Is it Aaron you're concerned about?'

She said, 'He's important, like in the community and stuff, not just at the center. People really like him.'

Testing me, seeing how I feel about Aaron.

'Some people do, yes, but I'm not one of them.'

Again she gnawed on her lip, looked around, and hunched her shoulders like she was trying to pull in on herself. 'He's not what people think.'

'No, he's not. You're right.' I was relieved to talk to someone else who saw Aaron for what he truly was – a fraud. I took a breath, let it out slowly. I hadn't realized how alone I'd felt in my thoughts, and in my fears.

'We were only there because of our parents – that's why Nicole went back. They wouldn't leave, and she missed them.' Before I could inquire further, she said, 'As long as I'm out here, they won't have anything to do with me.' She looked at her child, playing in the crib. 'They've never met Dillon.'

'I imagine that's been very hard for you.'

She sighed and turned back to me. 'My husband, he knows about my time in there. But he doesn't like to talk about it. He and Dillon are my family now.' I wondered at that, if those were his words or hers, wondered what kind of husband wouldn't let his wife talk about something that was so obviously important.

'When did your family join the commune?'

'Nicole was ten, and I was twelve. Our younger brother died of leukemia, and our parents joined a support group. There was another woman there, Joy, she'd also lost a son, and she told them about a retreat she'd gone to that helped.'

Joy. I remembered her well. I wondered if her child really had died or if her story had just been a ruse to connect with new recruits.

I said, 'Does Aaron get many members from support groups?'

'I guess so – a lot of them have lost family. We also get street kids and drug addicts. Aaron doesn't charge them. He just picks a few each year to come live at the commune, people he says need our help the most.'

Fear made my back stiffen in my chair. Would he find Lisa? I forced myself to relax. Lisa wouldn't go near a spiritual center.

Tammy was still talking. 'He says most people's problems come from a fear of death, that's what causes anxiety, depression, drug addiction, and all that. He said that if everyone understood what a beautiful place they'd go to when they died, they'd live better lives down here.'

Unless they had the bad luck to meet Aaron.

I said, 'The commune seems to have expanded into other countries.' I didn't want to tell her how much I knew from my online research, preferring to hear it from her. 'When did that happen?'

'Aaron said that we needed to reach more people. More bad stuff was happening to the earth, and we needed to help. He picked members and sent them around the world to start new communes. He always knew who was the most committed to their practice, or if anyone said anything against the commune.'

'Do you know how he might've been able to do that?' I had my suspicions, but I wanted to see what she thought.

'There are cameras in every room – even the bathrooms.' I flashed to Heather's reaction to the cameras at the hospital, now understanding. 'He says it's so we let go of our inhibitions. Some of the members knew spots on the grounds, or in buildings, where they could talk in private, but he still found out what they'd said. He said he could read their energies, but I think he just had spies.'

He probably did. I remembered Aaron's uncanny way of always knowing who was wavering or spreading doubt. That person would be singled out by Aaron in the next cleansing ceremony, forced to confess, then ignored for a few days. A couple of days later another member would be given special privileges.

She said, 'If someone was talking about leaving, he'd be really upset.'

'Upset how?' My mind filled again with the image of Joseph kicking that man on the ground, the machete coming down while Mary struggled.

'He'd take the member into his office, meditating with them and talking to them for hours and hours, until they'd agree to stay. He'd also have other members talk to them – sometimes people could be really mean. They used a lot of guilt, like saying that you wouldn't get to see the people you love on the other side after you die. If a member ever did leave, they'd call them nonstop.'

'What happens to members if they break a rule?'

'Usually we just weren't allowed to talk to people, even if they were standing right beside you. Or they had to get an adjustment.'

'What's an adjustment?'

'Sometimes it was just talking with Aaron, but if he didn't think you were getting the message, you had to go for a full adjustment. They had these electrical things that sent currents through your brain and cleared you out. They said it's like you get cysts, where energy gets trapped in your cells, and it disrupts your health and your thinking, so you have to break it up, then release it.'

It sounded like he was experimenting with some sort of biofeedback or brain-wave system.

Tammy said, 'That wasn't so bad, but then it got worse.' She looked over at her son. 'He started putting people underground.'

At first I thought I'd heard wrong. 'I'm sorry, did you say—'

'He has isolation chambers built under the center. He doesn't let you out until you've surrendered to your fears and let go of your past.'

My body stiffened, horror at her words, and something else, an uncomfortable feeling that I wanted to escape from, but I didn't know what was causing the unease. I took a breath, stayed in the present. 'Doesn't anyone refuse?' I knew how closed off cults could become, how over time members could, and did, tolerate numerous abuses at the hands of their leaders, but I was still surprised so many people went along with Aaron's crazy ideas.

'People said that the adjustment really helped them – and they did seem happier after. Some people would pay so they could go through it again. They have a special area in the basement called the Adjustment Room.'

'What about the other chambers? Where are they?'

'In the basement too, but I never saw one. Only the senior members and the office staff can go there without permission. Everyone else has to wait for Aaron to decide if they're ready. It's a privilege to enter the Isolation Chambers.'

'I thought it was punishment?'

'It was at first, but then a couple of the members who'd gone through it said they left their body and had visions, like of their spirit selves and stuff.'

It sounded to me like they were having autoscopic hallucinations. 'How long did he keep them down there?'

'Sometimes for days. And they weren't allowed food or anything.'

Which would explain their visions, but he must be able to get air to them somehow.

Tammy said, 'Now people *beg* to go down. He uses it as a reward – but he says that he's the only one who can communicate with the other side. What everyone else sees is just a window, but he can open the door.'

I shook my head, stunned at how far Aaron's mind control had spread, wondered if it had increased in other ways. 'Does he still hold Satsang?'

'Yeah. Every week he has new chanting sequences and we had to memorize them. He also makes video podcasts, for when he's away. We weren't allowed personal computers – there are just the ones that the office staff uses to run things. So they'd play them for us on a big screen in the meditation room.'

'I heard that they also have a store?'

She nodded. 'Near downtown. They sell organic food, books, CDs, and jewelry. That's where people can also sign up for retreats. Sometimes they give out food. That's how we meet a lot of homeless people and street kids.'

Tammy was warming up, looking visibly relieved to be sharing her experience. 'He doesn't do many personal vibrational-healing meditations anymore, only for people he has a vision about. But there are speakers in the rooms, so he can talk to us. Sometimes he'd come to the kids' school and lead us in chants. He said our minds were more pure and open to the earth's vibrations.'

I thought of children clustered around Aaron, kneeling at his feet. Then I remembered kneeling before him, his hand pushing down the back of my head.

Tammy was watching me. It took a moment for me to find my voice again and gather my thoughts. The next part was going to be difficult.

'There was something else that I wanted to share with you today.' I cleared my throat, took a sip of my coffee. 'Aaron ... he also sexually abused me when I was a child.' Tammy's eyes widened. I continued. 'He convinced me that I had to let him do things to me, or my mother would get sick. When I remembered what he'd done, I started getting concerned that there could be more girls ...'

For a minute, I thought Tammy might cry, but she focused on her son, blinking hard, trying to regain control.

'He told me that I was special and that he could help my family,' she said. 'But I couldn't tell anyone. It had to be our secret.'

I nodded, feeling a mixture of sadness and anger, over

our lost innocence, at how he'd abused our trust. Everything she was saying all too real and familiar.

She said, 'He also said that if I didn't help *him*, he wouldn't treat my parents or sister anymore, and they could get cancer.'

So he was still using the threat of illness to manipulate people. After already watching their brother die, it would've been a powerful motivator. My voice gentle, I said, 'Did you ever tell your parents about the abuse?'

'We tried, but they didn't believe us. They said it was an honor to have a private healing with him.' Her eyes filled with tears again.

'I'm so sorry, Tammy.' It was a sad fact that many parents didn't want to believe their children in these cases, especially if it involved another family member or a respected member of the community.

'I know they're just messed up, because of him, and because our brother died, but I don't know how you can't believe your own kid.' She looked again at her son. 'If anyone hurt Dillon, I'd kill them.' Tammy turned back to me. 'Joseph found us after we went to the police.'

So Joseph *was* still alive. I wanted to ask about his position at the center, and his mental health, but Tammy answered that question with her next sentence.

'Something was wrong with him. He'd always been kind of creepy, but he was ranting, saying crazy stuff. Like that if we didn't recant our stories, the Light was going to punish us. We were scared he was going to hurt us, so we told the police we'd made it up. Nicole was still freaked-out and went back.'

'But you didn't?'

'I'd met my husband by then. He saw Joseph outside my house one day and told him that he'd kill him if he came near me again. We didn't hear from him after that.'

I remembered when my father had shown up to claim us. It seemed like they were all for pressuring people until there were any confrontations with angry fathers or husbands. They were careful to fly under the radar.

Tammy's tone had been proud, happy to have a protective husband, but then it changed to sad as she said, 'It's hard, not being able to talk to Nicole or anything. She was my best friend.'

I gave her a sympathetic smile, and said, 'I imagine you miss her a lot.' I waited a moment, then asked, 'Did you ever see Aaron with other girls?'

She nodded. 'Sometimes he'd be really nice to a new girl and ignore me or Nicole so we'd know what he was probably doing. But the weird thing is I'd be jealous, like it meant I wasn't special anymore or something.'

'It's normal to want to feel special, but that doesn't mean that you wanted his sexual attention. You shouldn't feel ashamed of those feelings.'

Tammy looked a little relieved. 'I think sometimes that's why Nicole went back. She wanted to be there, where that stuff was normal, because then she didn't feel so weird about it. Out here, she felt more ashamed . . . and dirty.'

I felt sad, thinking of this young girl struggling on her own with these emotions. 'Some people have difficulty adjusting to a new environment with less structure, where no one is telling you what to say or do all the time, especially without your family and friends for support. That may be another reason Nicole chose to go back.'

'It was tough sometimes. I'd remember how scary Joseph looked, and I'd have nightmares about him showing up to take me back. I still do.' She even glanced at her door, like he might hear her speaking his name.

I said, 'Was Joseph ever violent at the commune? Or what about Aaron, if someone did something wrong, or wanted to leave?'

'Not that I remember . . . ' She squinted, thinking back. 'The counselors just consult with Aaron, then he takes that person for an adjustment.'

'Who are the counselors?'

'Members who've been there a long time,' she said. 'They're sort of like our mentors, and they helped us when we were having problems. Sometimes they told us how to help the other members. Mostly, if someone did something wrong in meditation, like drank water early or went to the bathroom, we weren't allowed to talk to them.'

'Did anyone else ever try to leave? How did you get out?'

'We worked at the store and made some friends on the outside. We were scared because when other people had moved out, Aaron said that terrible things happened to them on the outside, like car accidents and violent crimes, or getting some bad illness. And the ones who came back said that things *were* harder on the outside. Like they had no money and couldn't get a job – a lot of them would start doing drugs again. They'd come back all messed up.' She was quiet.

'What if anyone got sick?'

'We weren't allowed medication, but everyone smoked marijuana. We weren't supposed to talk about that with anyone who just came to retreats, only people who became full members. He said outsiders wouldn't understand.'

I nodded, thinking over everything.

She said, 'Now that you've told the police your story, are they going to arrest him?'

'They interviewed him, but without more witnesses, they can't lay charges.' I explained the process.

Her face dropped, surprised and disappointed. 'So nothing's going to happen?'

'Not unless more people share their stories. If you wanted to reopen your case, now might—'

'No.' She'd started shaking her head. 'I'm not going through all of that again. Their questions, it was brutal. My parents . . . they'd never forgive me.'

'I understand how it can feel as though you're the one who's done something wrong. But if Aaron's arrested, it

268

would break the hold he has on the members, and the center would probably shut down. Even if he flees the country, he'd be away from your sister and your parents. You might be able to reconnect.'

'I hadn't thought about it like that before.' Her baby started crying in his playpen, and she walked over and picked him up, bouncing him on her hip. She said, 'I have to get him down soon. Do you mind if I think everything over?'

'Of course. I'm curious, though. Why were you willing to meet with me?'

'I've never talked to anybody else who, you know, lived with them.'

We held gazes. I said, 'Thank you for letting me come here today and speak with you. It also helped me to share my story with you.'

She gave a small smile, but added, 'I still don't think I want to talk to the cops about it again. I'm sorry.'

'Take your time. You don't have to make any decisions tonight.' I took some paper out of my purse and wrote down my number. 'I know this is painful. And there are a lot of things to consider.' I slid the paper across the table as I said, 'If you ever want to talk, give me a call.'

'Thanks.'

Still standing by the playpen, she held her son tight as she looked away and nuzzled his hair. The baby gave me a gummy grin.

*

Outside in my car, I sat for a moment and stared back at her house, thinking about Joseph's last visit to her home. Was I being reckless? Putting myself, Tammy, and who knows who else at risk? I thought again about Willow, possibly lying in a lonely grave in the forest, no one but birds and animals a witness to her death. Then I reminded myself that we still didn't know for sure that Aaron had harmed her. If he had, it was a different situation. She was a runaway, not someone who would easily be missed. He would have a harder time denying his involvement if something were to happen to me or anyone else I spoke with. Still, I locked my doors and glanced around, looking for anyone else sitting in their vehicles. The street was quiet.

Chapter Twenty-four

I'd hoped that I'd hear from Tammy soon, but as a day turned into a week, I began to accept that she would likely never pursue criminal charges against Aaron. I couldn't blame her; it was a difficult process. I'd called Corporal Cruikshank and told her what I'd learned, but she said that it was all hearsay, so they couldn't act on it unless it came from Tammy. She suggested she talk to her, but I had a feeling Tammy would shut down if she felt pressured and asked that she wait a few more days. I also didn't want to call Tammy again without any additional information, or upset her, but I was worried about how she might be feeling since our visit. It might have opened a lot of pain for her, and I wasn't sure how much support she had from her husband. I was still debating my options when my worst nightmare came true.

I was sound asleep when one of the nurses in emergency called.

'Sorry to wake you, Dr. Lavoie, but your daughter, Lisa, was brought in unconscious tonight. You're listed as her emergency contact in her records.'

I bolted awake. 'Is she okay? What happened?'

'A witness reported she was vomiting and, as he said, "jerking around" before collapsing, then losing consciousness. There's no evidence of head injury, so we need to know if she has any allergies or takes any medication.'

'No, no allergies, but—' I hesitated, remembering Lisa saying, *I'm clean.* 'She has a history of drug abuse.'

I remembered her first overdose on methamphetamine when she was sixteen. She'd been hallucinating and started to hit me while I was driving, nearly killing both of us. There might have been more occasions when she was an adult that I never found out about. If she was treated and released quickly, they would have no reason to notify me. But this time they called, which meant it was serious.

The nurse was still talking. 'We haven't been able to ascertain why she lost consciousness, so we're treating her with supportive care.'

'Is she awake?'

She lowered her voice. 'She's in a coma.'

I sucked in my breath and stood up so fast the room spun. My heart thudded fast and frantic. A coma, my daughter was in a coma.

'I'll be there as soon as I can.'

After I pulled on some clothes, I grabbed my keys and ran outside to my car, startling the cat, who'd been hiding in her box, and sending her fleeing. My hands gripped the wheel all the way to the hospital, my knuckles white. I had no awareness of any other cars on the road, or even what route I took to the hospital, my mind filled with terrifying thoughts. Why had Lisa overdosed? Did seeing me send her into a downward spiral? My stomach sickened at the idea.

When I got to the hospital, I spoke to the doctor, who told me they'd moved Lisa upstairs to Intensive Care. There was no change in her condition. When I found her, she was on one of the beds, a curtain pulled around her, with only an IV and a ventilator keeping her company. Nurses floated around the unit, checking on various patients, speaking in hushed voices, while monitors beeped. Lisa's eyes were closed, her skin pale. I held her hand in my own, feeling shaky from the adrenaline pumping through my blood. *She's okay. She's right here. She's going to be fine.* I repeated the mantra over and over, but I still couldn't make my heart believe the words. How much drugs had she taken? Would she live only to have brain damage?

I pulled a chair close and sat beside her, studying her hand in mine, the long fingers, the short nails. They were filed, and I wondered at that small bit of vanity. She was taking care of herself, which she didn't do when she was actively using drugs. Her skin was also clear, no acne. Again, I wondered what had happened to cause her overdose. I studied her sleeping face, the rise and fall of her chest, praying for the first time in a long time to a God I wasn't sure existed.

Please don't take my baby. Give her another chance.

Two hours later, I was still sitting with Lisa's hand in my own, when I felt her thumb twitch. Then her eyelids flickered. Was she starting to regain consciousness? Lisa's eyes shot open. She stared at me, pupils dilated, eyes terrified. She focused on something just over my shoulder, and her heart rate went wild, the monitor beeping rapidly as she yanked her hand away and tried to pull her ventilator out. I stood and grabbed her arm, saying, 'Stop, you'll hurt yourself,' but she thrashed around and pulled her arm free. She managed to rip the IV out, spraying me with fluid. When I finally got a grip on her, she fought harder, making guttural moans through the ventilator. I lost my hold, and she lashed out, her forearm hitting hard across my nose. Then behind me, footsteps.

Two nurses rushed to Lisa and held down her arms while she moaned and grunted in panic, her eyes rolling back in her head, the whites flashing. I backed away from the bed, my adrenaline still pumping and my blood roaring in my ears as I watched them fight with the madwoman on the bed. My daughter.

It took them a few minutes to calm Lisa, saying, 'You're in the hospital and you were brought in unconscious.

There's a tube down your throat so you can breathe, but you're safe. We'll let you go when you calm down.' She finally stopped fighting and nodded, signaling her understanding. They relaxed their grip. She was still breathing rapidly, but she was also looking around the room with more awareness. The nurses shut off the supportive breathing, then monitored Lisa's oxygen levels while they asked her to squeeze their hands, or move her eyes in response to a question. They told her that they had to leave the tube in for a little while longer, until they confirmed she could keep breathing on her own.

A half hour later, the doctor came in with the respiratory technologist, and once they confirmed that Lisa was ready, they removed her breathing tube. The doctor then asked if she was okay with my being there while he talked with her.

Her gaze flicked to me, and I thought she'd refuse, but she said, 'S'okay,' her voice still raspy from the hose.

He then proceeded to ask some basic questions, and she answered them all fine. But when he asked what drug she'd taken, she looked confused again.

'I didn't . . . I didn't take anything.'

The doctor made a note. 'What's the last thing you recall?'

Her face began to pull and twist as she struggled to remember. 'I don't know . . . it was earlier in the day. I was at the wharf, then it's all blank.'

The doctor said, 'We ran a drug screen when you were

first admitted, and it didn't show the usual suspects. But the sudden arousal, aggression, and memory loss all fit with GHB, which isn't one of the things we generally test for. We've seen a few cases of it recently with the street kids, though ...' He paused, with his eyebrows raised as he waited for her response. I knew what he was getting at.

When Lisa first started using drugs, I'd done some research and was familiar with GHB, or gamma hydroxybutyrate, which is a central nervous system depressant, popular with people frequenting nightclubs and raves. Also called liquid ecstasy, or liquid x, in small doses it was a stimulant and aphrodisiac, known to create euphoria. In high doses it could cause dizziness, agitation, visual disturbances, depressed breathing, amnesia, unconsciousness, and death. It was also nearly impossible to detect in a urine sample, so we'd never know for sure.

Lisa also knew what the doctor was insinuating. Her face was flushed and angry-looking as she said, 'I'm clean.' She glanced at me, her expression saying, *I know you told him.*

The doctor made a note, his own face expressionless. 'Do you remember anyone handing you a drink?'

I didn't understand why he'd asked that, until I remembered that GHB was also known as a date rape drug. Had Lisa been *raped?*

While I was putting it together, so was Lisa. Warring emotions crossed her face. First confusion, then fear, and soon anger. Her eyes filled with tears as she said, 'No, and I don't want to talk about this anymore.'

I said, 'Lisa, if someone hurt you—'

The doctor interjected. 'There was no sign of sexual trauma.'

Lisa said, 'I said I didn't want to talk about it.'

It was clear she was hiding something, probably remembering meeting with her dealer or a friend, but I didn't want to press. There was no point.

The doctor finished his exam, during which Lisa remained mostly mute, then explained that they'd like to keep her in overnight for observation.

She nodded her assent, then turned to stare at the wall.

I said, 'I'm just going to the bathroom. I'll be right back, okay, Lisa?'

She didn't answer.

When I came back into the room, Lisa had fallen asleep. I sat beside the bed, taking her hand in mine again, knowing that as soon as she woke, these little affections would be refused. I studied the small half-moon scar on her pinkie finger that she'd gotten as a child when she'd caught her finger in the door of our camper. She'd screamed and cried, and never slammed that door again. Maybe this time she'd finally hit rock bottom, a terrifying close call, which might just give her that final push to seek proper treatment. I wanted her to come home with me and focus on getting better, but I couldn't push her into that decision. I smoothed her hair back, noticing it was soft and silky, so she'd been taking care of that as well. I gazed down at her, my eyes filling with tears.

What happened to you?

I sat beside her for a while, then asked one of the nurses to inform the psychiatric unit that I wouldn't be able to come in the next day. The head nurse brought me a blanket, and I nodded off in the chair. Hours later I heard a movement in the bed and startled awake. Lisa was watching me.

I said, 'Hi, baby. How you feeling?'

Her voice still raspy, she said, 'My throat's sore.'

'I'll get you some water and ice chips.'

As I handed her the cup, she said, 'When can I get out of here?'

I waited while she swallowed some of the water and rested her head back on the pillow, then I said, 'You'll probably be released tomorrow.' I glanced at my watch. It was already three in the morning. 'Just a few more hours.'

I approached the next part carefully. I didn't want to ask her what happened – it would put her on the defensive. I also couldn't demand she come home with me. I longed for the days when I could just scoop her up and carry her in my arms. But I had to allow her to come to the decision on her own. I said, 'Would you like to stay with me for a little while?'

She looked like she was considering it, her eyes

thoughtful, but there was something else in there. Fear? I resisted the urge to alternately insist, cajole, force, argue, and beg.

She whispered, 'Okay.'

My body flooded with relief. Before I could get too optimistic about our progress, she said, 'But you can't ask me a bunch of questions.'

I nodded, accepting her terms, then asked if she needed anything. She wanted to go to the bathroom, so I helped her out of bed, then we watched TV until she fell back asleep. Though it was an awful situation, I was happy to be with my daughter. Even this little time with her was more than I'd had in years. Mentally, I prepared for the next few days. It wasn't going to be easy. If she'd started to use again, her moods would be erratic. She was likely to lash out, and if the past had proved anything, I would be her favorite target.

When she was little, she'd been so sweet. Though never a chatty child, she was very affectionate, always tucking her hand into mine, or crawling onto my lap unbidden, snuggling in bed between Paul and me. She was also kind, caring for all our animals, but also her friends, often inviting one who she didn't think was happy over for dinner. For a while she kept losing clothes. When I finally asked her about them, she said that she'd been giving them to a friend at school whose parents were having a tough time. I'd been proud of her thoughtful, loyal nature, but I worried that someone might take advantage of her giving ways. I'd said to Paul one day, 'I'm scared she's going to try to save the world.' He'd stopped what he was doing, and said, 'I wonder who that reminds me of.' I'd laughed, and had also been thrilled that she had some parts of me in her.

That was a long time ago.

I fell asleep myself for a couple of hours and woke when I heard Lisa stirring. While she had a shower, I went up to the ward to make sure they were able to find someone to cover me. Michelle was at the desk, her gaze sympathetic as I approached. I wondered how much she knew.

Michelle said, 'Is everything okay? I heard your daughter was sick?'

Though I liked Michelle, I didn't want her to know about Lisa's problems, so I said, 'She'll be okay – I'm taking her home now.' Then I picked up a binder and started going over a few things about my patients, making it clear that I wasn't going to share anything else. Michelle was cheerful, but I could sense the curiosity in her, and a hint of hurt that I wasn't confiding more. I felt bad, but I wasn't going to talk about my personal issues at work. I'd just finished up and was walking by Kevin's office when he stuck his head out.

'Thought I heard your voice.'

'Hi, yes, I'm just leaving though.'

He cocked his head, studied my face. 'You all right?' His eyes were so concerned that I found my own stinging. I blinked hard.

'It was a rough night. My daughter was admitted.' For some reason the words that had been so hard to share with Michelle fell off my lips. 'She overdosed, probably on GHB. She'll be okay, but I don't know for how long . . .'

'Oh, no.' He opened the door. 'Come in.'

'Thanks, but I have to get her home.' By the time we checked out it would be late morning, and I was exhausted from my night spent in a chair.

He stood there, the door still open, his expression kind. 'You sure?'

'Maybe we can talk tomorrow.'

'Absolutely. Here, let me give you my cell number.' He quickly pulled a business card out of his wallet, handing it to me. 'Call anytime, okay?'

'Thanks.'

He gave another reassuring smile. I tried to smile back, but exhaustion was making me weepy, so I quickly turned away.

In her room, Lisa was pulling on her boots, her face pale from the effort. She paused to catch her breath.

I said, 'Do you need some help?' and reached for her feet at the same time as she bent down to try again. Her hand brushed mine. We both stopped. She held my hand for a fraction of a second before releasing it. For the second time that morning, I had to fight to hold back tears. I sat in the chair beside the bed as she finished pulling on her boot and laced it up.

She glanced over at me, and I saw a flicker of something in her eyes, like she wanted to say something, but she looked away, and the moment was lost.

After she was cleared to go home, I wheeled her out to my car. I held out my arm for her to brace against when she climbed in the passenger seat, but she ignored it. We were silent during the ride home, both of us exhausted, though my head was spinning with questions. I wanted to know where she'd been living, *how* she'd been living, what happened the night before, was she using again, did she still want to quit? Nothing I could ask, but I also couldn't bring myself to chatter about nonsensical things either. As the silence mounted, I turned the radio on.

When we pulled in the driveway and got out of the car, Lisa stood for a moment, admiring the house.

'Wow, Mom. This is gorgeous.'

My mood lifted at her casually calling me 'Mom' and liking my house. It was unrealistic to expect it might mean she'd be willing to stay longer, but still, I hoped. I grabbed her packsack out of the trunk. Whoever had called 911 had left it behind with Lisa. I wondered if it was the same person who gave her the drugs. Did they even consider staying with her before leaving her in the alley like a piece of garbage? I shook off the anger. All I could control now was this moment.

As we passed by the box where the stray had been sleeping Lisa said, 'Is this for Silky?'

'No, she passed away in the summer – a few weeks after I was attacked.'

Her mouth pulled tight, and I wondered if she was upset I hadn't told her about the cat – she used to sleep with her when she lived at home.

I said, 'I would've told you, but . . .'

'S'okay.' But I had a feeling it wasn't okay at all.

Inside, I showed her the guest room. She stood in the middle and surveyed the room, the white duvet and pillows, the bamboo bed frame, dropping her packsack onto the floor and tossing her coat on the side chair. 'It's nice.'

Again, I was inordinately pleased. 'I'm so glad you like it.'

She walked over to the bed, spotting the stuffed white dog I'd bought for her. Her back was to me as she picked it up.

I said, 'I saw it and thought of you . . . It was for your birthday.' On that weekend, I'd lit a candle, blew it out, and made a wish for my daughter.

'I'm going to take a nap, okay, Mom?'

Her voice was thick, like she might be crying.

'Are you okay? Do you want some—'

'I'm fine.'

It was a clear dismissal. I slowly closed the door behind me. When I peeked in later she was sound asleep, but there was rapid movement behind her eyelids, making me wonder what demons chased her dreams. I'd meant to read on the couch while waiting for her to wake, but I also fell asleep. I woke hours later with her standing over me. I sat up with a start. 'Are you okay?'

The house was dim, but she'd turned on a couple of lights. Outside it was almost dark, so it was probably early evening. Wind coming in from the ocean pushed the bamboo against my windows as rain tinged against the glass panes.

Lisa said, 'You can stop asking me that,' and sat in the chair across from me, pulling the wool throw off the back and wrapping it around her body. I noticed she'd made herself toast. There was also a plate on the coffee table in front of me, with a steaming cup of tea, and she'd turned on the fireplace. I was pleased at the cozy domestic scene, the scent of burned bread in the air, that she remembered I like honey on my toast. I took a sip of tea, eyeing her over the rim of my cup. Her hair was a tangled mess, the crease of a pillow in her face. I smiled, remembering how when she was a child, she used to be afraid she was getting wrinkles. But she never cared much about her looks, or fashion, sometimes trying on my things, but she'd preferred to dress me. She'd carefully apply my makeup and brush my hair, her hands gentle, loving. She'd say, 'Here, let me, Mommy.'

As though she were the adult and I the child. Sometimes I'd wonder if that's what happened. Did I treat her too much like an adult?

Feeling my gaze on her, she turned away from the fire and looked at me as she said, 'Do you think there's life after death?'

The question shocked me, but I tried not to show it as I slowly set my cup back down and mentally prepared my response. It wasn't something I could easily answer, and a question that I'd asked myself in the days after Paul died. But I didn't think that's what Lisa wanted to hear now. Her gaze was intent, her body ready for combat. I chose my words carefully.

'I hope there's something beyond this life, yes.'

'You *hope*, but you don't believe it.'

Another challenge. One I decided to ignore. Keeping my voice neutral, I said, 'What do you think? Do you believe there's life after death?'

She glanced back at the fire, her face reflective, then she looked up at the photo of Paul on the mantel, of us as a family. She focused on me. 'When I was in the hospital, right before I woke up, I could feel Dad, like he was in the room with me. And then I heard that song he used to always sing.'

She didn't have to say anything further for me to know what song she meant. When Chinook's health started to fail, Paul would play 'Fields of Gold' over and over on the stereo, singing it as he went about his day.

Sometimes in the evening we'd look at photos together of Chinook as a puppy, of all our years with him, both crying, knowing we were losing our beloved dog soon, neither of us knowing that cancer would also claim Paul's life less than a year later.

Now I softly sang, 'You'll remember me . . .'

Lisa picked it up. 'When the west wind moves . . .'

We drifted off, our minds filling in the rest of the words in a silent chorus.

After a moment, Lisa said, 'When I opened my eyes, I saw him. He had a hand on the back of your chair, and he smiled at me, then he disappeared.'

Her eyes filled with tears, and she swiped at them, a quick angry motion. I remembered the flash of fear in her eyes when she'd first woken up, how she'd been looking at something behind me. She was probably hallucinating from the GHB in her system, or there was some other physiological explanation, but I didn't think for one moment that Paul's spirit had truly been there. I did, however, recognize that Lisa thought he was and that her vision was very real to her. I didn't want to take that away. She was waiting for me to say something.

I smiled and said, 'That's a lovely thought. I'd like to think that your father still visits us.'

'You don't believe me.' Her voice was flat and resigned, like she'd expected me to let her down. The thought saddened me.

'Lisa, that's not what I—'

She said, 'I didn't overdose.'

I didn't know how to answer, suspecting that she *had* overdosed but in the ensuing amnesia from the drug had forgotten taking it, so I simply said, 'Okay.'

'I *didn't* – someone gave me something.'

'Who? Was it one of your friends?' I tried not to sound accusing, but the tone was there, and my daughter, always intuitive, especially when it came to any censure from me, picked it up immediately.

'You still think I'm taking drugs. I told you, I *quit.*'

I took a breath, started again. 'You're my daughter – I love you and I want you to get well. I'm afraid that if you're still living on the streets, hanging around people who *are* doing drugs, you might start using again. Seeing you tonight, like that ... ' I cleared my throat. 'I'm scared I'm going to lose you.'

I tried to will her to look at me, but she was pressing her thumb hard against crumbs on her plate and licking them off. Quick, angry motions.

She said, 'I was doing fine until last night. I have it under control.'

I waited for her to elaborate, but she was staring into the fire again. I decided to drop it, hoping that over the next few days I'd be able to revisit the conversation. I changed the subject. 'I saw Garret recently.'

She took a bite of her toast, chewed hard as she kept staring into the fire. Her face unreadable, she said, 'Yeah.'

She didn't say it as a question, or like she wanted to

287

know more, but I still added, 'I gave him your father's tools – I didn't think you'd want them.'

No answer.

'He's got a photography studio now.'

Still no answer.

'And he was asking about you – he said we should stop by sometime.'

Now she turned. 'Did you tell him where I was?'

Thrown by the heat in her voice and confused about the source of it, I said, 'I didn't *know* where you were – but I did tell him that I'd run into you at Fisherman's Wharf. He was worried about you.'

This time she dropped her mug on the side table with a thump, her plate following after. 'Why can't you just stay out of things?'

'I don't understand what the problem is with my telling Garret about you. You used to be so close, and he misses you. He's your brother and—'

She stood up. 'He's my *half* brother. And we were close when we were kids, until the two of you started to gang up on me.'

'Gang up on you. You mean when we were trying to help?' Was that what this was all about? She felt like Garret and I had joined forces against her?

She laughed bitterly. 'Yeah, you were real helpful, Mom.'

'Lisa, can you please just sit down and explain why you're so upset?'

'Don't discuss me with him, or anyone. This is *my* life.' And with that she stalked off, leaving me staring at my half-eaten toast, my own fear growing. She'd almost died the previous night, and she still wasn't taking responsibility for the problems in her life – next time she could end up brain-damaged, or lying beaten or raped in an alley, if she didn't just die from the overdose. I followed her down the hall to her room, but when I knocked, all I heard was the shower.

Hours later, she still hadn't come out of her room, and it was obvious she planned to stay there all night. I left her alone, deciding it was probably better to wait until morning before we had another talk – hopefully we would both be more relaxed. But in the morning she was gone, having taken only the stuffed husky with her.

Chapter Twenty-five

Expecting to be home with Lisa, I'd booked the next day off, which I now spent cleaning obsessively while I mentally went over our argument the night before. I still wasn't sure what had caused it. Obviously, she'd been angry about my relationship with Garret – a surprise. Jealousy between siblings was common, but they'd been close, only growing apart after Paul died, when Lisa was pulling away from everyone. Did they have a fight I didn't know about? Or, perhaps, while I was struggling with the loss of Paul, I'd put too much responsibility on Garret. Lisa, not liking authority at the best of times, would've resented that.

While I was dusting, I noticed my purse had been moved. With a sickening feeling, I went through my wallet. I was missing fifty dollars.

The first time Lisa had stolen from me, I felt angry, betrayed, and worried. This time I just felt grief and sadness – and fear soon followed when I wondered what she was doing with that money. What if she bought more drugs and overdosed again? The thought almost derailed me, but I mentally pulled up my socks and tried to think about what I was going to do about all of this.

First, I went to the spare room and sat in the chair beside the bed, trying to think like Lisa and connect with her. I closed my eyes, breathed deeply, let my mind settle. Lisa had been hurt by something I'd said, but I couldn't put my finger on it. Also, she was upset that I doubted her, though in my defense she hadn't given me much reason to trust her. Why had she stolen the money? I heard her voice in my head: *You expect the worst from me, you'll get the worst.*

Saddened by the thought, I was about to leave when I noticed a corner of a paper sticking out from under the bed. I reached over and pulled it out.

It was a pamphlet for The River of Life Spiritual Center.

I stared at the brochure in disbelief. How did she get this? Did someone give it to her? My gaze fell on their final slogan: 'We Heal Your Body, Mind, and Spirit.'

Lisa was the perfect target: transient, estranged from her family, and at the moment, extremely vulnerable. I remembered her question the night before about life after death. She was looking for answers, and I hadn't given them to her – not the ones she wanted to hear. If she was already in the commune, would I be able to convince her to leave? She was an adult, so the police weren't going to help. Then the thought crossed my mind that Aaron might've specifically targeted *my* daughter. I'd made a report, and I'd been talking to former members. I'd also told Mary and Tammy that my daughter lived on the streets. What if they contacted someone on the inside? Would he use Lisa to manipulate me?

I made myself calm down. *Just take it one step at a time.* All I'd found was a brochure, which Lisa might've picked up anywhere. Before I projected too far in the future, I needed to find out if she was even at the commune or back on the streets. I considered phoning the center, but decided to contact Tammy first.

She picked up after a couple of rings. I launched into my story. When I was finished, I said, 'Did you by chance tell Nicole about my visit?' I was careful to keep my tone polite and not accusatory.

She said, 'No, I told you, I haven't talked to Nicole in years. No one's allowed to have cell phones, or email accounts. If they want to call out, they have to use the phone in the main room – and they need permission. Even if I left a message, she probably wouldn't call back. I didn't tell *anyone* you were here.'

So Mary wouldn't have been able to call anyone in the center either.

Thinking out loud, I said, 'If I call the registration office, would they tell me if she's staying there?'

'No, they're serious about protecting the privacy of the members.'

'If she enters the commune, I don't know what might happen. She just got out of the hospital.' I thought about Aaron's view of modern medicine. If Lisa had any after-effects from her recent overdose, would they get her help? I said, 'She's not well and needs to be with someone who has medical training.'

'I'm sorry. I don't know what to say. I wish I could help.'

'Thanks, but the only thing that will help is if we can just shut the whole place down. I don't know how we're going to be able to do that either.'

A sound on the other end of the phone, air exhaling. Then, 'I've been thinking lots since you were here.'

'And?'

Her voice became stronger as she said, 'I want to make a statement.' Then weakened again, 'But if we do this, do I have to testify? I don't want to have to look at him when I'm talking about what he did. And when I first left the center, I was pretty messed up and did lots of drinking. I don't want some lawyer making me feel like a piece of crap or the press ripping me apart. I have a kid now.'

'If the Crown decides to lay charges, they might be able to work something out so you don't have to go court.'

Another deep breath. 'I'm going to do it, but I need to tell my husband first. He's working out of town right now, so I can't talk to him for a few days. I'll let you know when I've gone to the police.'

'Thanks, I'd appreciate that.' I let out my own breath. We were finally moving forward.

'Good luck finding your daughter.'

I was going to need it.

Even though Tammy had said that the center wouldn't tell me if Lisa was there, I looked up their number on my iPhone. The woman who answered was polite but said they weren't able to give out information on their members. Next I checked my voice mail at the hospital, hoping against hope that Lisa might've left a message, but there was just one from Kevin, asking how I was. I called him back, and when he heard my voice he said, 'How are you? How's your daughter?'

'I don't know. She just—' I was mortified when my voice broke.

Kevin said, 'What happened?'

I told him about our argument, then about finding the brochure.

'I'm really sorry. Is there anything I can do to help? I have some time this afternoon. Do you want to go for a walk and get some fresh air, talk it out?'

'Thanks, but I'm just going to drive around and see if Lisa's shown up at any of the shelters.'

'If you need to talk later, you let me know. Meanwhile, hang in there.'

I said, 'I'll try,' and took a breath, blowing the air out of my lungs. 'I just pray that she's not at the commune already. She's so vulnerable right now.' I told him what Tammy had said, about going to the police. 'But I don't know how long it will take to move through the legal channels, or if they'll even arrest him.'

'If Lisa is at the center, you still have some time before she becomes too integrated. She could just be at one of the initial retreats, which she might not even enjoy. And if Aaron is arrested, Lisa will probably leave.'

I thought of Heather, how she'd gone to that first retreat and ended up staying for months, leaving her life, her friends, and her family all behind.

'I hope you're right.'

I took a drive but didn't see Lisa. Later in the evening, I headed out again, hoping some of the street folk had come back to the shelter. Though it was a sketchy time of night to be walking around, it was a risk I was willing to take. It was cold, so I bundled up and positioned myself at the edge of the building, with Lisa's photo in hand. When a group of youths clustered about the front steps, one young man with facial piercings and a skateboard noticed me. He looked friendly, so I smiled tentatively and started toward him. He left the group and met me.

'You looking for someone?'

I held out the photo. 'Yes, my daughter, her name is—'

'Lisa.' He nodded. 'We've hung out a few times. She's cool.'

'Do you know where she might be?' I held my breath. *Please, God.*

He squinted back at his group of friends, who were starting down the road. 'Last time I saw her was a couple of nights ago – she showed up down the alley, said she was going to crash at the Monkey House.'

'What's that?'

'It's down on Caledonia. The big white house. Careful how you go in there, though. You don't want them to think you're a social worker or a cop.'

'Thanks. Why's it called the Monkey House?'

'Because everyone in there has a monkey on their back. Good luck, lady.' He started to walk away.

If Lisa was there, did that mean she was using drugs again? I called out, 'A couple of nights ago, she overdosed. Did you know that?'

He turned around. 'Last I heard she was clean.' He shrugged. *Just another day on the streets.* Then he dropped his board and skated off to join his friends. So he thought she was clean too. Was Lisa telling the truth?

I drove down to the house on Caledonia and sat outside, wondering if I should've asked Kevin to join me. The problem was if Lisa saw him, she'd know something was up and would be gone in a heartbeat. I walked up to the house, took a deep breath, and pushed the door open. I was hit immediately with the scent of unwashed bodies, chemicals burning, and cigarette smoke. I made my way down a dark hallway, trying not to panic in the enclosed space. I faltered in one section, where someone had piled garbage outside a door, making the hallway a tight squeeze. *Don't think about it, just focus on finding Lisa.* I counted my breaths until my heart rate settled, then pushed on. I noticed that most of the rooms had only a bare mattress, where people were sleeping, or sitting up with glazed eyes. Garbage covered the wood floors. One woman glared at me, her face and arms covered with open, weeping sores. I quickly glanced away. In the next room a young First Nations woman, decorated in homemade tattoos, looked up and said, 'Who you looking for, sister?'

'My daughter, Lisa Lavoie.'

She narrowed her eyes, like she was thinking. 'There's a Lisa at the end of the hall. She's cute.' She grinned.

I hurried the rest of the way, nearly gagging on all the odors. The room at the end had a door. I debated whether I should knock, and then just pushed it open. Lisa sat huddled on an old mattress with no sheets, the cover stained. Old wallpaper hung down in big strips, and a cold wind pushed through the cracked window, the sill dark with rot and mold. Empty pizza boxes and take-out containers littered the room. She was wearing the clothes she'd left my house in: faded black jeans and a gray sweatshirt, the hood pulled over her head. With her coat wrapped around her for a blanket, she leaned against the wall, with her eyes closed and her packsack in her lap. Her face was so pale that I caught my breath, until she muttered something and shifted her body.

I said, 'Lisa?'

She started awake, staring at me. Her pupils were dilated, and she grabbed at her packsack and pulled it close, her jaw working and her gaze zipping around the room. She was high as a kite. I fought the urge to drag her out by the scruff of her neck and lock her in a room at home. Underneath my anger, I could taste my fear for her, my sorrow and despair. How could she do this to herself?

She said, 'What're you doing here?'

'I wanted to talk to you about the brochure you left at my house – the one for The River of Life. How did you get it?'

She avoided my gaze, just rubbed her arms, her body, jerky movements, scratching at her legs.

'These people aren't what they seem. You don't know how they can—'

'You're unbelievable,' she snapped. 'You're always trying to get me into a treatment center – now I'm trying to get help, and you're still not happy.'

She was right. I'd been pushing Lisa for years to get help for her addiction, but I'd never expected that she'd seek it from the center. I had to be careful here, had to make my point subtly. 'Lisa, I knew the leader when I was a child. They start off saying they want to help you, but in the end they hurt people. Especially girls. Their leader—'

'You want me off drugs, don't you? They helped some

other kids I know from the street. Why can't you ever let me do things my way?' Her voice broke. She stared down at her knees, her face flushed and angry. She'd always hated crying in front of anyone. When she was little, I was the only one allowed to hold her when she was sobbing. She'd push everyone else away.

I knelt on the floor in front of her. 'Lisa, I want to support your decisions. But I also want you to know everything about these people first.'

'*Now* you want to protect me. Where were you before?'

'I've always been here—'

She started laughing, a high-pitched sound. 'You were so busy learning how to help all those other people, you didn't notice – you didn't protect *me*.'

My blood whooshed in my ears, everything slowing down, her words coming at me from a distance. My psyche was already bracing itself, sensing I was about to hear something that was going to hurt.

'Protect you from what?'

'Someone screwed around with me, *Mom*. God, are you really that blind?'

I sat back hard on my heels. My mind trying to wrap around what she had just said. Did she mean someone *molested* her? I met her eyes, her belligerent glare daring me to deny it, and saw the shame and hurt underneath her angry words. It was true. I tried to speak, to say something, but my pulse was beating hard and fast, my

299

thoughts crashing together. Finally, I grabbed at one, my breath coming out in a rush as I said, 'When? When did this happen?'

'Little late to pretend to care now. I'm too far gone, in case you haven't noticed.' She dropped her head back, her laugh bordering on hysteria.

My heart thrummed in my chest. *Who'd hurt my baby?* I was almost in tears, near to panicking, but I grasped at some control. 'How did ... Was it one of your teachers?' Her expression was blank, resigned. She'd already decided I was going to fail her. I thought back to all the times she'd stayed late at school, the weekend camps with friends and their fathers. Then I got it.

'Did a counselor hurt you at the treatment center?'

She shook her head but then stared down at her packsack, zipping and unzipping one of the pockets. As a child, whenever she was hiding something, she'd always played with her zippers. I was right. Everything fit.

She said, 'Doesn't matter now.'

'It *does* matter – of course it matters.'

She looked at me. 'Get out, Mom. Just go home.'

'I'm not leaving you now—'

'You okay, Lisa?' A large man, with tattoos up and down his arms and long, dark hair in frenzied curls, stood at the door. His eyes had a wild look that signaled he was also high on something.

'My mom's just going.'

I turned to look at Lisa and wondered who'd replaced

my daughter, because I didn't know the angry woman staring back at me with hatred.

She said, 'I don't want to see you again. Get the fuck out of here.'

I heard the hurt in my voice as I said, 'Lisa—'

The man stepped toward me. 'She doesn't want you here, bitch. You better get out of here fast, or I'll help you out.'

I stood up. 'Don't threaten me. I'm talking to my daughter.' He took another step toward me. I looked back at Lisa, wondering if she'd call him off. But her head was lolling back, her shoulders twitching. She was already gone.

When I got home, I sat on the couch with my coat still on, staring at my unlit fireplace. I was cold, but I couldn't find the energy to get up and flip the switch. I'd let Lisa down in the worst possible way. I remembered her words: *You didn't notice – you didn't protect me*. She was right. How could I let this happen? How did I miss the signs? I was a doctor, her *mother*. I was sure that it was a counselor at the treatment center who'd abused her. She'd been young, maybe too young to be in a center. Had I been in such a rush to get her in a program that I didn't stop to consider whether it was the right one for Lisa? I was a fraud, all these years trying to help women, and I hadn't seen the truth of my own daughter.

It sickened me when I remembered one young

counselor at the treatment center, how familiar he'd seemed with Lisa. He'd told me to be strong when she called crying that time – not to enable her – and then she'd run away. She'd been trying to escape, and I'd stopped her. Why had she never said anything? Did she think I wouldn't believe her? It hadn't been that long after her father died. Maybe she didn't want to upset me.

I wanted to go to the treatment center and rip the place apart trying to find who'd hurt my child. The idea of some man's hands on her, of her feeling alone and scared, tore me to shreds. But without Lisa exposing her abuser, I couldn't do much. I wondered about calling the police, but they couldn't do anything either. I didn't even have a name. Finally, I took a hot bath and made myself go to bed.

I was still awake hours later, listening to the wind as it roared in off the ocean, when I heard a crash in the back-yard. I sat up, heart pounding, straining my ears to focus on the sound. I pulled on my housecoat, grabbed the bottle of mace I keep in my night table, and crept out into the body of the house. I padded into the kitchen, then peeked outside. I saw the problem right away. The wind had blown over the patio umbrella, and it was now rolling around, knocking into everything. I threw on some clothes and headed outside, braced against the storm. I'd wrestled the umbrella into the shed when the wind slammed the door behind me. The shed was black.

I tried to find the cord for the light while adrenaline pumped through my blood. *I can't breathe.* My shin slammed against something hard and I backed up a few steps. *I have to get out of here.* I knocked into some planters, sending them down around me. In a blind panic, I launched myself in the direction of the door, my hands grasping the knob. Wind and rain hit my face as I sprinted back to my house.

After I'd closed the door, I leaned against it, trying to catch my breath, my heart still beating loud in my ears. Rain dripped down my face, mixing with tears. What had happened back there? My claustrophobia had been triggered, obviously, but there was something more to the panic, an intense terror, even stronger than the time I'd tried to get my bike out of the shed. I hadn't been able to use any of my coping mechanisms. There must've been something about the shed.

Of all the memories that had come back since I'd met Heather, the reason for my claustrophobia had yet to be explained. I'd assumed it was related to the barn, but maybe it had been something else. I thought back but couldn't remember there being a shed at the commune. I contemplated going out to the shed with a flashlight, making myself stand there until the fear abated. Exposure therapy was effective in treating numerous phobias. But when I opened the door, the yard was pitch-black, and all I could see were the eerie shapes of trees and plants moving wildly in the wind. I closed the door and locked it.

That night it rained hard. In the morning I surveyed my backyard, checking for damage from the storm, picking up fallen branches. That's when I saw the footprint near the shed in some soft dirt. I stared down at it. Was it mine? It looked larger, but it was hard to tell, rain had blurred the edges. I crouched down, took a closer look. There almost seemed to be a faint tread. My shoes had a smooth sole.

Chapter Twenty-six

On my way to the hospital, I reminded myself of all the people who could have left the footprint, the meter readers, the lawn-care company I'd called for a quote. For all I knew, it was probably mine. I was reading too much into everything. Right now I had bigger things to worry about, like my daughter and my patients.

I talked with Jodi, the anorexic girl, and her parents, about her treatment. She had committed to another meal plan. I also spent some time with Francine, who seemed calmer, though she kept asking me where all her paintings had gone and called me Angela, asking if I remembered the time we went to Mexico. It's better not to contradict dementia patients when they confuse you with someone else, so I just asked her to tell me about her favorite part of Mexico. She looked so happy, sharing her stories about snorkeling in the Caribbean Sea.

The distraction worked for a few hours, but when I

broke for lunch, I sat in the cafeteria nursing a cup of tea and thought about Lisa. I still couldn't believe I'd missed the signs that she'd been abused, and I wrestled again with the same questions. What kind of mother was I? What kind of doctor? She'd been having difficulties before I put her in the first treatment center, but it had gotten a lot worse after. I'd been in such a rush to cure her that I increased the problem. Now her behavior after treatment made more sense, her refusal to talk to me or Garret, her increased drug use. It broke my heart that she hadn't confided in me, that all these years I'd been helping other people while my own daughter was suffering—

Stop. This wouldn't help Lisa or me. I had to find a way to speak with her before she joined the commune. Should I just give her a few days? I was still thinking when Kevin appeared at my table with a cup of coffee in his hand.

'Hi, I was wondering how you've been making out.'

I motioned for him to have a seat. 'Not that great.'

'Did you find Lisa?'

'Yes, but I'm still very worried about her.' I told him what had happened, leaving out what she'd said about the sexual abuse. I wanted to respect her privacy, and I was also still working it out in my own mind.

'It must've been hard to see her like that.' His expression was kind.

'It was, especially hearing how serious she sounded

306

about joining the commune.' I thought about the pain in her eyes when she admitted she was trying to get help, the desperation. I'd also seen that look in Heather's eyes when she talked about how Aaron believed everyone could heal themselves, how weak he had made her feel. What lies would he tell my daughter about her addiction?

Kevin said, 'Did you share your misgivings about their techniques? Or anything about your own experience with them when you were a child?'

'I tried, but she didn't want to hear it.'

'Do you think she might be more receptive another time?' He lowered his voice, the tone soft.

I thought about what he said. Lisa had been very high, the wrong time to talk about anything. 'Maybe I should go there again tonight. But it might be too late . . .'

Kevin said, 'If she does go to a retreat or joins the center, at least she'll get clean. Then she might make different decisions with her life. It sounds like she's starting to accept responsibility for her addiction.'

'I hope so.' I paused and smiled at him. 'I'm sorry, you probably just wanted a relaxing lunch, and now you've ended up hearing all my problems.'

Kevin shook his head. 'No, I'm glad to help. You want some help tonight?'

I considered his offer, but even if I was able to get Lisa out of the building, she'd take one look at Kevin and think I set her up. 'Thanks, but I should go alone. She'll respond better.' I rose to my feet. 'I should get back to work.'

'Okay, shoot me an email later so I know you're not in a ditch somewhere.' His words were joking, but his face was serious.

'Sure.' I was surprised that I was pleased at the idea of someone worrying about me. I'd forgotten what it felt like to be accountable. 'Thanks for the talk.'

'Anytime.'

I glanced back as I left the cafeteria. Kevin was staring down at his mug, looking lost in thought.

After work, I had a shower, then dressed in casual clothing, careful to remove my earrings and all jewelry, and made my way back to the Monkey House. I'd wanted to hit it earlier in the evening, before it got dark. I sat in my car, watching the comings and goings. Maybe it would've been a good idea to bring Kevin, but it was too late now. I grabbed my iPhone, holding it ready in my hand – and kept my other on the bottle of mace in my right pocket. Then, locking the car behind me, twice, I made my way into the house.

A few people stopped what they were doing and stared at me, clustered in little groups, their eyes vacant, reminding me of zombies in some horror film. When I got to the room where I had found Lisa before, it was empty. I stared at the bare mattress, fear shooting through my body. Maybe she'd just changed rooms. A woman's voice close behind me said, 'You looking for your daughter?'

I spun around. It was the First Nations woman from the day before.

She held out a hand. 'Give me some money, and I'll tell you where your girl's at.'

I had left my purse at home, tucking only the bare essentials from my wallet into my jeans. I pulled out a twenty. She motioned for more. I shook my head. 'It's all I have.'

She snatched it out of my hands. 'She left with those people from the center.'

My vision began to narrow as my heart whooshed in my ears, the scents of the building, unwashed bodies, drugs, and urine, thick in my throat. 'Do you mean River of Life?'

'Don't know what they're called.' She shrugged, scratching lazily at her arm, her fingernails scraping against one of her sores. She stopped and studied it for a moment, picking at the edges. She looked back at me. 'They started coming around, handing out their flyers and shit, trying to cure us.' She laughed. 'They sure like your daughter – talked to her a few times.'

Description, just focus and get a description.

'What did they look like?'

Another lazy shrug, staring at my pocket like it might produce more money. I waited, she met my eyes. I stared her down. Finally: 'Some old white dude with gray hair and some younger chick.'

My breath stopped in my throat. Did she mean Aaron? 'Did you hear them use any names?'

'No – there's something freaky about them. I tried to warn Lisa, but she wouldn't listen, said they were going to help her.'

The irony wasn't lost on me, the drug addict warning my daughter about what wasn't good for her. I wondered if she'd offered her a hit at the same time.

'Thanks for the information.' I pulled one of my cards out of my pocket and held it out. 'If you see her, or if those people come back, call me at this number, please. There's a reward if the information helps find her.' She snatched the card, peered at it like she was trying to read the words, then tucked it quickly into her armpit, her eyes darting around as if someone might steal it from her.

As soon as I was back in my car, I searched my contacts in my iPhone and found Daniel. I didn't know if his phone was still in service, but he picked up on the first ring.

'Daniel, it's Dr. Lavoie. I was wondering if you're back at the center.'

'No, I'm still finishing that job. They paid me in advance and—'

'I might need your help.' My words rushed out, pushing past all normal pleasantries. 'Lisa, my daughter, I think she's at River of Life.' I heard the name repeat in my head, still couldn't believe Lisa might be in that place, with Aaron.

A long silence.

I stared back at the run-down building.

'Are you sure?' he said at last.

'No, and that's what I need to find out.' I gnawed my lower lip, bit it hard. How long had Lisa been using again? It was hard to know if she'd suffer severe withdrawal symptoms. 'She's not well and might need medical treatment. I thought, if you were at the center, or if you knew how to reach anyone inside.'

'Is she sick?'

I didn't want to share about her addiction. 'She's just gone through a health scare recently, and I want to make sure she's okay.'

'They don't give out information about members.'

'So I've been told. If you called, would they tell you if she was there?'

'They wouldn't tell anyone. The whole center runs on the principle that people can leave their past behind and start again.'

Frustration made my voice sound angry as I said, 'People should be able to contact someone inside. What if there's an emergency?'

'You could leave a message.'

'I've been told that members are discouraged from communicating with the outside world, family or friends.'

'That's true. It's better they stay focused on the workshop. But if you leave a message, and she doesn't call back, then you know she's happy there.'

If she didn't call back, more likely it was because she didn't want to speak to me. But how would I know if she actually got the message?

Daniel said, 'She might not even like it. Lots of people aren't ready for the program and leave after the first weekend. Nobody's held against their will.'

He sounded confused, like he didn't understand why I was so worried. He was right, in some ways. Technically, Lisa could leave any time, but I knew that fasting and no sleep could change someone's perceptions of reality.

'Maybe, but I'd feel a lot better if I at least knew if she was in there, or still on the streets. If I were to go there myself, what might happen?'

Daniel said, 'The registration office is closed at night, but they wouldn't tell you anything anyway. You'd probably have to make an appointment with Aaron.'

I thought about the report I'd just made with the police, wondered if Aaron would even speak to me and what it might do to my case if he did.

I said, 'I don't think he'll see me. Do you have any other ideas? I'd feel a lot better if I knew she was okay.'

Another long, echoing silence. Finally, he said, 'Give me a couple of days to finish this job, then when I move back, I'll see if she's there.'

Despite my desire for knowledge of Lisa, I was still concerned Daniel was making a mistake. 'Did you think over everything we spoke about?'

'I'm still going back.' He sounded defensive, then grudging. 'If I see her, I'll let you know.'

'Thank you,' I said. 'I really appreciate this, Daniel.'

There was silence, then he hung up.

After I ended the call, I sat in my car for a while, watching people come and go from the house, debating my options. If I went to the center and made a scene, would they let me see Lisa? Not likely. Even if I did speak to her, would she leave? I thought of how she had forced me out of the flophouse the night before. I just wished I knew if she was okay. I started up my car and drove to the police station. When I explained to an officer what had happened, he just said, 'I can appreciate your concern, but your daughter's an adult. There's nothing we can do.'

Frustrated, I nodded. I was tired of being told there was nothing anyone could do – tired of *feeling* like there was nothing I could do. As I walked out of the station, my cell rang. It was Kevin.

'You okay?'

'Yes, I'm fine.' But I wasn't fine. Not even close.

'When I didn't hear from you, I was worried. Did you find Lisa?'

I told him what I'd discovered at the Monkey House and what Daniel told me about the center.

Kevin said, 'I have to agree with him. If she's at the center, it is better she draw her own conclusions, any interference by you might just make her want to stay longer. Can you give it a couple of days and see what he finds out?'

I let out my breath, watching the traffic zip by and the plumes of my breath on the cold air. We talked a little while longer, and he reminded me that once Tammy made her statement, Aaron could be arrested, which would hopefully make Lisa look at the center with new eyes. My best bet was to wait.

I leaned back on the headrest. 'I'll see what happens over the next couple of days, but I should get home now. I'm tired, cold, and hungry.'

'Why don't I come over with some miso soup? I have a favorite Japanese restaurant near my house. We can talk this over some more.'

'I'll be okay . . .' But then I imagined walking into my empty home, fear of what could be happening to my daughter my only company.

Kevin must have heard something in my voice because he said, 'Of course you'll be okay, but I know how I am when something's bothering me. It's always better if I have another mind to bounce ideas off, so I can make sure my perception of the situation isn't clouded by emotion. Then I make my decision.'

My professional pride stung at the implication that I couldn't control my emotions, and I wanted to defend myself – but when I stood back and considered my current desire to break into the commune with a loaded gun and hunt down Aaron, I realized that Kevin had a point. My sheer panic over wanting to keep Lisa away from Aaron was definitely clouding reason.

'Yes, please come over.'

Chapter Twenty-seven

I gave Kevin my address and sped home to quickly tidy while he was picking up the food. Though my home is usually clean, I wanted the security of a last-minute check. I rushed around, shoving the books and notes that were piled up on my kitchen table back into my office. The doorbell rang.

It was Kevin, wearing a maroon rugby shirt and jeans. I took his jacket and, as he walked past me into the house, caught the scent of soap and cologne, noticing that the back of his hair was damp – so he'd also tidied up. He looked around admiringly as he made himself at home in my kitchen and set the take-out bag on the counter. 'Your home is very nice.' He turned and smiled.

I tried to smile back as I got down some bowls. 'Thanks.'

We met eyes. His voice turned somber as he said, 'I know you have a lot on your mind. I just want to be a friend and support you through it.'

I felt a mixture of relief and disappointment at his words, wondering at the latter. I turned to put the kettle on and said, 'Do you like green tea?'

Behind me, he said, 'Actually, I brought us some sake. I thought you might need something stronger.'

I set the kettle down. 'You're probably right.'

It had been a long time since I'd had miso soup, or sake, and both sent a warm glow through my body as we sat at the table and talked. I shared my feelings about the scene at the Monkey House, while Kevin carefully listened. Afterward, he confided that he'd had a younger brother who became an addict. His brother eventually got his life together, and they were very close now.

Lulled by the sake, we moved into the living room, the fire unwinding my muscles even more. I began to think that maybe Kevin was right. Even if Lisa had gone to a retreat, that didn't mean she'd stay after it was over. She'd dry out, then hopefully make some changes with her life. She wouldn't be as vulnerable since the center was drug-free except for marijuana. Lisa was also older than I was when we joined the commune, and she was strong-minded, a fighter. She probably wouldn't even finish the retreat once she found out how many rules there were. They wouldn't have time to mess with her. Daniel had even said himself that lots of people left after the first weekend. Meanwhile, all I could do was accept that I'd done everything I could and there was nothing else to try.

As I studied Kevin by the firelight, his hair shining and his brown eyes reflecting the flickering flames, he told me about some of his travels. I watched his hand on his glass, his ease of movement as he brought it to his lips again and again. He had just finished explaining some of the meditation techniques he'd learned in India, when I said, 'You've obviously done a lot of traveling. Did you go on your own? Or were you married?'

'When I was younger, but I was single when I was traveling. That was one of the main reasons I went on the trip, so I could do some soul-searching.'

'Divorced?' I imagined him with someone he met while at university, but they grew apart as they began their careers – a common occurrence.

'Nope, widowed.'

I stared at him, my drink halfway to my mouth. He was a widower too?

Kevin, his face vaguely amused, said, 'You okay?'

'Yes, sorry. I was just surprised I didn't know that.'

'I haven't told anyone at the hospital.'

Another surprise. He seemed like such an open book I wondered what else he wasn't sharing. I also realized his hand was on the back of the couch. If I leaned backward, my neck would touch his skin, but I didn't move. Instead I said, 'Did you know that I'd lost my husband?'

He nodded. 'Someone mentioned it.'

I wanted to ask who, but had a feeling it was probably one of the nurses, remembering that we'd talked about it once when the hospital had a fund-raiser for cancer. I said, 'How did you lose your wife?'

'It was about six years ago. She was coming home from the school – she was a teacher – and a drunk driver hit her head-on.'

I shook my head. 'My God, I'm so sorry.'

'Thanks, I appreciate that. I was in bad shape for a long while. We were ready to start a family, so I felt like I'd lost everything at once.'

I nodded, understanding all too well. When we lose someone, we also grieve over all the things that will never be.

He said, 'I joined a support group, made some good friends, and pulled through it.'

'Have you had any relationships since?' I held my breath, in anticipation of his answer, wondering what kind of response I was hoping for.

He turned slightly so he was facing me, his arm still resting on the back of the couch. I could feel the heat of his body, the sensation of his skin so close to mine, sending a shiver from the base of my spine up to the back of my neck.

'Nothing serious. I just haven't found anyone I really connected with. It was always too easy to keep them at a distance.' He took a sip of sake, then added, 'I was starting to wonder if maybe I was never going to feel strongly about anyone again, but then . . .' He paused, his cheeks flushed slightly.

I said, 'But then?'

Still looking hesitant, he held my gaze. 'I met you, and I realized that maybe it was possible.'

My chest tightened, the moment slowing, everything that he was thinking and feeling reflected in his eyes. My face must have signaled something because he reached over and took my sake glass out of my hand while his other arm dropped from the back of the couch to my neck, his fingers splaying at the nape, gently turning my face toward his. He leaned forward, pressed his lips to mine. I also leaned into the kiss, tasting warm sake on his tongue, heat spreading through my body. His hands tangled in my hair. Mine reached up and curled around his biceps, feeling the hard muscles there. He led the way, teasing and gentle, then more passionate. My own ardor grew, my breath coming faster. Then I remembered Lisa's words. *I could feel Dad, like he was in the room with me.*

My mind filled with the image of kissing Paul, suddenly aware of the different feeling of Kevin's mouth. I opened my eyes, and caught sight of Paul's photo on the mantel. I pulled back, trying to catch my breath, disoriented, like waking from a dream, my thoughts sluggish. Kevin was watching me, confusion in his eyes, and also concern, his breath ragged.

I stood up. 'I have to . . . I have to get something from the kitchen.'

In the kitchen, still flustered, I started picking up our

dishes and running hot water, thinking, *You can't just leave him sitting on the couch. You have to say something.* But what was I going to say? *I'm afraid that my dead husband can see us?* I felt a presence behind me and turned around, brandishing a scrub brush like a weapon. Kevin's dark eyes were soft; his hand reached out to my wrist, holding me in place. He said, 'Did you want me to go home?' It was the vulnerability in his face that did me in, shy, a little hopeful. I shook my head, not able to find words to explain the mix of feelings running through my body. I tugged my wrist free and dropped the scrub brush into the sink behind me.

He stepped forward, wrapped his hand around mine. My slippery fingers entwined with his, the scent of lemon soap filling the air. He pressed his body against mine, the hard edge of the sink bending me backward slightly, his mouth covering mine, soft and gentle. In my mind a quote came forth, *Life is for the living.* It was something Paul would say to me when I mourned the loss of one of our animals too long. I stepped outside of myself for a moment, stepped outside of the guilt and the fear of letting go, the fear of betraying Paul.

What do you want, Nadine?

I wanted Kevin to stay the night, wanted to feel his body holding me close in the dark, wanted the wonder and joy of exploring a new person.

I took Kevin's hand and led him to my bedroom.

*

In the morning, I woke with a start when I felt a large male arm wrap around my body. My face warmed as images from the previous night flashed through my mind, each more erotic than the last, wondering how to handle the situation. It had been a while since I'd had to deal with the 'morning after.' I eyed my housecoat hanging on the back of the door, wondering if I could get to it before Kevin woke. Kevin, sensing I was awake, pulled me tight against his chest. His mouth nuzzled my neck, sending shivers down my spine as he said, 'Good morning.'

'Morning.' I wanted to lean back into his embrace, wanted to enjoy the moment, but the other part of me, the part that was no longer silenced by sake, wasn't sure how far I wanted to take this, how far it could even go.

Kevin said, 'I can hear your thoughts from here.'

I said, 'Oh? And what am I thinking?'

'That you'd love to have dinner with me this week.'

My nerves came back alive, the sense of things moving too fast, standing on an edge of a cliff and it crumbling beneath my feet while I tried to backpedal.

'I don't know . . . I have a lot on my plate right now.'

He was silent for a couple of beats, then said, 'I really enjoyed spending time with you last night, Nadine – and no, not just in bed.' He sat up behind me. I turned, so I was on my back, looking up at him. He smiled down. 'But we can take this as slow as you want, okay?'

I nodded. 'Thanks.' Wondering what 'this' was to him.

A one-night stand? A casual sexual relationship? Friends with benefits?

He said, 'Can I at least have a cup of coffee before you kick me out?'

I smiled back. 'I think I can make that happen.'

We had coffee, sitting at the table together, an easy familiarity already growing between us at the simple mundane ritual, passing the sugar and cream, our hands touching, sneaking peeks at each other over the rims of our mugs. I talked again about my concerns for Lisa, which had also come roaring back with the morning light. Kevin still thought I should wait another couple of days, and I could see the sense in what he was saying, but it didn't calm my fears. Saying good-bye to Kevin at the doorway sent another wave of awkwardness through me, but he just pulled me in for a hug and gave me a kiss on the cheek.

As he started down the stairs, he said, 'You let me know when you're ready for that dinner, okay?'

I nodded and watched from the corner of my front deck as he walked down the driveway to his car, which he'd parked on the other side of the road. I heard a car start up farther down the street, then the sound of screeching tires. A truck roared past my house just as Kevin reached the end of the driveway. A couple of more steps out into the road, and it would've hit him. I let out a gasp and clutched the railing. He turned around, our eyes meeting. *Did you see how close that was?* He gave a don't-worry-I'm-okay wave, but my heart was still beating fast as he drove away.

I was almost sure it was the same truck I'd seen slowing down in front of my house.

I called Corporal Cruikshank and explained about the truck, mentioning that I had seen it before, and that I'd found a footprint in my yard one morning and was getting some hang-ups. She took down the description of the truck, but I wasn't positive about the make or model. She said I should try to get a license plate number next time, and be aware of my surroundings when I left my home. I had a shower and made the bed, all the while trying to convince myself that the truck had probably belonged to one of the college kids who lived at the end of the street. They often raced up and down, and I worried they would hit someone or an animal one of these days. The night I saw them outside, they'd probably just been texting or adjusting the stereo. But I was having a hard time believing it.

I wasn't working that day, so I busied myself with chores. Though, I did take a drive by the Monkey House in case the drug addict had been lying, and Lisa was still there. I even checked inside again, but someone else was now staying in the room where I'd found her before. I also stopped by the hospital to grab a book from my office, wondering if I might run into Kevin. There was no sign of him.

Later that night I was cleaning up after dinner when the phone rang, showing a private caller. 'Hello?' I repeated it several times, but was only greeted by silence. I said, 'Lisa? Is that you?' Then I heard a click. I set the phone back down, a bad feeling in the pit of my stomach. What if it had been Lisa? What if she was hurt, or sick, and couldn't speak? Again I considered going to the commune and demanding to see her. I thought about Kevin's words of caution. Damn it all. I had to know if she was okay.

I was in the process of getting my purse and keys together when the phone rang again. This time it was Steve Phillips.

'I was able to get hold of a friend with a cadaver dog. He was planning on doing some training exercises anyway, so he's going to come up to Shawnigan tomorrow, and we'll take a walk down by the old commune, see what we sniff out.' There was an edge of excitement to his voice. 'Did you want to join us?'

'Please.' My blood surged with new hope. If they found something at the site, they might bring Aaron in sooner. If there was enough bad press, the retreats might even shut down. I explained to Steve what had transpired the day before.

He said, 'It's possible they targeted Lisa.' I sat down on my hall bench, fear taking my legs out from underneath me. 'But she could've also got that drug addict to make up the story to throw you off. Either way, if she's in there, she probably won't like you showing up. I've got a grown son. He was hell on wheels in his twenties. He always did the opposite of what I wanted – just to piss me off.'

'Unfortunately, she's the same.' I set my keys down beside me.

'My son, he came out of it all right. Maybe just give her some time.'

'Lisa's had a couple of close calls.' I flashed to the image of her pale in bed after her overdose. How many more could she survive? What if something went wrong at the center? 'What time should I come up in the morning?'

I had to do something.

That night, I woke abruptly with every nerve alert, sure that I'd heard a noise. I lay quiet in the dark, my heart thudding as I strained my ears. What was it? Something outside? The truck slowing down again? There was nothing but silence, then the feeling that I wasn't alone. Someone was standing nearby.

I reached up and slapped the light switch beside my bed, grabbing for the phone and my mace at the same time. I rolled off the side of the bed, crouched in a defensive position as I faced my room, ready to attack. There was no one there, just the faintest whiff of lavender floating in the air, like a memory.

Chapter Twenty-eight

The morning was dismal and wet. I was glad that I'd dressed in jeans, hiking boots, and my warm goose-down coat when I got out at the driveway of the old commune, the rain sneaking in under my skin, turning my hands red with cold. Steve's truck was already parked on the road, and behind it, a black SUV, with tinted windows. Inside, a dog barked. Steve and another man, also lean and tall, but with a hard-lined face and snow-white hair and mustache, were standing near the SUV, stainless-steel coffee cups in hand, steam billowing up into the cold air. As I walked over to them, the dog barked short, deep warnings.

Steve introduced me, and I shook his friend's hand as he said, 'Ken.'

As soon as Ken got his German shepherd, named Wyatt, out of the back of the truck, the dog was working, sniffing the ground in a back-and-forth pattern, anxious on the end of the long rope. Ken explained that they would do a preliminary search first, to see if the dog picked up on anything, then a finer grid search in some likely areas. He warned me that if there was a body, it had been buried for so long the dog would have to be within a couple of feet to pick it up.

I followed behind as we headed down the trail, feeling safer this time with the men and the dog. Ken called out commands, his voice seeming loud in the quiet forest, while the dog worked the ground as they moved closer to the barn.

The river roared in the background, and the surroundings drifted away as the scent of wet forest, leaves, and dirt enveloped me, bringing with them a new memory.

I'm down at the river. Aaron orders me to stand naked against a tree, the bark wet and rough against my skin, while he stares at my body, slapping my hands with a switch if I try to cover any part of myself.

He says, 'Separate yourself from your physical body. Feel the sensations, but don't attach to the discomfort, just observe. Control your shivering.'

At first, the pain of the cold and the humiliation is excruciating. I think I'm going to scream from it, but then I focus on the sound of the river, a bead of rain dripping off a leaf, chanting my mantra in my mind, until I'm able to separate from the pain, aware of it, but distantly. Then it doesn't matter what he does.

The sound of Ken calling his dog broke me out of the

memory. Still shaking off the lingering shame and anger the memory had roused, I skirted the edge of the old barn. The rain made the wood slick and wet, the scent of old barn and rot even stronger. Ahead of me, Steve was waving his arms, trying to catch my attention. I walked toward him. He was standing at the side of the barn, pointing to the ground. 'This the spot?'

'That's it.'

The dog was pacing back and forth in tighter and tighter circles, then started pawing at the dirt. He took another couple of sniffs and sat, his eyes focused on Ken's face. A shiver spider-walked up the base of my neck.

Steve and Ken began to dig, while the dog and I watched. The rain was coming down harder now, and I pulled my hood up over my head, moving a little in place to keep warm. Neither man showed any sign of stopping, grunting in exertion, their breath billowing out. My body was stiff, my hands tucked into the crooks of my arms, everything in me *waiting, waiting*. My mind filled with images of bones, stark and white in the wet earth. Steve stopped, stood straight, still staring down. I held my breath, my legs carrying me closer.

He glanced at me and said, 'Just stretching,' then rubbed his back. I stopped, embarrassed. They dug a little while longer, and the tension began to ease in my body. It would take them a while to get down deep. The earth was heavy and wet, and they had to work around roots and rocks. I started to wander around again, keeping them in sight. They struggled to break up one root, then paused, looking down at something. Their voices low, I couldn't hear them over the river. My blood whooshing in my ears, I started back toward them.

Steve turned in my direction. 'Looks like the body of an animal, maybe a goat or something.'

The air came out of my chest. 'Oh, thank God.'

Ken said, 'We'll just do a general search over the area, and see if Wyatt shows some interest anywhere else.'

I nodded. While Ken and Wyatt worked, Steve followed behind, and I had a better look at the commune. More memories came back when I got closer to one of the cabins, noticing the groove below where I used to hide. I dropped to my knees, peered into the dark, then turned and looked out at what my vision would've shown – mostly the campfire. I walked behind one of the cabins and stared out into a clearing, remembering when we'd chant as a group, our breaths exhaling as one. I skirted around the edges of the field, hearing Aaron in my mind.

I can end all your suffering.

I stopped at some plants on the side, an image coming to mind: a sea of red poppies in bloom. Aaron had told us their color symbolized resurrection after death, and we'd harvested the seedpods, probably for opium. I reached out and touched one of the leaves. My body flooded with another new memory.

I'm down on the ground. Aaron's hand is wrapped tight in my hair, his breath panting in my ear as he starts undoing my shorts. My hands reach for help, finding only poppies, their sick, sweet scent filling my nostrils. The air's so hot that I can hear the bark crackling on the arbutus trees as it peels back in the sun. Fragments break off and drift down, spiraling closer like brown butterflies.

Steve's voice snapped me out of the memory. 'Nadine.'

I was disorientated, a leaf crumpled in my hand, still caught somewhere between the past and the present. When was I in the field with Aaron? What else had happened?

Steve spoke again, louder now. 'Nadine?'

I dropped the leaf, brushing its juices from my palms as I turned. 'Yes?'

'Wyatt did a preliminary search, but he's not alerting anything. We'll spot-check a few areas, but he's starting to lose interest.' He noticed my arms tight around my body. 'If you want to get going, I can—'

'I'll stay.'

I followed Steve back to the center of the commune, then kept close as Wyatt worked the field in a grid, and along the riverbank, anywhere it might be easy to bury a body. The dog was moving slower now, his tail drooping.

Finally Ken said, 'He's done for.'

I walked with them to our vehicles. As Ken put Wyatt back in the truck, I said, 'He's a beautiful animal. My brother has a shepherd, too.'

331

'Yeah, they're good dogs.' Ken reached in and gave Wyatt a scratch.

Steve gave me a look. 'How is Robbie?'

I startled. 'You know my brother?' I wondered why he hadn't mentioned it the first time I came up.

'When I was still on the force, I had to break up a fight he was in at the pub.'

I wrinkled my brow. 'What was the fight about?'

'Don't know. The other two guys took off. It took a couple of us to settle Robbie down, and he wouldn't tell us what happened.' He held my gaze. 'He had a pretty bad temper.'

Something about the way he said it felt like a warning, which confused, then angered me. 'He was younger. He's worked through his issues.' I had no idea if that was true or not, but he was my brother.

Steve nodded, and then smiled. 'We've all got issues.'

I followed the men back to the main road, but they kept going straight to the village, and I turned toward my brother's. In case it got back to him that I was in town, I wanted him to hear it from me first. I also wanted him to know about Lisa. He'd always had a soft spot for her, and if he'd had any memories of the commune that he wasn't sharing, he might change his mind knowing she could be at risk.

He was working in the shop again. Brew gave a woof and bounded over to me, sniffing at my legs for traces of

Wyatt. Robbie straightened up from the workbench where he'd been sharpening the blade on a chain saw, the tool still in his hand. He looked over my shoulder, studied the mud on the car. I watched his face, the way his jaw muscles tightened.

I said, 'Hi, I wanted to let you know that Lisa might be at The River of Life Center.'

He turned back to me, his face confused. 'Whatya mean?'

I told him everything, then added, 'If she's gone there, she could end up staying. So I'm hoping that the center will get shut down. Tammy, the woman I found, she might go to the police, but she's still struggling with the decision.'

'Does Aaron know you're talking to people?'

'I don't know, maybe.'

'He's not going to like this.'

I thought about the truck rushing past, the hang-ups, the feeling of being watched, wondered again if it was someone from the commune. 'No, you're right. He won't, but there's not much I can do about that.'

Robbie picked up on my tension. 'Has he come after you?'

'I've been getting some strange calls and a couple of drive-bys.'

'You should just back off and forget—'

'He's hurting people, Robbie. You wouldn't believe the things he's doing now. He's got these chambers, where he basically starves people, and—'

'He's *starving* them?' His face was stunned, his mouth open, eyes wide.

'Yes, in isolation chambers.' I told him everything Tammy had shared.

Now he was pacing, back and forth, like a boxer in a ring without an opponent.

'Fuck. I told you – they're messed up.'

'That's why I have to do this. There's a woman, her name's Mary. She was from the commune, and she still lives out by the river. Did you know that?'

He looked wary again. 'No, but Mom used to go see some woman.'

My turn to be shocked. Mary hadn't mentioned anything about spending time with my mother after they'd left the commune.

Robbie was studying my car again. 'Where did the mud come from?'

'I met with a retired police officer out at the commune. Steve Phillips . . .'

Robbie turned back to the saw and began to sharpen, the tool making a rasping sound in a steady rhythm. 'Yeah, I remember Steve.'

'He remembers you too.' I paused, waiting for him to inquire further, or give me some acknowledgment, but the rasping continued.

I added, 'He said he busted up a fight you were in years ago.'

Now Robbie turned around, his face angry. 'I told you

not to talk about me to cops. Why the hell would he tell you that?'

'He's retired, and I didn't ask. He brought it up. He has a friend who has a cadaver dog. We searched the commune site, and—'

Before I could get the words out Robbie said, 'You searched the site? What for?' His face was shocked.

'For Willow.' Then I told him about Mary's finger.

Robbie shook his head. 'I don't know anything about that, but Willow, she got the hell out of there. Last time I saw her, she was hitchhiking on the logging road back to town – the morning she split from the commune.'

I was confused. 'How did you see her? Weren't you sleeping?'

'I'd gotten up early to go fishing at the big pool down by the bridge. I was just coming back when she was leaving.'

I paused, thinking it through. 'But you still don't know if she made it out. If she couldn't get a ride, she might have returned and—'

'No, I saw one of the logging trucks stop for her – a red one.'

His last statement connected with a thud. I thought of Larry, of his big red truck and his leering at pretty seventeen-year-old girls. Was it possible he picked her up? Heat infused my face. All the time we'd been out there searching, and Willow was probably living somewhere with three grandkids by now.

I waited to see if Robbie would add anything, but he was quiet. I was ashamed to realize that I wanted to be right about this, wanted to believe that I hadn't just been chasing ghosts. Now I feared I'd been wasting everyone's time. I still had a few questions.

'Why didn't you tell me you were friends with Willow?'

He gave me a what-are-you-talking-about look. 'I was friends with everyone in the commune.'

'You were more than friends.' I didn't really know if it was true, but something made me say it.

His face flushed, and his mouth tightened. 'I was *more* than friends with lots of the girls. What's your point?'

What was my point? Was I actually accusing my brother of lying to me?

'I just wondered if you knew anything else that might help me find her.'

'What's going on with you? I didn't know anything else about her, okay. She was just some chick at the commune. I hear from you once a year, and now you're on me every day about this shit. Why do you care so much about her?'

I hadn't seen Robbie this angry in years. 'I'm sorry. You're right, I've been pressuring you.'

Robbie's shoulders relaxed slightly, but he still looked upset. I watched Brew, who was watching Robbie, his eyes anxious, a low whine starting from his throat. He came over and sat near Robbie's feet, bumping against him. I wondered myself why I was so obsessed with finding Willow. Then it came to me.

'I guess because I wasn't able to help my patient, I've fixated on Willow.'

He nodded. 'Are we done with this? I'll hose your car off.' I knew it was a peace offering, but I still felt frustrated. My brother was shutting me out, again.

'Thanks. That would be great.'

As he rinsed off my car, I remembered that I'd also wanted to ask him about Levi. He'd reacted badly to my previous questions, but he'd been friends with Levi, so I didn't think it should be a problem. I said, 'Steve also told me that Levi moved back here, and he runs the ski school. Did you know that?'

He kept spraying the car in swoops. 'Yeah, I knew he was here.'

'I might go talk to him.'

'What do you want with Levi?'

'I told you. I'm trying to find witnesses. Why did you tell me that no one from the commune lived here anymore?'

This time it was an outright accusation: *You lied to me.*

He didn't bother defending himself, just kept spraying the car. I was starting to get angry with his avoiding my questions – avoiding me. I moved around the hose, standing within his eyesight. He still didn't look up.

'What happened? You two used to be close.'

'People change.' He finally met my gaze. 'Don't talk to

337

him about any of this unless you want it all over Shaw-nigan. He has a big mouth.'

'So you've never spoken to him since he came back?'

He paused, a tiny hesitation, and then said, 'Nope.'

My brother had lied to me again.

After I left Robbie's, I thought over our conversation. His desire to keep me from talking to Levi was obvious, but I wasn't sure why. I didn't want to break whatever tentative relationship we were forging. But I had a feeling Robbie was hiding something – something that Levi knew. Part of me wasn't sure if I wanted to open this door, but I'd already come too far to pull back now. In the end, still wrestling with my loyalty to my brother, I decided to take the long way around the lake and drive by the marina to check things out and maybe spot Levi.

As it happened, just as I neared the marina, I noticed a man pulling up to the dock in a ski boat, the flash of his ginger-colored hair catching my eye. Was that Levi? I took a closer look. It was definitely him. Now I also realized whom I'd seen that day at the pay phones by the store.

I slowed my vehicle to a crawl, still debating whether I should talk to him. He leaped out and began tying up the boat, then turned, like he'd felt someone's gaze on him, and surveyed the parking lot. Our eyes met. At first he looked confused, then a startled hint of recognition, followed by more confusion. He knew me, but he wasn't sure how. I pulled over and parked the car. He continued to tie up the boat, glancing in my direction once in a while.

I walked toward him, my stomach suddenly tight and rolling, my hands clammy. Blaming it on the sway of the wharf, I took a few deep breaths and planted my feet square. 'Hello, Levi. I'm not sure if you remember me . . .'

He stopped what he was doing and took another look at my face. I was about to give my name when he said, 'You're Nadine.'

So his confusion hadn't been about not recognizing my face, but something else. I'd misread his expression. Another person who didn't want to be reminded of their time at the commune?

'You do remember me?'

'You look just like your mother, thought I was seeing a ghost.'

I was feeling the same way. I flashed to the image of Coyote's limp body, mouth hanging open, slack as the water ran out. I shook off the thought.

We studied each other. I was uncomfortable, but not sure why. Then a gust of cold wind blew off the lake, making me shiver. Levi noticed, saying, 'Did you want to go into my office?' He gestured behind me. I turned and saw that he had a cabin beside the lake, with its own private dock and wharf, where boats, Jet Skis, and paddleboats were lined up, most of them covered for the season.

'Sure, that might be better.'

In his office, which was in the front room of the cabin, I spotted a door leading off into what I assumed were his living quarters. He offered a coffee, from an old coffeemaker that had seen better days. I passed and watched as he poured himself a cup, then sat behind the desk, tapping his pen on a pad of paper. He had an aged-surfer look about him, his face weathered from sun. He also radiated a wired-up energy, his eyes never quite meeting mine, and he was thin, almost gaunt. He sniffed, tossing his head in a quick backward motion. Drugs?

He said, 'So what brings you up here?'

I noticed the use of the word 'up.' So he knew I lived in Victoria. Who'd he been talking to? My body stiffened, but I kept my tone friendly as I said, 'How did you hear I moved to Victoria?'

He narrowed his eyes, like he was thinking, shrugged. 'Don't know, someone must've mentioned it.' I thought about the day I'd seen him on the phone outside the museum, suspecting he'd gone over after and asked about me.

'I was just visiting Robbie.'

'What's he up to these days? Still running the excavator?'

I nodded. So he knew a little about Robbie. I didn't want to show my cards, but I wanted to test whether Robbie had lied or not about talking to him. 'Things seem to be going well for him, but I guess you already know that.'

Another tap of his pen. 'Haven't seen Robbie for years, just his truck around town.'

I decided to cut to the chase. 'Why did you leave the commune?'

He stopped tapping but smiled his goofy grin, reminding me of the happy kid that he was, at least until his father died, and the grin had become scarce.

'That's kind of a personal question.'

'So you don't want to answer it?'

He laughed. 'I don't care, just thought it was a funny question. I left because they were freaks.'

'I heard some bad things have been going on there.'

His smile faded a bit. 'Aaron, he's twisted, man. Like really twisted.' His voice took on a bitter tone. 'He'd preach all this stuff about freedom, but then he kept a tight rein on all the pot and everything. I hated that place.'

Aaron had called marijuana our salvation because it was the closest we could come to experiencing the bliss we'd find on the other side. None of the members were allowed any for personal use, and it was only doled out by Aaron. If Levi had a drug problem, as I suspected, it would have been difficult for him at the center. I also sensed there was something deeper to his anger, an embarrassment, and I wondered if he'd been made to leave.

'Can you tell me more?'

'I try not to think about that time, you know? I like to just live for today.' He gestured toward the lake. 'That's my religion now.'

Living for today or running from the past?

I said, 'Is your mother still there?'

'No, she died before I left.' When he ran his hand through his hair, his sweater gaped at his forearm, showing a crescent-shaped scar. He caught my stare and quickly pulled his arm back down, watching me now, the smile gone, like he was waiting for me to make a comment. I thought of Mary. Had his scar also been a punishment? This time no memories came back, but still the feeling of unease.

I said, 'Your scar. Did you get that in the commune?'

He laughed. 'Nah, just drunk and stupid on the boat one night.' He laughed again, but something didn't feel genuine. Before I could put my finger on the reason or ask for details, he changed the subject. 'So why you want to know about the commune? You writing a book or something?'

He said it like a joke, but again I had a feeling he might've talked to the girl at the museum, and now he was trying to find out what I was up to.

I decided to go with the straight approach, maybe shock him into answering truthfully. 'For years I've suffered from claustrophobia and memory loss.' I explained about psychogenic amnesia, leaving out Heather and just

342

saying that a recent event had triggered memories of being sexually abused. 'I've been trying to find people who used to live in the commune, to see if there could be more victims.' I also decided to keep Tammy and Mary to myself for now.

He sat back in his chair, his face a portrait of shocked dismay. 'No *shit*, oh crap, jeez, I'm sorry to hear that.' His eyes seemed honest, but the way he said, 'Man, that's terrible,' like he was trying to convince me he was upset, had me wondering. He added, 'What's it called again? Memory suppression?'

I nodded. 'That's right.'

'And they just come back on their own?'

'Some. Some of them I have to focus on.'

'Isn't that stuff kind of hard to prove in court?'

'Yes, well, that's why I'm trying to find possible witnesses.'

He said, 'Wish I could help. I remember you spending a lot of time with Aaron. You guys were always down at the river, but I never saw anything, you know?' His expression was one of disappointment, his tone saying, *Sorry I can't help more.* Still, I thought about how the courts would look at those facts, how they would look to anyone else. *He was a nice man, just trying to teach her to swim. She's making it all up.*

I blinked a couple of times, cleared my throat. 'What about after, when you moved down to Victoria. Did you witness any sort of physical violence or abuse? You mentioned they were "freaks." Care to shed some light on that?'

He'd been rocking back and forth in his chair, but he stopped abruptly. 'I told you, I don't like talking about that stuff, okay?'

So, yes, he'd seen something.

I said, 'Okay. I can respect that. I didn't mean to stir up anything. I know how painful those memories can be.'

He looked away, got up, and poured himself another cup of coffee. I wondered if I should mention what Steve Phillips had told me about Levi seeing a woman with Finn. But as Levi splashed a small amount of coffee on his hand, cursing and bringing the burn to his mouth, I had a feeling I might have exhausted his patience. He'd recanted his story for a reason, one that I didn't think he'd be willing to divulge. Not yet anyway.

As he sat back down, I said, 'Do you remember Willow?'

He nodded, his goofy grin back in place. 'Yeah, she was real nice. Man, your brother had the hots for her.' He laughed. 'When she split, I thought for sure he'd go after her. I was kind of hoping he would – leave the other girls for me.'

He broke into a big swoop of laughter at his joke, his face flushed. But under his joviality, I sensed a lot of truth. Had Levi been jealous of my brother? Was *that* what sparked their arguing that summer and the eventual demise of their friendship? It didn't sound like he had any additional information on Willow's whereabouts, but I still said, 'Have you heard from her?'

'Willow?' His head bopped back in surprise. 'Hell, no. Not since she split that morning.'

'You saw her leave?'

'No, the last I saw her, she was . . .' He squinted, like he was thinking back. 'We were all out on that reflection walk, but I don't remember if she was there.' She wasn't, but I waited for him to search his own memories. 'When we got back, we all went swimming . . .' He was quiet, thinking, then shook his head. 'Nope, don't think she was at the river, either, so I guess the last time I saw her was before the walk.' He focused back on me. 'Why you asking about Willow?'

'She was just someone I remembered. I liked her a lot.'

He said, 'We all did. Man, I wonder what she'd look like now.'

His face was thoughtful, imagining an older Willow. I observed him across his desk, his aged skin and wind-blown hair, catching sight of my own reflection in the window behind him. For a moment I could almost see the ghost of our younger selves: my black hair in braids, his youthful, lean body and gap-toothed grin. I also thought of Willow, with her tanned skin and husky laugh. Did she have short or long hair now? Had she aged well? Was she happy?

'Yes, I wonder what she looks like too.'

*

I'd taken my leave after Levi picked up a call that was obviously going to take a while – he'd started to list various pricing options for rentals to the person on the other end while he rolled his eyes at me. I'd taken one of my cards out of my purse, writing on the back, *Call if you want to talk about the commune,* and also included my home number. He glanced at it when I passed it to him, giving me a thanks-for-stopping-by dismissive smile.

As I followed the path back up to my car, I looked back at the cabin and could see Levi through the top window. He dropped my card into the garbage.

Chapter Twenty-nine

Later that evening, though all my doors were locked, I felt exposed and uneasy. I'd been talking to a lot of people about the commune, stirring things up. Aaron had many loyal followers, not to mention people who'd probably invested in the center. It was a successful business, and they wouldn't want someone messing it up for them. I reminded myself that the police were more aware of the center now and that Aaron was smart enough to keep a low profile. Still, I checked all the doors and windows again, shaking my head at my paranoia. I was trying to distract myself with gardening shows on TV when the phone rang, startling me and causing me to spill my tea. Nursing my scalded finger, I picked up the phone on the fourth ring.

'Hello?'

A harsh voice, muffled and distorted, said, 'Stop now, or you'll be sorry. You don't know who you're fucking with.' He hung up.

Shaken, I stared at the phone in my hand, 'private number' showing on the display. Was it someone from the center? I couldn't tell if it was a woman or a man. The voice sounded like it was being altered by a computer, which only made it sound more terrifying. I pressed *57, hoping they could trace the number.

I sat on the couch and tried to think things through. It seemed my earlier fears might be more accurate than I'd anticipated. Somewhere along the way, I'd angered someone. I considered what I should do next. The threat had been upsetting, but if it had been from someone at the center, I still didn't think Aaron was going to hurt me, not for a sexual-abuse case which he knew would probably be dropped. If something happened to me, he'd be the first suspect, and he wasn't a stupid man. However, it was possible he was trying to scare me off before there was any negative publicity for the center.

The phone rang a second time, spiking my pulse. I waited a moment, gathered myself, and then looked at the call display. This time it showed a number that I vaguely remembered, but I still answered with a cautious 'Hello?'

'Hi, Nadine. It's Tammy.'

'Tammy! How are you?' I sat back on the couch, relieved.

'Not good.'

She sounded stressed, anxious. Concerned about her, I

sat back up and quickly said, 'Is everything okay?'

Her voice now thick and nasally, like she was crying, she said, 'My husband doesn't want me to talk to the police.'

I leaned back in my chair. Disappointed but not surprised, I said, 'And what do you want to do? Do you still want to speak with them?'

'I don't know. I see his point. He's just scared for me and Dillon. People think the center is so great, and Aaron is this important guy with tons of money. He just doesn't want me to be dragged through the mud, with all the newspapers and stuff, everyone talking about it. He doesn't think people will believe me.'

The way she said it, the sad tone told me that she was also disappointed, in her husband or the truth of the matter, I wasn't sure. But he was right – she would have an uphill battle. Many people wouldn't believe her, and if it did go to trial, it would be an emotionally exhausting process that would put a lot of stress on her life and marriage. I knew this all too well.

Now that the search hadn't turned up anything at the site, and Tammy wasn't willing to talk, the chances of ever building a case against Aaron were dwindling rapidly, but it was also important that Tammy feel good about her decision. I said, 'Tammy, I know how hard this must be for you. Going against the wishes of people close to us is extremely difficult. But sometimes we have to do what feels right to us, even if it means upsetting others in our life. I respect whatever decision you make, I just hope you do what's best for you.'

She lowered her voice. 'I have to go.' Muffled sounds in the background, like an argument: a raised man's voice and Tammy's, pleading.

I said, 'Tammy? Are you okay?'

A man's voice answered. 'Stay away from my wife.'

He hung up.

I sat in my dark living room, my heart hammering in my chest. I was worried about Tammy, but I didn't hear anything that I could call the police about, and if I phoned back, it could just cause more problems for her. I hoped that she was okay. When my system had settled down, I decided what to do next. There was one more person I could try to reach. I took a moment to calm myself, then phoned Daniel. It had been a few days, and he hadn't called with any news of Lisa, so I wasn't sure if he'd moved back to the center yet, or if he'd even still have his cell. He answered on the second ring.

'Daniel, it's Nadine. I was just following up on our last conversation.'

'Sorry, the job is taking longer than I'd thought. I promise, as soon as I get to the center, I'll look for Lisa and let you know.'

I dropped my head onto the back of my couch as tears pricked my eyes. 'Thanks.' I took a breath. 'No one else I've talked to has been able to help.'

His voice was curious. 'Who have you been talking to?'

'There was another victim, with a family member at the center. But she isn't ready to speak to the police, and she can't contact her family on the inside.'

'She probably just knows her lies will be found out. If you'd ever been to the center, you wouldn't believe any of these accusations.' His voice was confident, proud. 'Aaron's a brilliant teacher. You just don't know them.'

'I *do* know them, Daniel.'

I caught myself before I revealed more, hoping that Daniel might not have picked up on my slip, but he was quiet. Then, speaking slowly, as though he was still putting it all together, he said, 'Wait . . . Were you a member? Is that why . . . ?'

Now it was my turn to pause, wondering if it was a good idea to tell him anything more. How much did I want him to know? I scolded myself. How can I expect others to share their stories when I'm still scared to talk about my own?

'I lived at the commune in Shawnigan when I was a child, with my mother and brother.'

'Really?' He sounded stunned, and confused. 'Why didn't you say anything before?'

'It wasn't appropriate given the situation.' It still wasn't. I was opening myself up to a lawsuit if Daniel ever did decide to sue the hospital.

Daniel said, 'If you know them, then you know that the center isn't doing anything wrong. They're good people.'

I had already stepped out of my comfort zone, I might as well go all the way. 'Daniel, I was one of Aaron's victims. I made the report.'

Dead silence. Then, his voice angry and cold, he said, 'Did you tell Heather these lies? Is that why she was so upset? What did you say to her?'

I saw the dangerous turn his thoughts were taking. He was one step from blaming me for her suicide. 'I never told her any of this. She didn't know.' I held my breath, hoping I hadn't just lost Daniel. He was my only chance.

Daniel said, 'Don't call me again.'

Chapter Thirty

The next morning, I came in early before my rounds so that I could talk to Kevin and get his advice. He'd phoned once since he left my house, but I'd been outside in my yard and missed it. I hadn't had a chance to return his call, and I wasn't sure yet what I wanted to do about that situation, but I had decided to go to the commune. If Lisa was there, I'd deal with it – I just needed to know one way or the other. But, and I hated to admit this, I was worried about facing Aaron.

Late the night before, I'd received two more harassing calls, both stating the same sentiment – they wanted me to stop. If I didn't acquiesce, I was going to regret it. The police were looking into it, and I still suspected they were empty threats, but no less unnerving. Meanwhile, I was hoping Kevin would accompany me to the commune. When I got to the hospital, though, his office was closed, and Michelle told me he was at an all-day seminar. I called his voice mail and left a message, asking him to get in touch with me later.

For the rest of the day I focused on my patients. When I got home, I checked my messages, hoping that Kevin had called, but my voice mail was empty. Before driving out to the commune, I contemplated my decision again, wanting to be sure. I thought about the recent threatening phone calls and considered whether it was dangerous for me to go alone. With all the potential witnesses at the center, I didn't think Aaron would risk hurting me. Worst case scenario, he might refuse to see me. I decided to take the chance.

Though I was anxious to go there right away, I took a few moments to mentally prepare myself. My insides were vibrating at the thought of facing Aaron again. I forced myself to eat something light, dressed warmly in jeans and a turtleneck, and made sure my iPhone was charged. I also called Connie and left a message telling her where I was going. It was starting to rain, so I drove carefully on the winding coastal road out to Jordan River while I went over my game plan. I had no idea if the main office would be open, but I was hoping they'd at least let me talk to Lisa. I'd threaten to call the police if I had to, though I wasn't sure if that would hold any water. When I neared Jordan River, I slowed down. A truck came up fast behind me and passed on a narrow corner, sending my heart into my throat. Several more miles down the road, I spotted a few wooden buildings in a field on my left. Then I saw the large sign hanging over the gate.

THE RIVER OF LIFE SPIRITUAL CENTER.

I pulled in the driveway and parked in front of the main building, which looked like a luxury resort, with cedar siding, manicured hedges lining the driveway, and stone paths winding through gardens. The building was U-shaped, curved to take advantage of the view toward the ocean. The front entrance was stunning, with flag-stone steps and large cedar posts framing the wood door, a couple of wrought-iron benches and potted plants on either side of the entranceway. There were also pretty outdoor lights lining the walkway, but no one was on the grounds. I noticed a small sign pointing to the office around the side and assumed it was in the smaller build-ing to the right. I got out of my car.

A few pickup trucks were parked in the center of the commune, with dirty, mud-splattered farm vehicles, and a tractor pulling an empty trailer. Behind the buildings, there looked to be a barn, but I could only make out its roof, and in the wind, the wet scent of manure, hay, and animals. Near one of the fields, an old plow had been abandoned, moss growing over it, and in a puddle I spotted a child's wooden toy train, its wheels broken. I remembered reading in the brochure that they had a school and an early-childhood educational depart-ment.

As I followed the signs to the office, I slowed my pace, my feet crunching on the gravel, wondering which building housed Aaron. I glanced back, feeling myself being watched, and noticed a child's face peeking out from above a windowsill. A little boy, with a pale face and big eyes, his blond hair all in curls. He gave me a cheeky grin, then disappeared, the curtain dropping back in place. I wondered how many more children lived at the commune.

I found the office. There was a doorbell, with a sign saying *Please ring after hours*. I pressed the buzzer, which emitted a pleasant peal of chimes. I caught sight of a camera up in the corner, the red light blinking, and remembered Heather's fear in the hospital. *He sees everything*. After a few minutes, the door opened. My body tensed, waiting for Aaron to appear, but it was a young woman, long-haired and clean-faced, in jeans and a white sweater.

She smiled. 'Can I help you?'

I smiled back. 'I hope so. My daughter is missing, and I'd like to know if she's staying here. I'm very worried about her.'

Her expression kind, she said, 'I'm sorry, but we can't give out information on our guests.'

I said, 'I'd like to speak with Aaron then, please.'

She studied me. 'He doesn't see people without appointments.'

'I think he'll see me. I knew him when I was a child. If you could let him know that Nadine Jaeger is here, I'd appreciate it very much.'

She nodded, then said, 'I'll ask. Would you like to come in and wait?'

'Please.'

She led me inside. The office building was cozy and inviting, with tiled floors in earth tones, more wood beams, and a counter made from a long slab of cedar, stained a natural shade. Behind the counter, I could see some phones, a fax machine, a computer, and other business equipment. There was a door behind the counter that obviously led to some back offices. The front office opened up on the right to another smaller room, where there were books and crystals and CDs, and some basic sundries, like a gift shop at a resort. The woman motioned to some chairs and said, 'I'll see if Aaron will meet with you.' She disappeared into the back. I sat down on one of the chairs, noticing a small table with a scattering of magazines, mostly on health and meditation, living an organic life.

Finally, nearly fifteen minutes later, the door opened. I held my breath expecting to see Aaron, but it was the woman again. She walked toward me with a smile. 'If you'd like to follow me, Aaron will speak with you.' I assumed that Aaron's offices would also be in this building, but she turned and exited out the front door, saying, 'This way, please.'

We walked back to the main building and entered through a side entrance. So she must've phoned Aaron from the other office. I followed the young woman down a hall, my eyes taking in everything. So far, the commune seemed simple on the inside, almost rustic, in keeping with the West Coast-resort feeling. The floors were earth-toned tiles, the walls a flat white, the odd tapestry hung here and there. Broad cedar beams were fitted into the ceilings. The air was perfumed but not overly, just a mixture of the wood and something natural, like an essential oil. It reminded me of a spa I'd been to in the past. Doors opened off the hallway, but they were mostly closed. One that was gapped revealed a simple room: wooden single bed in the corner, one chest, a chair, the bedding all in white.

A few more doors down, we passed a room that looked like it was for ceremonies; mats on the floor radiated out from a dais. Large windows behind showed the wind lashing a tree in a courtyard. I could well imagine Aaron standing there, promising to end your suffering forever if you just followed his teachings. Then I envisioned his bringing up members to confess their sins, saw my daughter sharing her darkest secrets, baring her soul for this man to tear apart.

We walked by another room, and I caught a quick glimpse of chairs clustered around small tables, children's drawings lining the wall, and a blackboard. The schoolroom. When we came to the end of the hallway, the woman turned right and stopped in front of a wooden door. She knocked three times. A man's voice, low and calm, said, 'Come in.' It was Aaron.

The woman entered right away, but I faltered at the idea of seeing Aaron again. Then I felt a rush of anger, at how small and vulnerable this man made me feel – how he'd violated me.

Aaron was sitting behind a large cedar desk, rows of bookshelves on either side of him, and in the center a window, which I imagined had an ocean view. Massive cedar beams crossed the ceiling, and a cozy fireplace blazed in the corner.

To the left was another wooden door, and I wondered if that led to his private chamber. I imagined young girls in there with him and felt ill at the thought. Finally, I focused on Aaron, the man my memories had been avoiding for decades. He was studying me, his hands clasped in a thoughtful pose, a friendly smile on his face, like he was welcoming an old acquaintance. He was dressed in a navy blue sweater and wore a large wrist-watch that looked expensive. His face was lined, but he looked healthy, with a tan. The years had been good to him.

The young woman said, 'I'll leave you alone,' and closed the door softly.

Aaron stood up and came out from around the desk. Just the image of him looming over me sent me back to being a child again. I forced myself to stand straight, reminded myself that I was no longer powerless, though my legs were vibrating with adrenaline.

'Nadine, so nice that you came to see me.'

My stomach turned inside itself at his words and the tone of familiarity.

'I didn't come to see you. I came to ask about my daughter.'

He nodded, his eyes boring into mine. I forced myself to maintain eye contact, trying not to remember the things he made me do to him. His skin cold and wet from the river.

'Yes, Lisa. She's doing some excellent work, finding her spiritual path again. She was very angry inside . . .' He shook his head.

A jolt of panicked rage shot through me. So she was at the center – and he knew exactly who my daughter was, which increased my belief that he had targeted her. I wanted to knock the smug look off his face, the serene smile. But my daughter was here, and if I upset him, he wouldn't tell me anything else.

'I'd like to talk to her, please.'

'I'm sorry, but that wouldn't be good for her. She's focused on healing right now.'

Another wave of anger. 'How about we let her make that decision?'

'Lisa has turned her spiritual guidance over to me.'

'I'm her *mother*.'

'But are you the right mother for her?' The hurt nearly brought me to my knees. He saw me flinch, saw my shame. 'I'm sure you've asked yourself the same thing. How did she end up on the wrong path? Living with those people? She lost her spirit.' He shook his head. 'Such a beautiful girl, so much soul, but so much pain inside.' He tapped his heart. 'She needs to release it.'

A sick memory flowed over me. His hands searching under my shirt as he breathed into my ear, *You need to release your fear, free your body.*

I stepped forward. 'If you've touched her, I'll—'

'You'll do nothing.' He also stepped forward. 'Lisa is ready for spiritual awareness – she's willing to do whatever it takes. Are you?'

'My spirit doesn't need to be saved – yours does. I remember what you did to me as a child.'

'You went to the police.'

No denial, but no acknowledgment either.

'And I'm going to keep going to them.'

He gestured to the room. 'But nothing's happened. I'm still here.' He inhaled and reached above his head with both hands, then let out his breath in a long exhalation as he lowered them back down and clasped them in front of his heart, before dropping them to his sides. He looked at me, his face peaceful. 'The Light's always watching. And he knows I've done nothing wrong.'

'It's wrong to touch underage girls.'

'If what you're saying is true, the police would've arrested me.'

My impotence enraged me. He was clearly smart enough to consider that I might be wired and was gauging his answers accordingly.

361

He added, 'You became a doctor. It must've been difficult after your husband died.'

How did he know so much about me? Did Lisa tell him? The idea of them talking about me, the things he might've said, terrified me, but I held my tongue.

'Lisa told me you don't believe in life after death, or that our loved ones return to visit. Just because you can't see something doesn't mean it's not there.'

I wasn't playing this game with him. 'I'd like to talk to my daughter.'

He smiled, then picked up the phone and spoke softly into it. 'Please bring Lisa Lavoie to me. Thank you.'

He put the phone down and said, 'Why don't you stand by the fire, you look cold.'

Another memory crashed into me. We were at the campsite with everyone, after swimming in the river, and he'd wrapped his towel around me, pulled me down to sit on his lap. My mother had looked away. Had she known? The possibility stunned me.

When I didn't move, Aaron said, 'You never trusted me, though I don't understand why. I've always cared about you and thought we had a special connection.' He held my gaze, and I felt the sick wrongness, the feeling I'd always had as a child, which was made even worse by knowing that in his warped mind he actually meant it. He said, 'Everything I did was to help you and your mother.'

'Help me? You're a sick pedophile. And I'm going to

362

make sure the whole world knows you're a fraud. This center will be out of business soon.'

He said nothing, just cocked his head, assessing me. Finally, his voice calm, he said, 'My members are loyal and grateful for my help. Your threats have no meaning.'

The door opened, and Aaron turned.

'Lisa, welcome.'

She was here already? Had they been waiting nearby? I spun around. An older man was walking in with Lisa. Her hair was brushed clean, falling down her back in thick waves. She was wearing black leggings and a long beige sweater.

I came toward her. 'Lisa!'

The man stepped forward and blocked me.

'Excuse me, please,' I said. Then I met his gaze and realized it was Joseph. Unlike his brother, the years had not been kind. He was gaunt and pale, dark shadows circled under red-rimmed eyes, and his hair was unkempt. He had the look of someone seriously ill.

Lisa had already passed by to stand at Aaron's side near his desk. Aaron reached out and put his arm around her shoulder, his hand resting on the back of her neck, thumb pressing against her jugular. Panic surged through my blood.

Ignoring Joseph for now, I said, 'Lisa, are you okay?'

She didn't even glance at me. Instead she looked at Aaron for permission to speak, her body language almost deferential and her expression admiring.

Aaron said, 'Go ahead, you can tell her what you told me this morning.'

Lisa now faced me, her eyes angry but her words calm. 'It's interesting, all the stuff I'm learning about meditating and spiritual awareness. I feel calmer now, like this is where I'm supposed to be, so I can get better.'

I studied her face, searching for signs of fatigue or stress, but she actually looked rested and healthy. I was relieved and also torn. I hated to hear that Aaron was having any positive effect on her, but I had to admit this was the best I'd seen her in years.

'Lisa, I'm glad you're okay.'

'I'm fine. I like it here. These are my friends now.' She smiled at Joseph standing nearby, who returned it, but there was something in his face I didn't like, a sweaty, feverish energy that made me wonder if he was in a manic phase. I remembered him kneeling behind Mary, the smile on his face as she sobbed.

I fought back a rush of fear. 'They seem like your friends, but if you don't do everything they want you to do, they'll turn against you.'

A flash of anger in Lisa's eyes. She was still there, she hadn't lost her spirit. Unfortunately, her anger was aimed at me. 'You're just mad because I'm not doing what you think I should be doing. I'm *happy* here. But you're still trying to control me. You think your way is so much better? You think your house is so safe?'

'My house?' What was she talking about?

She stopped short, looked at Aaron. He nodded. 'Like we discussed, to let go of your negative thought processes, you have to share every part of your life.'

She looked back at me, tears glistening in her eyes. 'It was Garret, Mom.'

'What was Garret?'

'That's who molested me.'

I sucked in my breath. *No, not Garret.* My mind raced, trying to take in her words, but all I could do was stare at her, my heart thundering with shock.

Lisa continued. 'It started when I was thirteen. You were always at the hospital.' She didn't say the last part with bitterness or anger. It was defeat. A child who'd stopped calling out long ago for her mother to help her. She said, 'A couple of days ago, he found me down at the wharf, bought me a coffee, said he just wanted to apologize. That's why I overdosed – he drugged me. Then it didn't matter anymore. You already thought I was using again.' An angry shrug.

Now I was also crying. 'Why didn't you tell me?'

'You'd make me talk about it, but I just wanted to forget it.'

'You can't ignore something like this, Lisa. You have to deal with it.'

She threw her hands up. 'Stop it, just stop it. You're always pushing me to talk about everything. I'm not like you. I don't *want* to talk about it.'

Aaron's hand pressed against her neck again. She turned to look at him.

He said, 'It's time to tell your mother what you shared in confession.'

'I . . . I don't. I'm not ready.' It was the first time I saw her falter.

'I thought you wanted to end your suffering and begin a new life?' He cocked his head, gave her a disappointed look that I was all too familiar with.

'I do. I just—'

She started sobbing so hard she could barely breathe. I'd never seen her cry like that. I stepped forward, wanting to shield her from all of this, to hold her in my arms. But she took a step back, retreating from me. I stopped.

Aaron said, 'If you want to let go of your anger toward your mother and move toward inner peace, you have to break free from your past.'

Lisa took a couple of deep, shuddering breaths, trying to rein herself in, then with tears still streaming down her face, she turned to me. 'It was me. I was the one who attacked you in Nanaimo.'

Her words hit me like a blow, and I almost stumbled backward.

Lisa, it had been Lisa.

I found my voice. 'Why? I don't understand—'

'I was there with some friends, and I wanted to score some drugs.' She looked at Aaron. He nodded for her to continue. She turned back to me. 'I was going to ask to borrow some money, but when I saw you there, I knew you'd say no ...' She started crying again, covering her eyes, too ashamed to even look at me. I was also crying, trying to make sense of everything, angry and hurt.

My daughter had left me lying in a parking lot. She had left me to die.

I said, 'Do you really hate me that much?'

Her face was raw emotion. 'No, I just ...' She looked back at Aaron, wanting him to answer for her.

He said, 'It's not about hate, Nadine. It's about breaking free. Sometimes, we need to leave negative energies behind and open our hearts to a new family.'

My anger surged again. 'Are you actually saying that I'm a negative influence on my daughter? You don't know anything about us, or our lives.'

'He sees everything.' Aaron pointed to the heavens.

So he still believed that the Light spoke to him. There was no way to argue with him. I had to just concentrate on Lisa. I had to get her out of there.

I faced Lisa. 'Baby, whatever you've done, whatever happened to you, we can work it out, okay? I love you no matter what.'

She wouldn't meet my eyes. I moved closer. 'Lisa, please don't shut me out. Can we just go somewhere and talk about this?'

Aaron said, 'She doesn't want to go anywhere with you.'

'She's going to have to tell me that herself.'

Lisa raised her head, met my eyes, her gaze again blank and flattened. She had disconnected from the emotions, put them all in a dark corner of her mind, where not even the strength of my love could force them out.

She said, 'I'm staying here. I want to be happy again.'

'This place won't make you happy.'

She stared back at me. It didn't matter what I said, even if told her about my own abuse. I'd seen that look in my patients' eyes. Nothing would reach her now.

Aaron said to her, 'You've taken some important steps toward your spiritual growth. I'm proud of you.' He kissed her temple in a fatherly gesture. Lisa looked up at him, grateful. I wanted to pull his hands off her.

I wanted to kill him.

He said, 'You can return to your room now, and I'll speak with your mother. It'll be all right.' He smiled at her.

Her eyes slid in my direction, gauging my reaction, or seeking something – I wasn't sure – but then she deliberately looked away as she passed by me.

I tried one last time. 'Lisa, please wait a minute. You don't understand. He hurt me – when I was a child.' I gripped her arm. She pried my fingers off and hurried down the hall. I stared at her back.

My daughter was gone.

Joseph was now blocking the door. I paused, feeling the energy in the room shift and turn darker now that Lisa had left.

Joseph took a step forward. 'It's time for you to leave.'

Aaron said, 'I'd like to talk to Nadine alone, Joseph.'

Joseph's face was calm, but there was a quick burst of anger in his eyes and a red flush at his neck. He hesitated, like he wanted to argue, but Aaron nodded, the motion dismissive, reminding me of someone releasing their pet dog from a hold position. Joseph bowed his head, closed the door behind him, and went through the other door out of Aaron's office. I caught a quick glimpse of a darkened room. I also noticed a camera in the upper corner of the office and wondered if someone was watching.

I turned back to Aaron.

He smiled, and, his voice calm, full of confidence, said, 'I can help you heal your relationship with your daughter, but you need to let go and trust—'

'I don't need your perverted help.'

He looked pointedly in the direction Lisa had left. 'Your daughter attacked you, Nadine. Nearly *killed* you.' I flinched at his brutal words, at the memory of lying in the darkened parking lot, wondering if I was going to die.

'She's young and she's in pain – you're going to destroy her.'

'You had your chance to help her. You tried for years, did you not? But she was living on the streets, killing herself with chemicals. Now, in a matter of days, she's sober, she's happy, she trusts me. Why didn't she tell you about her half brother? Why didn't she trust you? Haven't you been asking yourself the same thing?'

I listened to Aaron, my blood pounding hard in my ears. Wanting to walk away but transfixed, every word he was saying exposing all my secret fears.

Aaron continued. 'When you were at the commune, I imagined you'd be such a good mother. I'd watch you with the other children at the river, wondering what kind of woman you'd grow up to be. But your mother took you away. Now I get to see your daughter and be part of her spiritual development. And you're getting everything you'd wanted for your daughter, but you're still not happy.'

I finally found my voice. 'You're not what I wanted for my daughter.'

'You have to be in control. Just like your mother couldn't accept my leadership, you're now doing the same. You're not allowing me to be a gift to your daughter. You're trying to destroy her happiness, but I'm saving her life.'

'You *ruin* lives. You take vulnerable people and manipulate them into believing they'll never find peace unless they listen to you.'

'Isn't that what you do? Make people think they need therapy, or they can't handle their lives? I teach them that they have the answers already.'

He was too confident. I'd still never seen him shaken. There was only one person I'd ever seen him react to: Willow. Could I use that now?

'Is that what you did to Willow? Teach her?' I took a wild stab. 'I know you killed her.'

He didn't even flinch, just looked me straight in the eye, and said, 'Willow wasn't ready for my help. Lisa, on the other hand, is ready to change. The question is, Can you let her go? Can you put her spiritual needs above your own?'

I said, 'If you touch her, if you do *anything* to her, I'll make sure you spend the rest of your life in jail. I know I'm not the only one, Aaron. I'm going to hunt down every woman you ever hurt, and we will destroy you and this center—'

The door opened at the side of the office, and Joseph walked in. He was wearing a windbreaker now, like he'd been outside.

'It's not right, the things she's saying.' He pointed at me, then ran his hand through his hair as he paced. He must've been listening in from another room or watching the security cameras.

Aaron said, 'It's okay, Joseph. I have it under control.'

Joseph was shaking his head. 'She wants to hurt you. I can feel it.' He was speaking fast and anxious. The small office was filled with the scent of his nervous sweat.

I wasn't sure if I should speak, or if that might add to his agitation, but I decided to risk it. 'I don't want to hurt Aaron. I just want to talk with him.'

'I heard you! You said you were going to put him in

jail.' Joseph was pointing at me again. 'She said she'll destroy the center. We have to stop her.'

My heart was racing as adrenaline flooded my body. Joseph looked like he could turn violent at any moment, his body tight and coiled.

Aaron said, 'Everything's okay. You can go back to your room.'

Joseph looked back and forth between us. 'No. I can see it, the poison on her. It's climbing up her arm.' His eyes widened, and I had to fight the urge to look at my arm, to see what he was seeing. But I knew there was nothing there.

Speaking gently, Aaron said, 'She's not a threat. The Light is protecting us against her bad energy.'

Joseph hesitated, looking at my arms again, then his body relaxed slightly, like whatever he'd seen before was now gone.

Aaron said, 'Joseph, please leave us alone now.'

His face confused, Joseph nodded and left. He gave me one last look before he exited, his eyes red-rimmed and angry. I had the terrifying thought that if Aaron hadn't calmed him down, Joseph would've attacked me a second later.

I reached for the door behind me. I had to get out of there right now. Aaron noticed my movement and said, 'You can tell the police anything you want, Nadine, but nothing will happen to me or the center.' He smiled.

'We'll see about that.' I left quickly, half expecting him

to come after me, but I made it back to my car without mishap, not even running into a single member in the hallway on my way out. I considered looking for Lisa, but the building was too big, and there wasn't anything I had to say that she wanted to hear.

As I drove away, I thought about how easily Aaron let me leave. I was no threat. I was nothing to him.

Chapter Thirty-one

The rest of the way back to the city, my breath was tight in my throat and my hands were shaking on the wheel, my stomach sick with nerves. I drove straight to the police station. The officer I spoke with said they would talk to Aaron and Joseph, and that they'd also bring Garret in for questioning, but I already knew he'd deny everything.

Once I got home, I finally let myself cry. Now that I knew it was Garret who'd stolen Lisa from me, who'd sat at my dinner table smiling night after night, I felt betrayed, and even angrier at myself for not seeing the signs. So much was clear now. Her moodiness after each time he'd visited, her increase in drug use. I was hurt and disappointed that she hadn't confided in me. It had been such a chaotic time, trying to finish my residency, Paul getting sick. Had I really been there for her? I'd tried, checking in with her daily, asking how she was doing, spending time with her, going to grief counseling together, in which she'd sat mute, but had I *truly* been present for her? Was I just so blindly trusting of Garret that I didn't see him for what he was? I was also hurt – I'd loved him like he was my own child, opened my heart and life to him. Now I wanted to kill him myself, but I had to let the police deal with it.

It wasn't until later, when I was huddled in my house-coat on the couch, that I also let myself cry about the fact that my daughter was so lost to me that she'd been the one who attacked me. I thought of her visiting me in the hospital in Nanaimo, how she had turned away. Would we ever be able to get past this?

The police called early in the morning. They'd spoken with Aaron, who had claimed that I'd shown up, pushed my way in, and had been abusive to some of his staff members. They also spoke to Lisa, who'd denied that Garret abused her. I attempted to defend myself to the police, but I knew how weak my justifications sounded, and, worse, how it must look to them: the Crown wasn't going to pursue my case, so now I was making things up. The officer said, 'They've made it clear you're not wel-come back. We understand that you're upset your daughter is living there, but it seems like she wants to stay. It would be better if you just kept away in the future.'

They were right. There was nothing left for me to do.

That day at work, I threw myself into my patients' care – following up on Brandon's meeting with a career coun-selor and consulting with Jodi's dietician. Francine was stable, but still depressed and slightly agitated. I sat with her for a while. She called me Angela again, giggling about the nude painting she was working on and how we had to visit Mexico again soon. When it was time for me to go, her expression grew frightened, and she said, 'I don't like this hotel. I want to go home.' I reminded her that she was at the hospital, and she began to cry.

I rubbed her back, trying to soothe. When that didn't work, I spoke of Mexico, the clear blue water, the white sand, the tropical wind blowing and grabbing at your dress and hair as you walked on the beach, gliding across your sunburned skin in a caress. Finally, she fell asleep, a small smile on her sad face.

Later, Kevin stopped by my office briefly, saying, 'I got your message last night, but it was too late to call back. Everything okay?'

I said, 'Yes, I was going to ask you something, but I sorted it out myself.' I had already decided that I didn't want him to know what had happened at the center.

He gave me a questioning look. 'You sure?'

'I just have a lot going on at the moment.' I made a motion with my hands, pointing to all my paperwork. 'And trying to play catch up.'

He nodded and said, 'Well, have a good day.' There was a bemused expression on his face, and I wanted to explain further, but before I could say anything else, my phone rang. He gave a wave and left my office.

*

The following evening I was brewing tea in the kitchen, thinking about Francine, who'd finally been placed in a good nursing home with an art program, one bit of bright news, when I thought I heard a noise outside. I peeked out the window but couldn't see anything. Wondering if it was the cat, I pushed open the door. It fell closed behind me. I paused, calling 'Kitty?' as I looked into the backyard. There was no meow in response, nothing moved in the grass. I glanced to my left. The motion sensor light in my neighbor's yard blinked on, casting odd shadows. Had the cat set it off, or something larger? I strained my ears, listened for footsteps. In the distance I heard a vehicle start up, then drive away fast, its tires squealing.

That night I slept fitfully, waking every hour or so, my heart palpitating at the slightest creak in the house. The next day, I called another psychiatrist at the hospital to cover me, then phoned Corporal Cruikshank in Shawnigan. She told me that the officers had contacted her the previous evening, after they went to the commune to speak with Aaron, so she already knew what had happened.

I had a hard time not raising my voice in frustration when I told the officer that I had not made these events up. She was very professional, careful to keep her own voice neutral, and said that someone in Victoria would still be speaking to Garret. But she warned me it likely wouldn't come to anything unless

Lisa was willing to make a statement, which we both doubted. She then also suggested I stay away from the commune and let them handle it from now on. I was just making things worse and potentially damaging my case. I agreed.

I had also told her about the noise in my backyard, and the vehicle driving off. She suggested that I have a security system installed, for peace of mind. It wasn't a bad idea. After we hung up, I made a few calls to alarm companies and arranged to have one installed as soon as possible. I tried to busy myself around the house for the afternoon, but I kept stopping and staring into space, Lisa's words haunting me: *It started when I was thirteen.*

When I thought about Garret's hands on Lisa, every time I remembered leaving them alone, guilt tied my guts into knots. I couldn't stand thinking he got away with this – thinking he could do this to some other little girl.

I grabbed my purse and drove to his studio. When I got to his house, a young mother was walking her preteen daughter to their car, waving and smiling good-bye to Garret. What would've just seemed like a friendly return smile on his face before now disgusted me. I waited until the car drove off, then got out of mine and walked down to his studio, where he was framing some photos. When he heard my footsteps, he spun around, smiling when he recognized me.

'Nadine! You came to see the studio. Perfect timing. I just—'

'I know, Garret. I know what you did.' I'd come there in anger, wanting to confront and rage, but now I wanted to cry. This was a boy I'd watched grow up, a boy I'd held when he cried at his father's funeral. How did this happen?

He looked confused. 'What's wrong?'

'How could you?' My words were a plea, begging him to make me understand, though I never would. 'How could you do those things to Lisa?'

He stepped back, his hand out in defense. 'I don't know what lies she told you—'

'I know you abused her.'

I searched his eyes, hoping for a sign of shame – some remorse. But he'd recovered now, and his face was just angry.

'Lisa's a drug addict and a thief. She'd lie about anything.'

'She wouldn't lie about this. I *know* you did it – and that you drugged her last week. Your father would be ashamed of you.' Paul would have been devastated to find out his son was a child molester, one who'd abused his own sister.

'My father would know that I didn't *do anything*.' His voice was almost a yell now. 'My father loved me.'

'I loved you too – and so did Lisa. You took advantage of that.'

Garret was trying to get himself under control, taking some breaths, running his hand through his hair. 'Nadine, you know me better than this.'

'I *thought* I knew you.'

'I would never touch her – she's my sister. But she's messed up on drugs, and she lies when she's stoned. She was just saying this crap to hurt you.'

For a moment, I faltered. Was he right? Then I remembered the look in her eyes. No, Lisa may have lied about many things, but that wasn't one of them.

Garret leaned back against the table, pushing a frame to the side as though clearing a spot for his hand, but something about the movement didn't seem natural. Then I saw the photos on the table. One caught my eye. Anyone else would've just seen the shape of a woman's back as she huddled on a mattress. But I knew my daughter, knew every curve and bump of her spine. It was Lisa. I stepped around Garret and pulled it out from under the others, studied it in shock. It looked like the same room I'd found her in. When had the photo been taken?

Garret quickly said, 'She signed the release.'

Thoughts crashed into my mind. Did he take the photos after he'd drugged her? What else did he make her do? Is this what had pushed her to join the commune? Rage and helpless anger at how my family had broken apart swept through my body. I thrust out the photo, 'What is this?'

Garret said, 'It's a project I'm working on. Lisa needed

money.' He sounded defensive but also nervous. His gaze kept flicking to the photo.

'What else did you do to her, Garret?' My voice was steel, my body stiff.

'Nothing. I told you, she wanted money. She was still doing drugs. She lied to you about that too. She's sick, Nadine. She's an addict.'

He was lying again, blaming Lisa for everything, each word out of his mouth making me think of Aaron, of how they justify the evil things they do. And Garret was going to keep lying, to the police, to other little girls, to their mothers.

Still holding Lisa's photo in one hand, I spun around and ripped Garret's photos off the studio wall, hurling them to the ground, frames smashing and glass shards flying everywhere.

Garret was trying to grab my wrists as he yelled, '*What the hell are you doing?*' I yanked free. He lifted me from behind, dragging and pushing me out of the studio, while I clawed and kicked at him. I landed a good wallop across his mouth.

He dropped me on the ground, stumbled backward, his hand coming to his lip and touching blood. He looked at it, like he was stunned that I'd actually hurt him. 'I'm calling the police, you crazy bitch.'

I stood up on shaky legs, still vibrating from adrenaline, brushing dirt and broken glass off my clothes. 'No you're not.'

Our gazes locked. He looked away first.

I left him standing outside his ruined studio, while I walked with my head high to my car, still carrying Lisa's photo.

Chapter Thirty-two

The next morning, after a restless night's sleep, I woke groggy and sore, all my muscles aching. Thankfully, I was off that day and didn't have to go into the hospital. I poured a coffee to take to the back patio. I craved the light, the open air. The sun was landing on the top step, so I sat there, lifting my face to the warmth. I heard a small thud to my right, and my eyes jolted open as I spun in that direction, my body braced for an attack. But it was just the cat, having leaped off the railing. She watched me, her eyes blinking in the bright light.

I rubbed my fingers together, called her closer. 'Here, kitty, kitty.'

She walked along the bottom of the railing, pausing once in a while to bump her head against the wood. When she was a couple of feet away, she stopped to lie down in a patch of sun. I made another kissing sound. She rolled over, then pulled herself closer by her claws, a rumbling purr starting up in her throat. Joy spun through me, the sweet pleasure of being responded to by another creature. She was a foot from me. We sat together, basking in the sun. Her black fur looked warm. A light dusting of dirt, maybe from my garden bed, shone on the tips. I reached out and ran a hand down her back. She rolled over again, head bumping against my hand. Another thrill of pleasure. I scratched behind her ears. She rubbed her cheek against my thumb. I moved lower, put my whole hand on her chest.

Lightning fast, her claws came out and she wrapped herself around my hand, biting. I shook her off, accidentally bumping her nose. She leaped up to the railing, jumped to the fence, and was gone. I rested my head on my knees, my brother's words echoing in my head. *You pressured her.*

All my life I'd been fighting for, or against, something. Before, when things had gotten difficult, I'd always been able to comfort myself by thinking that at least I was helping people, at least I was doing *some* good on this earth – all the sacrifices were worth it. Now it seemed that all I'd sacrificed was my daughter.

Inside, I heard the phone ring. When I checked it, I recognized Kevin's cell number. I put the phone down. I wasn't in the mood to talk. Despondent, I decided to go for a drive. I didn't have a destination in mind, just let my car and my heart lead me until I found myself heading out of the city. This time, when I drove through Goldstream Park, I thought about a gas tanker that had recently overturned when a drunk driver lost control of the truck. Cleanup crews had worked for days excising the contaminated soil, but it was too late for the fish. The gas had oozed into their gills and killed them in minutes.

One terrible mistake, and it would take years to recover.

At the top of the Malahat, I turned toward Shawnigan, deciding to hike to the trestle and see for myself how the repairs were going. My body was still sore from falling at Garret's, but it wasn't a long walk from the gravel parking lot, and it might loosen my muscles. I was also hoping it would help lighten my mood, or at least my thoughts, so I could see clear of the fog surrounding me. When I'd parked my car, I grabbed my gloves and threw on some hiking boots I kept in the trunk, then started down the gravel road, remembering when it was still covered with railway tracks and ties, the wood hot and sticky with creosote in the summer.

When I'd reached the trestle, I stopped and admired the majestic site, over six hundred feet of crisscrossed wooden beams curving out across the river, meeting with the forest on the other side, mountain ranges and trees in every direction. I couldn't see the river – it was probably over one hundred feet below – but I could hear it. A few big machines were parked on the other side, and metal construction fencing blocked off both ends, but I found an area where I could climb under. I walked onto the trestle, now a boardwalk, remembering how as kids we used to dare each other to stay on until the train came, always running when we heard the whistle. The last train had crossed over in 1979.

Many things had changed since then.

In the middle of the trestle, I leaned on the edge of the top railing, feeling the breeze whistle down through the valley, carrying with it the scent of fir trees and forest, cold, crisp mountain air. I breathed it in, trying to clear my mind. But I couldn't stop going over every moment of Lisa's childhood, all the times I'd left her alone with Garret. I was her mother. I should've protected her, should've seen what was happening.

I was gazing down at the river, thinking of my own mother, when I saw a movement to my left. I glanced up and spotted someone walking toward the trestle. When I realized it was a lone male, my body stiffened. Had Aaron sent someone after me? I held my breath and let it out in a relieved rush when the man's features came into focus, and I noticed a German shepherd beside him. When Robbie finally reached me, his face was flushed and his breathing ragged, like he'd been walking fast.

'What're you doing up here?'

'I needed to do some thinking. What are *you* doing here?'

'I was working at a job site at the end of the road and recognized your car – you have that hospital staff-parking thing on your rearview mirror.'

I nodded. 'Right.' I looked back down at the water. 'Remember when we used to dare each other to stay on until the train came?'

Robbie rested his elbows on the edge of the railing, looked around. 'We never made it. Dad would've killed us if he knew what we were doing.'

I gave a small laugh as I leaned on the railing near Robbie, thinking that the train probably hadn't seemed as dangerous to us as our father.

He said, 'So what did you need to think about?'

While I considered how to answer, Robbie reached for his pocket, still searching for his smokes. When he didn't find them, he shook his head. 'Damn dog.' The damn dog looked up at him, circled a few times, then fell asleep.

I took a breath and spilled it all. I hadn't meant to share everything, not about Garret or what he'd done to Lisa, but once I started talking, I couldn't stop. When I told Robbie that I thought someone was watching my house and that I'd been getting threatening phone calls, his mouth tightened to a thin line.

At the end I said, 'I'm scared for Lisa. She's vulnerable right now, but I also have a bad feeling about Joseph. The way he looked ... He's close to the edge. I don't think it would take much to set him off.'

When I was done, we both stared down at the swirling river for a while. Far below, one lone tree limb spun around and around, caught in the current.

Robbie cleared his throat. 'I remember what happened at the commune.'

I turned. 'What do you mean?'

'Aaron, the way he looked at you. I didn't like you being alone with him.'

Now I remembered all the times Robbie had interrupted us when Aaron was talking to me, and how ashamed I'd felt, worried he'd find out my secret. I'd snapped at Robbie, told him to leave me alone – and he did.

Robbie continued. 'You were right. Willow and me, we were more than friends.' His face flushed. 'Guess you could say she was the first woman I really cared about – last one too ...' He drifted off, swallowed hard a few times. 'She was from Alberta.' So I'd remembered that part right. It wasn't much consolation. 'Her parents were dead, and she was being raised by an uncle and an aunt, but I got the feeling her uncle was trying to mess around with her, so she ran away.'

'Do you know if she really left the commune?'

He glanced at both ends of the trestle, then looked at Brew, like it was easier to talk to him.

'We met at the beach by Mason's Store. I flirted with her and told her to come back to the commune, that we had good weed. So she left her friends and climbed in the truck ... She trusted me.'

I held my breath, sensing what Robbie was telling me was taking all his courage, and that one movement on my part could stop his flow, maybe forever.

'But I screwed up. I let her down.'

When he'd paused for a long time, I whispered, 'What happened to her?'

'He buried her.' Robbie met my gaze, and the torment in his eyes broke my heart. He looked away, blinking hard and clearing his throat.

My blood was pulsing loud in my ears. Everything else seemed distant and muffled. The river a dull hum. 'She's dead?'

He nodded. 'Aaron wanted her vest. She wouldn't give it up – I told her it wasn't worth pissing him off over. He was already angry at her for arguing about spiking trees. I'd warned her that he'd use it as a way to make her leave.' A bitter laugh. 'I thought that was the worst that could happen.'

I remembered following Robbie and Willow down to the river after she'd disagreed with Aaron, wondering what they'd been talking about. Now I knew.

Robbie continued. 'She'd told him he wasn't the only person who could help people. He hated that. We'd had a fight the next day too, because she'd decided she was sick of Aaron's crap, and she wanted to leave anyway. She wanted me to go with her, but I wouldn't, not without you and Mom.'

As Robbie paused, I wondered why Mom finally did leave. Was it really because of social services, and to give her marriage another try? Or had she actually been afraid of Aaron? Was that why my father showed up with a gun?

He started talking again. 'Willow said she was going to take you with her. She wouldn't say why, just that you weren't safe there.'

I was stunned. I thought about how young Willow had been, only seventeen, and I was touched and saddened by her courage.

Robbie was still talking. 'I told her I'd call the cops and report her as a runaway. She was pissed off, said she expected better from me. That's when I got mad and told her she wasn't as smart as she thought, and I walked away. I looked back from the road and saw Aaron go after her, but I didn't follow . . .'

I held my hand over my mouth, waiting for the rest of the horrible story.

'I thought he'd talk some sense into her.' His voice was strangled with emotion. He paused, caught his breath. After a moment, he continued. 'Later, I'd cooled off and felt bad. I thought maybe she was right – we should try to leave with you. When I came back, everyone was still on the reflection walk, and I couldn't find Willow. Then I walked around to where we'd been digging . . .'

'Oh no. The outhouses . . .' I remembered now. The men had been digging holes behind the new cabins. That's what Aaron had been working on that day.

He nodded. 'One of the holes was filled back up. I grabbed the shovel and dug as fast as I could, got down to one of those forty-five-gallon drums we'd used for paint . . . I pried off the lid, and I could just see the top of her head.'

Tears streamed down my cheeks. Robbie was staring at Brew, his face expressionless, like he had to disconnect from his words to be able to speak them.

'I tried to feel her pulse. But she was already cold, and there was blood in her hair—' Robbie's voice broke, his shoulders stiff and his neck tight with the effort to rein in his emotions. 'Her nails were torn and her fingers all bloody. The back of the lid, it was scratched. He must've hit her, with the shovel or something, to stun her, but she was still conscious when he put her in there.'

'My God.'

Robbie was talking fast now, trying to get it all out. The horrible truth finally bursting free. 'I was going to call for help, but none of you were back yet, then Aaron came around the corner. I told him I was going to the cops. He said if I broke up the group, he'd have to punish me by taking away something that I loved. I knew he meant he'd hurt you or Mom. He said he didn't want to do it, but that the Light would make him, like it had with Willow. It was her fault she died because she wouldn't give him her vest. He had to protect the family.'

It hadn't been about the vest. He wanted her gone.

Robbie said, 'I told him he'd killed her. And he said no, he'd come back to release her.'

He came back to release her. I couldn't have known this story, but it seemed familiar, a hard knot of dread and

391

fear in the pit of my stomach. I ran my mind over the words but couldn't think of when I would have heard them before.

Robbie was shaking his head, his hands fists on the railing. 'He was so sick. You could tell he actually believed it – that it wasn't his fault that she died.'

I had no problem believing he'd convinced himself he wasn't responsible for her death.

'What did you do with her?'

'He made me put the lid back on the barrel, then we filled the hole, and he made me dig a new one for the outhouse. I sat in the woods all that night, watching over her grave, just kept hoping that it was a crazy nightmare. She's still there. I go there sometimes and tell her I'm sorry . . . ' He drifted off.

I said, 'What are you going to do? We can't leave her there any longer.'

'I know.' He shook his head, a quick angry motion. 'I was worried about him coming after you – he stops by every couple of years, letting me know he's keeping an eye on you, so I won't say anything.' That's why Aaron had let Robbie walk around for decades with this knowledge. He'd used me as the threat.

'Is that why you told me that you saw her hitchhiking down the road?'

He nodded. 'I wanted you to drop it. But you're already in danger now, and getting him arrested is the only way to keep him away from you and Lisa. I'll talk to the cops.' He searched his pocket again for phantom cigarettes. Brew looked at him with concern, his nose twitching, sensing the anxiety in the air.

'We can go to the police now. I'll take you.'

'Okay, let's do this. But I'll follow in my truck with Brew.'

As we walked back to our vehicles, we didn't talk much, but I could feel the first tentacles of healing, a subtle shift. So much made sense now. How he'd changed when we got home, the coil of anger that always simmered in his eyes. Why he'd never let himself get close to another woman.

When we got to the station, we were informed that Corporal Cruikshank was out and wouldn't be back for about an hour. The officer on duty said it would be better if we talked to her as she was already handling the investigation in Shawnigan. Robbie decided to wait at the station. When I said I'd stay with him, he answered, 'Nah. I'd rather do this on my own anyway.'

'You sure? I don't mind waiting.'

He shook his head. 'Just go back to Victoria and hang tight.'

I gave him my new Victoria cell number and he agreed to call after he was finished giving his statement. Before heading down to Victoria, I drove back to Mary's to tell her the news – Aaron's days as a free man were numbered. When I got there, she was digging in her garden. I stopped near the gate and climbed out. Mary turned at the sound of my car, squinted at me as I walked toward her.

I said, 'I need to speak with you again if you have a moment.'

'I thought about what you said last time, but I'm not talking to the cops.' She continued with her task.

'You might not have to. That's why I came here.'

She turned around, the spade in her hand. 'What's happened?'

I told her what Robbie had shared and that he was back at the station, waiting to give his statement.

'Aaron will never get out after this. As soon as the story breaks, other victims of abuse will likely come forward.'

She bowed her head and covered her face in dirty hands. She took a shuddering breath, like she might be crying.

I said, 'Are you okay?' I was confused about her reaction.

Speaking into her hand, she said, 'I want you to leave. I need to be alone.'

I wasn't ready to leave yet, not without an explanation. Something about her tears didn't feel right. 'Are you upset about Willow?'

She nodded. 'Willow had come to me for help, about her vest. She wanted to keep it. But I wasn't ready to go against Aaron yet.' She looked down at her missing finger. 'That was before this.' She looked back up at me, her eyes wet. 'I wouldn't help her, so she said she was going to leave the commune.'

I crouched down. 'You didn't know Aaron would hurt her.'

She said, 'I thought she was wrong, that she should give him her vest. I was caught up in everything he was saying, like all the others. I told him she was planning on leaving. I *told* him.'

So there might've been more to Aaron's reason for killing Willow. I wondered now if they'd argued, and Willow had told him she was taking me. 'The police might want to know that. It would help their case, show motive and—'

She stiffened, the pain in her eyes disappearing into anger. 'I already told you I'm not talking to the police. I want you to go now.'

She got up and walked toward the house, leaving the spade still stabbed into the earth.

Chapter Thirty-three

On the way home, I mulled everything over. I felt bad for Mary, but if she didn't tell the police what she knew, I wondered if I should fill them in. Even with Robbie's statement, there was a chance Aaron could get off because of lack of evidence. Lost in thought, I flinched when my phone rang. I glanced at the call display and felt conflicted when I saw Kevin's number again. Part of me wanted to tell him everything that had happened, but the other part wanted to wait until I knew what the police were going to do. After a couple of rings, the phone went silent.

I had time before Robbie was going to call, so I went into the hospital and did some paperwork in my office at Mental Health, hoping it might distract me. I'd also hoped to avoid Kevin until I'd had a chance to think everything through. I thought that he taught group on Wednesdays, but when I came out of the bathroom, he was coming down the hall.

He said, 'Okay, I'm getting the definite feeling that you're avoiding me. I've left you a couple of messages . . .'

'No, no. I'm sorry. I've wanted to talk to you. There are just some things happening in my life that I can't go into at the moment.'

He nodded, but he sounded a little annoyed. 'If you aren't interested in pursuing this . . .' He made a motion between us. 'You can just tell me.'

'It's not that. You're a wonderful person and I enjoy your company immensely, but I'm dealing with a lot of personal issues right now.'

His expression softened. 'I'd like to help.'

'I don't want to involve you in more of my problems.'

'I think I'm already pretty involved.' He smiled.

'You've been great.' I smiled back. 'But honestly, I don't think I'm ready for more than friendship – not when I'm dealing with so much. It wouldn't be giving us a fair chance. We already have enough complications.'

'Like what?'

I was flustered. 'Uh . . . We work together, I'm older than you.'

He raised an eyebrow. 'Really? You didn't strike me as the kind of person who runs from a few complications.'

'I'm not running away. I promise. I just don't think it's good timing until I sort a few things out with my daughter.'

'Well, the offer for dinner still stands, whenever you're

ready, or if you need a break from it all.' He gave my shoulder a squeeze. 'Hang in there, okay?'

As I watched him walk down the hall, I felt a moment of regret and pushed it away. It had been the right thing to do. I had to deal with this on my own.

I'd only been at the hospital for about thirty minutes, but I couldn't focus on paperwork, so I drove home to wait for Robbie's call. Meanwhile, I phoned Tammy, who almost hung up when she heard my voice. As soon as I said, 'Aaron's going to be arrested,' she paused. I told her that my brother was going to the police. Before I could say anything else, she said good-bye and quickly hung up, leaving me to assume her husband had walked in. I hoped she was okay.

When another half hour had passed without word from Robbie, I began to worry. It had been almost two hours since I'd left Shawnigan. I tried his cell, but it went straight to voice mail and he didn't have a landline. I told myself to give it some time. He might've been delayed at the station. I was sure they had lots of questions. I waited for another twenty minutes, then tried to call Robbie again. Still no answer. Something had to be wrong.

I called the station. Corporal Cruikshank said she'd come back to the station late and the officer at the front told her Robbie had gone home to drop his dog off and planned on coming straight back. That was an hour ago. My pulse spiked at that news. Where had he gone? I told her what Robbie had planned on sharing – and then, as we spoke, I began to wonder if someone at the commune had found out what he'd been about to report. Had Tammy contacted her sister? I voiced my fears to the corporal. She said that it was unlikely and that Robbie might've just changed his mind, or been waylaid somewhere. She also said she'd send a car out to Robbie's to check on him, but she added, 'Is it possible that he had more to do with the event? He might've had second thoughts . . .'

Instantly angry, I said, 'Not a chance.'

She just said, 'I'll let you know if we find him.'

I grabbed my purse and headed to Shawnigan. I had no idea what I was going to do once I got there, but I had to try to find Robbie. I slowed down as I approached his house, trying to see from the road if there was any activity or police cars outside, but his place looked quiet, almost serene in the afternoon sun.

I'd parked and was about to call the station again, when the officer from Shawnigan called. She'd been to Robbie's, and there was no sign of him – but I should keep her posted if he still didn't show up. Frustrated, I decided to have a look myself. I got out of the car and walked around, calling his name, and Brew's name, only hearing birds in response. The officer was right, there was no sign of him or his dog, but his truck was there. I knocked on his front door. Silence. I searched under the front mat for a key, didn't find one. Then I peered through his windows, trying to see if he was lying hurt somewhere. His coffee mug was on the table, a pad of paper beside it. I checked his shop, but everything was also still and quiet.

From the front of the shop, which was higher than the house, I could see where he'd been working in the field just below. The excavator was sitting near a mound of dirt that looked fresh, not yet dried out in the sun. That's what he was probably working on this morning. Then I remembered that he'd also been at a job site at the end of the road. I drove down that way. When I spotted Robbie's backhoe at a construction site, I stopped and talked to a carpenter, who said Robbie hadn't been there since that morning. I sat in my car, thinking. If Joseph and Aaron had come after him, where would they take him? The old commune?

I drove out there and checked the barn, the cabins, down at the river, calling Robbie's name, even searching the area where Willow was buried in case Aaron had decided to dig up her body, but the ground was undisturbed. I'd felt ill, seeing the dry fir needles coating the earth, knowing what was underneath that peaceful surface. I thought of Willow's body, curled up in a forty-five-gallon drum, and backed away from the area, alert to every noise in the forest, until I was safe in my car with the doors locked.

*

On the way back to the village, my iPhone finally got coverage and a call came through. I recognized the number right away.

'Mary, I can't—'

'I need to see you. I've been thinking about everything you said. I'm ready to talk.' She sounded upset.

'I'm sorry, but I don't have time right now. I'm trying to find my brother. I think Aaron's done something to him.'

'How . . . ' She paused, like she was trying to take it all in. 'How did he know he was going to the police?'

'I don't know. But Robbie never made it to the station.'

'Come get me. We'll look together – I might know some places. And if we have to, I'll go to the police with you and tell them what I know.'

'Be there in ten minutes.'

When I pulled in the driveway, the dogs didn't come running. Thinking they were just inside the house, I ran up to the front door and rapped hard. Mary whipped open the door, pulling on a coat. 'Come in for a second.'

'I don't have time—'

'I need to show you something.' Her face was anxious and pale.

I stepped in and she closed the door behind me. She quickly walked toward the kitchen, saying over her shoulder, 'I remember a place they used to hide up in the mountains. I can show you, on the map.'

I hurried after her – and stopped abruptly when I saw Aaron sitting at the kitchen table, with Daniel standing behind. Mary sat down across from Aaron, tears on her face. Something cold and hard pressed into my side.

Joseph was holding a gun on me.

I put my hands up, my blood roaring loud in my head as my mind tried to make sense of what was happening. Why was Daniel here? My breath left my chest in a rush when I realized he was also holding a gun, but it was by his side and he didn't look comfortable with it. He was staring down at his hand, his face pale, and his hair around his forehead wet with sweat.

'Daniel, what are you doing here?'

He met my eyes, then quickly looked away again, shamefaced.

My pulse hammered hard, my throat was tight with panic. My hands still in front of me, I shifted slightly, so I could keep an eye on Joseph, who'd deteriorated even further since I'd last seen him. His hair was greasy, his face pale, and his eyes bloodshot, like he hadn't slept for days. He looked jumpy, on edge. I said to Aaron, 'What do you want?'

'We need to talk.'

They'd brought me here for a reason, and I doubted it was just to talk. That shocking thought led to another. 'Lisa, is she—'

'Lisa's doing very well.' His tone was casual, almost friendly, no sense of urgency.

'What did you do with Robbie?'

'We tried to make him see why going to the police would be a mistake, but he wasn't ready to listen. It's up to the Light now.'

My breath caught in my throat. 'What does that mean?'

'When he's ready to surrender to his fears, he'll be freed.'

I didn't believe that Aaron ever planned on freeing my brother. Wherever Robbie was, he didn't have long. I faced Daniel. Maybe I'd have better luck with him. 'Please tell me where my brother is. He's done nothing wrong.'

Sounding overwhelmed, Daniel said, 'I thought we were just talking—'

Aaron said, 'Enough.'

Daniel stiffened.

I said, 'I told you, Daniel, they aren't what you think.' I still didn't know what they had planned, but I sensed that things had already gone further than Daniel had expected. 'You don't want to go to jail for anything this man has—'

Aaron said, 'Daniel knows where he belongs. He's my son.'

Shock staggered through me. I looked back and forth between the men. Could it be true? I said, 'He's your *father*?'

Mary finally looked up, her eyes focused on Daniel,

worry in her face. But it wasn't worry for herself – it was a mother's worry. Now I saw it. Yes, Daniel looked like his father, but he had his mother's green eyes. She must've been the one who warned them Robbie was going to the police.

I spoke to Daniel, confused. 'Did Heather know?'

Daniel shook his head. 'No one knew. I was overseas working at one of the communes. I didn't want special treatment.' His gaze slid to his father. Special treatment or not, he'd still wanted his father's approval. I noticed that Joseph's gaze also flicked to his brother, but then he stared slightly off to the side, his face attentive, like he was hearing or seeing something that no one else did.

I had to keep a conversation going with Daniel, in hopes of distracting Joseph, who was now starting to look agitated. His gaze moved all over the room and even up to the ceiling.

'Why did you marry Heather? For her money?'

He looked shocked. 'No, of course not. I loved her.'

'But Aaron encouraged you, he matched you up. He wanted you to marry her because she was wealthy – he *knew*, Daniel.' I threw out another quick thought. 'Did he pressure you to convince her to move back after her parents died?'

He hesitated, a look crossing his face that told me I might not be far off.

Then Joseph, speaking to the side again as though answering someone else, said, 'The Light said they had to die, and I was the one chosen to release them.' His voice had an odd, fervent tone, a terrifying intensity that signaled someone no longer in check with reality.

Daniel stared at the back of his father's head, shock in his eyes as he said, 'You *killed* them?'

Aaron glanced behind him. 'It was their time.'

Daniel was stunned – I could see the horror in his face, and the anger. I didn't know how much longer they'd be content to talk, but I had to keep them distracted.

I spoke to Aaron. 'You killed Heather's parents when she was still vulnerable from the miscarriage – you pushed her over the edge.'

Daniel's knuckles were white on the gun, a slight shake making the barrel tremble against his leg. He looked back and forth between me and his father. He was furious, no doubt about it, but would he do anything about it?

Aaron said, 'They weren't committed to a spiritual path. Her father was a lawyer – he worked for the logging companies.' Aaron sounded disgusted, and I remembered his long-standing hatred of logging. He added, 'Heather was weak.'

Daniel jerked back, his mouth open, and in his eyes, an expression of pain. He walked around the front of the table, to face his father. 'You did this? I told you Heather was still having a hard time and you *kill* her parents? That's *murder*.'

Aaron said, 'I did it because I love you. She was hurting

you. I could see your struggle – you were weakening, losing faith in our beliefs.'

Daniel looked conflicted, wanting, needing, to believe his father had good intentions and that he had cared for him.

I said, 'He doesn't love you, Daniel. If he loved you, he wouldn't have kept you a secret all these years. He's using you.'

Joseph shoved the gun in my side as he said, 'Just shut up – shut up.'

I held my hands out. Aaron stood up, took the gun from Daniel's hand before he had a chance to react, and headed toward me. My blood flooded with adrenaline. I backed up a step and shouted at Mary and Daniel. 'Are you just going to sit there and let them hurt me?'

Mary flinched, her face terrified, but didn't say anything.

Daniel said, 'What are you going to do with her? Can't we let her go?'

Aaron said, 'Her fear is blocking her from seeing the truth. She'll ruin everything we've worked for, all the good we've done. Joseph. It's *time.*'

Joseph reached for me. I kicked out, but he spun me around and pinned both my arms behind my back. I twisted and turned, rearing against him, slamming my head back, hoping to fracture his nose, but he dodged at the last moment. I struggled to break his hold, but nothing was working.

My breath came out in hard gasps.

I tried to calm down. If I broke free now, I'd get trapped in the house in minutes. If he was going to take me outside, I had a better chance of making a run for it. There was thick forest behind Mary's place, and I'd have cover if they started firing. But first, I had to get away.

Joseph began to drag me to the door. I struggled, but I was biding my time. Aaron followed behind with the gun. Daniel put his hands to his head, like he couldn't believe what was happening, and turned back to his mother, who was now sobbing. Daniel spun back around and followed us, but he looked panicky.

I said to Aaron, 'Is this how you do it? You make your brother do your dirty work?'

Aaron said, 'The Light wants me to use whatever tools are available to share his word. Sometimes his message flows through my aides.'

Then it came to me. 'You didn't kill Willow; you made Joseph do it.' I could see it now, the missing piece. Joseph back early from the walk, Aaron whispering in his ear, the dark and twisted thoughts, sending paranoid words into his head, feeding his fear, and unleashing him on Willow.

Aaron calmly said, 'My brother's on his own spiritual path.'

'You know he's sick.' It all fit into place. 'You knew what to say, so that he'd go after her.' Could I also manipulate Joseph somehow?

Joseph twisted my arms again, dragged me another couple of feet.

I gasped from the pain, trying to focus. No, Joseph was too loyal to his brother. I had to work on Daniel. It was my only chance.

'Daniel, he's murdered another girl before, and he's going to murder me. You'll be an accomplice.'

Aaron sounded annoyed as he kept moving us toward the door. 'Don't believe anything she says. She's trying to distract you.'

Daniel was still following, but his face was desperate and stricken, like he didn't know what to do or how to stop the events from unfolding.

We stumbled down the steps, the backs of my heels hitting each one. At the bottom, Joseph spun me around, then marched me toward the barn. Terror, loud and violent, began to shriek in my head. Was he going to kill me now? He tripped on a rock, and his grip loosened. I twisted hard and elbowed him in the gut, finally breaking his hold. I ran as fast as I could, my lungs screaming.

Go, go, go.

A body slammed into my back, and I hit the ground hard, my teeth going into my bottom lip. My mouth filled with the metallic taste of blood. Joseph pulled me up. I reared backward, connecting with his chin, sending a jolt of pain down my neck and spine. He grabbed me in a bear hug from behind, squeezing until I started to feel faint. Then he forced me toward the barn, my heels dug futilely into the ground, trying to slow the process, but I was off balance, being propelled backward. Helpless and grunting with exertion, I tried to get some air back in my lungs, breathing in big, panicky gasps. We were almost at the gate.

When we reached the barn, my entire system went into survival mode and I struggled like a wild animal caught in a net. Joseph grunted a couple of times as my blows connected, but he still didn't let go. I stepped down hard on his instep, gouging and biting at his wrists – fighting for my life. He almost dropped me again, and I managed to get one hand onto the barn gate, my nails tearing as he tried to pull me away. Aaron smacked my wrist with the butt of his gun. Pain shot up my arm and exploded behind my eyeballs. I screamed. Joseph slapped a hand down over my mouth and dragged me the rest of the way into the barn.

My body was paralyzed with terror now. My heart beating so hard in my chest I thought I might pass out. I could no longer fight. I was going to die.

We were at a door. Aaron opened it. It was dark inside, looked like a small storage room. The smell of stale horse feed and mold wafted out. Joseph force-walked me into the dark. I came back to life. My body heaving and jerking. I kicked up and out, braced my legs on the sides of the door. Now both their hands were on me, and they thrust me into the room. I fell onto the floor, my knee cracking on concrete. In front of me, there was a small freezer, not much bigger than me, old and covered with rust spots and filth. Joseph picked me up, holding me while Aaron lifted the lid on the bin. I fought in Joseph's arms, my breath panting out. Aaron grabbed my legs, and they dumped me into the freezer. I landed on a pile of grain, my body sinking into it slightly, my knees bent.

The lid was closing. I slammed my fists into it. *'Let me out of here.'*

Sounds from the outside. Aaron's voice, 'Where's the padlock?'

Daniel, his voice hollow and shocked, 'Why are you putting her in there?'

Aaron's voice, 'Joseph, just put the pitchfork in the latch.'

Another noise, something scraping against the side of the freezer.

I hit my hands repeatedly on the lid, kicked up with my feet. Finally, I paused, my breath jerking out of me in angry sobs. How was I going to get out?

On the other side, Aaron's muffled voice said, 'Daniel, go back to the house. It will be okay – we'll let her out when she's released her fear.'

I yelled, 'You're lying. You're never going to let me out. The police know I'm here – I called them on my way. They'll be here any minute.'

Aaron spoke at the corner of the lid, his voice so close I jumped in the dark. 'Now you're the one lying.'

I heard a few rustles on the other side, then footsteps walking away.

I was alone.

Chapter Thirty-four

As soon as they left, I hit and pushed up at the lid with my hands over and over and over. The plastic on the inside was old and brittle, breaking in places as I hit it. I peeled some off, ripping the insulation out, and pushed up on the metal of the lid. I still couldn't break through it. I also tried to use my feet to kick up, but I couldn't get enough force. Finally, my body bruised and battered, I had to rest, gulping for air, almost hyperventilating. The darkness pressed in, squeezing all the air out of my body. My legs were vibrating, my heart whooshing in my ears. The world tilted sideways and I thought I might pass out. Then I remembered.

We're in the field, picking huckleberries, while everyone else is on a walk. The air smells dense and heavy with heat. I'm wearing shorts and a loose T-shirt, but the sweat makes it stick to my body. I keep pulling it away from my front, not liking the way Aaron's looking at me. My hands are stained

412

red with berries, and I try to wipe them on my shorts. He's watching me, and says, 'I want to meditate.'

The berries I've eaten churn in my stomach, their sweet taste now bitter in my mouth. I know what he really wants.

I say, 'I don't want to do that anymore.'

'Don't you care about your mom?'

'You're not helping her. She's getting worse again.' In the last couple of weeks, she'd been moody and quiet, sleeping in her cabin all day, barely eating.

He says, 'In our meditations, she said that she's been thinking about killing herself again. I've been talking her out of it, healing her. But maybe I don't want to do that anymore either. Maybe she'd be happier on the other side.'

I stare at him. He's telling the truth, I can see it in his face.

He says, 'Lie down, Nadine.'

I get on my knees and lie on my back in the long dry grass. My eyes are already filling with tears. I try to think about the grass scratching against my leg, the buzz of dragonflies floating in the air nearby. But I'm scared.

He lies down next to me and presses his mouth against mine. My hands grab helplessly at the poppies. He undoes my jeans shorts, puts his hand down them and touches me between my legs. He yanks them farther down, and rolls on top of me, starts pulling down his shorts, and tries to shove himself inside me.

It hurts, and I cry out. He presses his mouth harder against mine.

I twist my face away. 'Stop. I don't want to.' I push at him

413

and hit him with my fists. I kick out, kneeing him in the groin. He yells, cupping himself. I pull up my shorts and take off running for the barn, looking for my mother, my brother, anyone who can help, forgetting in my panic that they're all on their walk. His footsteps are loud behind me. I make it partway up one of the haystacks when he grabs my foot, pulling me down, until I'm close enough for him to grip my hair, yanking my head back. I try to scream, but he slaps his hand over my mouth. He lets go of my hair, wraps his arm tight around my chest and shoulders, so my arms are pinned, squeezing the breath out of my lungs. Then he lifts me against the side of his body, like a sack of grain, and carries me to the back of the barn, where they've been digging a root cellar under the storage room.

He stops by the hole, turning his body so that I'm over the edge, my feet dangling, and removes his hand from my mouth. I look down. At first I don't understand why he's showing the cellar to me. Then I realize the hole is only a few feet deep and wide, and I think he's going to make me dig, as punishment.

Then he says, 'Do you see, Nadine? Do you see where you're going?'

Now I understand. He's going to put me in the hole.

I kick and struggle, but he's holding tight. He steps backward and swings me around, then grabs one of the old metal barrels that are stacked against the wall. With one hand, he pries the lid off. He lifts my body over the barrel.

I catch a flicker out of the corner of my eye, a shadow

414

moving by the door, blocking the crack of light. 'Help!' I yell, thinking someone is there, someone will save me. But only a flurry of birds rushes up to the rafters.

I bite at his arm, try to get my legs on the outside of the barrel, but he punches me hard in the temple. Stunned, I'm limp in his arms. He jams my legs into the barrel, uses his knee to press down on my back. I grasp at the metal rim. He raps my knuckles, bends my fingers back until I have to let go. He's grunting with exertion, scrambling for something, then the lid is coming over my head, and he's pushing down with all his weight. I'm screaming, loud, but it's muffled.

He hammers the lid in place with his fists.

There are only a few inches of air between my body and the lid. I'm surrounded by metal, my knees up near my chin, no room to move, to breathe.

The barrel is tipping. I land on my side. I stop screaming, trying to make sense of what's happening. Now the barrel is rolling, the sensation of falling. I drop with a thud, my body slamming into the metal sides. I gasp for breath.

For a second, everything's silent. Then I get some air, scream again and again, but no one comes. I'm hot and sweaty. It drips down my face. I'm panting.

I hear a thud, realize it's dirt hitting the barrel. I yell, 'Please, no, please let me out!'

More dirt hits the barrel. I get one hand up by my ear, push at the lid, but it won't budge. Thick heat presses in on me like a blanket, closing my throat up with each breath. I claw at the smooth walls, try to squirm my body around,

and it makes the air thicker, even harder to breathe. **I'm**
crying and gasping. I hear strangling sounds from my throat,
more dirt falling, over and over. Then silence. I'm moaning,
sobbing in broken whimpers.

A soft thud, like someone jumped into the hole.

'Please, please. Let me out!' I'm frantic, crying.

Aaron's voice, 'Are you ready to surrender to the Light?'

'Yes, yes. I'm ready.'

Silence again. Then, 'I don't believe you.'

Another thump as dirt hits the barrel. Shovelful after
shovelful rains down. I scream, a frantic high-pitched
screech, until I can't get my breath and start hyperventilat-
ing, tears and snot mixing on my face.

Finally, he stops, and calls down, faint through the dirt
and metal, 'Do you want to be released from your fear,
Nadine?'

'Yes,' I sob. 'Yes. Please. I'll do whatever you want.'

A pause. He's going to let me out. My body fills with
relief.

Then he starts throwing more dirt down. I can't tell how
much now, whether I'm almost buried, but the sound is get-
ting softer. I've peed myself. I think of my mother, of Robbie,
and my father. I'm going to die. I close my eyes, chanting in
my mind, Please, please, please, please, please, please.

The noise stops. There's nothing but silence. Has he left?
I'm dizzy, shuddering with sobs and panic. Seconds tick by.
I'm sure now that he's gone. I can't last much longer. I gasp
for air, but I can't get my breath.

Then a sound near me, something scrapes the top of the barrel. I tense. Another scrape, rhythmic, and I realize he's shoveling away at the dirt. A surge of hope, followed by fear. Is it just another game? I push again at the lid, beg with the last of my strength, 'Please. I don't want to die.'

Then the sound of metal against metal, the lid is being pried off. I blink up at the light, gasping and gagging for air. Half-blind, I can only see Aaron's shape in the light from the doorway. He reaches down, lifts me out, setting me on my feet, but I'm disoriented and weak, and I fall to the ground.

He crouches in front, clasps the back of my head, and looks into my eyes.

'You can't run away from me, Nadine. We're family now.'

I slur my words, my tongue and lips dry, my throat raw from screaming. 'I'm sorry ... I'm sorry. Don't hurt me, please.'

His hand on the back of my neck grips harder. He leans close, his body reeking of sweat. He's about to say something. Then, in the distance, we hear the singing voices of the commune members, coming back from their walk.

I open my mouth to scream.

He slaps me. My head rocks back, hitting the barrel behind it, stunning me again. He puts his hand on my mouth, grinding my lips into my teeth. 'If you tell anyone about this, I'll do it again – but I won't let you out.'

His hand presses harder. I taste blood. He says, 'I'll bury you alive. Do you understand?'

I nod, terrified.

He says, 'Wait for a few minutes, then go down to the river and clean up.' He leans close to my ear, his voice muffled and distorted and seeming to come from far away. 'Remember, tell anyone, and I'll leave you to die next time.'

He lifts me out of the hole, dumping me on the floor of the storage room.

Then he is gone.

After a few moments, I pull myself together, stagger away from the barn, through the back field, down to the river, going to a pool farther below the commune where none of the members swim. Crying and shivering as I wash myself in the frigid water. I wash my clothes too, spreading them across a rock in the sun, curl my naked and bruised body up into a ball, hiding behind a big rock, the warm sand wrapping around me. I fall asleep.

Hours later, when I come back to the commune, my mother asks where I've been. I tell her I've been at the river. That I split my lip on a rock.

I can't remember anything else.

Now, I forced my body to relax, to breathe in and out. I was terrified, my legs shaking, but I had to break this down into moments, analyze the situation, and take it step by step. *Take some deep breaths. You can get out of here if you keep calm.*

Aaron wasn't coming back for me. He had warned me years ago, and his rage was too great. This time he would let me die. Now that my eyes had adjusted to the dark, I searched for a crack of light at the edges of the lid, but I was just surrounded by blackness and the scent of old horse feed, musty and rancid. My head filled with terrifying memories of freezers being recalled in the seventies because so many children died, and all the warnings to never play in one.

I tried to calculate how much air I had, how long I could live. I knew that if I panted too much, I would use it up faster, so I tried to slow my breathing. I didn't think I had much time, the air already felt different, my head light and my blood seeming loud in my ears. I tried to accept the fact that there was a very good chance that I was going to die. I thought of my family. What would happen to Lisa? Would she ever know where my body was? Tears leaked from my eyes as I thought of Robbie, wondering if he was also buried somewhere, staring up at a lid, screaming for help. Would death come easy for us? Would we just fall asleep, or die gasping for breath, suffocating in our makeshift graves? Panic surged over me again, rage at my helplessness. I hit up at the lid, an angry shove that got me nowhere. I burst into tears, sobbing in the dark like I had as a child. I pressed my hands to my eyes, took some breaths, and tried to refocus.

I had two choices. Accept my fate, pray that Daniel would realize his father intended to kill me, and somehow overpower both men. Hope that Mary would call the police, that somehow, some way, I'd get lucky and survive this.

My other choice was to die trying to escape.

I bent my knees and, bracing my arms on either side of the freezer, kicked my heels into the wall. It didn't give. I tried to push against the side walls, the wall behind my head, and the lid. The freezer was solid.

I wondered if I would have more strength if I used my shoulders to push up. Angling my body and trying to double over in the small space, I reached down and braced my hands on the floor of the freezer. Then I reared up as hard as I could, using all the strength of my back. My neck and shoulders were in agony from the blow, my knees throbbed. But I thought I felt a slight give. Could the latch on the lock be rusted? Or maybe the screws that attached it to the freezer?

I pushed up hard again and heard a slight noise, like something might be giving. I pushed up again and again, sweating and grunting with exertion. I took a break, sucking in big gulps of air, scared about how much oxygen I was using, but then the thought: *If I'm going to die, at least I'll die faster.*

With the last of my strength, I slammed my back up against the lid, sending a jolt of pain down my spine. Then a louder, tearing sound, a feeling that the lid was loosening, like the lock was giving out. I pushed up again, using everything in my body. A rip of metal as the bolts started to pull out. Now I just had to push a few more times, straining up, almost standing in the small area, until the padlock latch finally tore out, and the lid flipped open.

I climbed out of the freezer, my back and legs screaming in pain. Hands out, I felt my way around the dark room, stopping to listen for footsteps. Then I was at the door. I'd thought Aaron would've blocked it as well, but when I gave a tentative push, it swung open. He obviously hadn't thought I'd be able to escape.

I crept around the side of the barn, skirting the edge of the forest, keeping the house in sight as I came around behind it. I didn't know how I was going to get to the vehicles – mine was at the front, but now I also saw a green truck behind the house. It had to be Daniel's. It looked familiar, and I remembered the truck that slowed down outside my place. Daniel must've been keeping an eye on me, maybe trying to protect his father. As I got closer to the house, I heard raised voices. I crouched behind a tree and listened. It sounded like they were fighting. Daniel was angry, saying, 'You said you just wanted to talk to them – you didn't tell me anyone would get hurt. When are you going to let her out?'

Aaron answered, 'When the Light says it's time. She's not ready.'

Daniel yelled, sounding desperate, 'She's going to die.'

Aaron was talking, his voice lower, like he was trying to

421

calm Daniel, but I couldn't make out the words. I hoped Joseph was also inside.

Staying low behind the tree, I thought about my plan. I was going to have to get all the way around the house without their spotting me and run to my car. When they heard the car start, they'd come after me, so I had to disable the truck too. Adrenaline gave me strength, narrowing my focus to only this moment as I crawled over, then slowly stood up, peering into the cab of the truck. No keys in the ignition. I'd have to rip out some wires. When voices rose inside the house again, I eased open the truck door, holding my breath as I popped the hood.

There was silence from the house, and I worried they'd heard me, then Daniel started yelling again: 'We can't do this – we can't let people die.'

I quickly yanked out every wire and hose I could get my hands on. When I was finished, I glanced over at the house and saw Mary by the back door.

She was watching me. We stared at each other. I was sure she was going to call the men, but she just gave a brief nod, then turned and walked back inside.

I ran around the house and climbed into my car, saw the keys dangling from the ignition. I started the car up and began to pull away. Daniel, Joseph, and Aaron came running out of the house. In the rearview mirror I saw Mary grab Daniel's arm, holding him back. The dogs were also running out, and one dodged in front of the car. I tapped my brakes, trying not to hit it, and swerved on the loose gravel, coming to a stop in front of a tree as I slammed on my brakes. I put the car in reverse.

Motion out of the corner of my eye, and I saw Aaron running toward me. He threw something at my window and I automatically ducked. Glass shattered and a rock hit my arm. Pain shot through me as I gripped the steering wheel and pounded the gas, trying to get around him. Joseph ran in front of the car. The gun in his hand pointed at me.

I hit the brakes, ducked again. Aaron reached his hand through the broken window, punched me hard in the side of the head. I sat stunned as he unlocked my door and put the car in park. I scrambled across the passenger seat, he grabbed at my legs, dragging me. I clung to the steering wheel. Kicked back with all my strength.

Where was Joseph? I glanced to the left. He was still standing in front of the car, the gun aimed at me, waiting for his next command from his brother.

I looked through the rear window, searching for help, an escape, anything. Mary was crying hysterically, hands over her mouth. Daniel was staring transfixed, his face full of horror and panic. And in his hand, he held the other gun.

I yelled out, 'Daniel, shoot him. You *have* to shoot him. Heather loved you. She wouldn't want you to let this happen.'

Daniel was crying now. The gun rose.

Aaron didn't turn around. He was still trying to pull me out of the car, so confident in his control over his son.

I heard a *crack*. And Aaron let go of my legs. I looked over my shoulder. Aaron was clutching his side, his face stunned as he crumpled to the ground.

Joseph walked over and stared down at him, the gun by his side, his face expressionless.

Daniel was running toward Joseph. He tackled him.

The men fought on the ground while I clambered to put my car in gear. Joseph broke away and ran toward the truck, Daniel hard on his heels.

Without looking back, I stomped on the gas and tore out of the driveway.

Chapter Thirty-five

I drove as fast as I could on the narrow gravel roads, fishtailing around one corner and nearly going over an embankment. When I passed an area of logging, I noticed a large excavator and flashed to an image of Robbie's excavator at his house down by the septic field – the dirt pile fresh. Now something stuck out as odd. I tried to bring back the scene in my mind. Another image came forward: The lids for the new tanks were covered. From what I knew of septic systems, it was better to leave the lid exposed. And the septic wasn't even hooked up yet.

What if they buried him in the tanks?

When I got to Robbie's, I ran to the excavator. I was right: The lids for the tanks were under the mound of dirt, but the pipes out to the field were uncovered. One came up beside the mound. I heard something, a muffled sound from the end of a pipe. I focused on the sound, called, 'Robbie?' Then I heard the noise again, a faint call for help.

I yelled down, 'Hang in there,' and called 911, shouting directions.

I grabbed a shovel from the shop and began digging, yanking off my coat and tossing it to the side. It would take forever to move enough dirt to remove the lid. I looked at the excavator. Were the keys still in it?

I climbed onto the machinery and found the keys still in the ignition. In their haste, they must have forgotten them. I turned on the big machine, the diesel engine loud and drowning out the thudding of my heart. I hoped I still remembered how to run it. My hands sweaty on the levers, I tried to bring the bucket up, but I kept digging it farther into the ground, catching it on a boulder. Finally, I figured out how to lift the bucket, then scoop the dirt and move it to the side. When the hatch was in sight, I shut the machine off and ran over to the tank.

I began to try to tug and pull at the concrete lid, but it was almost two feet by two feet – and heavy. How was I going to get Robbie out?

I looked back at the excavator resting near me. Could I use it somehow? I caught sight of a heavy metal chain under the seat, with two hooks on either end. I dragged the chain over to the bucket, attaching one end on the teeth and the other on the hatch. Then I clambered back onto the machine, and jerking and bobbing, my hands still unsteady, I brought the bucket up. I lifted the hatch off, with a whoop of relief, and

426

dropped it to the side. I shut the machine off and ran back to the opening, kneeling as I yelled, 'Robbie, you okay?'

My brother's voice floated up. 'Brew – he's hurt.'

'I'm coming down.'

I lowered myself into the tank, which didn't look deep, bracing my arms on the sides of the opening, worried I would land on Robbie. But when he saw my legs he said, 'I'm over here,' from the other end of the tank. I dropped with a thud and found myself in an area about four by eight. In the dim light from above, I noticed Robbie lying in the corner, his back propped up on the wall of the tank. Brew was lying beside him.

Now I also realized that Robbie's shirt was off and he was holding it in a bundle against Brew's shoulder. The animal's breathing was rapid, his side rising and falling, air coming out in a *chuff*.

Robbie said, 'Can you help Brew?' His voice was tight, rushed, the words tripping over themselves in their haste to get out.

I crawled over, saying, 'Easy, boy,' when Brew whined. I checked his pulse, using the femoral artery on the inside of his thigh. It was weak and thready. The tank was filled with the scent of blood mingling with dog breath and fur. I could also smell Robbie's body scent, sweat and dirt, diesel from his excavator.

Still speaking fast, Robbie said, 'Brew attacked Joseph. I tried to stop the bleeding.'

427

I felt along Brew's ribs and under his front leg. My hand was covered with warm sticky blood. I examined his gums. Even in the dim light, I could see they were pale gray. I pressed the flat part of my finger against them, checking his capillary refill time.

Five seconds. Far too slow.

The bullet had probably hit a small vein and he was bleeding internally. If it had been a main artery, he would've died in minutes. The heavy breathing was not so much pain as his body working hard to make oxygen. He'd just get sleepier and sleepier until he finally passed out, and then died. Likely soon.

I said, 'It doesn't look good, Robbie.'

'Fuck.' He rested his head on the back of the wall, looked upward. 'Fuck. Fuck.' His voice was thick, like he was fighting tears.

My own eyes filling with tears, I said, 'I called 911. They're on the way.'

'Is Brew going to make it?'

I looked back down at the dog. His breathing had gone shallow. His eyes half-closed, his tongue lolling. 'No, I don't think he has long.'

'Shit.' Robbie took a deep breath, like he was trying to brace himself, then carefully lifted the dog up, so he was partway across his lap. Brew gave Robbie's hand a small lick, then closed his eyes all the way. His breathing slowed.

'Good boy,' Robbie said. He bent down and pressed

428

his lips to Brew's head, gave him a hug. 'You want to go for a walk? Let's go for a walk, buddy.'

Brew let out a sigh. A few moments later, he was gone.

We sat in silence, my hand still on Brew's side, while tears rolled down my face. I looked only at the dog, trying to give Robbie some space, but I heard him sniff a few times and clear his throat. There was a sense of emptiness in the tank now, a hushed soundless quiet that made every movement seem louder. Brew's body was already cooling; his life was over. Still, I stroked his soft fur, mentally saying my own good-byes, thanking him for being a friend to my brother, remembering him trotting over, bumping his wet nose into my hand.

After a few minutes, Robbie wiped his face, leaned over, and whispered something in Brew's ear. He then eased Brew's limp body off his leg, gently resting his head down on the ground. He sat back up, with a groan.

I said, 'Are you okay?'

He wheezed. 'My ribs – I think some are broken.'

'I should have a look.'

In the dark, my hand touched Robbie's side, but I couldn't feel any blood, or protrusions.

He sucked in his breath. 'Shit.' He rubbed at his chest. 'I keep getting these fucking pains in my chest.'

Was he having an anxiety attack? 'What does it feel like?'

'This pressure. I can feel it in my arms and jaw, around

my back too. Like someone's squeezing me. Hurts like shit – makes it hard to breathe.'

Oh, no.

'You could be having a heart attack. Are you feeling light-headed?'

Almost on cue, his head dropped forward, and he slumped down.

'Robbie!'

I quickly moved Brew's body to the side and lowered Robbie so he was lying flat, checking his vitals. His breathing was shallow – then stopped. I started CPR immediately, saying in between chest compressions, 'Come on, Robbie.'

Please, God. Please help us.

In the distance, I heard sirens.

I rode in the ambulance with Robbie down to Victoria. They had him on oxygen even before they got him out of the septic tank, and gave him chest compressions all the way to the hospital. They brought him back a couple of times, but they were still giving him chest compressions as they wheeled him into emergency. For the next while, I paced the hallway, waiting for news. All I could think about was how many years we hadn't stayed in touch, how many years I'd thought it was just easier that way.

The police had sent cars to Mary's, but I didn't know if they'd made any arrests, or if Aaron was even alive. Finally, one of the doctors came out and told me that

430

Robbie was stable and responding. They were going to move him to ICU while they ran some tests. I was allowed to visit with him briefly, but he was on pain control, which was making him sleepy, so we didn't talk. I just held his hand, telling him he was going to be okay. His face was pale, but he managed a smile.

Kevin, worried about why I hadn't shown up back at the hospital for a staff meeting, which I had completely forgotten about, called my cell when I was in the waiting room. Still in shock, I told him that my brother had had a heart attack. He came by to bring me coffee, and when he saw the police outside Robbie's room, he knew there was more to the story. I filled him in, then he sat, flipping through a magazine, while I paced. My feet keeping time with my thoughts: *Will Robbie make it? Is Lisa okay? What's happening at the commune?*

The doctor came to talk to me again. 'Looks like he had a narrowing of one of his arteries. We'll do bypass surgery in the morning and put in a stent. If all goes well, you should be able to see him tomorrow evening, and he'll be home in a couple of days.' Before the doctor left, he added, 'He's probably had this problem for a while – he's lucky he was with you.'

After the doctor had gone, I held my hand over my own heart, sagging back in the chair.

Kevin reached over and rubbed my shoulder. 'Don't worry. Anderson's one of the best cardiac guys in the country.'

431

I gave him a smile. 'Thanks, and thanks for sitting with me.'

'Of course. Do you want another coffee?'

'I'm good. I'm sure you have appointments. I don't want to keep you. I'll probably be here for a while.'

He nodded, but said, 'I can reschedule. I don't mind staying.'

I said, 'No, please. Really, I'm fine on my own.'

He looked at the magazine he was holding, ruffled a few of the pages with his thumb, then said, 'When you told me what had happened, it scared me.'

'I'm fine. Little banged up, but I'll be okay.'

'I know, but it made me realize something.'

'What's that?'

'Even though I don't want to lose someone again, I still want to have a relationship in my life. I think it's worth the risk. I think *you're* worth the risk.'

'I'm sorry, Kevin, but I told you. That's not what I want right now.'

'You told me that, but I'm not sure if it's true.'

'It's true.' We held gazes for a moment, then I looked away. 'I've had a lot happen in the last twenty-four hours. I need some time alone, to sit and think.'

'Of course. If you need me—'

'I know where you are.' I said it with a smile, but the message was clear.

He dropped his magazine on the chair, also gave me a smile, and then headed to the elevator. After he left, I picked up his magazine and flipped through it, then stopped and looked at the coffee he'd brought me, now cold. I thought of his offer. I'd wanted a fresh coffee, wanted his companionship, but I'd still said no. What was wrong with me? Why had I reacted so negatively to his kind offer?

Then I thought of Francine, a sad, elderly woman wandering the halls, lonely, speaking to people from her past. A life lived with many friends and travels, a successful career, but no one left to sit by her side.

Chapter Thirty-six

The police called later that evening. They'd arrested Aaron at the scene, and, still in custody, he'd been rushed to the hospital for a gunshot wound. He'd lost a lot of blood and was recovering on the same ward as Robbie, but with an armed guard. Daniel and Joseph had escaped. The police weren't able to search the commune without a warrant, and at the moment they didn't have enough evidence that either of them might be hiding there to get one.

They were now contacting authorities in other countries to keep an eye out for Daniel and Joseph, in case they fled to one of the foreign communes. They'd also arrested Mary, but she was refusing to talk, still protecting her son. She did admit it was her car he'd made his escape in, after Joseph had taken the truck.

The next morning, Robbie had his surgery. I wasn't working, but I tried to busy myself at the hospital, so I'd be around in case anything went wrong. Finally, Dr. Anderson paged me that Robbie was in recovery and starting to wake up. The procedure was successful, but he'd had another minor heart attack during surgery, so they wanted to keep him a few days, just for observation. I could see him now.

I walked into Robbie's room and slowed as I neared his bed. His eyes were closed, and my pulse spiked when I noticed how pale he looked.

He opened his eyes when I reached his side. 'Some nurse took my damn hat.'

He smiled at himself. Hating his vulnerability but knowing that I'd get the joke. Robbie had never liked to be without his baseball cap – only time I remember him not wearing one was at funerals. We'd had far too many of those.

'I'll get you another one.' I smiled back, relieved to see he was in good spirits. I'd been worried about depression – something men often experience after a heart attack, especially because he'd just lost Brew. I felt a wave of sadness, thinking of my brother going home to an empty house. Almost like he'd read my mind, Robbie's smile also faded, and we held gazes.

I said, 'I'm sorry about Brew. The police brought his body out of the tank and Steve Phillips took him to the vet. Do you want him cremated?'

Steve had seen all the police cars going to my brother's place and followed behind. I'd only spoken to him for seconds before climbing into the back of the ambulance, but he'd promised to look after Brew.

Robbie nodded and looked away, fiddling with the bandage on his chest. His voice thick, he said, 'Can I have some water?'

I handed him his cup, helping him with the straw. When he was done, I set the cup back on the side table and sat down in the chair. Trying to pull myself together from the upset of seeing my brother with tubes coming out of him, I took a moment to unwind the scarf from around my neck, then stuffed it in my pocket.

Speaking low, almost in a mumble, Robbie said, 'You did that in the ambulance.'

Thinking he might be groggy from pain medication, I said, 'Did what?'

'Took off your scarf and shoved it in your pocket.'

I narrowed my eyes, tried to remember what he was talking about – the trip in the ambulance still a blur. The only time I remembered taking off my scarf was after he'd flatlined and they were giving him chest compressions. The stress and heat in the ambulance had made me feel like I was strangling.

'You were unconscious . . .'

'It was more than that.' His voice was impatient. 'You know I wouldn't make this shit up. I saw you – like I was above you. You took the scarf off so fast you ripped your earring out. It's under that stretcher I was on.'

Now I remembered the pinging sound, so focused on Robbie that I'd ignored it. I sat back in the chair, stunned into silence. How did he know that?

He said, 'I don't want to talk about this much – it scared the crap out of me, okay? And don't go telling a bunch of people. They'll think I'm nuts.'

Still trying to process what he'd just told me, I said, 'Okay . . .'

'It was kind of like what Aaron described. I was outside, I could see you, and hear your thoughts. You were really scared – I tried to talk to you, but I couldn't. I felt calm, though, and really peaceful.'

He had to have been hallucinating. I was about to explain that it was probably a neurological response to the lack of oxygen, then stopped when I realized that most hallucinations produced from an oxygen-starved brain would cause confusion or disorientation, not a calm, peaceful image. And I couldn't explain how he knew my earring had fallen off. Even if he'd still had auditory response, there was no way he could've seen me remove my scarf.

Robbie stared back up at the ceiling, blinking hard. 'Something happened to me in that ambulance. I don't know what it was, or why it happened.' He met my eyes. 'But I'm not afraid to die anymore.'

I thought of Paul, thought of my mother and father, about my own fears of death. Then I realized I'd climbed down into that septic tank without a moment's hesitation. Being forced to conquer my fear in the barn had set me free.

I was overwhelmed by emotions and thoughts I

wanted to take out and look at when I was alone. 'Well, you're not dying on my watch.'

He smiled, but then his face turned serious, the lines pulling deep around his mouth. 'I should've protected you better when we were kids.'

'You did protect me – the best you could. You were only sixteen. Your job wasn't to look after me. Our parents should've protected both of us.'

Anger washed across his face. 'You're always blaming them for everything that happened when we were kids. They tried their best.'

I wasn't surprised at the disconnection between my memories and his. I'd seen it many times in therapy, two siblings having a completely different opinion of their childhood. It was classic in a dysfunctional family, where the abuse was never discussed and the abuser always defended. But it made me sad. That the silence, and all things we don't talk about, still separated us.

I said, 'I loved them too – but they had a lot of problems.'

'You don't even know what it was like. You were never around.'

And there it was: the resentment. I'd moved away, and he'd stayed.

I tried to calm down, fighting my urge to defend myself for breaking the cardinal rule of our family – unhappy or not, never talk about what was really going on. My trying to seek personal happiness, to rise out of the tears and black eyes, the screaming and crying, was the worst betrayal of all. I'd developed ideas, spoke the language of feelings, and worst, I'd been impatient and angry with them for not wanting more, for not trying to join me in *my* world. And they'd felt it.

I wanted to explain that leaving was the only way I could survive, that our family was mired in pain and denial, and that I couldn't pretend anymore, couldn't keep the silence. But Robbie had just had surgery and shouldn't be getting upset, so I kept it all in, again, and said, 'You could've left.'

'How, Nadine? How the fuck was I supposed to do that? So Dad could beat Mom to death? So he could fall down the stairs one night?'

Robbie's face was red. The old anger finally coming to a head. My attempt to skirt the surface of our issues had failed. And it wasn't the first time. In this intimate moment, death's shadow still lingering between us, I realized that I always felt this in our conversations, had always done *this*. Thinking that I was holding back, but still my urge to push, to heal and fix, so people could be what I needed, was always there. In my tone, in the subtle way my tongue pushed the words out of my mouth. And my brother, the only person who'd shared my blood *and* my story, knew what I was really saying, even when I wasn't speaking at all.

So now I said it out loud, for the first time in our lives. 'They weren't your responsibility. They were adults.

They made their own choices – and so did you. I'm not going to let you blame me for that.'

The beeping of the monitor signaled the emotions warring in Robbie's body. Then something changed in his face. He rested his head back on the pillow, his breathing still heavy but his heart rate starting to slow.

After a moment, looking up at the ceiling, he said, 'You're right. I could've left. But I didn't want to drive over there one day and find Mom dead, hanging from a rafter or something, Dad passed out in his own puke. I always thought if I just watched over them, I could stop it, I could make everything be okay. But they both died anyway.' He paused for a beat. 'Maybe I just used them as a reason for not having to deal with my own shit. I never could take a chance, not even for Willow.' He turned his face toward me. 'I was glad you got away. I liked thinking of you in your nice house, with your family.'

Tears were leaking from my eyes. Robbie's were also damp, his mouth a grimace as he fought back the tears. I'd been wrong. He did know, he did see.

I said, 'When we love people, we want to help them – even when they don't want it. But sometimes we just end up hurting ourselves.'

He said, 'You've done well, though. I'm proud of you.' And he was. I could hear it in his voice. The anger I'd felt from him all these years wasn't because I'd followed my life's path: It was because I'd pushed him to do the same.

I thought of Lisa, wondered if that was the root of all our problems.

I said, 'My family wasn't perfect either. I made a lot of mistakes with Lisa.'

'What happened between you two?'

'I don't know ... Maybe too much happened.' I told him about Garret. Then about my own memories in the barn with Aaron, while watching Robbie's monitor and pausing when his heart rate spiked, reminding him to breathe.

When he'd calmed down a little, he said, 'That bastard – hope he gets the crap beat out of him in prison. You should tell Lisa what happened to you.'

'Maybe. If she ever speaks to me again.'

'You haven't heard from her?'

'No. I'd hoped she'd leave the commune once Aaron was arrested.' I explained what I'd learned from the police. 'But I have a feeling she's still there.'

He grew paler, starting to look tired. He rested his head on the pillow, his eyelids drooping. 'Keep me posted, okay?'

'I will. But I should let you get some rest. See you in the morning.'

After I left Robbie's room, I called the sergeant. The police still hadn't had any sightings of Joseph or Daniel. Joy, who apparently ran the commune alongside Aaron, wouldn't let them search the premises, and they still

441

didn't have cause to get a warrant because neither of the men had been seen entering the building. The sergeant suspected they were probably off the island now anyway, but he said they'd still get Robbie protection – he was a key witness in Willow's murder. Now that he was awake, they'd also take his statement, and they were assembling a forensics team to search for Willow at the old site. She was finally going home.

I didn't understand why none of the members, especially Lisa, had left the commune now that Aaron was under arrest. The sergeant told me that it was possible most of them didn't know what had happened. They didn't have phones, TV, or internet access. Their only information came from the staff, and they were obviously keeping everything quiet until they were able to speak with Aaron.

In the parking lot, I sat in my car for a moment, staring at the hospital through the thick wall of rain that had started thundering down, and thought about my conversation with my brother. It scared me, how close I had come to losing him – and his story about my earring. Everything on the other side of my window looked distorted now, flashes of colors and pale faces as bodies rushed by, but I couldn't make out features, couldn't bring their edges into focus. Aaron's words came to mind. *Just because you can't see something doesn't mean it's not there.*

The hospital was a gray blur, through my tears and the rain. I wondered which room was my brother's, thinking how at peace he had seemed when he spoke about how he'd nearly died. Then I thought of Paul, of those last moments before he took his final breath and died in my arms, how serene his face had looked as he let go of me. Now I realized I was the one who had never really let go of him.

That evening I spent a lot of time thinking about my life – and how it had also nearly ended. Then I made some decisions. I arrived early to visit Robbie the next day, and after he fell back asleep, I made my way upstairs to Kevin's office.

At my knock, his voice rang out, 'Come in.'

I hesitated. Would he want anything to do with me after I'd been so aloof? I'd never know unless I tried. I took a breath and opened the door.

He looked up in surprise, started to stand. 'Nadine . . .'

I motioned for him to stay seated and took the chair across from him.

I met his gaze, thinking how handsome he looked as he brushed his hair back with one hand, his forearm muscles flexing. I said, 'I owe you an apology.'

He cocked his head, a small smile playing about his lips. 'You're just figuring this out?'

'I'm a bit slow sometimes.' I stepped out on the edge of my emotions, stood teetering for a moment, jumped. 'You're right. I have been running away. I guess I'm scared . . . of this, of what it could mean.'

'I'm scared too. That's a good thing. I like the way you make me feel.'

We held gazes again, a slow thrum of nervous excitement hitting right below my heart. But there was something I had to make clear.

'My daughter, Lisa. She's still in the commune, and she's my number one priority right now – and forever.'

He nodded. 'Of course.'

'That being said, if you'd like to spend some time together, I could use a friend.'

He raised his brows. 'A friend?'

'A *friendly* friend. I'd like to see where this could go.' I raised my own brow, pleased to see his answering smile. 'We could start by having dinner again?'

'I'd like that.'

'Maybe I'll even audition for your band. I play a mean tambourine.'

'Let's not get carried away now.'

We both laughed, then he reached across the desk and held my hand.

This time there were no flashes of images, no guilt about Paul. But I remembered, when Paul was alive, how he'd try to steal moments like this at the clinic, catching my hand as I sped by, but I'd pull away, intent on my task.

Death makes you wish you'd done everything differently, had been in less of a hurry. This time I would enjoy the journey.

Life is for the living.

444

Chapter Thirty-seven

I'd just gotten home from the hospital and was unlocking my door when a police car pulled in my driveway. A tall man, with gray hair, dark eyebrows, and a deeply lined face that made him look tired, got out and introduced himself as Sergeant Pallan. He then told me he was handling the commune investigation. His eyes were serious and sad when he took off his sunglasses. I searched his face, my breath increasing, my chest tight, sensing that he wasn't there to ask me questions.

'What's wrong?'

'We need to talk, and I think we should go inside.'

It was bad. Whatever he wanted to tell me was really bad. The world distorted. My depth perception off, I stumbled on the doorsill as I led him into the house. *Please, don't let it be Lisa. Don't let her be dead.*

I made my way to the kitchen table, pulled a chair out, and eased my body down. I put my elbows on the wooden surface and rested my mouth against my fists, pressing my lips into them, trying to stop the scream building there. I was aware that my legs and hands were shaking, but peripherally, like a doctor assessing my condition. *Shock, you're going into shock.* I was already a stranger to myself.

I searched for words, made them come out my mouth. 'What happened?'

'Early this morning there was a fire at the commune and—'

'My daughter?'

'We don't know . . .'

I started to moan into my hands, a low, keening sound. Shock cocooned my body, everything slowing down.

The officer said, 'I can call someone for you.'

'Tell me what happened.'

'It might be better if you had a friend—'

'Tell me.' I bit out the words, anger and tears mixing on my face.

So he did.

There were only a handful of survivors. Two members had escaped through a broken window – one, a female staff member, was in the hospital with a bullet wound, the other was suffering from third-degree burns. The man who took care of the grounds had been down at the far end of the property mowing the lawn, so he'd also been spared. Another surviving member had been coming back from a horseback ride and was still in the distance when Joseph pulled up. She continued to the barn and began to take off her horse's saddle. There was silence for a while, and then gunshots.

Terrified, the girl had hidden in one of the stalls, with no way to call for help. She'd been watching the building with horror when she heard a loud whoosh and saw flames shoot out of the windows, quickly consuming the wood siding.

A few moments later, there was an explosion, and every building was engulfed in flames. The girl had released all the animals, then hid in the field until the police and fire trucks arrived.

It took them hours to put the fire out. At least one hundred and fifty people had died, twenty-five of them children. There might have been even more casualties but there hadn't been any workshops or retreats running at the time.

The members who died had all been locked into the meditation room, herded like sheep for a slaughter. Joy was the surviving member who'd been shot. She'd helped Joseph gather everyone, but when Joseph grabbed her keys and locked them all inside, then said he needed gasoline, she realized something was wrong. She'd tried to stop him, but he'd shot her and left her in the hallway. She'd crawled to her office and barely made it out the window before the gasoline had ignited some chemicals kept in the storeroom and triggered the explosion.

The police didn't know what happened to Joseph and

whether he was still on the loose. It was going to take months for them to identify the bodies. Joy had tried to list all the members that she knew for sure were in the meditation room, but Lisa wasn't one of them. Joy couldn't remember seeing her at all that morning or in the previous two days; nor could the other survivors. She was missing.

I kept staring at the officer, watching his mouth move as he explained that there were resources available to me, but nothing was connecting.

I put my head down on the table and sobbed.

The days after the fire were a haze of jumbled images and memories. There were moments where I'd be standing in my kitchen, staring at my hand clutching the soapy sponge, trying to understand. How could Joseph have killed all those people? How could I be washing dishes and doing laundry when my daughter was still missing? I knew grief would shield you from the worst and leak the pain out in small doses, but I remember thinking, *No, this is as bad as it can get, surely it can't hurt more than this.* But it could, and it did.

Most days I'd walk slowly around my house, feeling as though my entire body was beaten and bruised, trying to accomplish simple tasks. I'd break it down into moments: put on slippers, pull on housecoat, brush teeth. Then I'd stare at the woman in the mirror, and grief would spill out of my mouth in strangling gasps.

I'd dealt with death before, understood its process. But the loss of so many, combined with the agony of waiting to hear if Lisa was one of the victims, was something I never could've prepared for. And I cried for all of them.

Sergeant Pallan endured my frantic late-night calls when I asked him again if they'd searched everywhere for Lisa. *Could she be in the basement or one of the chambers,* I'd say. But he'd always tell me that she was still missing, then he'd gently add that it would take a while to identify all the victims – many of the bodies had been badly damaged in the explosion. But I couldn't accept that her body was also in the morgue, not until I had proof. I'd speculate in an endless loop of possibilities: She'd left the center before the fire, or she'd witnessed the event and was now hiding somewhere, fearing for her life.

In all of them, she was alive, she had to be alive.

From the hospital, Aaron insisted that his brother had acted alone, but the police suspected that he'd had a plan in case there was ever a problem. There didn't seem to be any other valid reason for the commune to have had certain chemicals. He claimed he was devastated by the tragedy, but he was finding comfort in knowing that his members were at peace. I knew it was a lie, that he was not only aware that his brother had a mental disorder, he'd fed his paranoia. He couldn't stand the idea of the truth coming out, of all his members turning away from him. I saw now that his fear of rejection had shaped everything he'd done all along, building the commune, the family he'd never had, protecting it at all costs, even if that meant destroying it in the end, so he didn't have to face their abandonment. I was glad that he'd likely spend the rest of his life in jail, rotting in a small cell.

With Joseph possibly still alive and Aaron able to give commands – some members from other countries believed in his innocence – they kept an officer patrolling by my home. They were concerned Joseph might be fixated on punishing me and completing whatever other tasks Aaron had given him. It was a very real fear and one that I shared. I lived in a state of suspense, waiting for *something* to happen, for Joseph to show up, for Daniel to be caught, for them to find Lisa. I called the police daily, looking for updates.

One of the survivors sold their story to the newspapers, then the others followed suit. When the reporters found out my daughter, a former drug addict, was also presumed to be one of the victims, and that I was a respected doctor, they began to follow me around. 'How did you feel when your daughter joined the cult?' 'Did you see this coming?' 'Do you think she's still alive?'

After the murders, and facing accusations of being an accomplice, Mary broke down and finally shared her story. She'd known she was pregnant when she left the commune, but had hoped Aaron would never find out. Her parents passed away a few years later, and she inherited a great deal of money. Aaron had seen the obituary.

He came up to Shawnigan, demanding a donation, and quickly realized Daniel was his child. He'd allowed Mary to keep him without a custody battle, while she contributed each month to the commune, but he wanted visitations. When Daniel was in his teens, he ran away to live with his father.

When the police investigated further, it became clear that Aaron had made some bad financial decisions and was facing bankruptcy. The land he bought was the final blow, draining the commune's accounts. Heather's parents had millions in family money, which is why he'd rushed their murder. When the police checked the commune's phone records, they discovered that Heather's parents had called shortly before their death. Joy revealed that Heather's father had discovered how much money Heather had given to the commune and threatened to sue them for coercion. Joy had passed on the information to Aaron – and the parents' whereabouts. They'd never been told that Heather was in the hospital.

It was Daniel who had been calling my home and making threats, trying to scare me away from his father and the commune, from everything that he believed in. The police also told me that the member who'd been coming back from horseback riding the day of the fire was Emily – the young girl who Heather had gotten to join the commune. I'd found a small measure of solace in thinking that Heather would be happy Emily had lived, but my own guilt still ate me alive. Morning to night, ghosts whispered in my ear. *You set this in motion. You made this happen. Why didn't you just leave it alone?*

I'd pushed against the wind and caused a tornado.

When Robbie was released from the hospital, he stayed with me for a few days; sometimes Kevin would join us, bringing dinner. I took a leave of absence from the hospital. I spent most of those days pacing my house, calling the police, watching the news, and forcing myself to eat the food put in front of me. Then I'd lie inert on the couch, falling into an exhausted sleep. My dreams were filled with images of my searching for Lisa but never being able to get to her in time.

Two weeks after the fire, Aaron was transferred from the hospital to jail, where he'd await trial. There'd been no signs of Joseph, so the police stopped patrolling by my home as often. Desperate to get away from my terrifying thoughts and keep busy somehow, I started to ease back into work. Michelle was a great support. She'd encourage me out into the sun to eat our lunch in the park across the street. Sometimes we'd go for a walk after work to get some fresh air and talk about Lisa. There still hadn't been any sightings of her either, and though some of the bodies had finally been identified, hers wasn't one of them.

I decided to talk to Aaron. I wasn't sure if he'd accept me as a visitor, but I should have known his ego couldn't stand missing a chance to impart his so-called wisdom. We stared at each other through the glass, the cold phone in my hand. He was pale and washed-out, unshaven. He finally looked his age. My head filled with things I wanted to say, to yell and scream at this man who had caused the death of so many people, who might have killed Lisa. But I had to be careful, calm. He was the only person who could give me any information.

I said, 'Where's my daughter?'

He shrugged. 'Where are any of us? The universe is infinite, Nadine.'

His casual response infuriated me. I leaned forward, almost touching the glass, forgetting my vow to be calm. 'Don't give me any more of your bullshit. Was she still at the commune? Did she leave before the fire?'

He was silent, a serene smile on his face. He was not going to answer. I wanted to cry in helpless rage. He knew. He knew exactly what happened to her. It was the last thing he had over me, the last bit of power. But I had power too.

'Your brother is *dead*, Aaron.' I bit out the words, my voice harsh and unforgiving. We didn't know if that was true, but I wanted to shake him up, hurt him like he'd hurt me. He didn't even flinch. Did he know something?

I added, 'He was the only family you had, the only person who loved you. Soon, your remaining members are going to lose interest, will find someone else to believe in, not a lonely old man sitting behind bars.'

He was still calm as he said, 'There are others who want to learn how to change their lives.' He looked around. 'There are many here who need my help.'

My voice turned cold. 'You're forgetting something, Aaron. Once you're sentenced, you're going to prison. And when the inmates find out that you like to molest little girls, you're the one who's going to need help. You're the one who's going to be screaming alone in the dark, begging them to stop. But they won't.'

He still held his smile in place, but I saw the fear in his eyes. It was all I needed.

I hung up the phone.

Garret was arrested. When the police had gone to talk to him, one of his clients, a young girl, had seen them at the studio. Later, she told her mother that he'd taken nude photos of her before, and she wondered if she was in trouble. The mother reported him, and others soon followed suit. When they searched his home, they found vials of GHB and naked photos he'd taken of other homeless females while they appeared to be drugged. He'd obviously enjoyed the sense of power he had over a woman who was out of her mind, posing them however he wanted, usually in a degrading manner. They also found more photos of Lisa on his hard drive. I hoped Lisa knew her abuser was finally going to pay for his crimes.

*

454

Often after work, Kevin and I would go for a drive down-town – searching for Lisa, putting up posters. I knew it was foolish, that we would get more false leads than any-thing else, but I needed to do it. Sometimes I'd think I could feel her nearby, as though her spirit were still on the streets and in those houses. Kevin and I were still just friends, until one day when he was too tired to drive home. I'd felt myself coming back into my body then, felt the tears beginning to dry.

The cat, along with my daughter, was gone. In the days immediately after the fire, there had been so many people around my home, new voices and scents, she'd bolted. We'd left kibble outside for weeks, but she didn't come back.

Tammy and I spoke a few times. She'd left her husband and was still struggling with the loss of her sister and parents. It would take a long time for her to heal, but she was strong and making plans for her future. They finally removed Willow's remains. I imagined the barrel being brought up from the ground, rusted and covered in clods of earth, her bones released from their imprisonment at last. It was hard not to think of her without remembering when Aaron had buried me, the sound of the shovel going into the ground, the dirt hitting the metal, the breath leaving my lungs, knowing that Willow had endured the same fate. But she hadn't made it out. Sometimes I wondered if that's when Aaron learned he liked burying women, liked to hear them scream, or if there were others. Willow didn't have any family, so Robbie and I planned to purchase a plot at the same cemetery as Paul's. When the police released the remains, we'd hold a service for her.

And we would plant lavender around her grave.

In the middle of May, about a month after the fire, I again started to get the sense that my house was being watched. It was subtle at first. I'd be outside, moving a garbage can, or taking the recycling out, and I'd have the feeling that I wasn't alone. I'd pause and look around, all my nerve endings alive and ready to run, but never saw anything, so I put it down to stress, or just an overzealous reporter.

One night I came home from work and was getting out of my car when I noticed a movement to my left. I stared hard at the cemetery, catching sight of a shadow quickly walking away. I ran into my house and called Kevin. He came over and had a look around, but didn't see anything. I reminded myself I'd been tired and jumpy, that it was likely someone taking an evening stroll.

A week later, I was in my potting shed when I realized my pruning shears had been moved. I always kept them hanging on the wall, but they were down by one of my bonsai trees, the one I'd been working on recently. I studied the branches. Fear shot through my body. Someone had cut one of them off.

Chapter Thirty-eight

The police had a look around and even fingerprinted the shears, but the handle had been dirty, and only my print showed up on the blades. It had to have been me that cut the branch, but I had no recollection of doing it. Kevin and I talked about my increased anxiety and considered the possibility that it was paranoia, a delayed post-traumatic stress reaction. I'd almost been killed, along with my brother, and I was struggling with immense guilt over all the lives that had been lost. I was also trying to accept the fact that my daughter had probably not survived the fire. It had been over a month, and there had been no sightings of her, no calls on any of the posters we put up. I still clung to hope, remembering how adept she was at changing her appearance and disappearing from the world, but this time I feared my daughter had disappeared forever. Even if she was just missing and hadn't died that terrible day, in the end my daughter was gone. And I needed to find some sort of closure.

There was a memorial at the scene of the fire. Now that the initial investigation was over and human remains had been removed, there was a metal chain-link fence and an officer guarding the entrance. People had been coming by for weeks, leaving flowers and trinkets outside the fence, lighting candles. I wanted to bring my own gift, and I also asked Sergeant Pallan if I could visit inside the commune site, something they'd allowed a few family members to do. Sergeant Pallan got permission to bring me there. Kevin also came with me.

I'd never driven by the site before, unable to face it, and I thought I was prepared now, but when we pulled through the gates, and I saw the charred remains of the buildings, I sucked in my breath, like I'd been punched hard in the center of my stomach. I covered my mouth as my eyes filled with tears, shaking my head at the devastating sight, the harsh reality of all those deaths. As we got out of the car, Kevin said, 'You sure you want to do this?'

I nodded, looking around. It was warm that day and the first thing I noticed was the smell, the sick odor of fire and smoke, not a pleasant, woodsy smell, but a mixture of everything that had gone up in flames. What had once been beautiful buildings and lush grounds now lay sprawled out, ripped open and gutted. The foundation was visible, some walls and parts of the building still standing, black and misshapen. Trees near the burned buildings also showed their scars, blackened trunks and branches. Crime-scene tape fluttered in the breeze.

We placed our bouquet of flowers with the rest piled outside the gate, a sea of grief that stretched the length of the site. We also took some time to read the poems and sentiments that people had tied to the fence. I cried at the photos of the victims that had been left by loved ones, with mementos, stuffed animals, a child's toy train, which made me think of the little boy I'd seen in the window.

When we were finished at the memorial, I walked around carefully through the wreckage, making out the shape of the buildings, where some of the rooms might've been, crying when I thought of the last time I'd seen my daughter at this place. We didn't speak much, Kevin and I, or the sergeant, and when we did, only in whispers, still sensing somehow that the dead lingered. The tragedy that had befallen that spot hung in the air, the energy of pain and death and fear remained with the buildings, and I felt it to my core. My stomach and body were weak and shaky and sick with it. I tried not to let my imagination take over, but I couldn't stop the flashes of brutal images running through my mind, people screaming in pain, the terror they must have felt in their last moments. I reached out a hand and touched one of the walls, feeling the wood turned to charcoal, rubbing it in my hands and letting the fragments drift to the ground, staring at the ash below my feet. *Dust to dust, ashes to ashes.*

Then, finally, the one image my mind had never been able to face until this moment, my daughter's possible death. The smoke trapping in her lungs, the screams of agony. I doubled over, clutching my stomach, sobbing. Then Kevin was beside me, his arms wrapping around me, holding me up as I broke down.

When my tears had subsided, and I could stand, the sergeant took us down a metal ladder that had been left, leading to the underground chamber. Though it was warm that day, we all felt the chill, the empty chamber with the door hanging open, the toilet dug into the ground, the metal cot with its thin blanket, which had somehow survived the fire. I went inside, rubbing my arms in the dark, thinking of all the members who'd begged to go in there, fasting until they were hallucinating, desperate for their glimpse of the other side. I hoped that Aaron's beliefs had at least brought them some comfort as they faced their deaths.

When we left the commune that day, I was exhausted, resting my head on Kevin's shoulder as we drove home, my hand holding his. I'd hoped for closure, but I'd just found more questions. Why wasn't my daughter seen those last days? Had Aaron or Joseph done something to her before they came to Shawnigan? My head filled with terrifying thoughts. What if she'd been put somewhere else, but no one came back for her? I tried to remind myself that Aaron had been happy with Lisa. He'd had no reason to punish her, no need for revenge.

I was still thinking about it when Kevin and I picked up my car at the station, then drove to my home. We were partway up my back steps, Kevin carrying some groceries we'd picked up for dinner, when I heard a noise. I spun around and noticed the door of my potting shed banging in the wind.

Kevin followed my gaze. 'Did you close the latch all the way when you were in there this morning?' His voice was worried.

'I'm trying to think but—'

This time we both heard the footsteps running down the road.

Kevin dropped the bag of groceries and gave chase, yelling over his shoulder, 'Call the police.'

Kevin ran halfway down the road, but didn't catch sight of anyone. He returned to the house a few minutes later, panting and out of breath. When the police showed up, their dogs tracked a scent from my shed, through the yard, until it disappeared in the middle of a street a couple of blocks over. Whoever it was must've had a car waiting, which meant they had planned for a quick escape.

Chapter Thirty-nine

For the next week, the police stepped up their patrol, and Kevin spent every night at my house. We didn't know if it was Joseph, whose body still hadn't been identified, or maybe even Daniel, or another member who might be angry at me, but someone was keeping an eye on me. For what purpose, we still didn't know. If Joseph hadn't died in the fire, he had to be hiding somewhere. He would've been identified at any hotel, so I began to consider that Aaron might've had a safe house somewhere. There had also been a day's lapse between when I was attacked and when Joseph set fire to the commune. Where was he during that time? The police had already spoken with Joy, who didn't know of any other properties.

I thought about Levi. He was one of the original members and had been a guardian at the old site. Could he know something? I thought back to my talk with him at the marina. I'd suspected his anger and bitterness toward

Aaron had something to do with his drug use and possible eviction, but there might be something else there. It was obvious that he'd known more than he was saying.

I mentioned my suspicions to the police, who informed me that they had already spoken with Levi after the fire as part of their investigation, but that their interview hadn't revealed any additional information. I decided to try myself.

Kevin thought it was a bad idea for me to talk to Levi alone and wanted to go with me. I agreed, and we were supposed to go the next afternoon, but then he got stuck at work. I paced my house, thinking. Every day was a lost day. If Joseph or Daniel *were* hiding somewhere, I was in danger. I already knew someone was watching me – what was their next plan? Then there was the other thought, the one that I couldn't voice to Kevin, could barely voice to myself. What if Lisa *had* been taken somewhere before they came to Shawnigan? She could still be there.

I left Kevin a quick message at work, telling him I'd keep my cell with me the whole time, and drove up to Shawnigan.

When I stopped to tell Robbie what I was doing, Steve Phillips was there – Robbie and he were going fishing. We sat outside in the sun on an old log picnic table that Robbie had built, a fine dusting of dry fir needles our only tablecloth, while I explained my plan.

'I know he's hiding something.'

463

Robbie said, 'He still might not say anything – he was always a bit of a coward.' He paused, looking down for a moment, then said, 'Guess it doesn't matter now.' He turned to Steve. 'Remember that fight you busted up?'

He nodded. 'You put up a good struggle. Always wondered who the other guy was.'

'Levi, he owed a dealer some money. They were outside the back door fighting. I pulled the dealer off him. Then we went at it, while Levi ran like hell. By the time you got out there, the dealer had split too.'

Something clicked. I said, 'Is that how Levi got that scar on his arm?'

'No, he had that for years – one of the horses bit him at the commune. He was always sneaking into the barn. He had a pot stash hidden in there.'

Steve said, 'Why'd you cover for him?'

Robbie shrugged. 'I was young and dumb – still thought cops were the enemy.' He drained the last of his coffee. 'Let's go fishing.'

After I said good-bye to the men and promised to call them as soon as I was finished talking to Levi, I drove around the lake. I caught Levi just as he was opening his office door. He startled when he heard my footsteps, then relaxed when he saw who it was. 'Jesus, you scared the crap out of me.'

'May I come in?'

He must've picked up on the serious tone of my voice

because his usual goofy grin disappeared as he said, 'Sure, sure.' He opened the door, ushered me inside. 'Have a seat.'

I remained standing while he sat behind the desk. I studied him, taking note of the bloodshot eyes, the dark circles.

He said, 'You okay? I heard what happened out there with Aaron and everything. Then the fire, and your daughter.' He shook his head. 'What a mess.'

I said, 'Yes, it is. That's why I'm here. I was wondering if Aaron ever mentioned anything about a safe house. Maybe somewhere he went that no one else knew about?'

He shook his head. 'Aaron and I weren't buddies, you know. It's not like he confided in me about commune stuff.'

'You *knew* things, Levi.' We held eyes. 'You saw things.'

'I told you, I didn't know anything about Aaron's plans. I told the police the same thing. And I sure as heck don't know where Joseph is now.'

He was angry, which could be an attempt to cover his guilt, but I suspected he was telling the truth. About this anyway.

'You do know about something that happened in the barn at the old site, though, don't you?'

'Oh yeah, like what?' His tone was casual, but he'd started to tap one of his pens again. A nervous tic he wasn't even aware he had.

465

'Aaron forced me into a barrel and buried me. To torture me.'

Levi dropped the pen onto his desk. It rolled off. Neither of us moved to pick it up.

I said, 'I was terrified, so terrified I'd blocked it out for years. But when I was at Mary's, I remembered. And I remembered something else too.'

He rolled his chair back, leaned on the windowsill, trying to look calm and nonchalant, but his hands were tense as they gripped the arms. 'What's that?'

'There was someone else in the barn that day at the commune. I saw a shadow pass by the door. It was you. You scared the birds.'

When Robbie had said how Levi got his scar, it had all come clear. I'd just assumed it had been the birds that blocked the light for a moment, but now I realized it was Levi – he hadn't wanted to be caught with the marijuana.

Now I expected more anger, defensiveness, and denial from Levi, anything but what I got. He brought his chair down hard, his eyes filling with tears. Then a nod, and another. His body saying, *There, yes, I did it. It's out now.*

He said, 'I was in the loft, and I saw what Aaron was doing to you down in the field – then you running to the barn. I wanted to help, but I was scared of what Aaron would do if he found out I'd been stealing some of the pot.'

The thought of him watching and listening to me scream for help, but just biding his time so he could sneak out of the barn, made me want to reach across the table and slap him, but I was so furious I couldn't move.

'So you just left me there?'

'I waited outside until Aaron left, and then you walked out, so I thought you were okay. I thought you'd tell people after, like your mom or something.'

He paused, looking at me expectantly. Was he actually trying to justify his actions by blaming me? I waited him out in silence.

'I'm really sorry,' Levi said. 'I've felt bad about it for years.'

He felt *bad* about it? He watched a man attack me, then carry me into a room, where he nearly killed me, something so traumatic that I'd blocked my memories for decades, and he *felt bad*. Another wave of rage made me clench my hands.

He shrugged. 'You didn't say anything about it to anyone, so I figured maybe you didn't want anyone to know.'

What else had he kept to himself all these years? Then I remembered what Steve had said, that Levi had seen a woman with Finn, and a dark feeling unfurled in my stomach. I didn't want to be there anymore, didn't want to hear what Levi had to say, but I couldn't stop the words. 'Why did you retract your statement to the police after Finn died? You told them you saw a woman.'

467

'Your mother, she was dancing with Finn, and she took him into the woods ...'

I could see it now, remembering how she loved the little children, making daisy chains for their hair, then picking them up and singing as she twirled them around. I imagined her wandering off, in one of her foggy states, stoned out of her mind, showing the small boy a path and forgetting that she'd set him down.

Levi was still talking. 'She never came back with him. I told the cops when they were questioning everyone. Aaron pulled me aside, told me I had to keep it to myself.' He added, 'Robbie knew – I told him at the commune.'

Another piece of the puzzle snapped into place: Robbie's real reason for distancing himself from Levi, why he hadn't turned him in after the fight.

How did I ever think Levi fun and affable? Now I saw him for what he really was. An insecure kid who snuck around and stole drugs.

Robbie was right. Levi was a coward.

I turned and started to walk away.

He said, 'Where are you going?' Sounding scared, like he wanted to keep the conversation going. 'I'm sorry. I know I should've done more.'

I didn't answer, just kept walking.

Chapter Forty

After I talked to Levi, I still felt uneasy, like I was missing something. I didn't know if Mary had any answers either, but I couldn't leave Shawnigan without at least asking. Since she had been released, she was back at her farm. But the police were still keeping an eye on her – in case Daniel tried to contact her.

When I pulled in her driveway, she was running a hose to fill up a bathtub in the horses' corral while they drank. The horses pulled their dripping muzzles out of the water to watch me, their tails flicking at the flies on their hind ends. The air was scented with hot fir trees and dried manure, dust from the gravel road as a truck roared by. In the distance, I could still hear the river, but softer and slower now. I studied the barn, expecting to be assaulted with painful memories, but it just looked like an old building. Harmless in the spring sun.

Mary watched me come closer, a hand stroking the

blaze on one of the horses, who was drinking again, its back leg kicking up at the flies on its belly.

She said, 'I'm sorry about your daughter.' She didn't say it, but her eyes told me that she was also sorry about what had happened that day at her home.

I nodded. 'I'm sorry about your son.' Despite my feelings toward Daniel and what she'd done, she was still a mother.

'I've already told the police everything I know.' She turned back to her task. One of the horses was getting greedy. It nipped at the one beside it, squealing its annoyance. 'Cut it out, Midnight!' she said. The horses put their muzzles back in the tub, snorting and playing in the water.

'I'm more interested in what you haven't told the police. Someone has been watching my house and it could be Joseph. If he *is* still out there, then your son is also in danger. It would be better if the police find him before Joseph does.'

She was silent, her back still to me.

'Mary, if you know anything, you have to tell me. Too many people have died already, now both our children are missing. This has to end.' I started to cry.

She turned around, squatted low, and sat on the railing, leaning forward slightly and resting her arms on dusty jeans. She was wearing gum boots, and hay was mixed in with her white hair.

She said, 'I think about the fire every day, wondering if

470

I'd gone to the cops when you first came here, would they still be alive.' Her face was pale and heavy with guilt. She seemed to have aged another ten years in days.

I wiped my tears away, took some breaths. 'We can all play that game with ourselves, but we don't know what else Aaron might've had planned. Did Daniel know Joseph was going to set the commune on fire?'

She shook her head. 'He would've warned them.'

'And you have no idea where Daniel is now? Or Joseph? Did they have a safe house somewhere?'

She met my eyes. 'I don't know where any of them are. I'm sorry.'

I saw the truth in her face, the sadness, and felt drained by it.

'Levi didn't know anything either.' I leaned against the railing, watched one of the horses. 'I talked to him before I came here. He told me some stuff about my mother, things that happened at the commune.'

I felt Mary studying me. She said, 'You look like her, but you're a lot stronger. She talked about you all the time. She was here the night she died ...'

I turned to face her, caught off guard. 'I've never really thought about where she was going that night. Dad just told us she'd gone for a drive.'

'Kate and I stayed in touch. Not a lot, but sometimes when she was fighting with your dad, she'd come out here and we'd smoke a joint.'

I flashed to an image of the two women, sitting on the

back porch, their shared memories of living in the commune surrounding them, mixing with the sweet marijuana smoke in the air, following them wherever they went.

'What was she doing here that night?'

'You'd visited, asking about the commune. It stirred some stuff up for her. She'd felt bad for a long time about what had happened to Finn.' She said the last part like she was testing the waters, wondering how much Levi had told me.

'You knew she was responsible?'

She nodded. 'I was with her when Aaron told her what Levi had said. She was really upset – she'd been so stoned that she could barely remember walking off with Finn, but she knew she'd done it. She'd left him somewhere and planned on going back for him, but fell asleep in the field. She wanted to tell the police herself, but Aaron said social services would take you and your brother.'

My mind filled with a memory. Finn's mother had sobbed and fallen on the ground, screaming that they were stealing her baby. Now I remembered my own mother crying in the background, Mary's arm around her shoulders.

'Whatever happened to all the marijuana?'

She looked down, eyeing me from the side, still not trusting.

I said, 'I'm not going to tell the police if you had anything to do with it.'

She studied my face for a couple of beats, then said, 'There was a logging truck driver who used to come by – he liked the girls. We'd give him bales of pot, and he'd sell it for us, keeping a bit of the profit.'

Larry and his red truck. I remembered now, the sounds of air brakes the night Finn went missing. I said, 'So he got rid of it before the police came?'

She nodded. 'We took it up to the road, and he loaded it on his truck. After that, he wanted a bigger cut. That's when Aaron decided to leave Shawnigan – he didn't trust him. So I told him I'd stay behind to keep an eye on things.'

'My mother, she told me she'd wanted to leave after Finn died, but she never explained how my father knew to come get us.'

'She left a note for your father at the store. Told him that she wanted to come home, but she was scared of Aaron.'

'He wouldn't let her leave?'

'She didn't ask. When Finn died, we'd talked and she wanted out. She was going to tell Aaron, then I showed her this.' She held up her hand with the missing finger. 'That's when she got in touch with your dad.'

I remembered my father showing up, the rage on his face and the gun in his hand. There was something else I had to ask.

'Did she know that Aaron was molesting me?' My body tensed, braced for the blow.

Mary held my gaze. 'Not at the time. But after you came up here and talked, she didn't understand why you couldn't remember so much. Later, she started thinking about it more, how Aaron would take you swimming alone, the way he'd touch you, kind of possessive, how you changed that summer . . . '

I was crying again, wanting to stop the words out of Mary's mouth, but needing to hear them.

'She figured out that he'd probably done something to you. She was upset – and angry at herself for not protecting you. She was going to talk to you about what she suspected, see if it would help you remember.'

'So she was just speeding?'

'She'd been smoking pot all night, drinking some too, mixing it with those pills she was always taking. I told her she should stay that night, sleep it off and go in the morning. I was making up her bed when I heard her drive off.'

She looked down at her boots, dragged them through the dirt, clearing a spot, like she was trying to erase something. 'I heard the next day that she'd had the accident. I couldn't go to the police, because Aaron had Daniel.'

I nodded, looking at her house. For a moment I imagined I saw my mother on Mary's porch, walking down the front steps, ready to protect her daughter. She turned and blew me a kiss. Then she was gone.

Chapter Forty-one

Though we still didn't know if someone was out to harm me, I refused to live my life as a prisoner. The next day I was kneeling in my yard, weeding one of the garden beds, my cell within reach, when I heard a soft thump to my right. I jerked around, the trowel in my hand like a weapon. It was the cat. I hadn't seen her in months. She watched me lazily from across the yard, blinking in the sun. I pretended to ignore her and continued with my work. She strolled over and rubbed against my side, bumping her head on my elbow. I got up, slowly, but she still skittered away a few feet, ready to break into a run as she watched me brush dirt from my knees. I said, 'You hungry?' then walked toward the house.

I glanced back. She was following, but cautiously, taking a few trotting steps forward, then pausing. Inside, I put some tuna on a plate and went back onto the porch. She was on the top step. When she smelled the tuna, she cried plaintively, weaving back and forth between my legs, staring up at the plate.

'Well, little miss – you're going to have to come in and get it.'

Leaving the door open, I walked back into the house and placed the plate on the floor in the middle of the kitchen, then walked farther into the house, sitting at the dining room table with the newspaper, where I could watch out of the corner of my eye. The cat stood at my back door, meowing loudly. I ignored her, turned a page.

She crept in, body low, ears flicking back and forth. Then at the plate, she lapped at the food, purring so loudly I could hear her from my chair.

When she was done, she cleaned her paws, and still sitting in the same spot, examined my house. I turned another page, reading words that had no meaning, my breath slowing as I watched the cat. She stood up, stretched. I expected her to run back out the door, but instead she sauntered past me and jumped onto the chair near the fireplace. Lisa's chair. She curled into a ball. One amber eye blinked at me, then she tucked her nose into her tail and fell asleep.

Two weeks later they finally identified Joseph's body. I was glad that he couldn't hurt anyone ever again but frustrated that we'd never be able to find out if he knew what happened to Lisa. And if he was dead, who had been keeping an eye on me? I hadn't had more creepy feelings since that day Kevin chased the person down the street, and I hoped that was the last of it. But I still wondered if it had been Daniel or maybe another member with a grudge. Part of that question was answered the following week when Daniel was caught trying to cross the border into the States. He was arrested on the spot – and claimed he didn't know that his father had planned to hurt anyone. He also said that he hadn't been anywhere near me. I believed him, but he still had to stand trial for his part in the events.

A couple of days after Daniel was apprehended, I was on the couch, reading a book with a blanket wrapped about me, and the cat, now named Glenda, purring on my lap. I turned the pages with my free hand – if I tried to take away the one that was stroking her, I'd earn myself a growl. Someone knocked on my door, and the cat leaped off, making my heart jump. Thinking it was Kevin, who was on his way over, I opened the door.

But it wasn't Kevin on my doorstep. It was Lisa.

She said, 'Mom, I—' then broke off, crying.

I stared at her, sobs ripping out of my chest, my body shaking violently. I couldn't move, nothing would work, my limbs frozen, blood roaring in my head. She stepped forward, and I grabbed her, my forehead pressed into her shoulder, my hands gripping her so hard it must've hurt. I couldn't get my breath, couldn't form words, just loud gasping sobs as I held her to me.

Lisa was also vibrating. Her hair tangled in my mouth,

my nose was running, I tried to get some air, but I still couldn't control my body. I held the back of her head, stroking her hair over and over, rocking back and forth.

Finally, some words escaped my mouth in strangled sobs.

'Oh, God. Sweet Jesus. Thank you.'

It took us a long time to calm down enough to move inside. My body still shaky, and my head light. I had to stand for a moment, lean against the wall, tears still hurrying unbidden down my cheeks as my daughter held out a steadying hand. She looked good. Her hair windblown, but her clothes tidy, a new jeans coat and cargo pants. Her eyes were bright, though red-rimmed from crying. She'd gained some weight, her face filling out. I wanted to know everything, where she'd been, what had happened. But she was hungry, wanted to eat, then talk, said that it would help us calm down. And she was right, the activity bringing back some sense of normalcy to a surreal situation. We made some tea and toast, like we used to when she was a little girl. One of us buttering the bread, the other spreading the honey. I couldn't stop myself from reaching out to touch her, to stroke her hair, to assure myself that she really was standing there. Finally, we sat on the couch, our knees touching.

She started talking. 'The fire, Mom, it was so horrible – but I couldn't help them. I couldn't get them out.'

'You saw the fire? Where were you?'

'I was in the chamber. Aaron had put me there a couple of days before – he said it would answer all my questions, but it just messed me up. When Joseph opened the door and told me to go upstairs, I tried, but I got dizzy, and I had to sit down. He didn't notice. He was too busy running around and grabbing containers, then he left so fast he didn't know I was still there. I was so scared. I didn't know what was going on. Then I heard this huge bang, Mom. I started running upstairs. The hallway was full of smoke, and I could hear this awful screaming. I tried to figure out where all the people were, but everything was on fire. It was so hot.'

My mind filled with horrifying images, people crying for help, flames racing through the building, and Lisa trapped. 'I'm sorry, baby. I know you tried.'

'I had to leave them there—' She broke off in a sob, and I knew this pain would be with her for a long time, the survivor's guilt enormous. She pulled herself together, started again. 'I crawled under the smoke, and smashed one of the back windows. Outside, I saw how bad the fire was, and I knew ...' She paused, her face tortured with memories. She swiped at her eyes, taking some breaths. 'People died that day, lots of people. But I lived, and I just—' She shook her head, looked down at her toast. 'I just didn't understand why God would let me live after everything I'd done.' Tears were rolling down her face.

479

I wanted to comfort her, but I sensed she needed me to be silent. I rested my hand on her knee, gave it a squeeze. She set her hand on top of mine.

After a moment, she continued. 'I ran away, hitch-hiked all the way back to town. I was living on the mainland, doing drugs and trying to forget everything. One day I woke up, passed out with some guy, and I still didn't understand why I was alive. I started thinking maybe I was saved for a reason, like I was supposed to do something with my life.' She fiddled with her toast. 'I moved back and found a program.' She smiled at me through her tears. 'I've been sober for over a month now.' I smiled back. She said, 'It's been hard, really hard. I wanted to call you, but I needed to know I could get through this, that I was done for sure.'

I nodded, sad that she'd felt like that, but under-standing.

'I was also scared that maybe you wouldn't want to see me ever again, maybe you hated me for the things I said to you that last time.'

'No, Lisa, I could never—'

'Wait, Mom. Please. I still have to make amends.' She cleared her throat, started again. 'What I did to you, all those years. I made your life hell, and putting you through all this, I'm so sorry. I don't expect you to ever forgive me. But I'm trying to change. And I need help.'

I cupped her cheek, looked her straight in the eyes so

she could see the truth of my words, the love. 'Of course I'll help you. Whatever you need.'

She started to cry again. 'I'd come by the house sometimes, trying to work up the courage to talk to you, but I was terrified that you'd tell me to go away.'

I put it together. 'Were you in my shed?'

Her cheeks flushed. 'I was looking at your trees. I wanted a piece of one, so I could have something of yours to keep with me. I came back another time just to sit with your things.'

'So it was you who Kevin chased off?'

'Yeah, he was fast. I'd borrowed my friend's car.'

'It doesn't matter, none of it matters.' I hugged her to me. 'I'm just glad you're here.'

She relaxed into the hug. 'Can I come home?'

I closed my eyes, savored the words, the smell of my daughter's hair.

'You can always come home.'

Acknowledgements

I'd like to start by thanking my readers around the world for their support and encouragement. I truly appreciate all the great emails you send me and love staying in touch on Facebook and Twitter. This can be a lonely job, with hours at the keyboard, so it's nice to feel a connection with the people who are actually reading my stories, and not just the characters who are walking around in my head.

Every writer also knows how important it is to have good resources – we are lost without them. Again, I was very fortunate to find some great people willing to share their time and knowledge with me, even when I swore I just had 'one more question'. In no particular order: Stephanie Paddle, Dr. Jane Saunders, Virginia Reimer, Constable J. Moffat, Sergeant R. Webb, Mark Tucker, Jonathan Hayes, Ken Langelier, Marcia Koenig with the King Country Search Dogs, The Victoria Cool Aid Society, Deborah

Gunnarsen, Lisa Winstanley, Steve Unischewski, Sylvia (Murphy) Unischewski, Don Godolphin, Nina Evans-Locke, and Lori Treloar. Any mistakes are mine.

A special thanks to Tamara Poppitt of Poppy Photography, who spent a couple of days with me traipsing around Victoria and Shawnigan Lake and taking photos of all the locations in the book.

I also owe a huge debt of gratitude to Carla Buckley, a fabulous critique partner and friend, who weathers the storms with me, and who also shares my passion for snacks – both very important attributes. Again, I'd like to thank Renni Browne and Shannon Roberts for their insightful feedback.

Mel Berger, my brilliant and wise agent, deserves a big thank-you for always being there, encouraging me, and best of all, making me laugh.

I am so grateful to my editor, Jen Enderlin, who pushes me to dig deeper and reach higher, even when I'm grumbling and resisting all the way. Thanks to the rest of the fantastic group at St. Martin's Press: Sally Richardson, Lisa Senz, Sarah Goldstein, Sara Goodman, Loren Jaggers, Matthew Shear, and the entire Broadway and Fifth Avenue sales forces. In Canada, thanks to Raincoast Books for supporting me on the home front. I'd also like to thank my foreign publishers, who share my stories around the world.

My endless appreciation to my husband, Connel, who is with me through every up and down, and who also makes it all worth it. To Annie, my beloved dog, who started the book with me, but didn't get to see it end. I know she's still watching over me. And to little Oona, who joined our family and has inherited the task of dragging me away from my keyboard to get some fresh air once in a while, so I don't turn into a lump. A special thanks to my friends and family for their constant support and understanding, especially when I'm nose to the grindstone, trying to meet a deadline.

About the Author

Chevy Stevens grew up on a ranch on Vancouver Island and still lives on the island with her husband and daughter. When she's not working on her next book, she's camping and canoeing with her family in the local mountains. Her debut novel, *Still Missing*, won the International Thriller Writers Award for Best First Novel.